I0847029

Waldwick

Waldwick...The Hayflick Limit

Kenneth Linde

Waldwick Books
www.waldwickbooks.com
McHenry, Illinois

Waldwick: The Hayflick Limit

Kenneth Jon Linde

Waldwick Partners, Inc.
dba Waldwick Books
www.WaldwickBooks.com

July 2021

All rights reserved.

No part of this book may be used or reproduced in any manner whatsoever without written permission from the author.

Printed in Wisconsin, United States of America

Library of Congress Control Number: 2019900113

ISBN: 979-8-9852613-6-3

ISBN: 979-8-9852-6136-3

9 798985 261363

Reflections:

The daunting reality of sitting in front of the Senate Judiciary Committee accused of a myriad of crimes is almost inconceivable. The pressure of sitting face-to-face with a group of adversaries whose only objective is to dismantle your life's work seemed both overwhelming and appalling. Yet, here I sit, surrounded by lawyers, employees, family and friends, wondering how this all happened.

My mind is wandering when it should be focused. Yet, the shockwave of reality has taken my intensity and splattered it in all directions like a bug hitting the windshield of my truck at 75 miles per hour. My eyes are open, but my brain is not. My heart continues to pound and I feel its intensity in my ears and yet my heart is broken – shattered in a thousand pieces, as I ask myself why? Why did all this happen? My only goal was to help people lead better lives. It was not to unravel the structure of America.

I wish my father was here and yet, he's been gone so long! I wish my mother was here, but she too has departed. I wish Dr. Williams was here, but we couldn't save her life. I wish The Duke was here to help shield me from some of the blows I am taking. I wish Great Grandfather was here to share words of wisdom. Instead, I stand alone, the shoulders upon which I would love to lean are nothing more than memories of a time of innocence, a time of consequences, when I truly believed I could change the world, rearrange the world and make it better.

Words spoken are a blur. People in front of me, around me, behind me. Speak, yet nothing is making much sense.

Am I losing it? Has my mind split in two? How can it be, where so much that is so important, seems so insignificant?

I look to the right and left. I examine the faces of those whose lives I've touched – their eyes, their smiles, their frowns - people who have in turn, touched me and I ask myself, 'would they have been better off had they never met me - not climbed onto my roller coaster of life and gone on the ride where the ups and downs have been so extreme?"

I wonder! I wonder! I wonder! My mind reflects on all that's happened and I slowly shake my head to try and do everything I possibly can to focus on what lies before me.

I sit at the table blankly staring at my adversaries and yet my mind thinks not of the proceedings, but of the past.

I close my eyes and the world around me isn't today, but yesterday.

I am not here and now, but a reflection, like standing between two mirrors where each reflection is smaller and smaller and smaller, all the way to infinity.

Introspection:

I'm 52 years old and have been with my wife, Amelia for 30 years. Our three children, Derrick, George the 5th, better known as "V" and Melia are all in their 20's and somewhat on their own. I think about them and find their lives wonderful and interesting as does Amelia.

A great deal has happened. Some of it incredibly good, some of it profoundly bad. As I think back on George the First's book, "Waldwick", then my first journal, called "Little Spirit" and my second called "Driftless", I see that the world has changed and with it, so have I.

When I was 22, I was an idealist who really didn't know who or what I was. It took that first mid-life crisis to bring me to my senses. You see, it really is more difficult to have everything than nothing. My friendship with Rodney Whitehorse continues to this day. I am proud to call the members of the Ho-Chunk Nation my friends. I still cherish The Forest where I learned so much about life and respect the memory of Great Grandfather, who showed me that goodness can prevail. For some, there is no effect. For me, the inspiration seems to come from a divine source that reinforces my belief in God.

Whenever I can, I go back to Waldwick and walk amongst the memories that flood my mind and heart. I remember the goodness of the people and the earth and how they made me a better man. One time, I took it upon myself to take Amelia on a trip around the world in a balloon to the edge of outer space. We were able to look down on all that existed and see how insignificant so many of the things I thought were important, really weren't.

From Great Grandfather calling me Little Spirit, to the feelings I get whenever I enter The Forest, my love for Amelia and my trip into space, I realized that my goal in life was to help other people and, with the support of my family, shifted from the world of commerce, to the world of health. Our first project was developing Mediglove which allows anyone, anywhere in the world to have a basic physical evaluation with results automatically transferred to SIMON, our quantum computer, who communicates the data to the appropriate medical experts. In fifteen years, our product has been used by over nine-hundred million people and has been attributed to improving the wellbeing of people everywhere.

While several companies attempted to copy our design, the inclusion of twenty-seven different patents and the profound expertise of SIMON, has kept us on the forefront of technology and a leader in global healthcare. SIMON took the talent of those who programmed him and filled their accomplishments with a level of fecundity where, what would have been virtually impossible became plausible in a matter of moments. What is even more gratifying is that my MadCity Boys, as they like to be called, have remained humble and creative while working diligently toward changing the world in a better way.

The enthusiasm of their innerworkings deviates profoundly from the entire "me first" syndrome that affects so many others and it is a joy to experience their enthusiasm, promptness and politeness evolving from one common bond of respect for each other and the gift each one diligently gives to the betterment of all. The only time that it would get out of hand would be those events where too much beer would lead to raucous laughter and haughty expressions punctuated by a level of profanity consistent more with a group of drunken sailors than one of highly-educated geniuses. The genial atmosphere developed by the MadCity Boys, allows for the creation of the bond we have for each other and a reward for the desire and dedication that permeates our foundation.

Each of the boys had attained a comfort level they only dreamed of where the word millionaire has the prefix "multi" in front of it. While everyone is comfortable, there was still a blue-collar mindset consisting of pick-up trucks and blue jeans, instead of sports cars and Rolex watches, with only yours-truly apparent with my custom-made shoes. Within all of us, there was no avarice, nor need for self-promotion and the total commitment remains re-investing 80% of the proceeds from Mediglove into research and our ever-expanding role within the medical community, simply by integrating artificial intelligence with that of the world's leaders in medicine.

It appeared that the MadCity Boys' perception of me was like an genial uncle who held the group together through my passion to help others, while accepting that I am not on their intellectual level compensated by their unwavering belief that our goal was, is and shall always be, increasing the quality of life and not its duration.

The Chaos theory states that, within the apparent randomness of a complex system, one can always find underlying patterns, and some form of interconnectedness, along with what are called constant feedback loops, repetition, self-similarity and even patterns of self-organization. This means that what appears to be a mess really has some sort of structure buried within. While applicable as a mathematical concept, I call it life that we traverse on a daily basis that motivated me to accept my limited knowledge that once made me feel we had reached our ultimate goal until the MadCity Boys convinced me that we could travel further if we only allowed our minds to open as wide as our hearts as we began looking at areas where we could use our expertise to expand our impact on world health.

Mysteries Unraveled:

How to begin? First, I must speak of the Ley lines within The Forest. If I do not, nothing I write will make much sense. Until a point in time and space, I had no understanding of why The Forest on our property in Waldwick, Wisconsin had such a profound effect on me and other people. It was only because of a trip into space that the riddle was solved. As we circled the earth in a space balloon, we learned the following.

The core of the earth consists of molten iron. As the earth spins, centrifugal force is taking the earth's plates and cracking them due to internal expansion. In so doing, the sub-mantel allows a much higher level of energy to be present along the cracks, creating literal rivers of focused energy.

Ley lines on earth tend to form a web of fairly consistent paths around the planet. These lines are literally, 'rivers of energy', that not only flow through the earth but, as many scientists and ancients now believe, flow between worlds and universes.

Depending upon the location, Ley lines can either support life or be detrimental to it. Sometimes the lines are weak and never attach to others and eventually bleed off into the environment. However, in some cases, weaker lines attach themselves to stronger lines and become permanent additions to the grid, or 'web-work' as some people call them or a network of connected energy channels.

Because Ley lines don't normally run parallel with each other, they periodically intersect at what are called nexus points. Those points, where the combined energy is strongest, are called Earth Energy Vortexes and the combined energy can be positive, neutral or negative.

There are a few spots on earth where three Ley lines intersect. Now the relationship can have even different sets of permutations that can be so strong that, in some cases, such as in Scandinavia, cows will not lactate near nexus points, unless they are wearing a copper harness around their necks.

The power and strength of a Ley line, earth grid or vortex, is a personal thing that can affect an individual in many ways or not at all, and is not something that can normally actually be measured. Those who are affected often feel a level of spirituality, where the Ley line and its force are the conductors and the person's mind is the translator creating a propinquity otherwise unknown or more importantly, unfelt.

Virtually everywhere on ancient earth people knew that Ley lines existed creating earth grids and vortexes where positive energy sources were identified, sanctified and considered holy, supplying physical needs, curing ills and balancing spirits, which is something we sadly rely on chemistry to do for us today. Used as a place of communion with the Creator, our ancestors knew that these energy points uplifted one's consciousness and fortified the soul.

Anthropologists who have studied Ley lines also found something else. Under every valid sacred site there is water which is called 'primary water' created in the bowels of earth as a by-product of various chemical reactions that collects and is forced, under tremendous pressure, towards the surface of Earth, continuing its upward journey until it is stopped by a force greater than its own.

The vortex in southwestern Wisconsin, where three very strong positive Ley lines intersect, is the area that I have called The Forest. Here, my ancestor, George the First saved my best friend Rodney's great, great, great grandmother's life. This is the spot that had always been my respite where I could go and ponder my life and find peace. This is where my mentor, Great Grandfather's ashes were mixed with the earth and where his spirit lies. This, is where I have met with the Medicine Man who began to teach me the meaning of life as shared by his ancestors and why I am learning they call me Little Spirit.

I always wondered why The Forest has been so special to me. And, while there is no "absolute" answer regarding why one person is affected by the Ley Lines and the next person not, or even to what degree. My daughter Melia seems to have come up with a logical conclusion by summarizing the correlation between electromagnetic energy and the heart of all living beings where the heart contains a system of neurons that have both short and long-term memory. The signals a person's heart sends to the brain can affect their emotions.

Melia noted that because the heart sends more information to the brain, than the brain sends to the heart, the coherent heart rhythms, as she called them, help the brain not only in terms of creativity and problem solving, but also establishing the electromagnetic field that emanates around the entire body that changes as one's emotions change. Melia said, "Physiological or cardiac coherence, or coherent heart rhythm, is the relationship between the respiratory system, blood pressure and heart rhythms that indicates periods of stress, relaxation and rest. In other words, as emotions change, the relationship between one's heart rate, breathing and blood pressure change as well, which are all caused by changes in the electromagnetic energy and therefore the magnetic field of all living species."

Melia then took it one step further as she correlated the changes in the electromagnetic field and how they could possibly interact with the energy of the Ley lines. She noted that the emotions of each individual not only affect how they could be influenced by Ley lines, but to what level, simply based on the mood present at the time. What was critical was that, this not only existed in humans, but all living beings, which I felt was a profound observation.

I thought back to the times I went to The Forest and was most profoundly affected. I quickly realized it was when I was angry, depressed or saddened. In other words, when my own electromagnetic field had changed.

Melia added that the electromagnetic field radiates emotions to others, who then pick up the quality and intensity of the radiated energy. She concluded that this could be one reason why some people and animals are dynamic and appealing, while others have either a negative or no effect at all.

While the death of my father was a profound shock and loss to our family, the loss of Amy's mother, especially to the disease that had pervaded my wife, sent deep tremors through my soul, enveloping me in fear that its insipience would resurrect its ugly head in Amy. Many nights, I would lay awake with her nestled next to me, enveloped in the fear that her malady would transcend our children - fear that equated to the realization that without health, when you have everything, you really having nothing at all.

To evolve from a farm boy in Waldwick, Wisconsin to a member of one of the state's wealthiest families, was not what I had dreamed, nor ever intended. To evolve from writer to businessman, only to find a hole in my heart so big that blackness cascaded in, was not what was intended. Yet, it is what it is and Newton was certainly right - for every action there is an opposite and equal reaction.

My life became a reaction to the power of money and all that it can bring - both good and evil - dominating, exacerbating and controlling - modifying and adjusting perspectives. Money makes one subservient to its power until all that exists revolves around its accumulation and consequence.

Money provides opportunity and freedom to do what one wants and yet it creates bounds and limits that impede and control, usurping reality, making one subordinate to its lure. While my birth family was, is and will always be special to me, the power of my existence has become simply a segment of the wealth I enjoy. Perhaps, I should have seen it coming! Perhaps, just perhaps, I should have been stronger and simply said no, but the lure of freedom to have and do whatever you want, can be so narcotizing.

While there were dynamics that allowed Amy and I to begin as an extension of the power of her father, The Duke, events and circumstances pulled us ever closer to his realm. This was not intentional. It was and simply is, the reality that immense power can attract and modify anyone at any time, bending them, molding them, altering them into a morphed image of their former self physically, mentally, socially and ethically if need be, simply to sustain the narcotizing effects of having everything.

We have lived an external life, connected to the power through all the companies we own. However, the death of Doctor Williams pulled us in closer than ever before - not out of pity, but out of love. I remember Dr. Williams last wishes as if they were yesterday. She asked to be cremated and her ashes spread upon the waters surrounding St. Martin where she grew up and where Amy spent months in treatment for Leukemia. To grant her wish, Amy's dad, The Duke, Amy and I went "home' on his personal plane called Amelia X. The Duke put Dr. Williams' urn in her favorite seat, on her favorite plane, for her last ride.

We landed at Princess Juliana Airport and met Amy's Uncle Frank and Aunt Julia who resided in Phillipsburg. Uncle Frank had a boat moored near the airport and we went out into the ocean between St. Martin and Anguilla to say goodbye. Slowly, we made our way past Marigot and St. Louis and then past Happy Bay. As we rounded the point, Uncle Frank cut the engines and dropped anchor. Before us was a small inlet called Baie Maria.

Pointing towards the shore, "This is what your mother was named after," Aunt Julia said, speaking to everyone and no one. "Baie Maria or Marie Bay was your mother's favorite spot. We grew up in Grand Case and our momma would walk your mother and me down here to swim in the ocean and watch the sun go down. We had no money and so this was our form of entertainment and tranquility."

With that, Uncle Frank opened the urn and we each took a small scoop of what had been one of the finest women we had ever known and poured it into the ocean as I quietly began whispering, "The Lord is my shepherd; I shall not want".

I remember The Duke … who had remained quiet the entire trip whispering as we listened. *"He maketh me to lie down in green pastures: he leadeth me beside the still waters. He restoreth my soul: he leadeth me in the paths of righteousness for his name's sake. Yea, though I walk through the valley of the shadow of death, I will fear no evil: for thou art with me; thy rod and thy staff they comfort me. Thou preparest a table before me in the presence of mine enemies: thou anointest my head with oil; my cup runneth over. Surely, goodness and mercy shall follow me all the days of my life: and I will dwell in the house of the Lord forever."*

I looked at Amy and she at me as we closed our eyes and I whispered, *"Ashes-to-ashes, dust-to-dust, may you rest in peace and peace be with you."*

As quietly as we started, we were done. Uncle Frank started the boat's engines and asked The Duke if he wanted to go to their house near Orient Bay called House-On-The-Hill. The Duke politely said, No! All he wanted to do was go home. We were in St. Martin less than two hours. It was a gut-wrenching time to say the least. The plane ride home met with almost total silence, and life goes on, and life goes on.

The Duke carried Dr. Williams' urn home and placed it on a table in the living room next to her favorite plain red vase from Amy's and my wedding. Dr. Williams died on a Wednesday and every Wednesday morning from then on, The Duke went to the florist and purchased one white rose, brought it home and put in the vase and whispered, *"I love you, too."*

When a man, who has been so powerful, that a simple phone call could change the direction of many men, sat alone, I knew we needed to help him in any possible way. As we opened our hearts, we opened our lives and The Duke became more active in our family matters. At first, he was reluctant, shell shocked that his Marie had departed, leaving him all alone.

The Duke told me, "You know son, at first I was too busy to be lonely then reality dropped in as I sat alone listening to the refrigerator hum instead of Marie. We had a great life and never went to bed mad at each other. I made a lot of money and hope we helped the world be a better place. Not once, did I make a major decision without consulting Marie. I always had her by my side giving me her honest opinion about the decisions I was making. I always had her with me and then she was gone! Without her, I just don't seem to have a sense of purpose or direction. One is certainly the loneliest number!"

Douglas Williams was grandpa to our three children, dad to Amy and me, as life continued on as it does for everyone who loses a loved one. At first, The Duke's days were long and the hours filled with sadness. One certainly is a lonely number!

As I watched the man crumble, I knew we needed to give his life purpose, but didn't know how or more importantly, when we should do it. Amy and I spoke often of his circumstance and agreed he could not go back to the company he founded as it was simply too much for him. We then agreed that we could certainly use his expertise in our continuing development of the Williams' Foundation to improve the health of all living beings. We knew that the time was not right, but didn't know when it would be and so life went on - Amy running Wilco, me heading up the Foundation and The Duke slowly healing from the devastating pain that permeated his heart.

As we continued to mature as both a company and family, I knew I needed to put more trust in those loyal to The Duke, Amy and me, while allowing them to work on special assignments for the family. With The Duke traveling less and therefore requiring less time for a driver, we awarded his long-time assistant Dennis, leadership of the "airline", as we called it. Dennis was and remains a master organizer and, by using the Wilco marketing team, we were able to build a viable entity that was and remains a leader in prime transportation.

I always depended on Andrew as my right-hand man, but no longer felt his services were needed as my chauffer and bodyguard. Once again, I looked inward and realized that he could easily run the security division and he was promoted to a Vice Presidential level. For their dedication and commitment both Dennis and Andrew also became wealthy men. For their loyalty, built on the caveats The Duke set forth of mutual trust and mutual respect, they received the third side of the triangle … mutual reward.

Expanding Research:

Our core research team consisted of Luke - head of operations and dogmatic Peter - head of anything and everything to do with our computers. Mark designed and kept improving Mediglove. Working with John and Nate, from Peter's team, the trio kept pushing SIMON to greater and greater heights. We also had Matt and Philip on site who were responsible for communicating with and adding members to our research team and also Tad and James whose goal was expanding the use of Mediglove throughout the world.

I called the group the MadCity Boys with great affection, as their personalities were profoundly different, but their goals were the same - helping improve the quality of life for all living beings. While a unified team, they also maintained a fervor for independence that ran so deep they proudly professed they were a unified source of antidisestablishmentarianism, who professed an affinity against many established institutions and authorities. While initially concerned, I soon realized that their level of intellect allowed them to supersede the comprehension of the masses to the point that the question 'why' was a strong part of their vernacular and the glue that held the group together.

On many occasions, casual conversations dealt with philosophical questions regarding life, religion or relationships, whose level would elevate to some unfathomable proposition, only understood by those in the conversation and only then to be superseded by some form of discussion on sports, that would result in a raucous dissertation on which sport was the most demanding, which team was the best or which player represented the epitome of achievement. What was truly profound was the fact that they respected each other so much that the discussions remained just that and never became personal or irate and the goal was never one of a personal nature, as the emotional aspect was always held in check and never allowed to explode into a state of anger or rage.

The team also had an external support group that served somewhat as counselors, consisting of Stuart Goodman, our lawyer, who kept us within the confines of reality and Father Paul Moran, who was a Catholic priest in Madison, whom I loved because of his generous manner that was always kindly in action, purpose and speech who became Luke's best friend and our spiritual advisor.

Father Paul liked to laugh, tell jokes and drink beer and wasn't one to expound upon the ethos of the church. He always told people he was a life assurance salesman. Needless to say, it was an eclectic group, full of fun and mischief with the biggest trickster of all being Father Paul.

In order to achieve what we wanted to do, we needed the greatest minds, the most powerful tools and the most liberated environment within which to work. While Milwaukee had been home for several years, Amelia and I still had the condo in Madison. Based on that, I had an idea which I thought could help everyone and that was building the research center near Mineral Point, thereby creating an environment based on the integration of nature and mankind where every person was made to feel important and an integral part of the entire project.

We acquired another 360 acres of farmland of which 340 were saved for farming and melded into my brother Tommie's operation. We created our concepts and took it to the planning commission. When they saw what we planned and the caliber of people who would be joining the home team, the leaders of Mineral Point quickly realized our goal was to gentrify the town from a quaint village to one of the leading medical research centers in the world.

We needed focus and coordination so that the advances of one group could immediately benefit those of another. This was to be a team and not competitors. Using a corollary system that my resident geniuses developed, all inputs from the different research pods were unified on a daily basis in our shared Watsons so that the focus remained on the project - creating atom-sized, micro-chips that could save lives.

Every morning at 5:00 o'clock, SIMON distributed "Nanonews", the daily "newspaper" of all that had been accomplished in the previous 24 hours and how each development affected the separate research projects and the total program as well. Monthly, all departments were to elaborate on their subject matter in a length no longer than one page and do so in a language all others could understand. We realized that this was time away from research and yet, through structured communication, there was organization that allowed all parties to determine the aggregate level of achievement the projects were creating. Using Gannt Charts, we had monthly measurements of primary, secondary and tertiary objectives. If it appeared that one pod was falling behind or was stymied, additional resources were added to allow the group to keep up the frantic developmental pace we were achieving.

The whiz kids loved Nanonews, especially the sick jokes and those from Father Paul, to which I can't go any farther than sharing his favorite.

A man in Kansas decided to write a book about churches around the country. He started by flying to San Francisco and started working east from there.

Going to a very large church, he began taking photographs and making notes. He spotted a golden telephone on the vestibule wall and was intrigued with a sign which read "Calls $10,000 a minute."

Seeking out the pastor he asked about the phone and the sign. The pastor answered that this golden phone is, in fact, a direct line to heaven and if he pays the price he can talk directly to GOD.

The man thanked the pastor and continued on his way. As he continued to visit churches in Seattle, Phoenix, Salt Lake City, Denver, Oklahoma City, and around the United States, he found more phones, with the same sign, and the same answer from each pastor.

Finally, he arrived in Wisconsin. Upon entering a church in Beaver Dam Wisconsin and behold - he saw the usual golden telephone. But THIS time, the sign read "Calls 50 cents."

Fascinated, he asked to talk to the pastor. "Reverend, I have been in cities all across the country and in each church, I have found this golden telephone and have been told it is a direct line to Heaven and that I could talk to GOD, but in the other churches the cost was $10,000 a minute. Your sign reads only 50 cents. Why?"

The pastor, smiling benignly, replied, "Son, you're in Wisconsin now and that's God's Country so it's a local call.

To which Father Paul would always emit a chortle, even louder than my best friend Rodney's deepest laugh. Each month, the MadCity Boys would have a challenge to see who could write the funniest joke to add to Nanonews. We kept track and then would have the annual review to determine the grand champion.

I love that story and while the spirit was cooperation and a common goal, you could also see the bounce in the step of the group who had made progress and moved their Gannt Chart further to the right. I was the conductor and yet couldn't play a single instrument! I was the man with the money and the moxie to get others involved socially, politically and most important of all, financially. I had no idea what was happening, but certainly loved the hoorays that came over morning coffee when there was a major breakthrough. We had begun what we dreamed would be the Foundation of the world's greatest research center dedicated to the improvement of life for all living beings.

Renewal:

Several months after the death of Amy's mother, I felt the time was right to have lunch with The Duke to see how he was doing and what we could do to bring some level of joy back into his heart. In a period of less than two years, The Duke had retired and lost his wife. This profoundly dynamic man, who started with nothing and ended up worth over ten billion dollars, was a man without a mission, locked in a solitary world with no timetable or new achievements and literally nothing to do. Some call it retirement; I call it hell.

Amelia and I talked and agreed that the time had come. We needed to give him purpose. To this end, I called and a sad voice answered on the other end. "Dad" I beckoned. He instructed me to call him dad from the day he approved Amy's and my marriage.

"Yes, son," he said in a defeated tone.

"Why don't we have lunch?" I inquired.

I heard a deep breath on the other end. "Ok," was his only response.

"How about going to your club?" I asked, knowing he hadn't been there since Dr. Williams passed away.

Again, a deep breath and another, "Ok".

"Wednesday?"

"Sure, why not?" he said, as if he was simply giving up.

It had been a long time since just the two of us had been alone together. In the months since Doctor Williams' death, The Duke had aged tremendously. Gone was the sparkle in his eye and with it the spring in his step. Also lost was the commanding presence that made him the leader that many loved and others feared. Instead was an old man, now unsure of where he fit in the world in which we lived.

"I'll pick you up!" I said.

"Dennis can drive me!" was The Duke's reply, forgetting that Dennis was running the 'airline' as we called it, which consisted of our 25 leased and chartered airplanes.

"Let me drive. Just the two of us." I offered.

"Ok," was his response. How sad to see that he was agreeing to just about anything, as the dynamic man I once knew and loved, was withering away.

The Duke was a member of two Wisconsin country clubs - one in Milwaukee and the other in Lake Geneva plus the one in Las Vegas we had visited with my dad. Both Wisconsin clubs were as exclusive and as incredibly expensive as was the one in Vegas. The Duke didn't golf frequently, but said it was good for business. In addition, The Duke was a member of a very exclusive social club in Milwaukee that only allowed 100 members. Each year, names were submitted for consideration. IF and it was a BIG IF you were selected for consideration, you would need to be vetted and then IF, you met the criteria of the members, you might be invited to join.

It took The Duke twelve years before he was even considered and then six more to be invited. Eighteen years! But once you were in, you were IN! I don't know if it was because it was so hard to become a member that made it so valuable to him. I do know, it was the place he liked best. At "The Club" he rubbed elbows with other rich and powerful members of the community and considered the nearly twenty years to acquire his membership worthwhile. There's something about being on the outside, looking in that makes anything more desirous.

I remember when Amy and I went to The Club one Christmas with Doctor and Duke Williams and the historic building was simply incredible. With polished wood and crystal chandeliers reflected in huge mirrors and artwork that had to be worth several million dollars, just in the lobby, it reeked of opulence from a time gone by, when money still meant exclusivity and prestige.

Even though I had been there infrequently, I remembered the staff and how they all wore black trousers, pleated white shirts and bow ties that were also black, except for the month of December when they were red. It had been that way for over one-hundred years and nothing and I mean nothing, was about to change.

I also remembered that everyone had a brass name tag with their formal first name on it. There were no Toms, Dicks, Chucks or Sandys. It was Thomas, Richard, Charles and Sandra. Very proper! Very formal!

All members were called Mister and Missus and so The Duke became Mr. Williams and I became Mr. Terrill. Even with all of Amelia's and my money, there wasn't a snowball's chance in hell we could ever join the club.

The food was incredible and the drinks were always one level above top-shelf. The staff knew what each member liked to drink and was discreet when they had too much. There was a card room where cigars were smoked until it became against the law to smoke indoors and they did it anyway. This was their world, not yours and mine. They did what they damn well pleased, cutting deals and looking down on the masses from high above.

The who's who of the club ranged from judges and lawyers to families of former beer barons, manufacturers and earth shakers who made Milwaukee famous. The crazy thing was that each membership stood on its own. You didn't get in because of your family. All memberships ended when you either died or decided it was no longer for you. I have no idea what the annual dues were, but I know it cost at least a half-million dollars and you got invited because you stood for something that on the inside thought made it worthwhile.

Because The Duke hadn't been to the club since Doctor Williams died, there were a lot of condolences when we arrived, which he didn't really want. The Duke had made peace with the death of his beloved and all the condolences did was remind him, she was gone. I can only imagine what it's like to lose someone you love. When my dad left us, it took me months to accept it. The thought of losing a spouse or worse yet, a child, haunts me every day.

After the obligatory condolences, The Duke and I went into the dining room and Charles, the Maître d came over and shook The Duke's hand. I could tell by the look in his soulful eyes, he was touched by the fact that Dr. Williams was gone. As a black man in a rich, white-man's world, Dr. Williams represented more than just The Duke's wife. Charles had been at The Club for over 40 years and Dr. Williams was one of a very few people of color who ever walked in through the front door, instead of coming in through the back and not once, did Dr. Williams ever have to wear a uniform.

The Club had been good to Charles. Each member's Christmas gift was substantial enough to allow Charles to put his three children through college with the hope and dream that someday, they, too, would walk in the front door. Things had changed in so many ways and the fact that there were even people of color on the membership waiting list was a blessing.

Nicole, The Duke's favorite waitress, came over and smiled. She asked The Duke if he wanted his usual noon drink. The Duke shook his head in a somewhat embarrassed manner. Within seconds, a tall chilled Arnold Palmer sat in front of him. Half ice tea and half homemade lemonade with three ice cubes made from distilled water, just the way The Duke liked it.

A soft smile came to his face as he looked up at me and said, "I'd forgotten how good these really are," as he took a long swallow and set the glass down. We talked about the weather and the Packers, Brewers and Badgers and made small talk. Finally, it was time for me to get to the point.

"Dad, I've been thinking."

"About what?" he replied.

"About you!" I answered.

"Don't worry about me, son. I'm fine. You've got Amelia and the kids and the Foundation to worry about."

"I know, but I need your help," I responded.

"My help? I don't know anything about computers and magic gloves and all that."

"I know you don't, but you do know people and you have an incredible network of relationships throughout the country that I don't have. I saw that when you and I visited Washington and New York."

"I introduced you to all those people. You're following up with them, aren't you?" He asked.

"Yes, of course, but it's just not the same," I assured him.

"Then what?"

"I want you to come to work for me," I answered.

"What?"

"I want you to work with us to help smooth things out in Washington. We've got some ideas, but they're going to need government approval and that means having someone who has the political connections and clout that I don't have."

"What about Senator Fitzgerald?" The Duke asked, referring to the Wisconsin incumbent Senator who had been in office for decades and covered himself in what I called 'political Teflon' - that greasy, slimy, film that ensures that nothing sticks, including promises made and the only time the words 'Middle Class' are mentioned is when it's time for re-election.

I replied, "I burned that bridge with Peter and his presidential pardon. We both know Fitzgerald feels threatened and won't be my ally and that there is a high degree of resentment between all parties. We need more of the people you know, who trust you, that we can depend on to help us fight our fight. I'm quite concerned that the past will bite us in the butt now that seven years have passed since my Fitzgerald confrontation. We knew that the Senator had alleviated all indiscretions that I had shared with him to the point that I felt he was capable of Draconian actions to punish or even totally eradicate the Williams Foundation and even the Williams family."

The Duke sat back in his chair and frowned. "You want me to work for you?"

"Yup!"

"I would be your lobbyist?"

"Yup!"

"What's my pay!"

"Same as mine!" I replied.

"You mean a dollar a year?"

"Yup!"

The Duke shook his head no. "Son, you NEVER let anyone working for you, make as much as you do!"

"OK, fifty-cents a year!"

"Well, I was thinking seventy-five!" he replied, with a sly smile that had been gone too long.

I could see the fire beginning to slightly burn in his soul. He was about to have a purpose and acquire some new goals. It was as if he was waking up from a deep sleep and looking forward instead of simply looking back. There would always be a void in his heart and yet, if what they say is true, time heals all wounds. I hoped that I wasn't rushing things, but Amy and I both thought it was time.

A broad smile came across my face when The Duke said, "Nicole, bring George and me some scotch. We've got some serious business to talk about." As Nicole walked away, The Duke looked in my eyes and said, " Twice in my life I've lost the one I loved. Twice! Both times my love was more than life itself. I will always love Marie and what she meant to me, but it's time for me to move on for Amelia, you, the grandkids and, quite honestly, for me," shaking his head in the affirmative adding "and then there was Derrick."

"When do I get to start - boss?" He said with a slight smile on his face.

Nicole brought the scotch and we toasted my new employee. I excused myself and indicated I needed to use the restroom. I went to the bar and got four quarters and came back to the table and slid three of them across to him. "One year's wages in advance!"

He laughed, as we toasted our beginning and laid out the plan. I knew the healing would take time, but also felt we were taking the first step. Phase one would be basic training. Phase two would consist of the planning stages for our next venture. Phase three would be Duke Williams working his magic to make certain our plans weren't for naught.

"What about Dennis?" The Duke inquired.

"Sir, Dennis is running the airlines. Do you think you need him full time?"

"You mean I get to drive my own car again?"

"Yes, just like I do, if you want."

"It's about time. Jesus, I've wanted to do that for years!"

"What kind do you want?" I asked.

"A Silverado, just like your dad had."

"Next you'll tell me you want to go out to Penny's and get some blue jeans," I kidded.

The Duke's eyes lit up. "And T-shirts too?"

"If you want!"

"My God, I wanted to get back to normal for so long I can't believe it. This fall can we go to another Badger game, sit in the stands and get shit-faced again?"

"Yes, dad, we can do that, too!" I had tears in my eyes. The bubble had begun to slowly burst and Doug Williams, as he wanted to be called, had begun to come out of his self-inflicted depression shell and was like a little kid at Christmas simply because he felt needed.

Mourning has a way of taking people and making them something else. For some, they never return. For others, they become a different person. Doug Williams would never forget his wife, nor ever profoundly regret her loss. Yet, life needed to go on with a purpose. He was given that opportunity on that sunshine-filled, Wisconsin day, and my heart was filled with more joy than it had seen in an incredibly long time.

Basic Training:

The routine for the MadCity Boys revolved around project commitments and accomplishments. We got together every month "down on the farm", as they called the center, where SIMON, our quantum computer, was installed. One team, headed up by Matthew or Matt, as everyone called him, had a goal to increase the computational capabilities of SIMON and the Watson computers and make them work together, assisting researchers around the world, while scanning the entire global internet four times each day for any new concepts, ideas or data.

The second team, headed by Mark, was in charge of making certain that Medigolve continued to function at optimum performance. The team had developed new sensors that looked even deeper into the human body without penetrating it, thereby allowing the wearer to have a more comprehensive physical evaluation than ever before, including genetics and more sophisticated warnings for all types of maladies ranging from skin cancer to arthritis.

A third group, headed by Peter, was responsible for determining concepts that would allow us to develop new products geared at helping the world be a better place. These included non-invasive chips for animals such as elephants, lions, tigers and bears that not only would track where they were, but determine any form of danger they might be in.

It was agreed that Doug Williams would start at the next meeting and go through basic training. The team all agreed that The Duke needed to learn about the computer, how Mediglove was functioning and what our plans were.

Normally, I flew to the farm in the helicopter and went home that night. For The Duke's inaugural meeting, we agreed to drive, as dad Williams really didn't like the helicopter ride. It was great because Amy had a morning meeting in Madison and we could all ride together. I called The Duke and asked him to join us. It was proposed that he come to our house the night before and have dinner with the grandkids.

The next morning, The Duke, Amy and I would drive to Madison and hang out while Amy had her meeting. We would have dinner, stay at the condo that night and head out early the next morning for the farm. It meant a lot of downtime, where in the past, time was measured in six-minute intervals for The Duke, it gave dad Williams something to look forward to.

Around five in the afternoon, dad Williams drove into our compound on Pine Lake in his new Silverado. He was wearing blue jeans and a Wisconsin T-shirt and neither was custom made, even though he was still wearing two-thousand-dollar loafers, just like me. We had dinner with the kids where Melia, asked what he thought heaven was like.

Dad Williams looked at Melia and smiled. "I think heaven is a beautiful place where there are flowers and trees and everyone is happy. There is no pain or suffering. There is no sadness, just people who love each other getting together to enjoy each other's company."

"Is grandma in heaven?" Melia asked.

"If she isn't, then I don't ever want to go there." Grandpa Williams answered in the softest, sweetest, most sincere voice I had ever heard him express.

Derrick then asked, "What if there is no place called heaven?"

This caught everyone off guard and yet The Duke responded. "Then we need to make certain we do everything possible on earth to make it better here and that's what your dad is trying to do."

Derrick accepted the answer. I was relieved.

No one thinks that tomorrow will be worse than today. No one believes that calamity might strike and doom prevail. No one, and I mean no one, ever dreams that what they have will be taken away in an instant, like dust in the wind, blown helter-skelter and yet with every car crash, accident, diagnosis of terminal cancer or heart attack, reality abruptly changes course so that what was, will never be again.

I began to notice the little things in The Duke. Nothing major, just little things you disallow and move on with life assuming, hoping, praying they are nothing but anomalies in this thing called life.

The next morning, we had breakfast with the kids and headed for Madison in my SUV. The Duke asked why I was driving a Mercedes. I told him that Wilco had purchased the Mercedes dealerships in suburban Chicago and I liked the GL550 AMG. He wasn't aware of the second largest auto dealer transaction in corporate history and I justified it by the fact that when you have nearly 200 dealerships, it's hard to keep track of what you do and don't have.

We got to Madison in an hour and dropped Amy off at our Madison offices. She was meeting with some of the local politicians and I didn't want to be involved. I asked Doug what he wanted to do. He said he wanted to visit Camp Randall stadium. It was late July and there was no football game.

"There's no game today!" I mentioned.

Dad Williams looked at me like I was an imbecile. "Of course not, but there is Bucky's Locker Room and I need some more Wisconsin clothes."

Whew! I was relieved to be called an idiot.

After almost buying out the store, we picked up Amy and went to the condo, parking in slot 805 - The Duke's spot for so many years. We rode the elevator up to our floor and The Duke headed straight for the patio and called us out onto the deck. "This is the most beautiful view there is. This is why I love this place. Look at Lake Monona! Look at the sailboats! Isn't is beautiful?"

I looked at Amy and she at me and neither of us knew what to think. Here was a man who had been everywhere, done everything and met everyone marveling at sailboats on a small lake outside our condo.

As the day rolled on and dinner was approaching, I called and made reservations at L'Etoile, assuming that would be where dad

Williams would want to eat. I was shocked when he requested Paisan's right next door.

"I love their pineapple and shrimp pizza," he commented, as we rode down the elevator and walked the one-hundred feet to their door.

At Paisan's we sat out on the patio overlooking the lake as The Duke snarfed down his pizza as if it were his last meal. There was no talk of Dr. Williams, work or anything. He was in a totally different world. We walked back to the condo and I got out a bottle of Glen Dronach Revival 15-Year-Old scotch and asked him how many fingers. He smiled and held up three. I knew that it meant three fingers tall of the world's best scotch to be poured and used as his nighttime elixir.

We sat and all was quiet for several minutes and then he said, "Son, I can't thank you enough for all you have done for me. You are the son I hoped Amelia's brother would have been, had he not left us so long ago. You know, that broke Amelia's mother's heart when Derrick died, but you came into our lives and filled it with happiness."

I had tears in my eyes - tears of gratitude, tears of pride and most of all, tears of love. This powerful man, sitting at the kitchen table telling me, the poor, skinny, farm kid from Waldwick, Wisconsin that I helped heal two broken hearts.

$uce$$:

The following morning, Dennis sent one of our helicopters over from Milwaukee and returned home, so it was just The Duke and me as we started the drive to Waldwick and the farm.

Dad Williams had been to the Waldwick enough times that there was nothing special to see along the way and I really didn't know what the hour's drive would bring. It was a real surprise. What was supposed to be "just another ride" turned into much, much more than I had anticipated.

As we were passing Verona, I turned to The Duke and asked, "What is the secret to your success?"

The Duke looked at me and smiled, responding "which way?"

I must have had a quizzical look on my face as The Duke answered his own question. "I started out without a pot-to-pee-in or a window-to-throw-it-out. I vowed, I was going to make something of myself in business and with a family. My dad had a drinking problem and mother had polio. She walked with a limp, but she was one tough cookie who constantly gave me the latest books or magazines on how to make money or be successful. I can't remember a time when she didn't tell me, 'You're going to be someone, someday'!"

My eyes focused on the road as The Duke continued. "I knew I wanted to get ahead, but after Susan, my first wife died, I vowed it would never be at the expense of my family and so I came up with a plan that I have really tried to live by."

I glanced at The Duke and then back at the road as he continued, "First, I knew and accepted there would be good times and bad times, happy times and sad times. When times were good, I put away resources to cover when times were bad. This wasn't just money, but favors and experiences I felt I could call on when I needed them. I earned the reputation that I didn't ask for much from those to whom I had given a lot, but when I did, I expected them to come through. My mantra has always been, 'Do more now so that you won't have to do as much later'."

I nodded in agreement as The Duke added, "Second, I quickly learned that bullshit gets you nowhere. I never thought I was smart enough to lie, because one lie always leads to the next and then the next and then the next and soon your whole world is nothing but a bunch of lies, including your own belief that you can handle it. When the shit gets piled so high even you can smell it, it's time to be open and honest and ask for help. Trust me, if you're honest with others, they'll be honest with you."

I had a slight smile on my face as The Duke continued. "The next lesson came from the school of hard-knocks. Always, and I mean always, prioritize everything you need to do. Create a pyramid with three categories - what you must do, what you should do and finally, what you want to do, in terms of people, events and yourself. No one should ever have an empty list, personally, financially, socially or from a family perspective. Then, take all three categories and prioritize the items you put inside each category and you will have a set of goals. Focus on the first goal in each category until it is completed and then move on. If you try focusing on everything at one time, you will be overwhelmed and give up."

The Duke was giving it to me straight. He was getting wrapped up in what he was saying and added, "Your pyramid will be dynamic. As you go through life, things will change and priorities will vary and yet, if you remain true to yourself, the pyramid is there and each year, you will need to take stock of what you wanted to do and what you actually accomplished."

The annual Williams' meetings, now had a new meaning as The Duke added. "Never, and I mean never, rationalize or deny the event, circumstance or goal that you put on the list the year before. If you do, you're bullshitting yourself and the list means nothing. If you want to accomplish something, you must honestly judge your levels of achievement and failure and determine what you did and what you failed to do and most important - why did you win or lose. When you have prioritized goals like this, you will honestly reduce your stress and make decision-making easier."

Holy shit! All The Duke was doing was explaining why there was structure to the meetings and timelines and why there were always deadlines and then why his meetings all came in increments. Beneath it all, The Duke was showing me how incredibly organized he was and this was the underlying secret to his success. Everything was in his head! He kept stock of all the different variables, while the organization and structure were his way of knowing, every single day, where it was in terms of achieving his goals.

The Duke glanced over and smiled, lowering his voice to an almost indecipherable level and began speaking in a monotone, as if he was sharing his inner-most secret as he added that the difference between successful people and really successful people was simply the ability to say "No" to almost everything. People will come with their hands out or ideas they think will give them the world. In the end, all it will mean is slicing the pie into one more piece until there isn't a mouthful anymore."

The Duke looked at me, shaking his head and declared, "No matter how much money you've got, the one thing that you will never acquire is more time. Rich-or-poor, black-or-white, young-or-old, time is precious, simply because it is limited and has exactly the same value when you have everything or nothing. Never forget, if people don't respect your time, no one else ever will!"

Now I really understood why there were limits to his meetings and why punctuality was so paramount in all that he did.

The Duke looked out the window and finally turned to me and inquired. "Did I make mistakes? You bet I did! Do I have regrets? Most certainly! But I wouldn't change a God damn thing because the way you learn is by seeing, doing and making mistakes."

"If I have one major regret, it's the loss of my son Derrick. I don't know what I should have done. I don't know why it happened. I have looked back and wondered where I went wrong. I went to all of his events in school and wonder if I was fully present and involved or just there as a casual observer. Kids are a lot more observant than we give them credit!"

"As first Susan, then Derrick and then Marie, left me, I've asked myself 'did I show them my love by giving them the undivided attention they deserved?' This is the question that hangs over me every single day as both a husband and father and I thank God for Amy and you, as you have given me that second chance!"

The Duke shrugged his shoulders and concluded. "Money! After a while, it's just a way to keep score and nothing more. All it does is increase the options. However, with more options comes the opportunity for more mistakes and even more people who want nothing more than to take that money from you."

The Duke looked out the window again, adding. "Love and respect! Both of them are worth so much more than the next dollar on the table. Son, I know you've learned that lesson and I can sense the joy in your heart. I know that being my son-in-law is a tough job. I also know that Amy is blessed to have you as her husband whose shoulder she can lean on when she needs to because, being my daughter is just as tough as it is on you. These are the costs of power and wealth. Nothing is free! Everything has an admission charge!"

He took a deep breath and then said something he never said before. "When I met Marie, times were different. There wasn't the outward social acceptance of mixed marriages there are today. I didn't care. I loved the woman and anyone who thought otherwise was disavowed. I know there were looks and comments. I know there was indignation! I know people talked behind our backs and yet, she was the woman I loved, more than life itself. She was brilliant and noble. She was beyond reproach, who made me a better husband, father and man than I ever thought or dreamed I ever could be and that made it all worthwhile. I'm certain you still get 'the look" when you and Amy go out, but those people can simply go to hell. No matter what, the really important thing is that you two are happy and that doesn't come from material things, it comes from truly feeling wanted, needed and loved."

WOW!

The Farm:

After the exposition on life, it turned to business as The Duke drilled down. "Tell me what you're doing, son." The Duke said in all earnestness.

"Instead of me trying to explain everything, how about we wait and let the crew take you on a tour?" I responded.

This appeased him and the rest of the trip we talked about my mom, my brother Tommie and his wife, Hsu - the farm and Wisconsin football. As we pulled into the parking lot, I could see that we were the last ones there. The MadCity Boys wanted to make a good impression and got there early and were prepared.

When we entered the building, introductions were made to those The Duke didn't know. Andrew had driven over from Milwaukee. Luke had come from the old limestone house he and Indira had purchased on Front Street in Mineral Point and the MadCity Boys arrived shortly before us. I was surprised to see my brother Tommie in the group, but happy he was there.

At first, they all started calling Amy's dad Mr. Williams. He raised his hand as if to stop them. "Gentlemen, please! My name is Doug and I am an employee here. My job is a little different than yours in that my role is to try and keep you guys out of trouble," he said with a sly grin on his face. There was relief in the faces of all. This powerful man was simply one of them, or at least, that's what he wanted to be.

The boys took him on a tour of the facility. They stopped in each pod, explaining the equipment and how it all was coordinated to save time, increase efficiency, reduce the number of people, and, therefore minimize our operating costs. As we were standing there, one of the souped-up vacuum robots came into view and The Duke got a kick out of what all the boys had done to make it better, faster and more efficient. To say the MadCity Boys were less than pristine would be an understatement, but they made up for it with their passion, brilliance and humility.

Because there was such a huge investment in technology and equipment, the boys took extra time pointing out the security system and how all one-hundred researchers only had access to their own fields of work so that no one could steal the entire database. Peter pointed out that all access codes were "rolling", which meant they were only good for 30 days and then, had to be replaced. This ensured that no more than thirty days' data could ever be taken. Peter also noted that, even though SIMON was incredible, he was still susceptible and for that reason, every day's progress was transferred to a third-party "cloud" and stored elsewhere, to which, like everyone else in the world, The Duke looked up into the sky.

Luke proudly outlined how the building left no environmental footprint whatsoever. "We heat and cool the building using ground water that is pumped up from 265 feet and returned to the same depth. The water's constant 57 degrees goes through the ceiling in the summer for cooling and is used with an electric heat pump and run through the floor in the cold months. The windows were positioned to maximize winter sunlight and block the summer's heat and the foot-thick insulated concrete walls help save energy. We installed panels on the roof that collect solar energy and store it in batteries that power our system and even our bathroom waste is converted back into energy, as is that from the farm."

"I'm impressed," dad Williams responded.

Luke continued, as we climbed a set of circular stairs in the central pod that wound around SIMON's cooling tower. "We have seven exterior pods, each designed for a different form of research and each with their own Watson computer." Luke punched in the security code and placed his hand against the scanner and opened the door adding, " We are on the third floor of central pod and SIMON is located two floors below." As The Duke took in the unobstructed view of the farm and The Forest, Luke added, "By using a circular design to connect the pods, we can traverse each pod either directly or indirectly, while allowing maximum, seasonal sunlight within."

On ledges below the windows were sets of controls and gauges that The Duke inquired about. Peter added, "These are the operational brains of the complex. We can determine who is here and who is not, because each of us has a rice-sized microchip embedded in our wrist that gives us access to everything. We can also control the environment of each pod in terms of heat and humidity and also whether SIMON's core temperature is within optimum operating range."

Luke continued, "From here, we have the ability to open and close each separate pod and seal it from the rest. When no one is here, it's all done automatically so that any break-in, fire or calamity would be limited to one pod and not the entire structure." I watched as The Duke nodded in the affirmative as we took the enclosed circular stairway up one more floor and reached the dome where Luke added. "The MadCity Boys started calling it 'The Silo" and the name stuck. This is the central conference area. Once again, as you can see, it is circular with glass all around."

The Duke looked around as Tommie added. "Being elevated above the pods, you can see our farmland, Forest and the fields in every direction. We added the dome not only for light, but to improve acoustics and increase airflow and give the entire complex a 'farm-like' appearance."

There were all kinds of neat things besides its capacious nature that Luke had figured including the photo-voltaic glass, like that found on Amelia Two that blocked the light when you had a presentation. With that, Luke waved his hand between two small pyramids and the windows went completely opaque as LED lights around the dome came on, all of which made The Duke smile.

I added, "The central pod was designed with a capacity of twenty people, however, using immersive virtual reality lenses, we can have thousands of people participate in any meeting at any one time, from anywhere in the world.

From his facial expression, we could see that The Duke didn't comprehend what we were talking about.

"Here put these on," Luke offered, as he handed a pair of the lenses to The Duke.

"Is there anywhere on earth you haven't been that you would like to go?" Peter asked.

"I would like to go to Antarctica," The Duke responded.

Luke nodded and one of the boys took a laser pointer and moved it to Antarctica.

"Holy shit!" The Duke responded as his hands went out in front of him. "Oh, my God!"

The Duke was like a little boy as he exhorted. "This is fantastic!"

"Turn your head and watch what happens," Luke directed.

"Oh, my God!" The Duke replied as he turned around and realized he was immersed in where he wanted to go and what he wanted to see. The Duke was looking at the ice and penguins as Luke nodded and immersive sound was added throughout the room.

"Holy shit!" The Duke responded with an excited giggle that reminded me of Amy as he heard the penguins call out to each other.

Luke nodded again and small air vents sent a cold breeze down on The Duke, which got him laughing. In a matter of minutes, the MadCity Boys had taken a man who had been so many places and given him a thrill, simply by adding a puff of chilled air from SIMON's cooler for good measure.

"How about China?" Luke inquired, pointing the laser at Shanghai.

"Oh, my, God!" The Duke marveled. "I'm standing on the balcony of Mr. and Mrs. On the Bund - my favorite restaurant in Shanghai. Look, there, Pudong and the tower!" The Duke said pointing as if we were there. "And look, at all the people trying to sell you watches! This is amazing!"

Luke smiled. Amy had told him Mr. and Mrs. was The Duke's favorite restaurant and he instructed The Duke to turn around.

"Holy shit!' The Duke added as he was looking into the restaurant and seeing his favorite table as people turned and waived.

"When did you tape this?" The Duke asked.

"It's live!" Peter answered. "Dr. Chang is there right now and was gracious enough to put on his goggles so that you could see what he is seeing."

Luke continued, "We have linked all our researchers together so that, when wearing the lenses, they have the ability to not only converse with each other, but see each other as well. They can also share data and look at the same examples as if they were in the same room. This saves time and a lot of money because people aren't traveling all over the world. In addition, even though everyone speaks in their own language, the person they are talking to hears it in their native tongue as well and so we have no language barriers."

"Unbelievable!" Doug responded.

"Now let's take you into a living cell". With that one of the boys put his hand under an electron microscope and The Duke's mouth dropped open.

"As you can see, we have an incredible capacity to assist researchers speed up their discoveries and do so anywhere in the world."

The Duke pulled the lenses off and shook his head in an incredulous way.

"This is the future." Luke added. "Let's show you where we are today."

With that the formal part of the meeting began as the boys discussed the technology behind the Medigloves. They summarized all the companies who were trying to steal our designs and what steps were being taken to improve the product. On the wall was a counter that showed the number nine-hundred, fifty-six million, four hundred and eighty-one thousand, three hundred and forty-three. As we stood there, the number kept increasing.

"We should be over a billion users in the next few months. This means that over one eighth of the world's population will have tried on our gloves and we will have harvested their medical records, provided analysis and, in some cases, saved their lives."

The Duke sat back in his chair in amazement as Luke continued on. "At first, the NSA was against this project until we brought them here and showed them its potential - both good and bad. From the good side, we are doing nothing more than monitoring people's general health and making them aware when there is a small problem before it becomes a bigger one. No matter where they are in the world, SIMON can provide medical evaluation and direct the person for medical assistance when needed."

The Duke was shaking his head in amazement.

"From the bad side, we have all the physical records, including DNA of one-eighth the population and can assist in identifying anyone who has come in contact with our glove for any reason whatsoever. You can see how that comes into play. We are not Big Brother and yet we are more sophisticated. We can also be more intrusive and certainly more finite than the government ever thought we could be and this has them scared."

The Duke leaned back and understood where we were at. In trying to do good, we were also taking away personal liberty and any form of anonymity.

"Whew!" was all he expressed.

Peter continued, "We have other projects on the drawing board, but will need to have the government on our side to continue. Today, we wanted to show you where we were and also let you know that we have nearly 100 researchers around the world in our network who are cooperating towards improving the quality of life for all living species."

"I had no idea!" The Duke responded incredulously. "Simply no idea!"

We spent the rest of the morning reviewing what the MadCity Boys did and how every member of the team had a specific role they played. Each outlined what they had pledged to accomplish in the previous month, what they had actually accomplished and what their goals were for the upcoming month. When goals were met, everyone applauded. When they weren't, the entire team was given the reason why. There was always good-natured bantering between everyone and that made the meeting fun.

At noon, a soft bell chimed indicating it was time for lunch and all the technical jargon gave way to laughter and joking and a lot of fun. We sat outside and had grilled hot dogs, potato salad, chips and lemonade with some of Tommie's team from the farm joining in.

No one seemed to notice that The Duke was not in sight. We were to reconvene at two and he wasn't there. One of the boys indicated they thought they saw him heading into The Forest.

I offered to go and look for him. I walked down the cinder path past Great Grandfather's obelisk to the springs and saw The Duke sitting on the small bench that had been placed there.

"Dad, are you OK?" I asked.

He turned and smiled. "For this first time since we started coming here, I'm feeling what you have talked about."

"You mean The Forest?" I asked.

"Yes. I have a sense of awe, unlike anything I've ever felt before in my life and I know Marie is here. I can feel her presence. Derrick is so wrong, there is a heaven. I can feel it!" I watched as the tears trickled down his cheeks. "I can feel it, George. I know she is here!"

I slowly walked to the bench and put my hand on his shoulder. "I can feel it too, dad." I said in a reassuring way.

"No, I mean it, son. All my life I have pushed and pushed and pushed and for the first time, I can stop pushing and let life come to me. Thank you, son! Thank you for bringing me here."

He slowly stood and we hugged. His was a hug of gratitude. Mine was a hug of affection. This powerful man had felt what I always felt, sensed what I always sensed and believed what I always believed.

As we were walking back to the compound, The Duke stopped and looked at me. His eyes were glistening with soft tears as he put his hands on both of my shoulders and said, "Q, you **are** Little Spirit!" as my heart stopped for an instant, filled with joy.

E-I-E-I-O:

After the meeting, The Duke was offered a tour of the additional farms which provided time for Tommie and me to talk about the farm and how I felt we needed to vertically expand the operation by getting back in the cheese business. Selling raw milk wasn't generating the return-on-investment we needed and we had to look for ways to cover our costs. Tommie countered that every dairy farmer had the same idea and competition was brutal with over-production of cheese killing the profit potential. Dad taught Tommie and me the same lesson – 'the greatest thing you can ever learn are your own limitations' - I acquiesced to Dad's wisdom.

I asked Tommie how much land was being used to generate winter food, meaning primarily hay and corn for sileage. He indicated it took about 800 acres to feed the herd. I asked about switching from controlled feeding to grazing, knowing that we could cut the aggregate pasture into 30 smaller chunks and direct the cows daily to a different field. By doing so, the cows would eat fresh-grown grass every day and we could cut our operating costs while increasing the productivity of the land not used to raise silage by switching them to other cash crops.

Tommie noted that milk production would go down and that's the response I was waiting for. I already had our corporate economists do analysis determine the cost effectiveness of lower cost grazing versus the anticipated reduction in production and determined that our net revenue would take us from losing money to, at least, breaking even.

I also noted that I felt we should begin looking into hyponics. Tommie looked at me and shook his head, not knowing what I was referring to. I told him I had done some research on greenhouse growing and wanted to have our economists work with him on developing a business plan to determine the viability of taking unproductive land and building solar greenhouses to grow high protein plants.

Tommie must have thought I was nuts, until I pointed out that the world was in need of more protein and the answer didn't lie in chicken, pork and beef, but in developing vegetables that could enhance our protein consumption and do so with vertical greenhouse hyponics where weather wouldn't be the critical factor, even in Wisconsin.

There as a slight smile on his face. "You've been talking to Hsu, haven't you?"

"Yes, I've been talking with your wife, as has Luke," I said with a smile as I continued spewing forth all the data Hsu had provided. "Did you know that obtaining one pound of animal protein uses about 7.5 pounds of plant protein consumed by the animal as it grows? Currently, in America, 80% of all agricultural land is used for grain to feed livestock, so our 800 acres is spot on. Generating protein for our livestock could not only be cost effective, but provide a higher return-on-investment, without detrimentally affecting your way of life."

I asked. "Can you and Hsu take a week off and go to Wageningen, Holland?"

"Holland?"

"We think all the world's agricultural answers are here in the States when, in fact, one of, if not the world's top agricultural research hub is in Holland, where they are looking at alternatives to soybeans to create protein. If they've progressed as far as we think they have, we would like to partner with them and allow them to use SIMON to help with their research, while we build duplicate photo-bio-reactor facilities on some of our land around here."

Tommie shook his head in amazement, realizing his little brother was thinking ahead.

I added. "Our goal, initially would be to develop micro-algae cattle feed and do so in tubes that wouldn't require the use of the land and could be available year-round. If what we think is happening, is actually occurring, your current basic rule of one-pound-per acre of protein would be increased to around six-pounds-per acre, resulting in increased production efficiency and lowered operating costs and no weather-related downtimes. This means, the 800-acre factor could be reduced to about 150 acres. It would require a major investment, but I believe it would be worth it and I need your advice.

Tommie just shook his head, smiled and said, "And I thought you were just some journalism student who was going to work for the Wisconsin State Urinal," as he gently punched me.

I don't know if it was Tommie's punch or what, but it got me to thinking about alternative ways to use the land beside dairy cattle. Between lower per-capita consumption, crazy federal regulations, and increased international competition, dairy farms were becoming a thing of the past, replaced by the hated milk factories where cows were sequestered in the name of increased productivity. I guess, I should be thankful. Without fighting the one planned for Waldwick, Tommie would never have met Hsu and all that has transpired would probably never have started.

The question became, what next? If you've got 1000 acres, you need to produce something and that led to the thought of beef cattle as I noted. "Hay is hay. You won't need it in the winter, so couldn't you take the extra land and feed beef cattle on it?"

Tommie nodded in affirmative, but had a frown on his face.

Let's look at the entire process as it exists today. The farmer raises beef cattle and sends them to a feed lot where they are fattened and then sent for slaughter. Once that's done, the sides of beef go to a butcher, who cuts the meat into the select cuts and either sells it to a retailer or to restaurants. This means there are five profit levels built into the costs. If we became vertically integrated and fed, raised, fattened, slaughtered and butchered our own cattle, we could get a higher gross margin and still be at a lower retail price."

Tommie countered. "There are a lot of people doing that."

I responded with a smile, "I know, but I don't want to raise standard beef cattle. I want to raise Kobe-quality beef that we could market directly to restaurants."

Tommie looked at me and shook his head in disbelief as I continued, "when you eat with The Duke, money is no object. He simply wants the very best and a twelve-ounce Kobe steak will cost $150, $175, even $200 at a high-end restaurant and a Kobe hamburger can run $40."

Tommie was incredulous as I continued. "I asked the chef at one of The Duke's favorite steakhouses in Milwaukee what made Kobe taste so much better and he said, 'it tastes good because of the fat.' The meat is streaked so thickly with fat, the Japanese call it 'white steak.' When it's cooked, the fat melts into the meat, infusing it with flavor, making it the cream of the crop."

"The reason Wisconsin farmers weren't in the Kobe-style business is because of how long it takes to raise the cattle and what it costs to feed them. While traditional American beef cattle have a growth duration of about 18 months Kobe style cattle are fattened for about 26 to 32 months."

"So you would build the greenhouses, switch some of the allocated current dairy cattle land to hyponics and transfer grazing the hay fields to both beef and dairy cattle?" Tommie asked.

I nodded in the affirmative. "That's my idea."

"Why haven't other farmers done this?" Tommie asked.

"The start-up costs are huge", I countered. "Which bank do you know would loan a struggling dairy farmer fifty to a hundred million dollars to get going?"

Tommie and I both wanted to see an operation first hand and so a week later, we flew out to Montana and went to one of the ranches where we met Frank Larson, who was more than generous with his time and knowledge. Proudly looking out at the pasture at the what had to be a million dollars on the hoof Frank added, "It starts with the cows. True Kobe beef comes from the region surrounding the city of Kobe, Japan. For centuries, the cattle were used not for meat, but to provide the muscle for rice cultivation. Consumption didn't really take off until after World War II."

Frank said. "Legend has it that Japanese Kobe cattle are fed beer, massaged with sake, even soothed with soft music. Experts say beer has been used to stimulate their appetites and sake makes for a glossy coat, on which they are graded. But that's not how it's done in America, where we believe good genetics and measured nutrition are the main ingredients in creating quality Kobe-style beef."

"The American version of Kobe beef comes from the same breed of cattle raised in Japan. Called Wagyu, a Japanese name that means 'Japanese cattle', they began arriving in the United States in the 1990s, often aboard airplanes."

I wondered if they flew first class or in coach, but thought better than to ask.

"The beef we produce is considered better than prime, which is the highest grade given by the U.S. Department of Agriculture. Prime is for meat that is abundantly marbled with fat and is offered mainly at five-star restaurants."

I asked how he got started and Frank said he started with a small herd, 88 cows and 10 bulls, bought from a Japanese rancher. The rancher, flew them to the U.S. so he could sell embryos and calves more easily than selling steaks to Australia, which, along with China, is another country where Kobe-style beef is flourishing.

I asked, "Is it healthy beef?

"Absolutely", Frank replied, adding how he helped fund research backing up his claim which compared American beef to Wagyu beef that found that Wagyu was much higher in unsaturated fat and has high levels of oleic acid, which is the fatty acid found in olive and canola oils, that has been shown to lower bad LDL cholesterol.

Frank added, "The health aspect of this animal is what should be the standard for any U.S. cattle herd."

"What about hormones or antibiotics?" Tommie asked.

Frank shook his head. "We don't use them. There are too many people getting cancer and I believe the chemicals in the food they eat is one of the reasons."

I learned there were only eight restaurants in America serving Kobe beef from Japan, but hundreds serving Wagyu and Tommie and I were sold. We asked for an option on 50 calves for three years hence and Wilco paid a deposit of a quarter-million dollars. We were going to be in the cattle business, but it would take that long to build the greenhouses and get the hyponics established so the land could be transferred from dairy to beef.

The Next Phase:

On the flight home, Tommie was like a kid at Christmas. He understood the economics and that our variable costs would be reduced. He also understood that the cattle would be eating hay all spring, summer and fall and hyponics in the winter, but wanted to know about the beer and Sake the Japanese used to fatten the cattle before market.

I had a wry smile on my face and said. "Just a minute," as I stood and went to the liquor cabinet on Amelia II, punched in the not-so-secret code and gestured Tommie to take a peak.

This is The Duke's private stash. Some of this stuff starts at $500 and goes up to $10,000 per bottle."

"So? What's that got to do with beef cattle?" Tommie asked.

"You need to fatten the cattle for market, right?" I asked.

"Sure!"

"And what's the number-one grain to do that?"

"Corn!" Tommie replied.

"Corn, good old field corn, that you currently grind up with the stalks to make sileage."

"Yup!" Tommie replied.

"What do you know about bourbon?" I asked.

Tommie shook his head and shrugged his shoulders to infer that he had no answer.

I smiled and continued. "By law, bourbon needs to be produced in America and made from 51 percent corn." Tommie smiled as I added, "Bourbon must be stored in brand-new, charred-oak barrels, AND, to be called bourbon, the liquid needs to be distilled to no more than 160 proof and entered into the barrel at 125 degrees."

Tommie was beginning to see where I was going as I added, "We can grow corn and distill it into bourbon. At the bottom of the stills, there is a residue called 'setback' that accumulates. Setback consists of water, proteins, fats and fibers of the mash that are heavier than the alcohol and esters that float above. All we would need do is pump out the setback, dry it and feed it to our cattle. We make bourbon, they get fat. We have no waste."

"But I thought a diet high in corn created bloat or possibly fatal amounts of excess gas and liver abscesses?" Tommie questioned.

I answered. "You're right, the more hay or grass a cow eats compared to corn, soy and other grains, the less likely the animal will develop these digestive problems. Corn is high in phosphorous and low in calcium and Hsu said that because of this, they are also likely to suffer from kidney stones and she recommended a two parts calcium to one-part phosphorus ratio for better health which we can mine from the limestone we have in our own quarries."

I must have had a shit-eating grin on my face as Tommie just shook his head and smiled and asked. "That easy?"

"Hardly," I responded. "Bourbon regulations are strict. In the 1800's distillers spent a lot of time adulterating, diluting, and tampering with their whiskies. Finally, standards were set with the Bottle-In-Bond Act of 1897 which requires bourbon to be the product of one distillation season and distiller and distillery. The finished product can't be more than 160 proof or 80% alcohol and it must be then bottled and stored in bonded warehouses, under the U.S. government supervision, for no less than 4 years, making the government the guarantor of the bourbon's authenticity."

"You want to build warehouses, too?" Tommie asked.

"Nope!" I replied. "Instead of bulk mining the limestone as a food supplement or selling it for construction, I want to drill it out to create caves and put secure doors on them. We can sell then either sell the limestone or stack it to cover our drilling costs while creating controlled and secure bonded warehouses that will maintain constant temperatures year-round."

"You've got this all figured out, don't you?" Tommie asked, "But do you think it will sell?"

"In Wisconsin?" I asked, incredulously adding, "Here are some crazy numbers. Wisconsin has the highest percentage of any state, when it ranks alcohol consumption with nearly 75% of all adults saying they drink. Wisconsin ranks seventh in per-capita total alcohol consumption at nearly three gallons per person for those over the age of 18. Believe it or not, New Hampshire is first, where they drink nearly five gallons, per year, which is even more than Nevada."

I continued, "I thought about other alcohol options such as beer and wine and found that in Wisconsin, the average adult drinks about 1.56 gallons of beer and there are now over 100 micro-breweries. They also drink about a half-gallon of wine of which there are over 50 wineries. What's really interesting is that Cheese-heads also drink nearly 1.25 gallons of hard liquor, which puts us in the top three states in per-capita hard liquor consumption in the U.S."

I looked at Tommie with a wry smile and added, "Here's what's interesting. I could only find one Wisconsin distillery producing bourbon."

"Tommie, we have a built-in market and all we need do is create a great product at a reasonable price. Because we have multiple uses for the same grain, which is the most expensive ingredient that we can amortize across multiple categories, it will make us very competitive, thereby allowing our retail partners to offer a premium product and at either popular prices or higher margins, which makes it even more attractive."

"You should be over selling cars for mom!' Tommie joked.

"I don't want to produce cheap booze. Instead, I had the MadCity Boys contact the University of Wisconsin about the best possible corn for bourbon and the Ag Department said they developed a hybrid corn called heirloom W335A in 1939 that was first intended as cattle feed. It's red in color and doesn't have the yield of typical field corn, but the sugar content is out of this world, which means better bourbon and fatter cows."

"How do you get the seeds? Tommie asked.

"First, The Duke and Wilco donate millions of dollars to the UW every year. Second, we can purchase starter kernels from their seed bank, plant them and expand the fields until we have enough to create the necessary setback volume to feed the cattle and distill our bourbon."

"In other words, you want to distill bourbon to create cattle feed and not the other way around?" Tommie inquired.

"Yup! In about ten years, we will see a return on our investment in terms of the bourbon, but the setback will generate a return in probably three."

Tommie just shook his head and smiled, adding, "Pop was right, you are a smart little shit. You've got this all figured out."

I smiled and nodded in the affirmative, proud of my logic adding, "I think so. By making the changes, we can reduce the reliance on dairy as our only income by developing the high-protein hyponics. We then take the now-extra land and use it to graze prime beef cattle that are fattened, using the setback from the bourbon we make. The major initial investment will be in the greenhouses, but we can use them as tax deductions and also grow organic vegetables. Then, when the cattle are ready, process them, including both wet and dry aging, and sell Waldwick Wagyu beef into restaurants in Wisconsin and Chicago who will also eventually offer our world-class Waldwick Bourbon."

We opened some of The Duke's $1500.00 bottle of Heaven Hill twenty-seven-year-old bourbon and each took a glass.

"To our success!" I offered, realizing this was a ten-to-twenty-year proposal.

"Success!" Tommie replied.

When we got home, Tommie and Hsu made plans to go to Holland and from there we had plans drawn up for the greenhouses, distillery and warehouses. The cattle were purchased and all we really needed was time to increase the acreage for the corn.

Tommie was busy. Luke helped him on site locations, while I contacted a certain friend in Black River Falls and proposed the Hochunk consider offering gourmet Waldwick Wagyu beef and fine Waldwick Bourbon in their casino restaurants. Without batting an eye, the CEO agreed and we had our first commitment. I only wished sales were always that easy. Just like that, the depression of being a dairy farmer in Wisconsin was replaced by the enthusiastic anticipation of an agri-business that would maximize the productivity of the land and the crops it grew.

The Next Step:

While SIMON was an incredible asset that assisted in basic evaluations and treatment recommendations for people all over the world, we knew we were only using a small fraction of his capabilities and wanted to determine where to go next. To this end, we began inviting guest speakers to address the team regarding their field of research, ranging from geology-to-paleontology, chemistry-to-physics, anatomy-to-physiology. In the end, the idea was to expand our horizons beyond what we knew. With the University of Wisconsin just 45 minutes away, the intellectual resources were simply astronomical.

In previous sessions, we had gone through the basics of anatomy and physiology and were moving into how the body functioned from both neural and chemical perspectives. To this end, we invited Dr. Rachel Brockett from the University of Wisconsin Department of Nutrition at University Hospitals to talk to us about the chemical composition of the human body and how what we ate affected our lives. We all sat back and allowed her to mesmerize us with her wisdom. With her permission, we broadcast her lecture via our IMVR system to those researchers who had the time and interest in her field of study. With that, we had an additional 78 people around the world plugged in, as each person's IMVR sent a signal that was indicated on our global map with a small LED light. Here is what Dr. Brockett said.

"You are what you eat. But do you ever recall munching some molybdenum or snacking on selenium? Some 60 chemical elements are found in the body and they are acquired by what we eat." With this, the MadCity Boys put down the potato chips they were munching and started paying attention.

"While a great deal has been learned, what all of the chemicals are doing is still unknown. However, we do classify 60 chemicals, where the more prominent chemicals are called macronutrients and those appearing only in levels of parts per million or less are referred to as micronutrients. While minute in quantity, they perform various functions including the building of bones and cell structures and regulating the body's pH, which affects the electrical charge necessary for all bodily functions, including thinking, and finally, driving chemical reactions."

The MadCity Boys were paying attention. No doodling or even looking out the window, as Dr. Brockett continued. "Roughly 96 percent of the mass of the human body is made up of just four elements: oxygen, carbon, hydrogen and nitrogen. We need oxygen simply to live, as it is the air we breathe. Hydrogen and oxygen combine to obviously form water, which makes up about 60% of our body. It's practically impossible to imagine life without water. We drink it, bathe in it, swim in it and virtually live in it. The rule of seven says that we can go seven minutes without air, seven days without water and seven weeks without food. That's how important water is to our existence."

Dr. Brockett continued, "Carbon is also synonymous with life. Carbon's critical role is due to the fact that it has four bonding sites that allow for the building of long, complex chains of molecules. Moreover, carbon bonds can be formed and broken with a modest amount of energy, allowing for the organic chemistry that goes on in our cells."

The MadCity Boys seemed stunned by this revelation as Dr. Brockett continued. "Nitrogen is found in many organic molecules, including the amino acids that make up proteins and nucleic acids that make up DNA."

Dr. Brockett took out the electronic pen and wrote the names on the overhead. "Beyond the big four, there are two more primary chemicals that are more than 1% of our mass. The first is calcium, which is the more common of the two and found in our bones and teeth. Calcium plays another important role in controlling bodily functions, such as muscle contraction and protein regulation. The final major element is phosphorus, not only found predominantly in our bones, but also in the molecule ATP, which provides energy in cells for driving chemical reactions."

Dr. Brockett added calcium and phosphorous to her list on the board and continued on. "Beyond the big six, as I call them, are fifteen more chemicals that are found in small percentages, but play critical roles in our overall health and wellbeing."

Dr. Brockett stopped and looked at the boys and added, "when a person has an unbalanced production of any chemical, it causes issues that can be addressed by the addition of drugs to their diet that compensate for too little or too much of the chemical being present. It is this imbalance that serves as the primary foundation for the drug industry."

The doctor then continued by discussing the industry and how many noble people dedicate their lives to the betterment of others, simply to have it all taken away by those more interested in the bottom line. I could feel her frustration and sincerity and listened intently as she added. "According to the Journal of the American Medical Association, nearly 60 percent of Americans, twenty years old and older, use of at least one prescribed drug, while the prevalence of poly-pharmacy, which is the use of multiple prescriptions, is found in about 15% of the population, with the number of individuals using prescription drugs for treatment rising every single year. In other words, the pharmaceutical industry is and remains a growth industry powered by one thing - return-on-investment, supported by our government in many ways."

Dr. Brockett stopped and slid forward so that she was sitting on the edge of the table that had been in front of her and continued, "Once upon a time, the only drugs advertised on television were nonprescription products like Alka-Seltzer and Bufferin. Now, however, powerful prescription medicines for serious or even life-threatening diseases, are routinely advertised on the evening news where people are encouraged to *ask your doctor* if a certain drug is right for you."

You could sense the disdain in Dr. Brockett as she continued. "According to Kaiser Health News, the pharmaceutical industry has substantially boosted its spending on direct-to-consumer advertising in the last five years to an estimated $6 billion per year. Many of the medications that are being promoted are extremely expensive and can cost from a few thousand, to hundreds of thousands of dollars per month. The critical thing to remember is that the drugs are not designed to cure you, only to maintain you, so that you have to keep buying the drugs month-after-month, year-after-year, until you die."

Dr. Brockett paused and took a drink of water. I don't know if it was because she was thirsty or for effect. Either way, what she was about to say was incredibly dramatic.

"Prescription drug commercials are very sophisticated productions. The music and images are designed to create a sense of enthusiasm for the medication. It should come as no surprise to learn that drug companies don't want to spend a ton of money frightening people out of taking their expensive medicines."

The doctor was burrowing down and wanted to make certain everyone was convinced by what she said as she added. "To usurp FDA regulations about disclosing risks, as well as benefits, the ad agencies have come up with some surprisingly effective strategies. Voiceover actors are hired who have learned how to deliver really bad news in a calm and reassuring way. When they get to the scary stuff, there is often a subtle change in style. The announcer tends to speed up while reading a long list of side effects. The video that accompanies some of the nastiest adverse reactions, including death, is often designed to draw attention to beautiful vistas, interesting activities, pets or people smiling. They've got it all figured out!" Dr. Brockett said shaking her head in dismay.

"If you think Congress will ban these prescription drug ads anytime soon forget it. The pharmaceutical industry is one of the biggest lobbying groups in this country and their massive funds support Congressional campaigns. Some of us would think that the television networks and magazines would simply say no to drugs, but the money flowing in is too lucrative and too easy to get to simply say 'no'. Doctors don't like the ads and actually had the

American Medical Association put out a statement against the direct-to-consumer messages as misleading and even dangerous."

"Who's winning the war?" the doctor asked and then answered her own question. "More Americans are seeing more ads than ever before. More money is being spent on lobbying than ever before. Congress is being given more money than ever before. Where is it all coming from? The answer is quite logical. It's coming from the cost of the drugs being prescribed and is probably why Americans pay more for prescription drugs than any other nation in the world."

"It's a money machine for all those involved. More people are being diagnosed with chronic illnesses every day. Sadly, while much of the national concern has been on high cost specialty drugs, medications that are required to treat more common conditions have skyrocketed in price and are having a financial impact on millions of Americans, not only in what they pay for the drugs, but the cost of health insurance, as well. Imagine where you would be without health insurance! Imagine what a profound effect it would have on the rest of your life if you were diagnosed and needed a drug that cost a few dollars to create and you were paying three, four, five thousand dollars per month just to stay alive."

The Dr. looked down at the floor and then at her audience. I believe she was measuring what she was about to say. "I am honored to be in your presence. You have shown a level of decency and integrity, nobility and honor that is simply vanishing in our world today. I don't know how to say what I am about to say, and please don't take this the wrong way. Your decency is simply going away! Due to your passion, you all seem to believe in the old-fashioned concept of the free press operating in a world that operates on a set of rules and boundaries that simply don't exist anymore."

The boys were uncomfortable in what the doctor said as they shuffled in their seats while she continued. "Sadly, the decent world is gone along with national interest in what is right and disdain for what is wrong. What remains are the three 'C's' of reality - conglomerates, corporations and cartels, all existing to control who and what we are and what we think is right at wrong. Be damned, goodness! Be damned, righteousness! Be damned, decency! All replaced by bottom lines irrespective of right and wrong, good and bad. There is no such thing as government. It has become a mere facade based on shadows that are created so well that most people still believe in the illusions."

I swallowed hard. My mind paused for a moment and wondered, just wondered where I stood. Did I create shadows? Was the simplified innocence of The Forest nothing more than a dream of what once was and what could be, only to see the roar of chainsaws of commerce ready, willing and able to eradicate life as we knew it?

There was a deep silence in the room. Dr. Brockett was getting her message across as she continued. "What is important for you to realize is that every living species has a need for the correct amount of chemical intake to lead a healthy, active life. Simply relying on drugs for the answer leaves out the entire concept of improving one's diet or adjusting the amounts of certain foods needed to compensate for any shortfall. American's always seem to take the easy way out. Instead of a healthy diet that provides the vitamins and minerals, we purchase multi-vitamins. This is what we are trying to address: identifying specific foods that will allow us to obtain the proper dietary balance, without relying so much on drugs."

Dr. Brockett stood and looked at the group. "We know what the problems are. We understand we cannot convince everyone to skip what's not good for them and eat healthy all the time. What we are trying to do is develop holistic diets and exercise plans that will reduce or eliminate the need for additional chemicals being added to the body. However, there is another way and it is called holistic nutrition which is the complex interplay between the physical, chemical, mental and emotional aspects of life, as well as the spiritual and environmental aspects of one's life and entire being."

"With SIMON's knowledge and nearly one billion respondents, you could bring personalized, non-biased health and nutrition information to the world. You have the ability to educate the public on the cost/benefits of eating unprocessed locally-grown, fresh, plant-based foods instead of what we eat today simply by showing the value of taking quality nutritional products and using them to manage chronic nutritional deficiencies and toxicities associated with lifestyle and environmentally-related health problems many people globally face."

Dr. Brockett paused for a moment and a sincere expression crossed her face as she added. "SIMON could recommend different foods that consist of vegetables indigenous to the area that would compensate for needed chemicals, thereby minimizing the need for the processed chemicals found in pharmaceuticals. This would not only save money, but reduce the dependence on manufactured solutions."

I could see the MadCity Boys had one more perspective on what we were trying to accomplish. Little did I realize, I was about to let the tiger out of the cage as we would be directly competing with some of the most powerful companies in the world. Instead of a casual look, their wheels were spinning as they thought of ways to program SIMON to address chemical imbalances and seek out alternatives to people's need through dietary changes.

As her presentation ended, Dr. Brockett answered all the questions posed about diet, chemicals and human responses. I asked her if she would like to join our team as a consultant. She said she was honored, but indicated her time was already spread too thin. I was disappointed. I told her the offer would always be open and she was welcome to come back and work with us in developing software that would allow SIMON to recommend proper foods to those who were identified with chemical shortfalls when they wore the Medigloves.

I thought the meeting was over when Peter and Mark asked for a few minutes of Dr. Brockett's time. I looked at the two of them and must have had a quizzical look on my face, but saw the gleam in Peter's eye and knew something was up.

"Dr. Brockett, would you mind putting these IMVR lenses on please?" Peter asked.

Dr. Brockett looked at her watch to tacitly indicate she was running out of time, but abided as Peter nodded and directed SIMON to upload what he called "ROVER" into the lenses.

"Wow!" was all Dr. Brocket could exclaim. "That's - that's beautiful. What is it?" she asked.

Mark replied "It's a pattern designed to include not only all the colors of the spectrum, but also different line width's and intensities while adding shadows. Something like an old-fashioned kaleidoscope. We took twenty different reflecting surfaces that are tilted toward each other so that the objects on one end of the mirrors are seen as regular symmetrical patterns when viewed from the other end, due to repeated reflection. We then connected the device to a set of very slow-moving motorized gears and recorded over one-thousand different patterns that were correlated by SIMON and just played for you."

"It's gorgeous" Dr. Brockett said, taking off the IMVR's.

Peter looked at her and smiled, adding, "The reason for the colors, patterns, line thicknesses and shadowing was to measure your visual acuity. In the process, we measured your eye's color separation capabilities and clarity at different lengths, but also your delineation capability, as it applies to contrast."

"You mean, I just had a basic eye exam?" Dr. Brockett questioned.

Mark shook his head enthusiastically as he asked SIMON to print the eye exam results and handed it to Dr. Brockett adding, "It wasn't just a basic eye exam. We were also able to measure your eye fluid levels and the associated pressure as it applies to glaucoma.

"Incredible!" was all Dr. Brockett could say as she looked at the print-out.

"But there's more!" Mark added.

I stood perplexed. These guys had just revolutionized eye exams and there was more?

Mark had that excited look on his face that comes from discovery and added. "We wanted to see what else we could learn and turned to the retina and believe we've made a discovery."

Peter smiled and continued. "We read about the studies being done on retinal screening and thought 'what the heck?' so we programmed SIMON to look for anomalies in the retina as well. In so doing, we came to a discovery that the retina of the eye is an area that can actually provide early warnings of other maladies where we've been able to detect to beginning buildup of amyloid plaque in the brain."

Dr. Brockett's hands went to her mouth. "If what you're telling me is what I think you are, with a basic eye exam, you can also provide a pre-marker for the on-set of Alzheimer's disease?"

Both Mark and Peter nodded in the affirmative.

"Oh, my God!" Brockett responded incredulously. "Oh! - My! - God!"

Mark continued. "It's not a cure! However, if what we are learning is correct, it will mean, not only identifying those with the malady long before it becomes debilitating, but determining therapies at a much earlier time of the evolutionary span and believe will lengthen the duration of mental acuity."

"In other words, potentially defer stages two, three and four?"

Again, both men nodded in the affirmative.

I sat in total shock! The boys were out-doing themselves as I sat shaking my head in profound disbelief leaning back and thanking God.

Peter continued, "We believe this process will result not only in affordable and portable eye exams, but eliminate the need for Alzheimer associated PET scans and thereby reduce evidentiary costs."

Dr. Brockett shook her head. "So, instead of the PET imaging test to reveal how tissues and organs are functioning, all you would need to initially do is put on the IMVR's?"

Again, both Peter and Mark nodded in the affirmative.

"Incredible! Simply incredible!" the good doctor added with her hand to her mouth, shaking her head in disbelief.

There was a deep sigh in the room with proud smiles all around. It's always fun to be on the winning side and watching someone who probably thought we were just a bunch of nerds, have her proverbial socks knocked off.

With the ROVER introduction, I realized that, if the tests validated what Mark and Peter concluded, adding the IMVR's to our business plan would not only result in taking global health maintenance to a much higher plane, but provide a tool by which those with such an incipient malady as Alzheimer's disease could begin their fight sooner and even make those totally unaware of its threat, cognizant of its existence.

The pilot was waiting with the chopper and Dr. Brockett was lifted back to Madison. Fifteen minutes after she said goodbye, Chopper One landed on the UW Hospital helipad and said goodbye to the good doctor. Dennis called me later and reported that Dr. Brockett was simply awestruck by what she'd seen and learned that one sunny day, *"down on the farm"* by a bunch of passionate nerds and me.

The ride home centered around the doctor and Rover. As I dropped The Duke off at his house he looked at me and smiled. "Son! I cannot tell you how proud I am of all that you are doing! I know Marie is looking down right now with a great big smile on her face, knowing you are truly making a difference."

I had tears in my eyes. Tears of gratitude! Tears of humility! Tears of the realization that my hopes and dreams were coming true and I was becoming the man I always wanted to be.

Time was flying by. We spent nearly a year working on Rover. Dad Williams flew to Washington numerous times to talk with people in power, but big pharma had more leverage and a lot more money than a bunch of geeks in Waldwick, Wisconsin.

We waited a while and then, The Duke got on Amelia X and gave it one last shot in Washington for my sake. When he returned home, he gave me a lesson in life that I will never forget when he reiterated, "Son, pharmaceutical companies aren't in business to cure people. Their goal is to maintain them. If they cure someone, those people wouldn't need to buy their products. They want to keep them reliant on the drugs as long as they can to maximize their return-on-investment and they will use all their money, influence and leverage to make certain it stays that way. We are perceived to be a threat to their business structure where everyone involved is making tons of money. From the chemical companies to the distributors, retailers and politicians and you just want to just step in and cut everyone out. That's just not going to happen!"

"What about the FDA?" I asked, already knowing the answer.

The Duke looked incredulously at me and continued, "Like most regulatory agencies, the agency started out with good intentions of controlling an industry. Then, as time went by, the big boys found out which politicians were on the committee that controlled agency staffing and started funding their elections and asking for this person or that person be added to the agency staff until, in the end, the agency is simply a mouthpiece for the industry and not a watchdog."

The Duke looked down at the ground and then at me. I could tell he was being sincere, but most of all, his guard was down. "Remember when Marie was so sick and you had to break into the FDA system simply to allow her to have one last shot at living?"

How could I forget?

The Duke took off his glasses, folded the bows and put them in his shirt pocket as he continued, "I think the big boys are running the FDA. They want drug tests to take a long time because they can catch up to any innovation faster than if a new drug, device or procedure were to just show up overnight. Imagine, if you knew what your competition was doing today and given a ten-year preview of what they had planned, and that's the short run, when the drug company is awarded a patent extension."

He shook his head. "You wanted to go in for the fight. I wanted to help, but the big boys are bigger, tougher and certainly more ruthless than you and I will ever be."

"But what about Mediglove?" I asked.

"Like Rover, it's an appliance and not a drug and no one knew who we were and that's why it initially got through. Try it today and it would take years to get approval because you caught the market with their pants down and they aren't happy that a bunch of wild-eyed geeks in Waldwick, Wisconsin beat them to the punch. Look at how many are trying to copy the product! It's insane! We're spending eleven cents out of every revenue dollar on legal fees, simply to protect what we've already got."

I knew The Duke was giving it to me straight. I sensed it would be a long shot, but actually believed that, if you were helping people, you had a chance. It was then I realized that conventional medicine is about money and not about making life better. "Buy this product and it will do this, but also realize, you will be their customer for the rest of your life!" Wow!

The Follow Up

A month later, it was time for the next MadCity meeting. As had become the practice, The Duke and I drove together, giving us time to talk, which I think we both enjoyed. The Duke noted that he was trying to start playing golf again and was using the Lake Michigan boat to go fishing. Some of his buddies from the Social Club were also retired and they started playing cards as well. He was keeping his days filled, but I am certain that walking into that huge, empty house at night, brought back memories and the abject level of loneliness that only comes with the number one.

The monthly meeting commenced and the MadCity Boys gave their reports and addressed how they connected with researchers regarding indigenous plants throughout the world. They outlined how SIMON was building the necessary database concerning edible plants, chemical compositions and required dosages predicated on human variables such as age, race, height and weight that could be incorporated with SIMON's database and Mediglove to allow for the prescription of holistic dietary supplements instead of processed chemicals. We all knew what we were doing wasn't for everyone, but also rationalized that helping people help themselves to better health, simply by identifying substances indigenous to their locale, could assist in minimizing their reliance on drugs.

There was a professional demeanor about the presentation, but I could sense a dreariness that comes when there is no passion. I found it interesting that, at lunch, we had salad, while the normal beer or lemonade had been replaced by water from our own Forest.

Our afternoon guest speaker was Dr. Albert Feinberg, a renowned expert on aging. This guy told us he was seventy-two years old but looked like he was in his forties. He had studied aging with Dr. Leonard Hayflick and was considered a world-renowned expert in his field. Normally, we didn't spend money on guest speakers as the helicopter ride was a big enough thrill. With

Dr. Feinberg however, there was a fee paid and we quickly learned it was worth every cent.

Dr. Feinberg was about my height with salt-and-pepper hair that was stylishly disheveled. He was wearing tan slacks, white shirt, brown tassel loafers and a navy-blue blazer. His piercing eyes poured out from behind his horn-rimmed glasses and he looked all the part of a college professor, which he was.

Because of his reputation, nearly seventy percent of our network researchers were "tuned-in" as we called it and the audience was several hundred people. 'V' had worked for months to get him to come and Nano news had repeatedly reminded everyone of the session. This was the 'biggy', we had all been waiting for to the point that both Hsu and Indira had taken the afternoon off from their respective research projects and sat in the front row, ready to be immersed in the wisdom about to be shared.

Dr. Feinberg began. "For decades, there were scientific theories about evolution and aging which was actually educated guesses based on existing physical and anthropological evidence. With the introduction of advanced DNA testing, scientists were able to trace their hypotheses back to a single individual. Known as 'Mitochondrial Eve', this prehistoric woman lived at a time when the human population was only about 10,000 strong and, while she wasn't the first woman on Earth — or Eve from the Bible — her DNA is present in nearly every human today."

"Pinpointing humanity's earliest common ancestor was nothing to bat an eye at. People think it's cool to find old bones and realize they represent a part of our evolution. From a scientific perspective, there's must more to the is being determined simply because scientists are more interested in what else Eve's DNA implied. They have concluded that all humans not only descended from a single individual, but that one individual came from Africa."

"Even with this common heritage, the millions of years of evolution based on action/reaction to the environment has created profound differences in the races of humans today, while still sustaining 99.9% of the same DNA throughout all of us. If people would simply understand this and accept it, perhaps – just perhaps, there would be less distrust, less hate and fewer problems here on earth."

Dr. Feinberg stopped for a moment to allow all that he shared to sink in and then began again. "There is a study of hereditary changes in gene expression without changes to the DNA itself that is called epigenetics. Scientists have known for centuries that changes in all living things are not smooth transitions, but occur in 'fits and starts' over long periods of time. If we go to a cellular level, we know that all living organisms are in a constant state of change – growing and degenerating, sustaining injury and - other than our teeth - repairing any damage, while reproducing and transforming itself by ingesting foods in the form of chemicals and converting those chemicals into different types of energy. From birth-to-death, human cells are constantly adapting to their environment or failing to adjust along the way."

Dr. Feinberg stopped for a moment and took off his sportscoat and placed it over the back of a chair. "All of this incredible activity involves birth, death and the orderly replacement of millions of cells per day that represent 1%-2% of our entire existence. Our bodies and the cells within it are in a constant state of flux, acting-and-reacting on, in and with the physical, mental and social environment in which we reside. It is what we call life."

With that Dr. Feinberg pressed the remote with his finger and an old black and white photo appeared on the screen. "This is Henry Chandler Cowless who created the theory of succession in 1899 regarding vegetation. According to his theory, many changes occur in an orderly fashion and can be predicted to some degree. In humans such things as gray hair and wrinkles can be predicted as we age."

"Dr. Cowless believed there are two classes of succession. The first is called 'primary succession' which occurs when a significant dramatic event changes the environment, such as when the asteroid hit in what is now the Gulf of Mexico, clouded the skies and cooled the earth. The other type of succession is called 'secondary succession' which occurs when an existing environment is severely disturbed by some traumatic event, such as global warming."

Dr. Feinberg stopped for a moment and removed his glasses for effect. "While Dr. Cowless was referencing trees and plants, the entire theory also applies to humans and this is what we are going to discuss today."

Putting his glasses back on, Dr. Feinberg continued. "If we are lucky and have the opportunity to grow old, we can witness the entire process of succession within our own bodies. First, you must accept that aging is done on a cellular level that affects almost all of the body' systems: the senses, digestive, cardiovascular, immune, skeletal and musculature systems included."

Dr. Feinberg stopped for a moment and then continued on. "I am 72 years old and am changing. My life is changing. My world is changing. My body is changing. But what if it didn't have to change quite as fast? Isn't life the balance between our quantitative and qualitative existence? While, like many of you, I do not believe in extending life, simply for the sake of its extension, I do believe in making certain that the time we have on earth has the highest possible level of robust health. Health, by the way, is derived from a myriad of things including the food we eat, exercise we get, environment we live in and rest we need. Yet, even with these four components, some will have a higher qualitative existence than others. Why?"

There was a pause in the audience. This is what everyone had come to hear about as Dr. Feinberg continued. "Research in the early 1960's by Dr. Leonard Hayflick determined that normal human cells, beyond stem cells that is, will only divide on average of 50 times before they stop. This has become known as the Hayflick Limit that can be obviously affected by disease and stress."

Dr. Feinberg put up an X/Y slide of a chromosome and pulled a white shoestring out of his pocket. "The basic composition of our chromosomes has what are called telomeres on both ends which are like the plastic tips on the ends of these shoe laces. You do remember shoelaces, don't you?" which got a light chuckle from his audience as everyone looked down at their feet.

"The telomeres protect chromosomes from damage and from fusing together. Every time a normal, non-stem cell divides, somewhere between 50 and 100 of the telomere cells cease to exist and the telomeres get shorter and shorter and shorter until they reach a minimum length, at which time the cell division stops altogether. This is called the aging process and is called the Hayflick Limit."

"There appears to be a genetic link to the both the initial length and number of telomeres each person has. This is why some people seem to age faster than others. Even more striking - many studies are finding that people with shorter telomeres are more prone to disease and even a shorter lifespan than those with longer telomeres."

Dr. Feinberg stopped for a moment and loosened his necktie. It seemed strange to even see one in the building, as none of the MadCity Boys or me ever wore one. Perhaps the doctor was trying to bridge the gap to those in his audience as he continued. "Scientists have been able to measure the length of telomeres and determine that stress can shorten them at a much faster rate than those of people who lead a less stress-filled life. This seems to be attributed to elevated levels of the hormone cortisol and may be one reason why stress can cause cancer. While it's impossible to eliminate all stress, identifying and then reducing stress, can slow the aging process and improve the overall quality of life and perhaps, just perhaps, prevent cancer."

Dr. Feinberg stopped and took a small drink of water and continued, "I mentioned that aging didn't happen with stem cells. What happens to them? Stem cells keep reproducing because an enzyme called telomerase repairs the stem cell's telomeres after each division. The interesting thing is that the telomerase doesn't affect non-dividing cells in the heart and brain and researchers believe that telomerase may even be one cause of cancer."

Feinberg added, "There is another component to aging that we need to examine that deals with the thymus gland which plays an important function in the immune system. The Thymus is classified as a lymphoid organ similar to the tonsils, adenoids and the spleen and is also considered an endocrine gland, like the thyroid and adrenal glands, such that it's a chemical messenger that emits hormones into the circulatory system that regulates other organs."

The boys were intrigued as the good doctor continued. "The thymus converts white blood cells into what are called T-lymphocytes or T-Cells where the "T" stands for thymus-derived cells that protect the body from bacteria, fungi, viruses and other pathogens."

"There are actually three different types of T-Cells. The first are called Cytotoxic T-cells where the word *cytotoxic* means "to kill" and these cells are responsible for directly killing infected or mutated, cells including cancer and viruses that enter the body. The second type are called Helper T-cells which are responsible for creating antibodies and activating other types of T-cells to address foreign invaders. The third type are called Regulatory T-cells which function as "police" to suppress both Helper and other T-cells to make certain the body doesn't overkill and do damage to healthy cells as well."

"Once the T-cells have learned to recognize specific pathogens, they travel to the medulla, which is the lower half of the brainstem that regulates several basic functions including respiration, cardiac function, vasodilation - which is the dilation of the blood vessels that controls blood pressure - reflexes like vomiting, coughing, sneezing, and swallowing where the cells undergo 'negative selection'."

"In the medulla, mature T-cells are introduced to the body's own antigens and/or other foreign substances which then induce an immune response which stimulates the T-cells. In most instances, only about 2% of the T-cells are released into the blood stream, where their job is to circulate and, when they encounter the molecular signature of the pathogen, attack the invader while also activating other immune cells while producing proteins known as cytokines that play a role in regulating the level of immune response."

"One of the challenges we don't understand happens with a systemic outbreak, such as the Coronavirus is that, for some reason, the number of Regulatory T-cells seem to not function properly, allowing too many T-cells to become active, thereby doing damage to normal cells affecting everything from the respiratory system to even the cells of the heart."

"What is unique is that the thymus reaches maturity "in utero" or before a child is born, and is at its largest and most active state in children. Starting at puberty, the thymus gradually becomes less active and the glandular tissue begins to shrink. By the time someone reaches their mid-60s, the thymus is largely inactive. By their mid-70s, or my age, the gland is no longer functioning. While there are still T-cells in the body, they no longer are as vibrant and aggressive as those made by the thymus and the aging body becomes more susceptible to infections and other types of diseases including pneumonia and cancer."

Stopping again and looking up at the audience, Dr. Feinberg posed the question. "What would happen if we could affect the length and/or duration of the telomeres or figure out a way to keep the thymus active? Could it mean that we could live longer or better?"

There was a pause to allow the thoughts to be pondered before Dr. Feinberg continued. "The profound question that arises is, can we, as a species, play God? Do we have the right to extend human life by manipulating the length or duration of a human's telomeres or creating a way to increase the number of T-cells in the body? If so, what is the limit and what are the consequences? Who is chosen to stay and who has to go? These are questions being pondered by bioethicists around the globe. In a world where the human population is decimating all other living species, do we have the right to take up more space simply to extend our individual existence, and if so, who get to decide?"

Again Dr. Feinberg's glasses came off as he walked slowly from behind the podium and directly in front of the audience. "This is why I sincerely believe we need to look at life only from a qualitative aspect, instead of a quantitative one! It would be a noble event if we could slow the aging process to minimize maladies and reduce infirmities without extending life."

Dr. Feinberg stuck his hands in his pockets and continued. "As has been the case with many childhood maladies such as Polio and Measles, Mumps and Rubella, our research deals with taking the illnesses of the aged and lowering or eliminating their consequence, without adding one single day to how long God has it planned that we exist on their earth. In other words - a qualitative solution and not a quantitative proposal. This is our goal! This is what I hope we can accomplish! This is why I am here today!"

The doctor looked around the room and then directly into the camera lens. "Before me, I am honored to be in the presences of some of the greatest research minds in the world who have created a collaboration based on your ability to give of oneself for the betterment of others. While this noble gesture has been part of mankind since its beginning, the use of one of the most powerful thinking machines ever created, allows you to take giant leaps instead of small steps and I commend you for this, especially because it's being done for the good of all living species and not their demise!"

We spent the next hour taking questions from the MadCity Boys and around the world. Everything was on the table and I believe even Dr. Feinberg was impressed by the depth of knowledge and commitment of the assembled team. Not once was the word "I" spoken. It was always "we" and this gave me an immense sense of pride.

After the give-and-take, Dr. Feinberg said goodbye and headed for the chopper to take him to Madison and his flight back to MIT on Amelia II. With his departure, the LED dots around the globe began to disappear and soon we were ensconced with just those who made up the local team. We all sat for a few minutes and digested what had been presented. And, like a fine meal, there was a profound sense of satisfaction regarding what had been consumed reflected in the smiles on everyone's faces.

As the silence of reflection became deafening, Peter spoke. "What if we could develop a nano-chip that could be implanted in the brain that would enhance communication between the brain and the primary organs?" Everyone had a perplexed look on their faces.

Peter continued. "If the human body produces so many different chemicals that control everything and drugs are used to replace stimulation of those chemicals, why couldn't we just create a chip that would allow the body to compensate for the inaccurate production allowing the body to have ongoing chemical balance?"

I inquired, "You mean, like being able to have the body create insulin so that those with diabetes wouldn't need to have shots?"

Peter shook his head in the affirmative.

"But how would the body react to having a nano-chip inside and where would it get the power needed to operate it?" I asked.

Peter raised his hands. "Hold it! We're getting way ahead of ourselves. First, we would need to determine what components are going to be required to create the chip, then we would need to outline what the chip would do and finally, we would need to determine how and where the chip could be implanted so that it wasn't a risk to the rest of the body and didn't have ill effects on the person, their wellbeing, nature or personality." Leave it to Peter to have already mentally examined the permutations and develop an operating objective.

The room rustled with electricity. The MadCity Boys were excited! There were enough programming skills in the room to solve the entire issue of how the chip would work. SIMON could examine all the permutations concerning design and development and chip capacity. Working with Hsu and Indira would give us insight into the biomedical aspects we would need to consider regarding a chip implanted in a human. Peter offered to head up the team and determine what groups of scientists were needed to help develop the chip and determine whether it would work.

Like everything else, the boys thought we needed a name for the entire project. After much debate, the boys elected to call it 'Project Frisco' simply because anyone from San Francisco hated when their beautiful city was called Frisco. I learned long ago, that the MadCity Boys had tremendous disdain for the egos of Silicon Valley and all they had accomplished. My rough, tough team of geeks were once again motivated and simply wanted to show the world that some social rejects from Waldwick, Wisconsin could create something more profound than they could and with that, Project Frisco began!

Offspring:

Our marriage remained solid after I realized and accepted what Amelia needed and that I too, had a mistress, better known as success. Yes, I had shifted out of the corporate world. However, the drive to accomplish simply changed direction.

While I was "sharing" my wife every now and then, other things remained the same. The question I always asked myself was how three children with the same parents, of which two are twins, could be so different? The youngest was our daughter, Melia. This wonderful daughter went through childhood marveling at the mysteries of life, wondering, pondering, contemplating how this and that and everything in between all fit together. As she reached an age of maturity, the little girl departed and a young woman appeared. While others dreamt of this and that, Melia's inquisition took her deep into the world of medicine and low and behold, my daughter, the silly one, who made us laugh, took after her grandmother and chose the world of Medicine. While others would venture into general medicine or even a traditional specialty, Melia evolved into the realm that Grandma Marie had ventured and delved into the world of Pediatric Oncology.

To make it even more specific, Melia evolved into Atomic Oncology and methods that would incorporate the use of lasers and even the wisdom of SIMON to identify and correlate procedures that would eradicate childhood cancers prior to their metastases and the eventual demise of a child.

To say that Melia was focused would be an understatement. It was laser-like and yet beneath the profound ability to zero-in on a specific particle of life, was the ability to expand beyond ever-increasing circles of knowledge, until she had encompassed a subject and brought it to her comprehension. Dedicated to her passion for medicine, life was not filled with the social aspects found in most young women. My hope and prayer was and remains that she finds someone, somewhere who can accept and understand a woman of profound intellect, completely dedicated to making the world a better place.

Our eldest son, by eleven minutes, Derrick, sustains the personality of his mother. He is incredibly intent and introspective, summarized in one word - serious. Whether questioning the existence of God or the value of wealth, Derrick had always been the least of our worries. We knew he would always perform to the greatest of his ability and understood that his frustration was not with others, but with the reality that he was human and as such, limited. Like Melia, he accelerated his educational process and graduated from high school early. By twenty-one, he was already in Cornell Law School, going there, not only because of its stature, but because Uncle Rodney had been so adamant about its quality.

Being one-fourth African American was the final reason. Cornell University, from its inception in 1865, had welcomed people based on who they were and not what they were or where they came from. As was the case with Amelia, we knew the day would come when Derrick would evolve into the leadership position of Wilco and take Amy's place as all the intrinsic components were there - intelligence, leadership and compassion.

Our third child - George the fifth, better known as 'V'. Well what can I say? Words like spoiled brat, self-serving, egocentric, do not do those descriptors justice. Expelled from high school, totally aloof and irreverent, 'V' was everything the others were not. Graduating behind his twin brother from high school meant nothing to him as long as he was having a good time. I remember back when he was a little boy and I was his hero. I did my best to teach and share my love and yet it never seemed to click. We were apart emotionally and he, even then, resented all that we were. By the age of thirteen, when my role was supposed to change from that of teacher to counselor, the resentment was still there. If I said 'up', he said 'down'. If I said 'good', he said 'bad'. If I said 'black', he said 'white' and so it was.

At age twenty-one 'V' had already flunked out of two colleges and we were informed he was being expelled from community college for having skipped so many classes, some of the instructors didn't even know he was attending. Amy and I were at wits' end.

One night, 'V' came home - half-drunk and roaring into the driveway in what was his fourth car in two years. It seems that when there is no cost, there is no value. As 'V' walked into the house, I was sitting on the couch waiting for him.

"Time, we have a talk," I announced.

"About what?" he responded.

"About you!"

"What about me?

"Your attitude!"

"What about my attitude?"

I had always been polite around the kids and yet this was going to be a serious conversation. The kids never heard me swear, nor raise my voice, but I knew I only had one more chance to try and save my son from familial oblivion.

"Your attitude sucks!"

He snickered.

"That's what I'm talking about. You think the world owes you everything and yet you are a fucking loser!"

'V's' head jerked back at my language and he stopped in his tracks. It was time to let the hammer down as I continued, "You think you're some sort of hot piece of shit and yet you are nothing! Takeaway mommy and daddy's money and you're nothing! You can't make it through one year of college! You don't even make it to classes at the community college. You have no sense of commitment to anything but yourself and those loser friends who hang on because you are the rich kid with the fancy cars who has to buy friends because no one wants to be around him."

This caught him off guard. I could see the anger rising.

I continued on. "I'm sick and tired of all your bullshit. You do nothing, accomplish nothing and are simply waiting for the day when your inheritance comes in. Little rich boy, who thinks he owns the world," I said in the most sarcastic tone I could create. "There's just one major problem. You haven't read the fine print of grandpa's will, where it says that when he dies, your mother and I get to determine if-or-when you get your inheritance and right now, my vote is never."

'V' looked at me in astonished amazement as I continued on. "You heard me, nothing!" I repeated the absolute for effect, "nothing unless your mother and I agree and right now you're not worth it."

"Fuck you!" as the insult slid under his voice.

Now I was really pissed! "Tell you what. Give me the keys to MY car!"

"What?"

"You heard me. Give me the keys to my car!"

"Your car? It came from the dealership."

"That your grandpa, mother and I own. Now, give me the keys!"

"How am I supposed to get around?"

"Ask your asshole buddies!"

The temperature in the room was rising and my Mini-Point badass temper was coming to a boil as my vitriolic mind spewed forth, "This is the end of the line. The free ride is over. Either get a job and start paying rent or get your ass out of my house."

"Your house?" he snarled. "Mom paid for it! Mom pays for everything." His verbal knife dug deep into my back.

"I'm going to talk to mom!"

"Don't you think your mother and I haven't discussed this? You're nothing! You do nothing! When are you going to grow up and become a man?"

Once again, I heard the expletive beneath his breath as my anger level went up another notch to a level only matched a long time ago when some ass decided to offend Rodney's wife, Ann, in the hospital.

I stood and looked him in the eye. "Time for you to see the world. Let's go!"

"Where are we going?"

"Makes no difference. Let's go!"

"I've got plans!"

"Tough shit!"

"Come with me now or get out of this house and NEVER come back."

We'd had other "discussions" but never like this. He realized this was much more serious than ever before and obliged.

I took the keys to the Corvette and headed for the driver's seat. I don't think he believed I could drive the beast. Quietly 'V' slid into the passenger seat. I could tell his demeanor was such that he could be easily angered to the point of becoming quarrelsome or even unruly, but I really didn't give a damn! I turned the key and slammed on the gas. We hit nearly 80 miles an hour before we were even on Highway 83.

I turned south and headed for the Interstate. Going west, I knew we could easily hit 150 MPH but didn't want to be interrupted by a speeding ticket and so I kept it in fourth gear at 80. Not a word was spoken as we headed towards Madison.

"I'm thirsty," he said.

Without a word, I took exit 267 and headed towards Watertown and eased into a gas station.

"You want anything?" he asked.

I just shook my head no.

A few minutes later he came out with nothing. "I need some money," he stated.

I silently stared at him as he continued. "I don't have any cash and they said my credit card has been cancelled."

"I guess you'll have to go without or go in the bathroom and drink from the sink," I replied. For the first time in his life, he felt the profound limitations of being broke, where something he wanted could not easily be had.

He got in and slammed the door and I took off again.

As we entered Madison, I headed south to the Beltline and the Park Street exit, towards the poorest part of town. As we left Park Street and got into an area called Hells Half Acre, I slowed to a crawl. The folks who lived there had to think it strange that a red, sports car, would be driving down their street and not stopping to deal drugs. I looked out the window at those looking back.

As we returned to Park Street and Badger Road, I pulled into the city bus waiting area and shut off the engine. I looked at 'V' and asked him what he saw.

He shrugged his shoulders, which profoundly irritated me.

"Are you that dumb or so self-centered that you saw nothing? Tell me what you saw!" I demanded in a tone that lambasted his response.

"A bunch of blacks sitting on their porches."

"A bunch of blacks?" I said incredulously. "A bunch of blacks?" The words spewed from my mouth in total disdain. "V's" head jolted back as I continued on. "Let's play a little word game - you and me!"

'V' had a quizzical look on his face as I detailed, "I'm going to say a word and you tell me the first word that comes to mind."

A slight sneer came across "V's" lips, which really pissed me off.

"Up!" I commanded. "Down" was the reply.

"Good" I directed. "Bad" was the reply.

"Black" I stated. "White" was his response.

"Brown" I murmured.

'V' looked at me and shook his head, as I said, "You said you saw black people and yet they weren't black. They were brown. You consider yourself white and yet your grandmother was of African descent. Your mother is half, what you call black, and you are one-fourth the same color. By using the term black-and-white you make them out to be opposites. To have them be different shades of brown, can't you see, we are all alike? Son, it is an incontrovertible fact that our family's society, culture and beliefs have impregnated your mind and done so to the point you won't let go and yet, you must!"

"Do you belong with them?" I asked. To which, there was another shrug on "V's" shoulders.

When your mother was your age, she didn't know where she belonged. Half-black, half-white! Did she belong with the rich white folks or with the sisters? I shook my head and asked, "What else did you see?" as my temper was rising.

"Squalor," Was his reply.

"Squalor? You mean poverty?"

He was softening. "Yes, poverty."

"Something you know absolutely nothing about!"

'V' just shook his head, which really pissed me off. "You think the universe revolves around you! It doesn't"!

I was on a roll and I wasn't going to stop. My Minnie Point Badass was at full broil as I stared at 'V' with a sneer on my face. "The universe is not just about rocks and gasses, atoms, protons and electrons and you. It is simply everything **and** nothing. Sadly, you and your friends are brainwashed! You look at all that is right, all that is good and all that is decent and do so with disdain. You have forgotten that all human existence is founded on our interaction with other humans that you continually lambaste and consider beneath you. Yet it is you and your friends who are languid – nothing more than poor players strutting and fretting upon the stage of life, believing the spotlight is on you when you're not the least bit significant to others, including right now, your family."

This got a jolt from him and after the words slid from my mouth, I regretted what I had said but continued on, hoping I hadn't hit too hard. "Positive relationships are the part of our universe that we must cherish most - family, friends, co-workers and neighbors represent just a few of the interactions that take place on a daily basis from which we define 'who' we are. Yet, you demean, degrade and denigrate these people simply because they are different than you. Because socialization is so critical to our wellbeing it isn't surprising to find that the most stressful experiences in a normal person's life center around those that strain or break social interactions. But for you, people are disposable, feelings perishable and relationships fleeting simply because they don't fit your realm at that time."

'V' was beginning to breathe deeply. I didn't know if it was anger or fear and yet I was a long way from being done. This was make-or-break time and I was going to have my say whether he liked it or not. "You don't even realize what you're doing to yourself or your family and how much it hurts your mother to see you act, think and feel the way that you do."

'V' defiantly retorted, "I've got lots of friends." Which raised my ire to an even higher level.

"You and your friends are superficial at best. You do things to attract attention and do so in unseemly and inappropriate fashion simply to degrade, diminish, shock or insult those you deem unfit for belonging to your misanthropic tribe of malcontents." I paused for a moment to allow my blood pressure to drop and then continued in a more scholarly tone. "You seem to be devoid of any modicum of decency and yet you are alone, unwilling to examine the benefits of being socially active and the risks of social isolation."

I paused for a moment and took a deep breath and then continued in a fatherly tone. "Son, socialization isn't limited to how many people you interact with as much as the satisfaction these social relationships provide. When a person feels their relationships are inadequate to satisfy their intimate and social needs, loneliness can happen, even when they are with others. Right now, when I look at you, I see one of the loneliest people I've ever known."

"Son, this loneliness can lead to an isolated life in a social world may and do so to the point that it becomes the basis of your existence and this is what I am truly afraid of. Look at those who kill! Many of them are lonely, social outcasts and their actions are nothing more than one final way to get attention!"

'V' was shaking his head. I didn't know if it was in disagreement or disbelief that someone had finally laid it out for him and it was time to go for the jugular.

I continued on. "What stops you from reaching out to others and expanding your relationships? I remember back to taking Anthropology at the UW and one word stuck with me, that I have done everything in my power not to subscribe to and that is Ethnocentrism."

There was a frown on 'V's' face and I knew he didn't have a clue, but when you've flunked out of two colleges and never went to class at a third, how could you ever understand. I continued, "Ethnocentrism is used in social sciences and anthropology to describe the act of judging another culture and believing that the values and standards of one's own culture are superior – especially with regard to language, behavior, traditions and religion. These aspects or categories are distinctions that define each ethnic group's unique cultural identity and that defines your entire group."

I looked at him and said, "'V', our country is **not** a unified nation. It's a conglomeration of sub-cultures – racial, religious, geographic, sexual and socio-economic to name a few. The net sum is that we have different opinions simply because the sub-cultures are 'different' in terms of beliefs, arts, traditions, capabilities, and habits. This isn't wrong, it's reality. It's amazing how the different races, religions, ethnicity, socio-economics and orientations can look at the same subject and have profoundly different opinions."

I shook my head in dismay and added. "We think we're one culture in America and yet the only thing that ties us together are the laws, which theoretically, are supposed to apply to everyone, but really never do. Laws are for poor people to abide by and for rich people to negotiate around which is one of the reasons why our country is so screwed up today."

As a parent, I was supposed to teach you. Unfortunately, I was too busy and taught you to look through the wrong end of social binoculars. If I'd paid more attention to you, I believe I would have done a better job of establishing right and wrong, good and bad, honorable and dishonorable, which I call 'personal accountability' that does **not** include entitlement and degradation of those less fortunate that we are."

I took a deep breath and stared at the road in front of me as I continued. "I'm not Lord God King, exulted ruler. I am a man, a husband and a father who has had his values shaped by his family, job and wife. I cannot expect that you will accept all that I believe in. All I can hope is that you use our values as the basis for creating your own."

"I realize and accept that nothing is cast in stone! What were the rules for mom and I ,are not the same rules for you and it's important to remember is that our culture is always in a state of osmosis that result in constant modifications regarding acceptable social behavior. Back in the 1950's there was segregation. In the North, white people didn't mind if African-American's got ahead, they just didn't want them living by them. In the South, while people didn't mind if blacks lived nearby, they just didn't want them to get ahead and so they had segregated schools. In 1960 with the advent of school integration, white and black students from the same community, who never really knew each other, began to interact, they began to realize that the other side 'wasn't really that bad'".

"We have no idea what it was like for Grandma Marie and The Duke". They were ostracized simply because of the color of their skin." To which "V's" mouth dropped open in surprise and then disdain. If it was sixty years ago and we were living in the South, you couldn't have been able to use "white" bathroom at the gas station or drink from a "white" water fountain, or eaten in a "white" restaurant or gone to "white schools" because you are one-fourth black. Sadly, today, some of that prejudice is still there, it's just hidden, but it is still wrong."

"But it's not that bad! 'V' retorted.

"For you no! That's because you're one of the lucky ones. While racial prejudice has been a part of American history since it began, today we see a tectonic shift away from abject delineation along racial lines to one more concurrent with socio-economic levels, where the higher the level of individual development educationally, financially and/or socially, the lower the level of racial reticence to the point that race becomes a secondary component - never forgotten - but minimized.

Whether it's the medical, professional, business or political leader, entertainer or athlete, the higher the level of attainment, the lower the level of racial delineation. Because of our wealth and social status, you're lucky, you're accepted. Take that away and you would be considered a social misfit – too dark to be white and too light to be black. Ask your mother, she went through it."

It was time to make my point. "If you want to be a better person, be a member of this universe and a participant in this thing called life. To do so, you will need to reach out to the lonely and simply let them realize they're not alone. You can touch their hearts and move their souls. You can look them in the eye and put a simple smile on their face and perhaps, just perhaps, help them break the cycle of singularity that permeates their heart by letting them see and feel that there are people who really care".

V's smart-ass, attitude was melting and yet it was still there. "Tonight, you got a taste of what it's like when you had no money when I told you to drink out of the bathroom faucet. You've been lucky and have had it good with everything handed to you. The mistake mom and I made was creating your assumption that it would always continue and yet, realistically you've done nothing to earn it." I paused for a moment and glanced over at 'V' and asked. "What else did you see?"

'V' shook his head from side-to-side as I let the world go silent for another pregnant pause. I continued. "Didn't you see people smiling and laughing? You haven't smiled or laughed in so long, I don't think you know how. Do you know why they smile? Because they have a sense of family and love - the two things you haven't shown in so long I don't think you know how. Whose better off? You, the rich white boy or those poor black folks as you call them? I bet on them, as they have something to live for and you have nothing except a bunch of parasitic friends and the BELIEF that you will inherit a lot of money that you can piss away."

I started the Corvette and roared out onto the Beltline towards Verona Road. Not a word was said. I hit the Verona exit in a matter of minutes and headed south on Highway 18 and 151 - the road I had driven hundreds of times. It was the road I had almost died on that changed my life forever. My goal was simply to save the life of my son. We drove past the small towns that had become Madison's suburbs and the small hobby farms, until the rolling hills of Iowa County came into view as we made our way to the Mineral Point exit and the north end of Shake Rag street where I added, "Your ancestors came down this road nearly 200 years ago with nothing but a dream. They scrimped and saved and did everything they could simply to live that dream. You have no dreams! You have nothing!"

My dissertation had taken the entire time it took to get from Madison to the farm as I pulled into the Waldwick compound. 'V' thought we would go inside. Instead I headed straight for The Forest path and talked while walking, as he followed. "The people who work here are dedicating their lives to making the world a better place. You, on the other hand, only care about getting drunk, making an ass out of yourself and finding the next woman to screw."

It was time for the ultimatum and so I beckoned with my hand as we walked deeper into The Forest. We made it to Great Grandfathers obelisk and the bench beside it. "Sit!" I commanded. Looking at the obelisk, I spoke again, staring up at the early evening sky. "Great Grandfather, if you are listening, please come to my son and share your wisdom."

I turned to 'V' and looked deeply into his eyes. "I'm leaving you here. I'll be back when I've calmed down. If you're still here, then all will be forgiven and we can start over. If you've departed, never come home again."

He sat stunned. I was simply walking away knowing that I'd said everything I could and believing it was now up to him. Tommie and Hsu were gone and so I drove into Mineral Point and had a quiet dinner at the Brewery Creek Pub. Afterward, I went up on High Street and had a couple more beers. I needed to calm down!

It was nearly eleven o'clock when I decided enough-was-enough and headed back to The Forest. I walked down the cinder path and 'V' was still sitting on the bench. He looked up at me and there were tears in his eyes.

"Dad!"

"What, son?"

"When you left and I was sitting here and this feeling rose up inside me. It was unlike anything I've ever felt before and I began to cry. All the anger! All the fear! All the frustration! All the sadness that had been building up inside of me just seemed to come out. I – I - I don't know how to explain it!"

"You don't have to, son, I've felt the feelings you felt and that is why I brought you here tonight."

"Dad, an old man came and stood before me. He had white hair and it was in a braid. He was wearing Indian clothes and spoke in a whisper."

"What about his eyes?" I asked.

"They were milky white."

My prayers had been answered. "It was the spirit of Great Grandfather. Please call him that." I said.

'V' continued. "Great Grandfather and I walked to the springs and he told me to drink from the cup. I did as I was instructed and a strange feeling came over me. For the first time, I felt as if I was at someplace special. I got the chills and the old man told me that it was all the anger, sadness and frustration leaving my body."

For many, there would be questions of sincerity. "V" had a reputation that way. It was when I looked in "V's" eyes that I knew the spirit was within him. Gone was the anger and bitterness!

Replaced by the gentle glow that only comes when one is at peace with themselves. While he had been blind, I had seen it in the eyes of Great Grandfather and knew that the truth was spoken as he had appeared and was truly in "V's" heart.

'V' continued. "Great Grandfather told me that I was still a boy and someday I would not only become a man, but a great leader. He told me my name was to become 'Two Feathers' and you would understand."

I sat down beside 'V' and looked into his eyes and explained. "Great Grandfather came to help you understand, just like he did for me. When I was about your age, I met with Great Grandfather several times and he taught me about life and most of all about goodness."

'V' responded as his head tilted back. "Great Grandfather explained that in order to become Two Feathers I would need to understand and respect four things, humility, generosity, compassion and forgiveness. Dad, I'm all screwed up. Derrick and Melia are so incredible and I'm just not them."

"No one said you need to be, son." I responded. "All you need be is yourself and greatness will come to you. You have all the tools! You just need to know what kind of house you want to build."

'V' looked perplexed by my last statement and so I continued.

"Life is like building a house. First you need to have a plan regarding what the house will look like. If it's too big, you will never fill it. It it's too small, you will quickly outgrow it."

I looked at my watch and it was nearly one in the morning. We walked towards The Forest edge and I stopped and turned back towards him and gently smiling, said, "If I found out that tomorrow would be my last day on earth, I would want to come here, be here and forever remain here, in both body and spirit. Come on son, let's head home" as I flipped him the car keys.

As 'V' drove, I told the entire story of Rodney, Ann, Great Grandfather, Luke and the Ley Lines and how we fought to keep The Forest. I shared with him my love of the land and my fears and finally, above all else, that my greatest accomplishment in life were my kids - all three of them.

We were nearing the Oconomowoc exit and I asked 'V', "Are you tired?"

"Not really," was his response. I guess the adrenaline was flowing through both of our bodies.

"Let's go to the office. There's something I want to show you."

We entered the darkened building and went into my office. I pulled down the case and handed it to my son. He looked inside and saw the two white eagle feathers as I noted, "These were given to me by the man you saw tonight. They are eagle feathers, the highest honor an Indian can receive and the greatest gift they can ever give. To the Indians, the eagle is a symbol of religious significance simply because it can fly higher than any other bird and to own them is reserved only for great leaders."

'V' examined the case and went to hand it back to me. I raised my hand to make him pause. "Someday they will be yours, until the day when you pass them on to your son or daughter as the Great Spirit directs you. With the feathers comes responsibility. Great Grandfather explained what you must become and now it is up to you to figure out how to realize the meaning of the name Two Feathers."

I added. "Humility! Generosity! Compassion! Forgiveness! If you are lucky, Great Grandfather will come again. However, don't rely on it. I last spoke with him nearly thirty years ago and since then he has not spoken to me once."

'V' was taken aback as he looked at the two feathers in the case and set it carefully on my desk. In twelve hours, we had gone from me threatening to disown him, to sharing one of my most prized possessions. He shook his head and asked, "How will I know when the time has come?"

I replied. "The feathers are not mine to keep and when the Great Spirit tells me the time is right, they will be yours. They were given to me as a symbol of my commitment to the betterment of mankind. They will not be yours today or even tomorrow, as they must be earned. Great Grandfather has spoken and some day it will be your turn. No one knows what the future will bring, but you have been chosen."

'V' sat down in the chair as I continued. "Soon you will have the urge to revisit The Forest on your own. The urge will come many times and it will be your respite from the perils of life. I believe that, like me, when you visit, you will be overcome by the tranquility and inner peace that will prevail. Do not fight your feelings. It is simply God leading you along the path. Drink from the springs and listen to the trees, as they will tell you the stories of those who came before you. Don't be afraid son! The Forest is a special place and you are a messenger. There will be days when you question all that transpires. There will be times when you will want to reject the responsibility. There will be circumstances and people who will challenge your commitment and yet, in the end, you will see that the path you take, will lead to profound happiness and satisfaction."

"You mean contentment?" 'V' asked, to which I nodded affirmatively.

I looked at 'V' and he at me and for the first time in a long, long time, there was life in both of our hearts. I stood and walked to the office corner. "Come here, there's something else I want to show you."

'V' rose and came to the office corner as I said. "This old chest belonged to the man you saw tonight. When I would meet with him, he would have me pull it up next to his rocking chair and hold my hands. As he spoke, his energy would enter my body and what he thought, I would also think. What he felt, I would feel. What he believed, I came to believe and it was then that I became Little Spirit. Pull up the chest and sit with me."

'V' did as he was directed. I put his hands in mine and continued on as Great Grandfather had done with me. "On the day Great Grandfather died, I came to the assisted living center and was given this chest. Not once, had I ever been given the opportunity to look inside until that day. As I stood in his empty room, I opened the chest and saw what it contained. No one but me has ever seen what the chest contains. Not your mother, nor your brother or sister. Someday, I will show you its contents and why you have been chosen, but it must be earned and not given, for it does not belong to me."

I could feel the energy between us traversing. I watched as my son's body quaked. I knew that all that had been within my soul, placed there by Great Grandfather, was being traversed into my son. "V's" head shook and his eyes closed as more tears rolled down his cheeks.

The stories that Great Grandfather had shared with me were being transferred, along with the pain and suffering that his people had endured. With it, came the anger and frustration that so many had felt. With that came the goodness and decency of a people so long ago who wanted nothing more than to live their lives in peace. I closed my eyes and my body also quaked. All that had been locked within me for so many years was flowing and there was a profound sense of relief as the story I had been told was finally being shared with another.

'V' and I sat in total harmony. As the transfer ended, our eyes opened and before me stood a different person. While the body was the same, gone was the boy and in his place, stood a man who now knew about life and was ready for what lie ahead.

I stood in awe. Before me was my son, who now contained a force field so great and so powerful that I was truly humbled by his existence. His energy field was now being transmitted and I could actually feel the interaction of his body and spirit as it coincided with that of his heart to create an aura that was being amplified, enhanced and expanded as one.

For an instant, the lights of my office flickered. The shared feelings took my body and shook it while everything 'V' had been, all that he had done and all that he could possibly do were being emanated in a tsunami of woven thoughts, emotions, experiences and fears that had been trapped for so long. I stood humbled as I realized that it was 'V' who had absorbed the sadness of an entire nation of people so long ago and it was 'V' who would help these noble people acquire the pride and happiness they had long sought .

I looked at my son and said. "Because of the us, Rodney's entire family exists. Because of that, I became a man who has dedicated his life to helping others. Because of Great Grandfather, our lives were forever changed. When you are troubled and need guidance, please come and sit on the old chest and feel the power within. When my dad and Grandma Marie died, I came here and called out for strength and guidance. When the three of you were born, I came here and thanked God for your existence. Yesterday, when our lives were so asunder, I came here and was directed to take you on the journey that we have taken. Someday, son, this too, will be yours to carry on all that is good."

With that, we hugged. Father and son - Little Spirit and Two Feathers, joined together on a journey as one.

There was a long pause and then 'V' asked, "What now?"

"That's up to you," I replied. "My hope is that you will come work at the Foundation. My dream is that someday you will take my place. I am totally certain that you will be much more than me, recognized and honored for all the goodness you have done for those whose lives you touch."

'V' looked at me and responded, "But I don't have any talent or education."

I replied. "There are only two things that matter and they are attitude and aptitude. You can learn, but the desire can only come from within your heart. What's incredible to me is that I don't think I've been what Great Grandfather said I would be and yet, I look at you and realize, understand and accept that, you my son, are the chosen one. Great Grandfather has already shown me that someday you will be a great leader. While I still have a long way to go before I reach that point where I feel I have accomplished what God has put me on this earth to do, I must share with you the caution bestowed on me that took many years for me to finally understand and accept."

"First, you must understand and accept that there is a profound difference between leadership and authority. People lead others because the others want to follow. People abide by rules established by authorities because there are consequences if they don't. The challenge we all have is determining who to follow and why. Those who lead must build the characteristics needed to have people want to follow them. As ridiculous as this may sound, you will either be a leader or a follower and virtually everyone ends up being both. As a parent, you lead your children. Throughout life, you follow teachers, politicians, religious clerics, whomever. The problem is that it takes inherent skills to be both a good leader and a great follower."

'V' continued to sit on the old chest as I stood and looked down.

"What can I do?" he asked, looking up at me.

"Learn! And as you learn, doors will open and your God-given skills will come forth."

I looked at his tired eyes and knew we both needed sleep and said, "Sleep on it and let me know when you make up your mind."

"Dad, I have already made up my mind! I want to earn the name of Two Feathers and carry on for Little Spirit."

Now it was time for tears in my eyes.

We drove home and as we walked in the door, 'V' gave me a hug and said. "Thanks, dad. I love you."

Those words burrowed into my soul. It had been so long since he had spoken them and they sounded so good. I quietly went to Amy's and my bedroom, undressed and slid under the covers.

"How did it go?" Amy whispered.

"Great Grandfather spoke to him," I replied

"Then all will be right?"

"Yes. All will be right!"

I slid down upon my pillow and looked across at the woman I loved and asked, "Have I shown you lately that I love you?" as I kissed her goodnight.

I could feel Amy looking at me in our darkened room and could feel her soft, gentle smile as she whispered, "Perhaps, I can be of some help."

The next morning 'V' and Amy had a private conversation dealing with her philosophy on life and how, her combination of what she called Mindfulness gave her a different perspective on life. I was afraid that 'V's" sense of self-worth was so ingrained it had become immutable, and yet, the soft smile of my wife and her sheer determination eradicated those doubts and she and 'V' began working together, discussing a depth of life and the value of living with internal peace.

Amy explained the term mindfulness as simply a straightforward word suggesting that the mind is fully attending to what's happening regarding what a person is doing and the space they are moving through. "Normally, a person's mind takes flight and they lose touch with their body to the point that, pretty soon they're engrossed in obsessive thoughts about something that just happened or fretting about the future that make them anxious."

Amy added that Mindfulness was the trained ability to be fully present, while being completely aware of where we are and what we're doing, and doing so, to the point that a person doesn't over-react or be overwhelmed by what's going on around them. She noted that, while socialization takes with many nuances and creates an inveterate situation, beneath the ordained level of existence lies a quality that every human being already possesses which simply requires the individual to learn how to allow have it to come into place and do so willingly. What she was saying made all the sense in the world and yet I knew that the thoughts and ideas would quickly dissipate if they were inculcated and accepted for what they were – changes that need to be made.

For Amy, the practice was automatic and unrelenting as it was part of her nature. I thought it would take continuous repetition for 'V' because he had such a long way to go.

However, Amy said that 'V' was very receptive and accepting what Amy shared with me the following. "When we are mindful, we can reduce stress, enhance performance and gain insight and awareness through observing our own mind, and increase our attention to others' well-being thereby providing time when we can suspend judgment and unleash our natural curiosity about the workings of the mind. When done properly, a person can approach all experiences with warmth and kindness—to ourselves and others."

In a few months, what had been a verbal commitment to me, began to see fruition. Gone was 'V's' narcissistic demeanor, replaced by a softer, gentler soul who looked deep into everyone's heart before speaking. In the absence of a smart-ass, insecure punk, arose a man of tremendous compassion, accentuated by the level of humility that actually enveloped me in awe. Not since Great Grandfather, had the aura I began to feel been present and I sensed that greatness what amongst our midst and greater things were about to happen.

The Meeting:

It was time for the annual Williams' family meeting. The date was set and the two-hour agenda established. It would be Amy, The Duke and me at the Wilco offices. The kids weren't allowed, as it was set to only be two generations and never three.

Andrew's security team scanned the room and Amy and I arrived about five minutes before the scheduled start. We saw that all the key players were ready to make their presentations - lawyers, accountants and advisors. The only person missing was The Duke. As a stickler for promptness, this wasn't like him. I looked at Amy who had a worried look on her face.

The Duke never carried a cellphone and so at 10:05 Amy called the house but there was no answer. Now, she was really worried and called Dennis. Even though he was running the airline, he was still loyal to The Duke and making certain everything was all right.

As Amy was talking to Dennis, the door opened and The Duke walked in. He was fifteen minutes late. I hoped that the excuse was traffic. His answer broke my heart. He had forgotten that the meeting was that morning. This was the most important meeting of the year and he had forgotten?

The lawyers and accountants and financial planners went through everything as I watched The Duke's mind wander. Either he no longer cared or was confused. I hoped for indifference and feared confusion.

Discussions turned to assets and returns-on-investment and the subject of the car dealerships came up. The world was changing and being in retail was more of a burden than it was worth. Amy and I sat and listened. This had been the cornerstone of the empire and we wondered what The Duke would think if we sold it off.

I looked at The Duke and he seemed indifferent. He had lost the passion.

"You kids do whatever you think is best," he added.

We looked at the inner circle and directed them to determine a strategy to sell off the auto group assets - all in one chunk or in pieces if we decided to do so. The committee could only recommend and so the process began.

As all the parts fell into place, we learned that the total net worth of Amy and her dad and the Foundation now exceeded twenty billion dollars. When you get to that level, money really loses its value. Anything and everything is yours except freedom - freedom to be and do - freedom to dream about tomorrow - freedom to be nothing more than normal, simply because you aren't normal.

My mind wandered back to my conversation with 'V'. *"Which is better to have nothing or everything?"* As The Duke once said, "You can buy anything, have anything, do anything except one very critical component that we all have in common and that's time. No matter how much money you have, a minute is a minute is a minute." The other aspect is health. While money allows for better treatment, it still doesn't eradicate the fact that rich and poor have one other thing in common - death!

At exactly noon the meeting was over. Lunch was served and it was time to go home. I looked at the little old man sitting alone and for the first time ever, I was worried.

"Dad, why don't you come out to the house?" I asked.

"No, Marie and I are going out for dinner tonight," was his response.

Amy's eyes closed as daggers of reality dug deep within her heart.

We got in the car to go home and Amy quietly whispered, "I'm concerned."

There was no need to address the subject of memory loss as The Duke had just spoken. The question became what to do about it. How do you go to a man with all the money and power you could ever imagine and tell him he was mentally slipping?

"I think we should call Dennis," was my response, and instructed SIMON to call Dennis' private number. While we were family-oriented as a company, we also knew that we needed to get hold of each other in times of emergency. For this reason, all senior executives had dual-line cellphones. The first line was for standard communication. The second was for times of real need, to which only recognized phone numbers were accepted. We thought this was one of those times.

All company phones had caller ID and Dennis knew it was me. I opened the line so that Amy could hear and let Dennis know that he was on speaker phone. "Dennis, we just had the annual family meeting and a couple of things came up that I felt you should be aware of that have us concerned." I could sense the fear in Dennis as I spoke. "First, The Duke was fifteen minutes late for the meeting and said it was because he forgot. Second, Amy and I asked him to come out to the house and he said he couldn't because he and Dr. Williams had a dinner engagement tonight."

There was a long pause on the other end as Dennis replied. "George, I've been noticing a few slips lately whenever we're together, but nothing that big. What do you want me to do?"

"When is The Duke scheduled for his next physical?"

"I'm not quite certain, but I think it's in a few months."

"Why don't we see if we can move it up? I'll have Cecilia make the arrangements. Is there any time that's more convenient for you?"

"George, you know that I will do anything for you, Amy and The Duke. Just have Cecelia call me and I'll make certain that I personally take him."

Amy spoke up. "Thanks Dennis, you are his most trusted friend."

"Thank you, Mrs. Terrill."

I chimed in. "I'm concerned about him driving and also his safety at home. Can you talk with Andrew and see what we can do? We don't want to over react but at the same time, we need to find out what's going on."

"Let me see what I can do, sir."

With that the conversation was over. Two hours later Andrew called and outlined a plan. He would take some of his most trusted security people and go to The Duke's house with Dennis. They would go under the auspice that The Duke's truck needed routine service and they wanted to upgrade the security system. This would allow the security team to check the property and remove the vehicle. Dennis would tell The Duke they would have someone ready to drive him wherever he needed to go until the truck came back. The plan was agreed to.

Three hours later Andrew called back and indicated they had activated all the cameras in the house except in the bedroom and bathrooms. He noted that The Duke was cooperative about the truck and actually invited the assigned driver into the house to eat lunch and play cribbage. Amy and I were relieved.

Cecelia pulled strings and two days later The Duke went in for what he thought was just his annual physical, not remembering that it had only been three months since he had been there previously. After the normal exam, a gerontologist came in and they began talking.

Fifteen minutes after The Duke walked out of the facility, we got a call. Our worst fears were coming true. Douglas Williams was in Stage II Alzheimer's Disease. I asked what the difference between Alzheimer's and dementia was and the doctor me informed that dementia is a general term for a decline in mental ability that is severe enough to interfere with everyday life. I thought to myself that he was also referring to the government, but kept my mouth shut, knowing that being a smart ass at this time was not appropriate.

The doctor added that nearly six million Americans 65 and older suffer from Alzheimer's which, he noted, was a degenerative brain disease that could lead to dementia. The doctor outlined the early warning signs caused by Alzheimer's disease which consisted of repetitive questions and stories, troubles with orientation and difficulties with complex daily tasks.

Amy had been doing her research and found that there were actually seven stages to Alzheimer's ranging from stage one where there was no impairment to Stage VII where the disease was terminal. Amy also examined the five stages between and realized we would be losing the person we both loved in a slow, gradual evolution from powerful and dynamic to lost in a maze, unable to communicate, recognize or share life's joys.

As we thought back, we both realized that The Duke was having difficulty finding the right words during conversations; was challenged in organizing and planning; had just about given up on remembering names of new acquaintances and would lose his car keys and personal possessions on a periodic basis. All of these were indications of the insipience that was about to take him from us.

The doctor added that The Duke was suffering from a moderately aggressive form of the malady where physical aerobic exercise and a Mediterranean diet consisting of small amounts of red meat, whole grains, fruits and vegetables, fish and shell fish and healthy fats such as nuts and olive oil would help. We were also assured that beyond the exercise and dietary changes, medications had been prescribed that would hopefully slow his decline.

The doctor also told us that emotional health was critical to slowing the onset. He noted that depression was a large risk factor such that those suffering from depression tended to be subject to a more rapid decline in memory and thinking skills. I immediately correlated the loss of Dr. Williams to dad William's decline and realized that death has a way of taking more than the one who has departed.

Sadly, we were also informed that the journey was a one-way street, and he would slowly slip away and Amy was devastated. We called a family meeting and let the kids know. Melia was stoic. Derrick the lawyer, had tears in his eyes. 'V' looked at me and put up his left fist and said, "Dad, the fight has only just begun. Let's see if SIMON and the MadCity Boys can't help."

The Prognosis:

'V' called Peter and told him the news that Grandpa had Stage II Alzheimer's and the doctors said there was little that could be done. 'V' asked if the MadCity Boys could meet with us at the compound and discuss using SIMON to determine the best course of action. 'V' was taking charge. I smiled. Even under the circumstances, he made me proud.

The MadCity Boys hadn't seen the new "'V", nor knew anything about all that had transpired. They just thought of him as this smart-ass, spoiled, rich kid. Because the Foundation had made them all very comfortable, while allowing them to retain their independence, they all recognized that their freedom, wealth and lifestyle were based on the benevolence of The Duke and Williams' family fortune, so they reluctantly agreed. Little did they know, they were in for the surprise of their lives.

The meeting was set for five days hence and 'V' and I took our new Airbus H160 helicopter to Waldwick. With our standard choppers, the one thing The Duke and I both found uncomfortable was the noise. While wearing noise-canceling headphones made it tolerable, I was always on the lookout for the newest, best and quietest ride possible. We had money down on Textron's first electric units, but I wanted the best that was available and so Dennis and I flew to Paris to see the Air Bus H160, which was billed as the world's first civilian helicopter made entirely from composite materials.

Dennis took it for a "test drive" and said the H160 was easy to fly, nimble and quite responsive, and the Helionix flight control system required fewer pre-flight checks, making it easier to get off the ground, thereby appeasing my insipient impatience. When I learned that it would take less than two minutes to get the helicopter into the air, I was ready to sign the papers.

Amelia XH, as she was christened, was initially designed to seat up to 12 passengers and two pilots and has a maximum take-off weight of 12,500 lbs. After Amy and the designers were done and we added additional acoustic insulation and our secret bar, we had a floating office that you could easily carry six passengers and two pilots, who could all have a pleasant conversation without headphones. I justified everything because the cruising speed of 177 MPH made the trip from the office to Waldwick in 20 minutes and increased the operating range to 550 miles while burning 15% less fuel and having auto pilot making.

Even with the new "ride" 'V' had a terrified look on his face regarding his presentation. He was never meant to be a gambler, but then neither was I.

"What if I'm a total failure, today?" 'V' asked.

I took a deep breath. We were getting close and I needed to continue.

"Leadership begins with respecting yourself by giving and defining your own value as a human being. If you don't respect yourself, it will be more difficult for you to respect anyone else. Having said that, I must add that respect must be earned and cannot be given. There's nothing free and there are no entitlements. You must create your own value."

Before 'V' could speak I continued – "But how do you do that? Within your realm, are the three components - the physical self, the mental self and spiritual self. From a physical perspective, it is critical that you maximize your potential health, which not only means proper diet, exercise and sleep, but also minimizing the risk factors that can be detrimental to your existence which includes smoking and drugs. Leaders understand that they must be able control themselves. They must be intelligent enough, strong enough and confident enough to simply say 'no'. We all think we can beat the odds, but they are against you."

I looked down at the green fields and continued. "What about the mental aspect? There are two forms - the intellectual and the emotional. From the intellectual side, you wouldn't be here today if you weren't considered intelligent and didn't have leadership qualities. However, your ultimate goal should never end up trying to be the best. It should only be to **do your best**. Why? Because we all have strengths and weaknesses, regardless of the category there will always be someone who is bigger, faster, smarter or more talented than we are. Accept this and relish the satisfaction that comes from knowing that you have done **your** best. If you do this, one of the critical components of self-respect will fall in place and that's being at peace with yourself. When you are at peace with yourself, you can be at peace with others."

I glanced at my son and smiled adding. "The final aspect of respect is the spiritual segment, which has nothing to do with religion. It has to do with knowing right from wrong, good from bad and only doing what is right and good, even when there are no consequences for doing wrong or bad."

"I think one of the saddest things that has happened to our society is that we have become a no-fault world. There's always a rush to assign blame. Real leaders don't participate in acute finger pointing. They don't participate in the blame game. Real leaders don't always think that someone has to be wrong or someone has to be at fault. There are times when this is the case, but not all the time."

"When a real leader makes a mistake, they admit it, learn from it and try not to do it again. Making the mistake over and over and over is reserved only for the insane and the government and not for those who want to lead others."

"Son, we've looked internally, now let's look at the other part of this segment of leadership - respecting others. How do we learn to do this? The first thing I sincerely believe is that you must eliminate adjectival classifications."

"What am I talking about? Defining, quantifying and qualifying individuals by race, religion, ethnicity, appearance, age and orientation and judging them by it."

"True leaders are blind to differences. They don't look at the "what" in a person, they look at the "who" in the person. Who are they? How can we work **together** towards a common goal? "

"When you demonstrate respect for others, you give value to their being and ideals. One of the best ways to show respect is to truly listen to another's point of view. Obviously, you won't always agree on every topic, but you should allow the other person the right to express their views. What's left of the First Amendment of our tattered-and-torn Constitution affords everyone the right to free speech – regardless of whether we agree with them or not."

"To be a great leader takes a tremendous amount of practice and patience that starts in the mind, the heart and the soul, which is amplified in the form of respect that is exemplified by the grace of being one **who truly cares.** To earn respect is one of mankind's most noble sentiments because it is always earned and never given."

"The third component is **Mutual Reward.** At one time I had several hundred people working for me and as I evolved I looked at those who directly reported to me and asked two questions…are you a problem solver? Can you work on a team? That boiled down to two criteria *attitude and aptitude.*"

"Did I make mistakes in judging people? Of course! That's when I began to realize why people fail - incompetence and indifference."

"Leaders learn that you cannot achieve success alone. To achieve, they empower others who are willing to work towards the same goals by trusting them to accomplish the agreed-to objectives who then recognize all members of the team for their contribution. 'We' has a much better sound to it than 'I' when it comes to success. However, when leaders fail the word, 'I' reflects a greater sense of commitment and sincerity."

"Leadership also means understanding the concept of humility! The first time I was fired. The first time I couldn't pay all my bills! The first time I insulted someone, humiliated someone or offended someone due to being argumentative or indifferent, is when I really learned the meaning of respect."

"Beyond trust, respect and reward are three structural aspects that are critical to effective leadership. They are organization, communication and passion where they involve establishing a clear vision of what your goal is and establishing those responsible for its achievement. Communication involves tracking your progress by providing information, knowledge and methods to realize your agreed-to vision, while sustaining the excitement, enthusiasm and momentum from that first meeting with those who follow." "How do I do this?" 'V' asked.

Holding up one finger I replied. "First, you take the mutually established ultimate goal and develop a timetable regarding when you all agree to reach your objective." Two fingers. "Second, you break the ultimate goal down into components determining what needs to be accomplished to reach the ultimate goal". Three fingers. "Third you develop a timetable for each component - a set of incremental deadlines, that allow for the ultimate objective to be achieved. There is a great visual method called Gannt Charts developed to reflect a project over time and protect against entropy as complex projects that rely on a myriad of individuals have a tendency to revert to total chaos, which was my greatest fear. Gannt charts reflect the status of each component and who is responsible for each task. With one form, you have the ultimate goal and what needs to be done to achieve that goal and by when."

We had already landed. The engines were cut and people were standing outside waiting for Amelia XH's door to open, but the pilots knew that I wanted more time and so we sat as they filled out their charts as I continued on. "Finally, all great leaders have one thing in common and that's passion. Passion is exuded in the form of enthusiasm and can be infectious. If you are enthusiastic and believe in what you are doing, you will have people who want to follow you. If you are positive and full of spirit, even when times get tough, people will want to follow you. If you look at the positive side and minimize the negative, people will also want to follow you, simply because our country, society and world today is filled with so much negative information. People covet any sense of joyful liberation that will seem like a respite from the dreary environment where everything seems so overwhelmingly bad when in reality, life is good."

The pause was pregnant, but I was oblivious. I wanted to make certain 'V' was prepared and so, with doors still closed, I continued with people staring at the new bird and wondering why the doors had not opened as I added. "Now that we have the characteristics and structure in place, we need to examine the challenges to leadership."

"First, what do you do when your integrity is challenged? Integrity means following your moral or ethical convictions and doing the right thing in all circumstances, even when no one is watching. Having integrity means you are true to not only yourself, but doing nothing that demeans or dishonors either you or others."

"A person's integrity is constantly being challenged both directly and indirectly. When a person ignores something that is morally wrong, when they don't express dissatisfaction with the way people or government treat others or when they witness the brutality of indifference, they are affecting their own level of integrity."

"Second, a good leader accepts people with different views. Leaders must understand, accept and work with others who don't hold the same views as they do. Leaders must accept that their energy levels and passion probably runs at a different pace than those around them and their thought processes are always in overdrive. However, when someone comes to a real leader with an opinion or point-of-view that is different, the real leader sincerely tries to examine it and see what makes sense and if they disagree, why they do so. It's amazing what happens when you take emotion out of it, as you can not only learn from different opinions, but even modify your own and make them better."

"Son, who's more intelligent, someone who knows ten times more than the general populous on two subjects or the person who knows twice as much as the general populous on ten subjects? There is a practice called focused learning where a person takes a topic, subject or situation and digs below the surface until they have a broader knowledge than the norm. For some it makes them more well- rounded, for others intellectual elitists. True leaders learn and become more well-rounded as it gives them broader perspectives on a myriad of subjects and therefore greater insight into the beliefs and opinions of others, thereby respecting their thoughts, values and opinions."

"Regardless of how hard people try, there will be times when there are difficult conversations. No one likes conflict and yet, true leaders enjoy virtually any conversation that does not contain derogatory emotion. Through conversation comes thought. Through thought, comes learning. Through learning, comes a breadth of knowledge that transcends the past and broadens the future. A real leader must encourage creative thinking within their organization or profession and this means never being satisfied with where you're at. Think of life like riding an escalator the wrong way. If you stop taking steps, you will back."

"The next time you see an individual who wants you to follow them, please remember the criteria – trust, respect and reward and then the structure - communication, organization and passion. From these, you will quickly be able to determine if you want to follow that person, challenge that person - including yourself - or find someone else who better serves your needs."

I was done and nodded to the pilots to open the door. Everyone knew not to ask what the conversation was about, but they all had a preconceived notion and it was 180 degrees from what they thought it was and that put a smile on my face.

After giving everyone a tour of Amelia XH, I asked if we could walk to the facility. I needed the exercise and I wanted 'V' to think about what I had said. While time was always of the essence, so is introspection. As we entered the facility, there was the normal handshakes and acquiescence to me, as I was still considered the alpha male. When everyone was seated, I announced that 'V' would head up the new project and do so with my blessing. You could have knocked the MadCity Boys over with one of Great Grandfather's feathers. To say the look of surprise was on their faces would be an understatement. To say there was doubt, made the look in their faces even that much more profound.

The Sermon:

'V' took to the lectern and quietly looked at the assembled group. For one very long minute there was total, uncomfortable, silence. As everyone's breathing slowed and all extraneous noise stopped, an empty cube of anticipation began to fill. Then 'V' spoke. "I am certain that my attendance here is a surprise to many. I am certain that even being allowed in this very room with so many great minds, who have accomplished so much, must seem like an insult to all of you who have dedicated your lives to the betterment of others. Over the past few years, I profoundly admit that I have had no direction and lived a life that today, I am embarrassed to admit. Yet, through it all, because of the love of my father and mother and their tolerance, I stand before you, a humble man, asking only that you allow me to dedicate myself to our mutual achievement and earn your trust."

'V' distanced himself from the security of standing behind the lectern and stood before the group. "As you can see, my grandfather is not here today, not because he didn't want to be, but because he wasn't invited. Not out of avarice or lack of respect, but simply out of love and gratitude for the man who has given all of us so much and asked for so little in return."

'V' continued. "My Grandfather has been diagnosed with Alzheimer's Disease." There was a soft murmur through the room. "The doctors say there is no cure and yet, I look out to you and ask, why? Why can't we, you and I, work with SIMON and the greatest minds in the world to see if we can't either stop this insidious disease or cure those who are afflicted with the malady throughout the world?"

'V' paused and then continued on. "You have done so much for so many. You have achieved more than anyone could ever believe and now I, while totally unworthy of your diligence, am asking you - are you willing to take that next step? Are you willing to see if we, as a team, can usurp the challenge before us and make the world a better place for all, where the quality of life isn't taken from those before their time?"

'V' added. "Where would we all be without the genius of Mark and Medigolve? One idea! One concept that you have all contributed to has changed the world! Where would we be without Matt and the Marauders who have nurtured SIMON and made him the greatest computer on earth, dedicated to the wellbeing of all living things? Where would we be without all of you who have dedicated your lives for the good of others, never asking, nor demanding the accolades you deserve? I am humbled to be in your presence and yet, God has called me and told me to come and so I am here."

The MadCity Boys sat in total silence. The person before them, the smart-ass punk - was delivering a motivational speech unlike any they ever heard before. I watched as hands went to mouths in amazement and eyes focused on the man before them as he continued by raising his arms in exclamation and saying. "This is a magical place where there is more to life than living."

'V' motioned with his hand and said. "Please come with me as we walk into The Forest so that I can continue."

The group looked at each other as 'V' headed for the door. I had no idea what was about to transpire and yet I hoped, no felt, it would be profound.

Slowly and quietly, the group walked the cinder path to where I had gone for respite so many times before. They all walked until we came to the few cobble stones that outlined the Foundation of the school where my ancestors had attended.

'V' continued. "We stand on hallowed ground where my father and my ancestors once learned about life - good and bad, right and wrong. We, as a group, must sustain that knowledge and use it to help those less fortunate than we are."

'V' walked to the obelisk and the group stopped once again as he continued. "A few weeks ago, I sat on that bench in total darkness. My father and I had an argument and he left me here and told me to think about life and what I had become. He assured me that he would return, but would not tell me when. If I was gone, I was out of his life forever. If I was here, perhaps - just perhaps, there would be a lesson learned."

"As I sat in darkness, an old man with white braided hair and milky white eyes appeared and spoke to me. He was a guiding light who provided the wisdom he shared with my father so many years ago. At first, I was a disbeliever and then, for the first time in a very, very long time, there was joy in my heart. You see, it was then I realized what is important in life is not what you have, but what you have given - not of material things, but of yourself."

'V' pointed to the ravine where George the First saved Rodney's ancestral grandmother and continued on. "At that very spot, my ancestral grandfather saved an Indian girl's life. At that spot, all that my ancestral grandfather had taken, was returned. At that spot, all that has been accomplished for our family began because, at that spot, the joy of giving exceeded that of getting and life began."

The MadCity Boys stood in awe as a sermon was being presented unlike any they had ever heard as 'V' continued. "One of my father's mentors is amongst you today. This man, took my mother and father on a balloon ride around the world and opened their eyes to its beauty and majesty, while he opened their hearts to the goodness they could provide. I cannot say thank you with enough sincerity or gratitude as that journey was the one that changed my father's life and now mine." All eyes were on Luke.

'V' looked around The Forest and then back at the group and exclaimed, "I never realized until sitting here alone what a special place this can be. For many, it's just a bunch of trees that my father and the Ho-Chunk fought to keep for the innocent. For others, it's just a Forest with no more meaning than any other. However, for a select few, to which I have been bequeathed, it's a spot where the powers of goodness can prevail, if one allows goodness to seep into their souls and give them purpose."

"Many of you have heard the story and yet, I must share it with you. Not of my ancestors, but about where you stand today.

While the lines can be either positive or negative and can run alone or intersect, there are only three places on earth that have what lies beneath your feet - the intersection of three positive Ley Lines that emanate a force more powerful than life itself"

The MadCity Boys stood in rapt attention as 'V' continued. "Captain Luke explained to my parents that the power and strength of a vortex, as many call it, is a personal thing, that can affect individuals in many different ways or not at all. It is not something that can actually be measured and yet it is there. I guess, like the entire concept of faith. In so doing and so believing one can develop a sense of meliorism where a person like me, begins to believe that the world is gradually improving through the combination of divine intervention and human spirit."

"V's" hands dropped to his sides and he almost whispered. "Those who are moved like I have been, sense a level of spirituality where the lines and their force are the conductors and the person's mind becomes the translator. For the first time in my life, I am at peace and hope you will come with me on a magnificent journey. Not everyone will feel a change, but those who do will be profoundly affected."

There was a narrow smile upon "V's" face as he continued. "Some of you know why this spot has such meaning to my father. Others have come here and stood in silence and felt the energy of the spirit that lives within. For those of you who, like me, never understood the significance, I will tell you this, it can be learned. When you begin to feel the energy, you, too, will bask in the beauty of innocence and be willing to commit to our endeavor with a fervor much greater than ever before."

"A few weeks ago, I came here as a disbeliever. I came here questioning the value of the land, expecting nothing more than solitude and a respite from my former life. As I sat here that evening, the spirits spoke to me and gave me strength and now I ask the Great Spirit to show you that you, too, are in a holy place, far superior to man. While we have acquired knowledge, we all must learn to acquire goodness that only comes from caring." With that 'V' raised his hands to the sky and looked towards the clouds. "Great Spirit, give us a sign that you are with us."

For a moment, there was nothing and then the soft summer breeze that had swayed the trees stopped, the birds fell silent and the insects that had permeated our meeting ceased to exist. For a moment, there was absolute silence and tranquility as the MadCity Boys stood in abject disbelief.

"Great Spirit, I still feel a sense of disbelief amongst some of those who are with me, can you please make them believe?" 'V' cupped his hands in front of his mouth and closed his eyes and then nodded. Opening his eyes, 'V' looked at the ensemble and told them to look at their watches. They all did and there was a gasp. Each watch had stopped at exactly noon. All second hands were frozen at twelve! All minute hands locked upon each other, pointing exactly at the same time. There was to be no motion, except the flow of energy between us and the earth upon which we stood. Everyone stood with mouths agape, some in awe, others in fear, some believing, while others were in total disbelief. The hour was upon them and they were made aware of the presence of a power much greater than their own.

"How many of you now believe?" 'V' asked. There was a quiet and polite affirmative nod from everyone. After an extended minute, the silence was pierced by "V's" command. "Follow me", as he walked the cinder path to where the pure water trickled from the springs.

"V's" tone-of-voice changed for a moment and became factual, reiterating what I had taught him about where The Forest existed and why it was special.

"Gentlemen, the water before you was created drop-by-drop, within the bowels of the earth, millennia ago from a time before my ancestors and those of the Indians, whose land this once was and is again. These drops of water have been forced towards the surface of Earth by the positive energy you have felt, where it springs forth devoid of any imperfection."

'V' raised his voice in exclamation. "We are here! We are at a spot where the purest of the pure comes forth as a testament to God's almighty benevolence. If you believe, drink the water with me. If you do not believe, I will ask the Great Spirit to stop the water's flow so that we can return to what was before, simply a group satisfied only with what they had already accomplished, unwilling to move onward and upward towards a dream of a better world for all."

The entire group stood in profound silence, frozen in awe. Then, led by Peter, each man came forth, one-by-one and cupped their hands in the cold water and put it to their lips. In a matter of minutes, the once self-confident group of free-spirits were transformed into believers. What had been nothing more than a grove of trees next to where they worked, became a shrine, where they felt the profound joy that I had felt my entire life. In an instant, their casual attitude and sense of satisfaction towards all they had accomplished dissipated as they realized they had only just begun.

I looked at my son and realized that the spirit was with him. I placed my hands in front of my face as if in prayer and gently bowed towards 'V', knowing that it was my only way of showing respect and gratitude for what had just transpired.

When everyone had sipped the water, we all walked back in total silence to the facility. It was as if the group had become monks and 'V' was their abbot. As we entered the auditorium, the MadCity Boys looked at their frozen watches and the hands began to rapidly move. Time no longer stood still, as they shook their heads in disbelief.

Quietly the group took their places with 'V' at the front of the room. Gone was any doubt! Gone was any disbelief! Gone was any reluctance! Everyone realized and accepted that there was a new task at hand … developing a way in which we could help those with debilitating mental challenges lead lives they had dreamed about.

'V' took a deep breath and gently smiled, as he stared at the assembly.

"Shall we begin?" 'V' asked rhetorically, not expecting any answer.

The MadCity Boys sat in complete, abject, silence and yet within their hearts beat a fervent state where the long languishing enthusiasm they had once felt was once again ignited into a towering inferno of spirit. With that, 'V' caught my eye and I knew our part of the meeting was over. Mission accomplished!

As the silent men sat in the silent room and stared at the silent young man before them, 'V' and I walked out the door and headed for the helicopter. "Just a minute, dad," 'V' whispered as he made a right turn and walked a few paces out of site of the windows of the compound to the edge of the cornfield and abruptly threw up.

The Plan:

I expected some response, but it had been two days and there was nothing. I knew time was critical and yet also realized that what had happened was so profound that any intercession by me could break the spell 'V' had created. As the week wore on, I became more impatient. On the fifth day, Ceclia came into my office and said Peter was arriving in a few minutes. I knew what I had to do and quickly moved the old chest in front of my desk.

Peter quietly knocked on my door and came in. I beckoned him to sit on the chest. He abided with a somewhat quizzical look upon his face and began to outline all that had transpired.

"After we visited The Forest with 'V', no one knew what to think or do. To say we were all moved by what we had seen, what we had heard and above all else, what we felt, would be an understatement. To use Matt's words, 'it was a religious experience'. For the first time, many of us who had no sense of religion, felt a sense of awe and a feeling of being in the presence of something vast and greater than ourselves. For those whose lives had centered around the concept of 'me' the rush they felt exceeded anything and everything they thought possible. Personally, I sensed the greatness, but never really believed in it. George, I don't think there is a single person who was there that day whose life 'V' didn't change. I can sense it. I can feel it and I, personally am profoundly grateful for the goodness that now fills my heart."

I responded. "My hope and dream is that 'V' takes the training and experience and uses it where I believe it will do the most good and that is in public service. Working with Rodney's nation, New York and Washington, should give him good insight." This got a chuckle from Peter. "As he learns and matures, I see my son representing people and Wisconsin. While he doesn't have the legal background most politicians have, he has all the other ingredients needed, plus one that many don't have - humility. He certainly doesn't need to worry about special perks. Instead, he can focus on doing what America really needs and that is developing programs and policies that help people - all people!"

"While so many politicians are desperate for campaign funds, 'V' has all the money anyone would ever need to run for office and we have all the business connections so that 'V' will never need to sell his soul to get contributions. All we need do is figure out how to thicken his skin so that he isn't trampled by the onslaught of dirty politics that seems to permeate our society and culture."

Peter leaned back, with a smile on his face. All the pieces of the puzzle were being put into place as I continued. "Peter, the Foundation is being built on knowledge and goodness and each day I am overwhelmed by your mentat nature that finds you capable of performing tasks at the speed of the computer, while doing so with the such a multifarious capacity that almost seem super-human. Yet, beyond the skills lies a man whose heart is filled with goodness and munificent in all aspects - time, treasure and talent and that's why you are the one I need the most, as only you can successfully sustain the goals and aspirations we have established. I told The Duke and he agreed, that when the day comes I decide to step down, you and only you are the one I want to run the Foundation."

Peter's mouth dropped open as I continued. "I don't know when that will be, but when the day comes, I will know because the passion I currently have will be gone. Growing up, I always wanted to be rich and have everything. We are wealthy and I have everything. However, there is still more I want and that's the satisfaction of knowing, deep in my heart, that I made a difference to my family, friends and the world. When the day comes when I sincerely feel that I have accomplished that goal or realize that I will never reach it, I want to step down, with dignity and let you carry on."

"We've got a lot of work to do," I said with a smile and with that, the meeting was over. "V's" career path was established. It was great getting to use some of the five-dollar journalism words I learned at the UW, knowing they would be easily understood by Peter. My only fear was that he would come back with a response I wouldn't understand. God, this dude was smart!

We've Only Just Begun:

We all assume that tomorrow we will be alive. We all assume that tomorrow we will be healthy. We all assume that tomorrow, those around us will be there. What happens when none of it exists? What do we do? How do we act, react, contemplate or even exist? When the team had been informed The Duke was diagnosed with moderately aggressive Alzheimer's Disease, cold reality jumped up and slapped them across the face. The doctors said they could slow the process, but not stop it. Slowly, the man who meant so much to so many people would slip into the abyss not knowing, not seeing, not feeling "now". My God! All the money you could ever need and yet, none of it worth anything if you don't have your health.

Our focus at the Foundation needed to change from general health to working on a cure or prevention of Alzheimer's or at least slow its onset. The MadCity Boys got together with 'V' and had a free-thinking session. It was agreed they had to think backwards. While chip implantation in dogs, cattle etc. had been around for decades, there was a microchip developed by a Swedish company called Epicenter who had begun the entire process of implanting chips within the human body to eliminate keys, passes and credit cards through a small insertion between the thumb and forefinger which was no bigger than a grain of rice that we had begun using at the Foundation for internal use only.

While the ethical question had raged. "Are we willing to sacrifice privacy for convenience?" the MadCity Boys thought this was the future and asked "what would happen if we could implant a billion Nanochips in the body, which would control the brain and its hundred billion nerve cells, without affecting thoughts and ideas, while never limiting big ideas, corollaries or contradictions? What if these Nanochips could send messages to the brain to tell it to respond to changes and threats? Couldn't the brain then use its arsenal of chemicals and neurons to fight disease and reduce damage? The brain would then be proactive and with it, self-medication would reduce or eliminate all sorts of maladies. Our dreams seemed limitless. Gone might be cancer! Gone might be neural disorders like dementia and Alzheimer's Disease taking with it insipient diseases like ALS, schizophrenia and all sorts of dastardly disorders. Taken one step further, couldn't these Nanochips be programmed to reduce aggression, eliminate crime and make society more socially compliant? The name bionic was created in the 1970's for a television show, as a combination of the word biology and electronics. Isn't that what we really wanted to do?

The web opened so many doors of communication affecting economic and social existence and we were using it to allow individual researchers to advance within their own fields. Couldn't we use it to recruit the greatest of minds to work together on the same project - better health and global peace?

A second meeting was called and I was invited. The macro objectives were established. It was time to begin compartmentalizing the goals into three categories -what we must do, what we should do and what we wanted to do, just as The Duke had instructed.

We knew it was going to be a long day as we sat and determined which scientific fields needed to be addressed that would allow us to not only create the product we wanted to develop, but determine where to place it within the body. Peter served as our moderator and used the white board in the silo to outline all the areas we needed to focus on. Even in our techno-advanced world, there was still something about the old-fashioned markers and an eraser that made the entire project seem more dynamic and attainable.

As the day wore on, the list got longer and longer and longer to include virtually every form of science there was. In the end, we looked at all five branches of science - earth and space, social sciences, life sciences, physical and the formal sciences to determine where we needed to recruit the right people.

There was a sense of accomplishment in the room as Peter pressed the "record" button on the whiteboard and his outline and twenty copies were printed on old-fashioned paper. At this point, I thought we were done until someone noted that all we had accomplished was outlining the sciences and not how the chips would actually be designed and developed. To this end, we knew we needed to add an entire engineering spectrum to our team.

Because the group had reached the limits of their expertise, it was suggested we ask SIMON for his assistance. This was what the MadCity Boys called a "duh" moment, when you have overlooked a simple, easy method to achieve your goal or acquire your information and the entire team went one-two-three - "duuuuuh!" in unison to which there was a loud guffaw!

Peter directed his Watson to send their notes to SIMON and then vocally activated SIMON and asked for a summary of the different types of engineering classifications. Once again, I marveled at SIMON's intellect and speed, as the entire summary was projected on the screen for everyone to see that included 64 different fields beneath the primary classes. I think everyone was surprised by the magnitude of the project and yet, when you're dealing with an invention that could change the world, you needed to make certain it was comprehensive in its design and development.

"Is everyone in agreement?" Peter asked, to the nodding heads in the room. "OK, SIMON, provide a list of the top three experts in the world in each of the sub-categories."

Once again, SIMON provided the names, credentials and locations of the prioritized list of candidates with their most recent photographs. In many cases, the names and faces were familiar as they were Nobel Peace Prize candidates or recipients. It was scary what SIMON could do!

Peter looked at the group and indicated that an introductory letter would be developed and remitted to those first on the list in each category. It was agreed, they would be given seven days to respond. Should we not hear from them or they weren't interested,

SIMON would go to the second person with the same letter and same criteria and do so until all slots were filled. In the matter of one day we had identified the people we needed on the team, why they needed to be on the team and those people who met the requirements to be on the team. Not bad for a bunch of farmers from Wisconsin!

As the meeting adjourned, I asked 'V' what he thought and he just shook his head and said, "Incredible".

"We've only just begun, son! We've only just begun!"

Way, Way, Away:

'V' stayed with Tommie and Hsu while I took the chopper home. The ride went smoothly and when I walked in the house, Amy was sitting on the family room couch.

"Well?" she asked looking at my exhausted face that was devoid of any emotion and lacking any semblance of a smile.

"Incredible!" I answered. "But, also incredibly complex."

"How's that?"

"We need to not only design and develop the chip, but the software and then decide where to place the chip in a person's body and then design the equipment that can do it. I'm glad I've got the boys and SIMON or we would have been there for a month just figuring out what resources were needed."

"Expensive?"

"I think it's going to cost a lot!" I replied sadly, shaking my head.

"How much?" Amy asked.

"I really don't know, but I'll guess somewhere between five-hundred million and a billion dollars."

"Wow!" was Amy's only exclamation re-directing to "How did 'V' do?"

"He's fitting right in and will be working with Peter and Luke on the bio-ethics aspect."

"Great," Amy said, standing and coming over to me saying, "You know what I've been thinking."

"What?"

"You've been working awfully hard and I think we need a vacation."

I looked down at the floor and then at her with a slight smile on my face. "And where would you like to go?" I asked.

"Can we go to House-On-The Hill?"

"Of course." I responded. I thought "it's her house, her plane, her company and her husband." When I get tired, no make that exhausted, I get cranky and feel sorry for myself.

"We haven't been there alone, in a long time and I miss it," Amy replied.

We made arrangements for the time away. It would give us nine full days on the island, which was the longest we had ever been gone. Dennis would fly us down and pick up one of our VIP's, who was on St. Croix and bring them back to Milwaukee, so that half the trip was all business. At $3,400 an hour, operating time, I still watched every penny.

The designated Friday, we boarded Amelia X. The flight was uneventful, even at nearly 700 miles per hour. Uncle Frank met us on the Princess Juliana tarmac. I think I was surprised by the degree of recovery from yet another hurricane, precipitated by one more degree added to the world's average thermometer. Other than Orient Beach, everything had been repaired and even there, progress was made. While it was all new, it was also a bit sad, as the memories we had with Rodney and Ann and how eclectic everything from Pedro's to Club Orient had been, were replaced by buildings and businesses that were a lot more "commercial" than the ones that had been destroyed.

Uncle Frank dropped us at the house and everything was as it should have been. We walked in and it was like we had never left. Keys for the Range Rover were on the hook, the refrigerator was filled with fruit and fresh flowers on the table and our clothes were still in the drawers. I asked Amy if she wanted to use her old room and she shook her head no. I inquired about her parent's room and the memories of her mother were still too fresh. Instead, we took the guest suite and settled in.

Amy went to her old room and climbed into a pair of her old short shorts and a boy's white ribbed undershirt with the wide-open sides. Amazingly, after all these years and three kids, the shorts and shirt still fit. Perhaps, a little tighter, but still a wonderful sight to see, bringing back memories of our first encounter at Devil's Lake in Wisconsin.

I changed into shorts that came down to my boney knees and ventured into the kitchen where I looked at Amy and smiled, making certain that she knew I approved. She worked hard at keeping fit and being back at House-On-The-Hill returned her to the comfort zone she desired. I don't know if thirty-year-old clothes were a reward or a barometer. Either way, I knew that fitting into them, made her happy.

I perused her top for even the slightest hint of protrusions and recalled when I'd never heard the term "pokies". I remembered Amy laughing at my ignorance when I asked her what the term meant. She giggled and explained that "pokies" was another name for "poking out".

"Poking out of what? I asked.

"Someone's chest" she laughed.

I had always discretely leered, when she had "pokies" and she always laughed when I had mine. From then on, whenever we would see someone - male or female, in that state, one of us would whisper - "pokies at - with the direction, outlined in hours of the day, where noon meant straight ahead, three o'clock to our right, etc. It was/is our little secret that made/makes us both giggle. It's funny how little things begin and how wonderful it is when they do can become little secrets between lovers.

As the day wore on, we got ready for dinner, which is always one of my favorite things to do on St. Martin. No matter where you go, the food is always great. Amy asked Uncle Frank to make reservations and we had a nice quiet dinner at L'Auberge Gourmande in Grand Case and went back to the house. Amy punched in the code to the wine vault that easily contained over $500,000 in wine and opened a chilled bottle of Louis Roederer, Cristal Brut 1990 Millennium Cuvee Methuselah. Little did I know one bottle of Champagne could cost nearly $20,000. Also, little did I know that there were all kinds of bottles in the vault that cost more as it seemed Amy had acquired her father's taste for fine wine.

"Here's to my wonderful husband." Amy toasted.

"Here's to my wonderful wife." I replied, not knowing what was going on.

"Here's to giving me my son back." Amy countered.

"Here's to giving me three wonderful children and the best possible life I could have imagined." I replied.

We drank our Champagne and made our way upstairs to bed. Between flying, eating and drinking, we both collapsed and fell asleep almost immediately, realizing we weren't twenty-one anymore.

Orient Beach:

Saturday morning, I awakened early, but then I always do. That's part of being a farm boy, I guess. I quietly went downstairs, into the darkness, where the only sound was the periodic hum of the refrigerator, keeping cadence to the twinkling lights below. I breathed in the warm, succulent air and thought to myself how lucky I was to have the wife and family I did.

I sat on the couch and looked at the Bible sitting on the coffee table where I had left it the last time we were there and remembered back to when Amy quoted from the book of Ruth. My hand caressed the soft, black leather sheath and I opened to where the gold piece of tapestry had been placed. It was Corinthians and I began to read.

"Strive eagerly for the greatest spiritual gifts. But I shall show you a more excellent way."

"If I speak in human and angelic tongues, but do not have love, I am a resounding gong or a clashing cymbal and if I have the gift of prophesy, and comprehend all mysteries and knowledge. If I have all faith as to move mountains, but do not have love, I am nothing."

"If I give away everything I own and I hand my body over so that I may boast, but do not have love, I gain nothing."

"Love is patient, love is kind. It is not jealous, it is not pompous, it is not inflated, it is not rude, it does not seek its own interests, it is not quick-tempered, it does not brood over injury, it does not rejoice over wrongdoing, but rejoices with truth."

"It bears all things, believes all things, hopes all things, endures all things."

"Love never fails."

"If there are prophesies, they will be brought to nothing; if tongues, they will cease; if knowledge, it will be brought to nothing. For we know partially and we prophesy partially but when the perfect comes, the partial will pass away."

"When I was a child, I used to talk as a child, think as a child, reason as a child; when I became man, I put aside childish things."

"At present I know partially; then I shall know fully, as I am fully known."

"So, faith, hope, love remain these three; but the greatest of these is love."

As I finished, I looked out as the faintest fingers of pink sunlight were poking their way across the eastern sky, sliding between the morning clouds upon the sea - parting them as if to reach out to me, beckoning me, calling me, reminding me that all there is, all that was, all that will ever be, means nothing without love. I thought of Stephen Hawking's line - *"look up at the stars and not down at your feet"* and smiled in a testament to such a great man!

Amy quietly came down stairs and we went out on the veranda where she sipped her espresso and snuggled next to me to watch the early sunrise - a typical day at St. Martin.

"Let's walk the beach" she offered. I quietly nodded in affirmation and Amy put her espresso cup in the kitchen and we went to the Rover.

"I'll drive" she said, taking the keys from my hands.

Slowly, we zig-zagged down the hill and turned east onto Highway N7. We went past El Rancho Del Sol, the French BBQ place where Amy shared so much and continued a few hundred yards down the hill and turned left into Au Village D'Orient. We had been to St. Martin dozens of times and yet, even though everything seemed the same - same trees, same guard shack, same scraped speed bumps in need of paint. It was always special, where the only thing that changed were Amy and me!

We made our way down to the shore as we drove past Le Piment, Good Morning bakery and the Bikini Beach restaurant and took a right down the "back road" behind KonTiki and Wai and the new shops that replaced those destroyed by the hurricane, parking the Rover behind the last shop.

Pulling on the tie of her belt, Amy began removing her cover before stopping short of total exposure. "We're going naked, aren't we?" she asked in an almost incredulous way. There is a fine line between inhibition and exhibition and Amy had always been indifferent towards her body, neither aroused or embarrassed by its exposure. Even after all these years, I was still somewhat surprised by her indifference. To her, she was ambivalent to who saw what, when or where. I guess the reason why there was no reticence was that we were standing at the edge of one of the world's most famous nude beaches and the thought of attire seemed almost alien. Yet, there was still reservation and a level of discomfort in me.

From our years together, I knew and accepted that she had more of a European outlook than most Americans in that the physical self was not the same as the sexual self. She had always been one who was liberated, but never one who was out of place. She would be naked when possible and made sense and yet, conservative when that too was appropriate. Amy raised our kids the same way and discussions regarding body parts and bodily functions were open, honest and without any form of erogenous verve. Even me, the conservative one, learned to accept that she was probably right, as consistent exposure and repetition took the tingle out of the human body by removing the correlation of exposure to sex.

I thought back to when we first met and her broken ankle and the mind games we played back then - left foot-club foot, left foot-club foot, came to mind and I smiled. I remembered our first visit here as a couple and keeping my promise of being 'unencumbered' as she called it, around the pool and on the boat. I thought of Rodney and Ann on their honeymoon and how Rodney had whispered that he and Ann had "gone skinny dipping" down at Club Orient and my courage level rose. This was not a hedonistic escapade, but an unraveling of the reservations that had been locked inside.

Why had so much of the "fun" of our youth faded? Like so many others, our marriage had dulled. Why had we broken the promises that we weren't going to be like other couples - "alone together, alone apart, if we began all over we might not start?" With that, my trepidation was gone and I pulled down my shorts and stood naked before my wife. There it was, her long-lost girlie giggle that made the entire escapade worthwhile, as Amy slipped off her cover revealing her naked body.

"You didn't think I'd do it, did you?" I inquired.

Amy grinned and shook her head. "Well, let's go for that walk, or are you still being conservative?" she inquired.

My wife had softened a bit around the edges, but was still in phenomenal shape. To many, she would be considered lissome. For me, the duration of existence had removed the sexual thrill and replaced it with an attitude of pride in the way she looked. Three days a week, every week, she was doing yoga and weight training, swimming and running and it showed with tight abs and butt. Even so, it seemed strange, looking at her naked, with palm trees as a backdrop. I quickly glanced down and saw the small rose tattoo she had inked when she was cancer clear. A smile creased my lips as I remembered her excitement when it first appeared, a testament to me and wondered if she would do the same today. I can only imagine what I looked like - skinny old me.

"What about the keys?" I asked.

Amy went to the back of the Rover and lifted the small rubber top of the bumper. Beneath, was a small compartment with the four-digit, serial combination that Uncle Frank had installed at Amy's request. She placed the keys in the receptacle, closed the cover and spun the dial, saying, "Now we're totally naked." She giggled.

I looked at her and she at me as she grasped my hand and we began walking towards the rising sun. We had long evolved from an amatory relationship to one filled with the profound acceptance of each other for what we were – two people – sharing our lives as one.

"Did you know that the first American movie to show nude men and women was the 1927 Best Picture, *'Wings'*"? Amy inquired. "Imagine, almost 100 years ago they actually showed 'everything' and won the Academy Award?"

I don't know why that came out, but I believed it was to put me at ease as we passed the spot where the small bungalows of Orient Beach Club had once stood, only to be replaced by three-story, ocean-front condos that were sold as time-shares. This section of the beach was clothing optional and the facility primarily appealed to the naturists. It always had been, but it was different - more commercial, less personal, I guess. Not quite as innocent!

It was a little after six and we were alone walking parallel to the lapping waves of the shore. I thought *"Oh my God, what if someone sees us?"*

Amy added, *"'Titanic'* had Kate Winslet nude with Leonardo DiCaprio drawing her in 1997. The censors wanted to rate the movie X, but the scene was so critical and so well done, they allowed it and the movie was given a PG13 rating."

"Georgie, will you take some naked pictures of me someday?"

"If that's what you want." I replied.

"I think that would be fun. Can I take some of you?"

Gulp!

"How about us together using the timer?" Amy inquired as she curled her arm inside mine.

Again, I replied, "If that's what you want."

"Perhaps tomorrow morning, or this week?"

"Ok" I said in mortal fear.

The rays of sunshine were already turning gold and the cadence of the soft waves upon the shore served as our symphony, reminding me that it would be another glorious day in paradise. Amy and I walked to the very end, stopping at the edge of the exposed reef that sheltered the beach from the ocean's roar. I felt the warm breeze eclipsing the wind of the ocean's waves and thought, how different from the calm of Orient Bay and how it was like life. I guess there are rough seas for everyone that can be calmed by reefs of love and laughter, built slowly and carefully as experiences grow.

Looking out at the waves, Amy turned and asked me, "Have I told you lately that I love you?"

I was surprised by the question and answered. "You show me every day."

"Have I been a good mother and wife?" she inquired.

"Of course!" I responded, wondering why the questions and trying to be totally positive.

"Will you love me forever?" Amy asked again.

"Certainly!" I replied.

Amy hugged me and kissed my lips and pulled back and said, "I love you George Terrill. You made me the happiest woman on earth and I want to thank you for that." With that, she pulled me close and put her hands on my bare, boney, butt - pulling me in even closer whispering, "I want to make love to you right now – long – sensuous - love" as she bit my left ear lobe.

Normally, I was the one accused of blabbing on and on and on. Today, I was the quiet one as she expounded on virtually everything. I glanced her way and hoped that all that was happening was simply a reaction to those times when there were questions and doubts, when everything in her life came crashing down. I felt I needed to respond in a gentle manner and did so by slowly, pulling back and looking in her eyes responding, "Have I told you that I love you?"

"Yes!" she replied.

"Have I been a good husband and father?"

"Yes!"

"Will you love me forever?"

Again, a nod of affirmation.

To her surprise, I then recited our wedding vows. *'Do not press me to leave you or to turn back from following you! Where you go, I will go; where you lodge I will lodge; your people shall be my people, and your God my God. Where you die, I will die —*

there will I be buried. May the Lord do thus and so to me, and more as well, if even death parts me from you!'

There was a deep, serious smile on Amy's face as she pulled me in again and gave me a kiss as her way of answering in the affirmative.

"Do you mind being naked on the beach," she asked.

"It's OK" I reluctantly replied.

"You said you would. Remember? Unencumbered!"

"I remember," thinking it would soon be over, before anyone saw us.

We walked west, hand-in-hand, to the imaginary dividing line where the rocks tumbled into the sea. This was the point where Amy once outlined, west of the rocks meant going topless or wearing a very little would be judged one way, while wearing the same thing on the east side of the rocks, meant being judged in a totally different manner. The haute couture of the times had certainly changed what was acceptable. While thong bathing suits had once been risky, on Orient Beach they were common-place. On St. Martin, social trends had evolved in such an inviolate manner as to make the area devoid of restriction. Depending on the time of day, one could walk without violation or fear of punishment.

So much had changed as women's swimwear became more revealing and I oft-times wondered if the day would come where women would walk into a store and dig down in an empty basket and select a bathing suit consisting of just air and actually pay for it. Different values and perspectives, delineated by a pile of rocks, where heretics roamed on both sides, pontificating their beliefs of right and wrong. I shook my head in disbelief.

The Green Stairs:

I felt uncomfortable with our first encounter - a man, probably in his fifties, naked and walking towards us. As he passed, his eyes looked at Amy's body, without ever making eye contact and then he was behind us. He was physically aroused by Amy, which made me both angry and proud. Where once a mixed-race woman was looked upon with disdain, values had changed and with it, so had the coveting of my wife.

After the smiles at our little jokes, or anyway I hoped they were jokes, Amy quickly changed the subject, pointing to the concrete stairway in front of us with the peeling, green paint and said in all earnestness that it was like looking at the headstone of a deceased friend, "This is where Pedro's used to be. They had the best grilled chicken in the world. It was also where you could come and see all kinds of people in different degrees of dress or undress - all getting along - accepting each other for who they were and not what they were."

"Before Hurricane Irma hit, the weather experts said it wasn't going to be a big deal. In Pedro's they had over 10,000 pictures from people all over the world and had moved them indoors. Then boom, 160 mile per hour winds, a twenty-foot sea swell and fifteen-foot waves and the building and pictures were gone and all those memories were wiped away!"

Was this a message to me? If so what was she trying to say? Amy never casually had tangential conversations. Her incredible intellect and legal mindset meant all topics had a purpose.

The bay was in one of its halcyon modes – calm, peaceful and carefree, just like I hoped we would be. I thought we might stop walking at the stairs and the escapade would be over. Instead, we continued walking further west as Amy suggested "Let's walk all the way down to the other end - past Kon-Tiki, Bikini, KaKao, LaPlaya, Waikiki and Coco Beach to Mont Vernon - All the way! As long as we're back around eight, we're fine."

I was mentally, socially and physically reluctant and yet I also sensed her insistence. We walked a few hundred feet and Amy stopped, pointing towards a small store on the west end of the retail compound with her saying, "This is about where Rodney and Ann were sitting when we came to meet them at Le String." It had been years and with new buildings and no palm trees, I had no idea and politely nodded.

Pensively, Amy added, "This is where you met Sydney and where that part of my life became known. You have accepted me as me and where I first realized how truly wonderful the man I was going to marry really was. You have allowed me to share my inner-most secrets and let me be me, never judging me, even when, well, even when things weren't going as good as they are right now."

Amy squeezed my hand and said, "This is the exact spot where I absolutely knew I loved you, George," squinting as she looked at me in all earnestness while adding, "To this day, there have been no regrets and I have marveled at your goodness and respected your integrity. I am so happy I met you and that you love me."

I stood somewhat aback by the profound exclamation and wondered why? Why had she said what she did? Most marriages end up in sequestered silence where what is, is all that remains, marking all there was and will always be.

I paused for a moment and added. "Amelia, you are the love of my life. I cannot imagine how it could be any better. I accept you for what you are and only hope that you accept me for what I am. It hasn't always been perfect and yet I cannot fathom what it would be like without you. I can only hope that, through all these years, I have shown you the depth of my love and pledge it will continue for as long as we both shall live."

There were tears in her eyes, moistening her gratitude and providing relief, while indicating her sincere acceptance of my pledge.

Quite seriously, Amy inquired, "Do you mind if we keep walking?"

"Of course not!" I lied. Even though, in those moments on the beach, I had grown somewhat accustomed to the fact we were both naked. It still seemed strange and initially uncomfortable, especially being aware there might be more people walking as well. It was then that something happened to me and, with each step I realized this wasn't the erogenous adventure I had initially feared, but Amy's way of stripping away all vestiges of reservation so that everything exposed consisted of true feelings, unbridled by any form of decorum. This was a cleansing act, where all the emotional veneer of indifference which had built up between us was being buffed away, layer-by-layer, bruise-by-bruise until the soft glow of acceptance shone through. As I smiled to myself, I began to realize the love was still there, as was my sincere belief that she was special.

"What do you miss most when we're not here?" I asked.

Her answer came quickly - "freedom"

I must have had a quizzical look on my face and so Amy continued. "I miss the freedom to be me. I miss not feeling as if I am being judged all the time. I miss the introspection that was so paramount to my existence." Looking down and then smiling her soft smile she added, "but I wouldn't change any of it, if it meant not being with you."

"If we lived here full time, how would it be different?" I asked.

"First, I would go back to practicing Mindfulness on a regular basis and ask you to come along. It's really one of the things I miss the most. They are so right, George! Do you remember? They can influence the very core of oneself'".

In other words, be naked and be healthy?" I asked.

Nodding in the affirmative but having a smirk on her face Amy added, "Because of the weather and social structure at home, I can't sit naked on the beach in January or I would freeze my butt off. In June, for that matter I can't either, because the restrictions are still there, as our society and the law deems otherwise."

"So you would want to run around naked all the time?" I pondered.

Amy shook her head 'no' and gave me a very serious look as if to infer that my conclusion was ridiculous. "Of course not! Only when I needed to meditate and practice Shinrin-yoku."

"You miss that too, don't you?" I asked, as we continued to walk.

"Immensely! Which is why I do yoga, but it's not the same. Here, we could walk and periodically do deep breathing and use all our senses. If we did this, you would see things you do not see, hear things you do not hear, smell things you do not normally smell and sense things you normally do not feel, that I want to share with you."

Amy was getting serious, very serious, adding "in doing this George, we could have a much deeper sense of both 'me' and 'we'. While I used it to focus on my fight back to good health, I feel it could help intensify our love for each other and do so on a totally different plane and perhaps narrow some of the differences we have."

I thought for a minute and tried to comprehend what she was saying. If I got it right, she was saying, "George, let's see if we can't try things so that we can make you happier, with one thing that is missing - yourself!" If this was the case, I was willing to try just about anything.

Amy stared out at the waves upon bay and said, "George, the human brain can do a lot to help a person or couple heal, if it knows where to focus. With the right combination, I believe we can resolve any differences, challenges and disputes simply by enhancing our own self-concepts and living a more-healthy, happy, married life."

Taking a deep breath and eliciting yet another soft smile that traversed her face, Amy closed her eyes and continued. "I told you a long time ago that I love the smell of the ocean as it is clean and crisp. Yet, when I focus, I can also smell the hibiscus and sea grapes and even the decaying seaweed that floats on the shore and this is what I want for you."

Great! Just what I always wanted - the smell of rotting seaweed.

Amy added, "When I really focus, I not only hear the ocean, but the breeze, the call of the birds and even the crunch of the sand as my body shifts its weight. What is different is that I've learned to focus on each of them, one at a time, like listening to an orchestra and being able to hear to just one instrument. In so doing, I can be in touch with nature throughout my entire body, to a point of relaxation and peace and do so to such a degree, that the rest of my body can help fight any battle and emotion."

With that, Amy closed her eyes, inhaled deeply, exhaled and listened to the sounds that encompassed her body, mind and soul. The lapping of waves! The shrill of the birds! The undulated pulsation of the wind - all naturally combined as a cacophony of tones - intricately woven together to create a harmony intended to simply reflect "now", exuding peace and tranquility and emanating a sense of being, reserved for those willing and able to simply let go - of their thoughts, emotions, fears, foibles and most of all nightmares, that impede tranquility.

Amy paused, if only for a moment and then added, "Sound is very close to the divine energy within us, such that, in its natural state, it truly resonates with God!"

My thought process was shattered, if only for a moment, as I wondered whether I could ever be so profound - so introspective - to experience nothing more than a sea breeze and equate it to eternity.

Amy looked so deeply into my eyes that her pupils bored holes into my soul as she added, "this is what I miss most George and why I love coming here and what I really want for you."

I took a deep breath, as did she. The warm, moist, ocean-air filled not only our lungs, but our body with recompense, as the evoked thoughts and emotions soaked our minds and souls - hers with nothing more than the attempt to lift her husband beyond here and now. Me - to justify all that I had been with hopes - no dreams - that tomorrow, just tomorrow could be a better day, where the generalities of existence would be punctuated by the sharp angles of perception that would allow me to think and feel and see more than ever before.

Amy looked at me while stating the obvious, "George, you're still wound so tight and I believe that you too could become more relaxed and drawn to your own, *'inner power'*. I sincerely believe that this is what helped me become completely indifferent towards so many things that used to bother me. I only want to take each day, experience and relationship and maximize it to the point that it helps me enjoy life to the fullest. "

My wife's stare returned to the ocean, then back at me, as she looked into my eyes to the point that, once again, her sincerity penetrated my heart. "I love you and I love it here. I love you because you are kind, generous and sincere - and most of all, because I know that you love me. I love it here because of the sense of freedom I have."

Before I could respond, Amy looked back out at the ocean and continued. "At sunrise, people allow you to be yourself with no judgment or altercations. You are free to be whatever you want and that's when I release my remaining inhibitions and realize who I am, by concluding that my physical self doesn't play any part of it."

A slight frown came across Amy's face, as if in revelation that a thought or memory which once existed reappeared, to which Amy exclaimed, "I know, I've given you pain, for which I am profoundly sorry. I only hope you understand and accept me for simply being 'me'. I've had many days when I feel incredibly guilty and have needed some assurance that you still love me, which you, my kind, loving, caring, generous man have always been able provide. As you agreed, there are no limits and yet, because there are none, there is also pain."

Amy's head bowed for a moment and then she looked at me. "Perhaps, just perhaps, my inclinations are simply reactions to my own inner fears and trepidations. While you never have felt worthy of all that you have, perhaps my weaknesses are simply a way to hurt the only person, other than my family, I've ever loved, which is you and do so simply because I don't feel worthy of all that God has been given me - wealth, love and a second chance at life."

I looked at her and repeated, "I am in love with you now more than ever Amelia! Now more than ever!"

Amy looked at me again and asked. "What do I do? I want you to love me more than anything else in the entire world. Yet, I don't know if I am strong enough to resist temptation when I am at my weakest points."

The Price of Admission:

We stopped for just a moment and Amy became quite pensive. "What I've done isn't for everyone. Yet, for me, it's made all the sense in the world. I get up every morning, look at my inked, 'survivor' and the dots on my shoulder and thank God I'm alive, vowing to be a better person than the day before".

Shaking her head in regret Amy continued, "Then I peer down at my little rose and why it was added and my day begins and sadly, promises are broken and damage is done. Without you, I don't know where I would be. When we met, I added a wonderful piece of my life puzzle. For all these years, because of you, I have had the joy I never felt I deserved and the complete and total concept of inner peace I aspired to. This has allowed me to live my life with tranquility because I absolutely know you love me and accept me for who I am!"

WOW!

As we "made the bend" as she called it and passed Bikini beach and reached Kao Kao, Amy looked at me and then at the sand and then out to sea. I knew she wanted to say something, but had trepidations finally asking, "Do you ever wonder why your parents named you what they did?"

I shook my head, "no" and was about to answer when Amy added. "You are the fifth generation and yet your father's generation stopped naming someone after George the First, who began 'Waldwick'."

I replied, I'd never really explained why there was a generational gap. Preferring to simply share that I was named George Terrill the Fourth in honor of George Terrill the First. Rarely did I mention a baby who died at birth from respiratory distress syndrome, who would have been my uncle and was supposed to be George Terrill the Fourth.

We walked a little further, reaching the jagged edge of sand where the night's high tide had deposited the seaweed and away from the shore. It was low tide and so Amy adjusted our course and we waded ankle-deep in the clear water.

"That must have been hard on your grandma," Amy replied.

I just shook my head in the affirmative, even though the subject was never broached. I answered, "I am honored to be named after two of my ancestors instead of one," adding a soft smile to my face.

"To have a child die before a parent has to be the worst nightmare" Amy added. I thought of Derrick and her parents and then our three, shuddering at the thought and concurred.

"How about you?" I asked. "Why were you named Amelia?" I think I knew, but wanted assurance my deductions were correct.

As we continued on, Amy looked down and then at me as she carefully tailored her response, replying "I asked my dad once and he didn't answer. When I was in my rebellious high school years, I asked again. At first daddy didn't want to answer."

Amy had called The Duke, 'daddy', something she had never done before. I knew what was about to be expressed was coming from deep within her heart.

"Daddy, said he and mom named me after Amelia Erhardt, just like you expected. He said they did it because they wanted me to have a hero to look up to. Daddy always wanted to be a pilot, but his eyes were too bad and so he looked at Amelia Erhardt and saw a brave woman who broke down barriers for herself and others."

"Mom and dad knew back then, it was going to be tough for Derrick and me, being mixed race. They knew the struggles we were going to face and the "looks" and sneers. They knew we would have trouble identifying with people and "fitting in" and wanted me to have someone beside mom as a role model."

"Daddy didn't dig deep enough! He, like most people, thought of Amelia only as an aviatrix and that was all. When he filled me in, I began doing my own research and found out about her marriage vows and also some gossip about her orientation. What you told me that first night we met, was stuff I already knew and to find someone who held her in the same level of esteem I did, was exciting."

"Until I went away to college, I had inclinations, but was straight as an arrow. Mom and I talked the famous mother-daughter talk and she was very open and frank. I think her medical background helped because she had segregated intimacy into three different categories – the physical aspect, the mental aspect and the social aspect. Back then, college age women were just beginning to look at sex from more than the emotional part and I guess, some of the things we did, were simply attempts at revolting against our parents, which was and is a part of growing up."

"Like most 'liberated' girls, in high school, I wondered what it would be like to be with another girl, simply because so much was written about it in magazines. However, I was always afraid that my parents would find out. Besides that, it was already bad enough being mixed race and not knowing where to fit in. To add another layer to the situation seemed almost impossible."

"When I got to college and became Amy instead of Amelia, I worked hard just to fit in. Yet, I found myself becoming 'curious' about my own identity including my sexuality. I took a Sociology course and learned that one-in-eight men and about one-in-four women had sexual encounters with partners of their own gender, but did not identify as gay or bisexual, whose numbers are around 5% for women and 2% for men. I did the match and realized that one in every twenty women were like me - curious, yet also inhibited, afraid to take that next step."

"One night, during my freshman year, we all had been drinking and when I came back to my room in the dorm, Carol was there and well, we both sort of let our guard down. At first, I was afraid and then enjoyed it."

"The next morning, when I woke up, Carol and I were sleeping together in her bed and, well, we started in again. This time, we were sober. At first, it was infrequent and then it became more consistent. At first, I felt embarrassed! Then, I began to feel more comfortable about myself. Carol and I kept it to ourselves, yet the rumors about us, were everywhere."

"The first time I was called a lesbian, it hurt and I tried to deny it. The first time I was called a Dyke, I shook my head and realized I would rather be called that, than what I had been called in high school, simply because of my race."

"But you're beautiful!" I retorted."

Amy responded, "Appearance doesn't have anything to do with race or orientation. Because you are attracted to the same sex doesn't mean it's easy."

Amy continued, "Carol and I kept it to ourselves. One night we went out and she took me to a gay bar and I freaked out. I was comfortable doing what we were doing, but didn't want to have yet another stigma on me."

We reached the rocks beneath the condos of Mt. Vernon and stopped. Beyond was an outcropping covered with grass and it was time to turn back. Nary a word was spoken as we reversed direction in total silence, allowing the thoughts of the discussion to soak in. We had gone about 100 yards when a young, attractive couple passed by, on their way to where we had been geographically I hoped, and not emotionally.

When the couple were out of listening range, Amy asked, "Did you find her attractive?" referring to the woman we had just passed. I could have lied, but realized this was about truth laid bare, in more ways than one and responded in the affirmative.

"What did you notice? Amy inquired, adding, "Her face? Her hair? Her breasts?

I answered, "yes!"

Amy continued, "her waist?"

"Yes!"

"Legs?"

"Yes!"

"Overall body shape?"

"Definitely!"

"How about Never, Never Land?" Amy asked, referring to where Amy had placed her small rose tattoo so many years before and had been "zapped", referring to the laser hair removal she had done previously.

I nodded in the affirmative.

"And?"

"And what?" I asked.

"And what went through your mind?"

I shrugged my shoulders.

"Be honest with me, George."

"I thought, I was." I replied.

"Didn't you, if only for a moment, think about having sex with her?"

I reluctantly admitted I had, but was embarrassed to admit it.

"It's normal, George! It's what happens whether we want it to or not."

"What about the guy?" Amy asked.

I shrugged my shoulders.

"Come on George, you had to notice."

I admitted, I did.

"What did you look at?"

"His face? His body? His physique?"

"I don't know." I replied, shrugging my shoulders, somewhat embarrassed.

"What about his 'package'?"

Now I was getting uncomfortable, admitting I had glanced and then looked away.

"Why? Amy asked.

"Why, what?"

"Why did you look away?"

"It's just a thing guys do. You don't stare at another guys 'package'. It always makes you feel uncomfortable."

"You mean, inadequate?"

"Sometimes, but that depends on the package." I replied.

"What about his?" Amy asked.

I gulped and answered. "I guess, he would need a lot of wrapping paper to send that package anywhere." Amy giggled, as I thought, 'my God, what a creepy conversation'!

Amy continued and I realized she was getting quite serious when she stated, "Here's where we're different, George. I looked at the same woman and observed the same things. I also had the same thoughts as you did flash through my mind."

"You mean?" I asked, not finishing the sentence.

"Yes, I found her sexually attractive and appealing and wasn't embarrassed by looking at any part of her and certainly didn't look away. And yes, sex did cross my mind."

"What about him?" I asked.

"Same thing!" Amy replied. "I looked at all of him, with exactly the same thoughts and feelings."

I didn't know whether to be angry, hurt or intimidated. As I kept my silence, Amy must have realized my quandary and added that she was first attracted by the physical attributes, adding that, 'in men, these attributes create a sense of security, where women subconsciously measure size and stature as a sense of both reproductive capability and protection'. I think she realized this made skinny old me feel inadequate and added she wasn't referring to the "package" when she was talking about size and that she, like most other women, go beyond the body and look for "good dad" traits such as gentleness, compassion and sensitivity as well. Whew!

"Any more about him?" I asked as we continued walking, asking if she looked *'down there'* and she said she did.

"What about, you-know-what?' I inquired.

"Wanting to have sex with him?" Amy replied.

I shook my head in the affirmative as we stopped again and Amy looked in my eyes and added, "this is where you and I are different, George. You looked at the woman and got a positive sexual charge. You looked at the man and felt uncomfortable. I looked at both of them and had the exact same, positive sexual charge."

I started with, "In other words -" and once again, Amy interjected, "yes, I would have, if it was the right time, place and circumstances."

Deep Water:

The "naked protocol" had been in place from the very first step and our deep conversation along the way made the environment secondary, so that our responses were automatic! As had been the case during the first encounter way back at Club Orient, when we came across other naked people, our eyes simply averted, as did theirs. I realized, this journey wasn't about thrills! This was, as Amy said it would be, the cleansing of one's soul, in a manner foreign to many, including me.

Amy's chin dropped and she gulped air as if she were drowning and continued. "I went for counseling and laid it all out to Doctor Goodman, who was a psychologist on campus, as there was no way I thought I could ever share everything with anyone - something I hadn't done until right now," pointing her finger at the ground and then me in exclamation.

"Dr. Goodman asked a lot of questions and I used a lot of Kleenex. I was messed up! All that was 'happening' and then Derrick! The pain was too much. Thankfully, Dr. Goodman split the three components into segments and we began discussing each one independently, until we had them out in the open and somewhat resolved."

"The first topic was the racial thing. She told me to accept my race and be proud of who I was. However, unless you live in 'here'" as Amy's splayed fingers slid up and down her torso, you can't understand. Regardless of where we are today, there is and will always be discrimination, simply because it's natural to examine differences instead of commonalities. When you are mixed race, this discrimination can result in a person de-identifying with his or her identity. Instead, they choose to self-identify with the more accepted monoracial race which, in my case, is white. Historically, black identity was also assigned to all biracial and multiracial individuals, regardless of whether they espoused this identity or not".

Amy continued, "Coined the 'one-drop rule' that went back to slavery that George-the-First explained, it was a means of hegemony, where an individual with just one black ancestor was considered black. It didn't matter who or where, just one drop and you were considered inferior. I thought back to George the First and Anna and realized what Amy was saying was absolutely right.

Amy added, "In addition to the one-drop rule, racial classification continues to be done through a process known as physiognomy which is the practice of making decisions about a person's race based on his or her physical appearance. 97% of self-identified biracial individuals, who believed they appeared 'more-black' were identified by others as black, whereas only 17% of self-identified, biracial individuals who believed they appeared more-white, were also described as being white and that's where I've fit in."

"Even though Doctor Goodman said, having parents of different color shouldn't matter. The challenge was always with whom did I identify? I was too brown to be associated with white folks and had too light skin to be considered black. When you are in your teens, all you want to do is fit in and no matter where I went, I was always being classified. Through the grace of God, many people who used to shun those of mixed race now accept us. We are still quantified and segmented, but at least we're not shunned or ashamed."

Amy continued as we walked, "Doctor Goodman added that I was actually one of the lucky ones, because mom was so well known and respected as a physician and daddy had money, which made a big difference. I guess wealth and power can overcome a lot of prejudice, except jealousy, which never goes away. The beauty of it all was watching how much mom and dad loved each other. No matter how bad it ever got, they knew they had each other! "

I took a deep breath and realized that when you come from a lily-white, little town and have few minority friends it's one thing. To live as one is quite another. Amy and I had been lucky, our wealth and subsequent power made all mean and defamatory words spoken, done behind our backs. Our kids identified with "white folks" even though they were one-fourth black. Thank God times had certainly changed, not because of who they identified with, but simply because they had a choice.

Amy paused for a moment, lamented, and continued, but with a completely different tone to her voice. "George, I've also "been" bipolar for the better part of my life. This is the one I feared the most, as the horror stories I read made me cringe and was the main reason I first went to see Doctor Goodman."

"Add to this the social structure of wealth and being blessed or challenged with a higher than average level of intelligence and the combination posed yet another set of problems. Everyone thinks it's great to be brilliant, but this was Derrick's demise that scared me the most, simply because the real challenge of intellect is confinement. When you're as intelligent as he was, you always need to make certain you restrain your thoughts and emotions knowing they could verbally destroy another person simply because, intellectually, you can!"

Man! Amy was REALLY letting her hair down as she continued, "I'll never forget what Doctor Goodman said, 'it's not that bad' as she explained that almost everyone who is bi-polar periodically enter into an elevated mood that results in hyperactivity in all forms, like the time you asked me to do research for you. The risk comes about when those feelings lead to engaging in 'pleasure-seeking' behaviors as Doctor Goodman called them, which end up with the person indulging in physical or social activities others either keep under control or to themselves."

Amy added, "like everyone who hears the words, 'you've got cancer' when you're diagnosed as bi-polar, you think the worst. Fortunately, I suffer from what is called Bipolar II. While Bipolar I **disorder** involves periods of severe mood episodes from mania to depression and back again, Bipolar II is a milder form of mood elevation, involving less-intense episodes of hypomania that alternate with periods of depression, which you have seen in me."

I must have had a quizzical look on my face as Amy expanded her dissertation. "Hypomania is a mood state characterized by persistent disinhibition and mood elevation or euphoria and is when I am most vulnerable in terms of my - my inclinations."

I knew what she was referring to as it was all beginning to make sense. Usually, she would be fine and then, boom, the moods would kick in and she would either go off the deep end and be a bitch or go crazy and need to have her physical urges satisfied.

"Dr. Goodman felt that I also had what was called "mixed features' where I can go through periods of simultaneous symptoms of opposite mood polarities during manic, hypomanic or depressive episodes. You've seen it in me George, when I have high levels of energy, sleeplessness and racing thoughts while still feeling hopeless, irritable and even suicidal and this is when I am most depressed, because I know that I am hurting you."

A soft smile crossed Amy's lips as she added, "Fortunately, my 'extreme' episodes are few and far between. Dr. Goodman said that there is also called Rapid-cycling that describes having four or more mood episodes within a 12-month period, which is what I thought I was suffering from until Dr. Goodman said the episodes needed to last for a minimum number of days in order to be considered distinct episodes and mine are random."

"Some people also experience changes in polarity from high-to-low or vice-versa a single week, or even a single day, meaning that the full symptom profile that defines distinct, separate episodes may not be present. This has to be terrible! I mean, how would people know how to act around you?"

I thought to myself of the times when I really didn't know how to act or what to say. I thought of the anger and frustration and the questions I asked, "what did I do"? I thought of the times when, no matter how I tried, I simply couldn't satisfy her and was finally beginning to understand that it wasn't me, realizing this was what she was trying to tell me.

Amy looked at me, shaking her head and stating, "George, I've been to the edge, but don't believe I've ever been totally out of control. When my peaks-and-valleys became more apparent and I was diagnosed, I got the usual "cry for attention" argument; the "making it up" comments and the "you need to just get over it" remarks. That's when I couldn't hold it in anymore and I would lash out. There was anger! There were periods of promiscuity! There were times when I really thought I was going crazy, simply because I couldn't be satisfied."

"Imagine what it's like to be aroused and know it can't be resolved. Imagine the incredible emotional burden when nothing, and I mean nothing, takes away the craving. This is what I periodically have gone through to the point where there were and remain times when I need physical gratification and can't think about anything else, yet know that there isn't enough, until the urges go away. "

"Before Dr. Goodman, I sincerely felt that no one wanted to look at me as a complex person, just a complex problem. I think this is what happened to my brother. He too was bi-polar, but had it worse and simply couldn't handle always being classified and therefore quantified and it killed him because all he ever wanted to do was escape."

A look of introspection crossed Amy's face as she continued, "Looking back at my social history, before I met you, I realized a lot of the reasons I sabotaged relationships that had more to do with the way my disorder made me than who I was, or who I was with. I would start a relationship in a manic state and the world would come crashing down as I slipped into depression. Each relationship came with the hope that whoever I was with would be able to help me when I couldn't help myself."

Amy continued, "After the doctor and I got past the bi-racial and bi-polar things, I felt comfortable enough to openly accept that I was also bi-sexual and Dr. Goodman didn't even flinch. Instead, she challenged me by asking why I felt the way I did."

I could tell this was really important to Amy and was being shared not only for my benefit, but hers as well as she continued "I threw the question back at Dr. Goodman by asking, 'haven't you ever wanted to take what you like physically and share it with another woman so that you can see how they respond? How can you ever learn what you enjoy if you don't explore? How can you ever expand your horizons if you're afraid to look over the next hill? What you like and what you enjoy, might be only a small fraction of what you COULD enjoy and how you COULD be fulfilled, if you only knew more about the options you have."

I took a deep breath as Amy continued, "I remember, Dr. Goodman was a bit taken aback by my inquiry, but I continued, stating what you once told me - 'There are so many people so hung up about what is right and wrong - good and bad - and what they should and shouldn't do, who are going through life miserable, frustrated, naïve and yet judgmental, because someone, somewhere at one time, said it was wrong."

"Mom said, what adults do should be totally up to them and not society, not culture and certainly not religion! What's right, is what makes people happy without making anyone else unhappy. What's wrong is when someone is either directly or indirectly made unhappy. As long as it consists of consenting adults, who don't purloin the innocence of children, people should do what they want and need to do to be happy."

Amy added as we walked, focusing not on what lie ahead, but simply the next step upon the sand. "People who self-identify as being bisexual experience two types of stigma, not only from heterosexuals, but homosexuals as well. Bisexuality describes how people feel, not necessarily how they act. They say a person can feel attractions to both men and women. However, many make a conscious decision to remain celibate or confine sexual activity to persons of one gender. Yet they still identify as being bisexual by themselves and others."

We stopped and I knew what was about to be said was very important as Amy looked at me and pondered, "Traditionally, orientation is normally classified by being involved in a sexual experience that revolves around some sort of physical contact." With that, Amy shook her head and frowned at her thoughts, as she continued. "I believe this is a somewhat outdated definition that constitutes an absolute, where either you have or have not participated with the same or opposite sex, which to me, is wrong."

I wasn't sure where this was going and yet found the profound willingness to share inner thoughts and beliefs almost beyond anything anyone had ever shared with me before. Amy was laying her soul bare so that I could understand who she was.

Amy looked at me and I could tell she was speaking from the heart as she added, "I've always hated the word 'bisexual,' because it put me in a box and I've always thought of myself as pansexual. Bisexuality implies a dichotomy, pansexuality suggests the possibility of attraction to a spectrum of gender identities. I don't ever think about someone being a boy or girl, just a person and that's what I always wanted to be. My eyes started opening in the fifth or sixth grade. My first physical relationship was in seventh grade and was with a girl who I saw simply as another human, who didn't identify as male or female. Looking at her, she was both beautiful and sexy, yet tough and vulnerable, while also feminine and masculine and I wanted to be just like her.

I looked at Amy and asked her point-blank, "does this mean that you are androgynous?"

She looked at me and furrowed her forehead as if I was some sort of dolt and replied, "Androgyny is the combination of masculine and feminine characteristics that are melded into one ambiguous form. I don't think I'm like that - am I?"

"No, you're all woman in my book." I replied as a compliment.

Amy didn't smile and sent a salvo my way as she continued. "But that's not what I am George!"

"Does this mean that you are sexually ambivalent?" I asked, not really knowing what I was talking about, but wanting her to finally, let it all out.

Amy looked at me and once again was prepared as she replied, "ambivalence is a state of mind. It's where a person has simultaneous mixed feelings and/or experiences, uncertainty or indecisiveness. I'm not that way, I'm not ambivalent at all. In fact, I'm probably just the opposite. I have strong emotional feelings towards you and yet physically towards both men and women. The only thing that has been removed is my desire to be with any other man than you. I love you and only you."

I felt a profound sense of relief as we stopped for a moment so that Amy could get her bearings both physically and emotionally, all emphasized by the frown on her face. I realized that a deep, dark secret was about to come forth and listened as she said, "For years, I sincerely believed I was demi-sexual because I couldn't experience any sexual attraction and I never had a strong emotional connection with that person. At first, sex was just the physical thing. I did it because everyone else was doing it and I thought, if I had sex, I would feel more normal."

"Until you, there was never any romantic attraction, because there was never an emotional connection. Then we met and I knew from that moment you were the one. If Frank hadn't been in the back of the UPS truck or you weren't still recovering from your accident, I probably would have wanted to have sex with you right then and there. I knew George! I knew! I'd never felt like that before and thanked God for allowing me to feel what it was like to have the passionate urge I had never experienced."

I was quietly honored as Amy continued, "the night we went to Milwaukee to dance, I wanted to have you simply pull over and let me pleasure you in every possible way. My urges were incredible! When you left me at the door, my dreams that night were incredibly erotic! I could hardly – actually I really never did hold back from mentally making long, erotic love to you over and over and over, just like I want to do right now."

Amy took her left foot and pushed some of the soft sand to the side as if clearing those thoughts from her mind and began again. "Is what I'm saying making any sense, George?"

I nodded in the affirmative, realizing that for the first time in our marriage she was trying to explain why she was the way she was. Amy looked at me with intense eyes. I know she was doing her best to justify who she was. What was sad for me, was knowing that it wasn't necessary. I accepted her for who she was and loved her no matter what.

The conversation ended, as we continued silently walking away from Mont Vernon and hopefully the intensity of what transpired. We were one - just two people hand-in-hand - deep within our own thoughts, yet sharing emotions that would blend us even closer than ever before.

I looked up at the rising sun and imagined Amy running the entire length each day, as she recovered from her battle and got tired even thinking about it and then Amy began again. "I sincerely feel guilty for stepping out of our marriage to find the periodic feminine intimacy I need. At times, it's very difficult to maintain our relationship at home and there are days when I am depressed and anxious because my attraction, behavior and identity are not in synch with what people think of me. It's like trying to place a square peg in a round hole. It seems like it's "OK" if you're straight or gay, but being part of so many minorities like I am, can make it feel, at times, like everyone has an issue with my existence."

Amy continued, as we walked. "I have been profoundly blessed. I have a husband who shows me every single day that he not only loves me, but respects **and** accepts me. You have no idea how many times I've asked myself, 'how did I find true love with you? I ask myself, how can I ever show you the depth of feeling which comes from sharing everything with you, when I believe no one person can give me everything I need? It's really, really, frustrating!"

I looked at Amy and responded. "Lies and deception are very destructive to relationships and I want you to know and accept that I have never lied to you nor deceived you. My life would have been incredibly different and certainly less rewarding had you not provided the support and love that has allowed me to experience what I have and realize what's really important. There are no regrets - none, not a single one."

Amy looked at me and replied, "George, you are a man of faith and yet religion is one of the major barriers to sexual self-acceptance and I will always be grateful that you have gone beyond what you were taught and accepted me. While there is a great deal of good, what the Bible teaches can also be twisted so that, at certain times in history, it has been read to support slavery, wife-beating, kidnapping, child abuse, prostitution, racism, and polygamy.

"The Book of Ruth" I interjected and continued, "sort of says what it's all about, doesn't it? Add in Corinthians and it appears to me that there are more important considerations to create stigmas about."

Amy nodded in the affirmative, adding, "The question people ask is, 'do you believe that an authentic self can be achieved by balancing two mutually exclusive needs, acknowledging, rather than denying one's feelings?'"

We stopped for a moment and I turned to her and said, "What you are doing right now is one of the bravest things I've ever seen. You've admitted you have conflicted feelings and yet, you have the strength to define the rules of behavior in our relationship, knowing that, by sharing what and how you feel, you were risking everything."

I continued, "I know you have attempted to avoid the things that trigger those attractions and feel guilty when they take place and yet, the more you share with me, the more I understand and the more I understand, the more I realize the torment you've been through. I know about the times when it hasn't worked and believe, I'm to blame! You see, I've thought about those times and there is always one common denominator - me! I made you feel lonely because I took you for granted and put myself first."

Amy looked down at the sand and then at me, as I continued, "In other words, what I thought were profound words so long ago, you already knew, when I told you I was willing to share you if need be."

Amy nodded yes.

Happiness:

I wanted to revert from talking about to me, back to her as I truly needed to know more and asked "What else did Dr. Goodman say?"

Amy responded. "She asked me to define happiness. I remember that I smiled and looked into her eyes and replied - 'to feel wanted, needed and loved!'" Since then, I've gone further by adding that happiness must include joy, contentment, tenderness and enthusiasm. With all that we have, I also know that money and belongings do little to affect our happiness."

Amy looked at me and the 'intense look' permeated her forehead as she shared, "Then Doctor Goodman added more factors that I have carried with me to this day when she said, 'Authentic happiness must include positive emotions, such as hope, contentment and gratitude. Dr. Goodman added that one key ingredient is nurturing relationships with others and the number one malady in America today is loneliness. Loneliness George! Not cancer! Not heart disease! Loneliness! Finally, Dr. Goodman said we all need to feel like we are a part of something larger than ourselves - that we all have a sense of belonging and accomplishing something. What's sad George is that our brains are wired to attend to and learn more from negative experiences than positive ones and this really impedes our ability to be happy."

I looked at her for a moment and then asked the question, "are you happy?" hoping and praying she would say 'yes'.

Amy nodded in the affirmative as she realized that we were on the same page and that all I ever really asked for, consisted of nothing more than her love of me.

My mind burrowed so deep in thought that the entire reality of walking naked on Orient Beach evaporated. People passed by and yet weren't even there! We were walking – talking - sharing, introspective and enlightening thoughts and secrets, yet doing so with such a deep regard for each other that all else was secondary - simply a blur in the sands of time.

"Because of Dr. Goodman, I no longer felt guilty for the negative thoughts about myself I once had. She was the one who shared the statistics and made me begin to accept who I was. That was when I began to minimize my attempts to ameliorate what I thought were my deficiencies and accept myself as me. This was a very difficult thing to do George. For years, I had tried to make a right from what I considered wrong and take actions that would make up for what I had long-believed were negative actions, when in fact, what I felt was neither negative, nor wrong, but just the way I am."

Amy clasped my hand and squeezed my fingers as we continued walking, interjecting that Doctor Goodman understood and accepted the philosophy that if it wasn't dangerous, demeaning or permanent, it really didn't matter what adults did or with whom, as long as all parties did so willingly. She also noted that the good doctor reaffirmed that, while there was probably a social stigma involved that made some mannerisms demeaning to some, the fact that two or more adults were willingly involved, made it acceptable.

Amy added, "For many people the way I am is an anathema. They can't comprehend what it's like and don't understand that what's normal for them is not normal for me and what's normal for me is so foreign to them that they find it repellant as if they were allergic to it. Yet, I witness the cruisers and how they ogle when they come by the busloads to Orient Beach only to judge others and not to accept the reality that people can be and the human body can be androgynous if allowed to be so."

We stopped for a moment and Amy said. "You know what else she told me?" It was a rhetorical question that Amy answered. "Dr. Goodman told me that sex for women had evolved from one of passion and/or submission to include forms of recreation and entertainment. She added that, what had once been taboo, was acceptable in terms of partners, practices and circumstances. I was shocked when she said that George! All the things I'd heard about, all the things I cringed but were secretly fantasizing about, weren't bad things, just different things and I hadn't shared with her, all the silly stuff my roommates and I were doing."

"Doctor Goodman added one more really important point, George! She said good sex included great laughter. Pleasure didn't need to only be physical, George. It could be fun! Fun George! Fun!"

I wondered what she was referring to, but really didn't want to know. Amy and I had always had a somewhat unwritten agreement when it came to talking about our 'physical' past and I didn't know if I had over-stepped the bounds when the only word out of my mouth was "Did?"

Before another word pursed my lips, Amy replied. "I took mom's advice and explored and, quite honestly, had fun. Through exploration, I was able to set my own bounds instead of what society and culture had in mind. Mom also told me, there was nothing wrong with being physically adventuresome as long as you didn't end up just being an object for others."

My mind was splattering in a dozen different directions – "others?" What did that mean, did I dare ask? Would she be offended? I decided to risk it – "Others?"

Amy replied. "Yes others. I wanted to see what it was like. For a woman, it's actually a lot easier than for a man. I wanted to experience everything and trying a lot of different 'situations'! In order to make sure I was never objectified, I had my version of the golden rule – 'Do unto me only what you will allow me to do unto you.'"

My mind was whirling as I probed a little deeper asking – "you mean?'

"Yes, not only 'different' things, but different sets of dynamics." Amy replied in a matter-of-fact way.

One would think that after all the years together I would know. Yet, she was really letting her hair down and I wanted to know more, if she was willing to tell me. Perhaps it was my prurient interest. Perhaps, I was trying to resolve the questions that had floated around in my head for so many years. I wanted her explain everything, not to judge her. Simply because I wanted to know. "You mean?" I somewhat sheepishly asked again.

I took a deep breath of relief as Amy added. "Exploring isn't strange or weird or perverted. In fact, those who are mentally *"healthy"*, savor the pleasure and remain unfazed by the experience. When it's over, they continue on with their life, realizing and accepting that all they've done is add another chapter to their experiences and expanded their references.

Amy's head slightly shook from side-to-side and a broad smile crossed her face, as some those memories of what she and her roommates had done flooded her thought pattern and I think she was contemplating whether to share things with me or not. She looked at me with a wry grin on her face and admitted. "We did have a lot of 'fun' back then, doing a lot of crazy things college students do."

Before I could respond, Amy added, "Our house was on a street that was mainly rented to upper classmen. One Halloween, we decided to have a progressive party, where you go from one house to the next and there would be prizes for the best costume, most outlandish – you know. The four of us decided we all wanted to go as the same thing. We thought about getting those micro mini-skirt kilts and going as prep school girls with the big glasses and all; then we thought about going as naughty nurses as Renee was in pre-med. We even thought about going as French maids, Playboy Bunnies - you name it. We really had fun goofing around thinking about it"

"Sandy was majoring in theater and asked if we would like to go as statues. She knew this guy who did bodypainting and we could go painted white from head-to-toe. We all thought that would be cool. Wear a bikini and get painted."

"Sandy had this guy come to the house who brought his body-painting equipment that included a small spray gun. He asked us if we wanted to just go as painted girls or looking like real statues. I asked what the difference was and he said 'hair'. I thought he meant on the tops of our heads. He meant body hair and explained that statues had smooth skin and if we wanted to look like the real deal, we'd have to shave. We all agreed that if we were going 'all in' we'd shave. I thought he meant our arms and legs, but he meant everywhere including what he called *'Never Never Land'* which is where the term comes from, when he asked 'you are going nude aren't you? I've never seen a statue in a bikini.'"

At first, we were all a bit reluctant - had a few drinks - and agreed that this would be a one-time event and so he got out what he called his 'fuzz buster' and did his thing on all of us. It was warm out and we went out in the back yard and he fitted us with plugs so that no paint would get inside us.

"He asked what type of paint we wanted. Cheap paint would crack and begin coming off right away. The good stuff would stay on all night but would need to be cleaned off with a chemical when we were done. At first, we were going with the cheap stuff until we all realized, we wouldn't be able to sit down or touch anything and so we went with the good stuff."

"Jack, Renee's fiancé came over and split a gut laughing. He was going to go as a scarecrow, but we talked him into getting his body painted and the make-up guy, used the fuzz buster on him and painted him like a toy soldier and he went as Renee's pull toy."

"It's amazing what a coat of paint does. None of us felt like we were naked. But then, that also could have been the alcohol. Needless to say, having four naked statues and a pull toy at the party set the mood and we won the grand prize. When the party ended, we all went back to the house, all climbed in the shower together and used the chemical to get rid of the paint and washed each other all over. It was a crazy night, but really, a lot of fun."

"Jack too?" I asked.

"Sure why not?" Amy replied.

I smiled at the image, as Amy continued. "I remember Renee's bachelorette party! My God! There was this one guy who thought he was God's gift to women. We thought it would be fun to have him come to the party instead of hiring a male stripper and see what we could get him to do. There were seven girls and him. We started drinking early and when he showed up, were already half in the bag and decided to be naked. I'll never forget the look on his face when Cheryl opened the door and let him in. He thought he'd died and gone to heaven. We took a lot of crazy pictures. We were all SO drunk!"

"The guy went along with it?" I asked.

"He played along and provided some pure debaucherous fun for everyone. It ended up with the guy spending the night with Renee. It was her last *'adventure'* before settling down. It sure was crazy night!"

"Did you ever get the photos developed?"

"We gave them to Renee as a shower present. I thought her mother was going to croak. Instead she laughed her butt off, not knowing what transpired with Renee."

Amy shrugged her shoulders as if to justify what happened saying, "It was her last fling."

I shook my head in amazement. The craziest thing we ever did in college was get drunk after Badger games and go bar hopping on State Street as Amy looked at me and proclaimed. "The problem with guys is that you're all wired to do one thing – spread your seed. When the fun begins, you only have one goal in mind and miss out on the genial aspects of simply letting go. I know that as we age, we become more 'reserved'. I know that things we are willing to do in college, we'd never do as we get older. Yet, as I look back on some of the things we did, I realize, it was really part of growing up and there was nothing wrong with it."

I asked Amy if she missed it.

"Not really!" she replied. "I did what I did and found you and realized the majesty of love and how much more it means than just sex. You, are my husband and I love you! I made a covenant that I have vowed to keep. Since we've been married, I've NEVER been unfaithful or had a deleterious association with another man. If you weren't here and weren't the center of my life and it was the right time, place and circumstance and I wanted to do it, I would be willing. But those aren't the circumstances, because I am totally committed to you."

Wow! This was getting crazy. Amy felt justified that, because she was married, it was wrong to be with another man, but it was OK to be with a woman. I remembered back to our first time on St. Martin and realized that what she said was nothing more than what I offered. What was transpiring began long before we met and she was perfectly willing to balance both lifestyles and provide full disclosure with profound transparency.

Simply Human:

We were getting into even deeper water from a metaphorical sense, but I knew we needed to go on, noting that nothing we experience ever ceases to exist. Some of our experiences are relegated to the unconscious, simply because they are irrelevant or unimportant at that time. However, at the same time, other experiences burrow into our soul, leaving an indelible mark that transcends who we are and what we want to be. What we know, becomes part of the experience of our conscious ego and therefore a part of us. Once having seen, we cannot un-see. Once we having known, we cannot unknow. Once having done we cannot un-do! Once having felt, we can no longer un-feel.

We slowed for a moment as another couple passed by. Amazingly, even though both parties were naked and totally physically exposed, we stopped talking so that they couldn't overhear our conversation or see our emotions. Gone was the reticence and shyness of our physical selves, replaced by the profound need to clothe ourselves in our thoughts and emotions, reserved only for us.

As the couple passed, Amy added, "what we are conscious of becomes an integrated aspect of our own reality and the fear and trembling we may have experienced when we leave behind the safety of consistency cannot be overemphasized. Change George, for most of us, is a terrifying experience, simply because each person is always profoundly desperate to know things will work out, even when reality says they won't."

"What about hope?" I countered.

Amy shrugged her shoulders and replied, "Hope is an attitude that a future positive event will materialize, even if it's unlikely. My return from cancer hinged on my hope that each day would be better than the day before. Because I had hope and could actually see progress, hope was as good as any of the medicines I took because it gave me the resilience I needed to endure."

In the end, Amy explained what Doctor Goodman told her. "If a person is willing, they can recognize the abyss established by their own values that have made them sad. If they want change can take place and, if the person is willing to release all the physical, social and emotional bonds that have affected them regarding the fundamentals concerning who they are, who they have been and what they have believed about themselves, they are able to change. If a person can do that, they can lead a fuller life. Yes! There will be mistakes! Yes, there will be disappointments! Yes, there will be heartbreak! However, it is better to have tried and lost, than never have tried at all!"

"George, I married you because you were and remain the only person who looked at me and saw more than a list of symptoms and consequences. In my heart, I believe you saw a person worthy of love and respect. It didn't matter what category I placed myself in, or how many there are, you have accepted me as me and because of that, I chose to love you for you. No matter how I or anyone with whom I share the same traits for that matter lives, life we will always be met with criticisms. I always just wanted to be 'normal', like everyone else."

We stopped again and looked deep into each other's eyes. This was a deep and serious conversation and it required more than words. Amy added, "What Doctor Goodman said next is the most important part. I remember her nodding in the affirmative at my self-analysis and repeating what I had said - happiness boils down to sincerely feeling wanted, needed and loved and that's what you have always made me feel. George, you shared these exact words when we here the first time and validated that I had chosen the right man to spend the rest of my life with."

I smiled and said "thank you" asking, "why did you stop seeing the doctor?" I asked.

Amy replied, "When my leukemia diagnosis came in, I had to stop. Doctor Goodman prescribed pills to smooth out the peaks and valleys and they're the ones you see me take every now and then, simply to protect me from me and from hurting you or the kids. I take my prescriptions and feel as if the peaks are eroded and the valleys filled in, realizing, I'm simply not me."

"After I came here, I tried to go "off meds" and back to counseling, but it was different and the questions the psychologist asked, while done with good intentions, were ultimately, incredibly condescending and humiliating, making me feel as if I were some kind of leper or an outcast, when all I wanted was to learn why? Why did I think and act and feel the way I did? Why were my needs and values so different?"

Amy and I stopped again, indifferent to the world around us, not caring if others walked by or not as Amy said, "George, I watch the way the world comes at people who are different with fear and contempt and it makes me sick. Being bipolar is incredibly hard for a plethora of reasons, but I've never felt scared of being that way. I'm a human being, the same as them.

When God made me, I wasn't meant to fit neatly into one category or even several. I decided a long time ago that the only way to live life to the fullest was to just be myself. This means I may fit into some categories neatly, others not so much and some not at all. If people ever learn to respect those categories and the people who inhabit them, the world will be a better place.

My dream is that hopefully someday, all people will actually value someone who is different and have the inherent ability to embrace that difference. Then and only then will they understand that differences are what make the metaphorical world go round."

I nodded in the affirmative. My God, what an incredible level of introspection! As we walked again in silence, I began to reflect on the instances and the realization of why Amy's responses and moods were the way they were. I then asked Amy, "does anyone else know?"

"About what?"

"About your - about everything!" I lamented.

"Mom knew! She knew before I did and was the one who recommended Dr. Goodman. It's an inherent ability most mothers have. We can sense when things are 'different'".

Amy paused for a moment as if to get her bearings and determine whether she should continue. She closed her eyes, took a deep breath and put her hands to her mouth as if in prayer and added, "Mothers know".

"Did she know about - about everything?" I asked, not wanting to be too descriptive.

Amy looked at me and nodded, replying, "Yes everything, before I did."

"And?"

"And what?"

"She accepted it?" I asked.

This got an incredulous look from Amy as she replied, "mom loved me and accepted me for who I am. Just like I accept you and the kids, knowing there are things I would like to change, but accept the ways things are."

I closed my eyes in profound relief and let out a deep sigh, knowing that I didn't need to carry Amy's secret's alone, asking, "What about your dad?"

Amy's head jerked back as she answered, "daddy's clueless and that's the way it's got to be."

"Why now?" I asked. "Why, after all these years, are you telling me now?"

"I haven't shared this with you because there has always been an assumption on my part that it would make me less capable of being faithful in our relationship, simply because all my needs can't be fulfilled by you! I tried! I really tried! But I failed and I'm telling you now because I love you so much and just - want - to - say - I'm sorry. Sorry that I have failed you."

Tears roiled within her heart and splashed upon her cheeks. My heart was broken, not by the news, but by her profound sadness as she reiterated, "this is all my fault!"

"Your fault?" I strongly countered. "Don't you think I've wondered why you are the way you are? Have you ever asked yourself why I accept it? Every time 'something' has *come up,* I've tried to learn more and each time I came to the same conclusion, it's – not – your - fault! It's who you are and therefore you can't fight it. If you try, you will always be frustrated and unhappy.

I've always been short and skinny. Is that my fault? I can't be taller! Is it my fault I can't change my metabolic rate, nor the color of my eyes? They are what they are and that's what makes up me, you, the kids - everyone! Amy, I love you. I always have and always will. I don't and won't judge you. All I ask in return is that you don't judge me."

I continued, "I've always tried to support you and understand what's going on, while appreciating your strengths and accepting your weaknesses, where those strengths profoundly outweigh the weaknesses. Along the way, I've learned that, when you are living with a person you love, who has a medical condition, where doctors and scientists really don't know the exact cause, you need to look for possible and potential solutions to minimize the effects. I also realized that, unfortunately, there aren't always going to be answers, as every action has a reaction and I am willing to accept the actions because I don't want to ever lose the strengths you have that make you great."

I paused for a second and peered deeply into her eyes. What I was about to say was really important. "Amy, if there is no choice, there can be no fault and if there can be no fault, there should be no shame. There's nothing to be embarrassed about! There's nothing to feel guilty about!"

"Shame happens when we believe we haven't lived up to the ideals of society or someone close to us or some spiritual code, all of which we know are changing. There's nothing to feel guilty about, simply because your inclinations are normal for you and you have hurt no one, including me. Because of this, there should be no remorse and no need for reparations."

There were tears in Amy's eyes as she wiped her cheeks and whispered, "I'm so sorry I haven't shared all of this with you before. I'm so much in love with you - more today than yesterday, but not as much as tomorrow."

As we hit the "curve", it was already getting hot, in more ways than one I guess. Amy asked if we could go in the water to cool off. We had no towels and obviously no clothes and even the wizard me, realized we really needed neither. The water was warm and the waves gentle and so we walked out to where we were up to our necks in more ways than one, thereby allowing the water to cool our bodies and wash away any lingering tension.

Amy looked at me and smiled, saying, "I love you for who you are and what you are and most of all, for understanding. I know it's not perfect! I know many men couldn't handle what you do. I know it hurts and I only hope I make I up to you in other ways."

I looked at her and pulled her into me, pressing my lips to hers and feeling her body against mine. Instead of talking, I initiated a long, deep kiss that communicated what I really wanted to say…"it's Ok! It's OK! It's OK!"

We stayed in the water long enough for the young couple to pass. As we returned to the beach, we were now following them, as the warm breeze dried our bodies.

"Nice ass!" I nonchalantly whispered.

"Which one?" Amy replied.

I guess I caught her off guard when I responded, "both of them" with a chuckle.

This was the antidote we both needed as we walked the last vestiges of the beach hand-in-hand as the gap between the couple and us lengthened. Words were not spoken. We were both silently awash in thoughts that represented the culmination of our walk upon the beach.

As we reached the spot where our morning began, the young couple continued on into their zone of social safety called anonymity, oblivious to the thoughts and secrets they'd evoked in our souls. Our pace slowed and, as we walked those final steps, I realized that this venture hadn't at all been about being physically naked, it was about being exposed emotionally. All the questions! All the wondering! All the frustration that had built up over the years had been stripped away and we stood revitalized, excited by each other, just as we had been so many years before.

We stopped for a moment as our hands unclenched and Amy took one long, last glance at the ocean. Taking in a deep breath of the morning air, I slid behind her and put my hands on her shoulders and shared the view she was admiring. Slowly, my arms went forward and I put my hands around her waist and pulled her in. At first there was a start as Amy felt my body press against hers and then relaxed, realizing this wasn't a physical expression, but one of love. Out of acceptance, Amy's arms crossed and she pulled my hands tighter across her abdomen, thereby pulling me closer to her body and soul.

As we stood there - watching nothing, feeling everything – I relished

the belief that the emotional lacquer built up over 30 years together, that had dulled our emotions and eroded our attraction was gone and, in its place, there was peace.

For an extended period of time, we stood watching the rising sun break from the ocean's grasp, enmeshed - not physically, but emotionally - not for gratification - but melding as we once were - filled with the wonderous joy and excitement simply for each other.

Softly, I put my chin upon Amy's shoulder. There was a gentle sigh of acceptance on her part, as her head tilted back and I whispered three soft words I knew would last forever – "I – love – you!"

Nanospheres:

The Madcity boys had concluded what was needed in terms of chip design and called a meeting to bring me up to speed. Experts from all over the world had joined the team with the promise that any recognition and reward would be equally shared. The goodness of mankind was being exemplified.

Initially, the boys wanted to develop an operating system that was specific to each organ within the body so that the system would communicate with a chip located in the brain and be paired with Nanochips to manage the chemical elicitation needed to satisfy any chemical imbalance. Working with the University of California San Diego, the team was developing a system where the Nanochips could be placed in a serum and then, using an electromagnet, 'moved' from where it was injected to the desired organ. The whole system seemed incredible and yet so logical.

As the MadCity Boys progressed, they realized the challenge was much more profound than initially planned. Being the geniuses they were, they simply began developing an operating system that incorporated the nano-chips and one major controlling chip, they called a nanosphere they hoped would serve as the mainframe for the project.

The goal became to create a form of augmented reality, designed to enhance the real world by superimposing elements that would not only enhance our senses of sight, touch, smell and touch, but work with the autonomic system that controls our body. This would be a profoundly difficult task and yet the boys felt we had the resources and brilliance needed to take a giant step forward.

In order to do this, the team began outlining what the Nanochips needed to be and what they needed to do. Macro outlines were developed and then, within each outline, sub-categories identified, until the team had a comprehensive structure summarized. I could spend the next two hundred pages outlining what they wanted, but it probably wouldn't make any more sense to you than it did to me. Instead, I picked out some of the ideas and have it here for you.

While Moore's law correctly predicted that the number of transistors on a chip would double every two years, the goal was a quantum leap forward, not only in capacity, but in both size and operating capability, that was to be powered by the electrical system within the human body. This meant first developing individual Nanochips, where the boys explained that a Nanochip was defined as, "an integrated circuit so small, in physical terms, that individual particles of matter must play major roles, so that more processing power can fit into a given physical volume with the less energy required to run it". The boys noted that a Nanochip could work faster because the distances between components were reduced, thereby, minimizing what is called *'charge-carrier transit'* time.

To begin the process, the team knew they would need to better understand every organ in the body and create a system that would allow for permutations without consequence. For this they turned to the Englebart concept of virtual reality and began creating immersive three-dimensional environments that allowed the participating medical, mathematical and scientific minds to work side-by-side in examining the development of each Nanochip so that each was specific to the organ and function of that part of the organ it was responsible for.

On the team were global specialists, researchers and physicians who knew how each specific organ worked and what needed to be done to improve its efficiency. When it came to the brain, experts on each region were added so that the brain committee consisted of the sum of intellect that could better understand and guide others when it came to the chip design. Being somewhat, no make that, totally in the dark, I asked for a brief summary on how a computer chip worked.

Peter outlined how chips worked when he said. "Until recently, each computer chip was constructed of silicon and metal. The computer chip is nothing more than an integrated circuit which contains millions of transistors that make up what is called a processor that is aligned to create an electrical signal. When several chips are placed together with different amounts of memory storage space on them, you create what is called the central processing unit or CPU."

"Each chip uses a language to communicate and perform activities called the assembly language. There are three main functions of all computer chips. First, the chip uses an arithmetic/logic unit to perform mathematical equations. Second the chip needs to move memory from one chip to another and finally, the chip needs to make decisions and create instructions based on those decisions."

Peter continued. "There are two main types of memory that a computer chip uses: ROM and RAM. ROM is read-only memory and is used for permanent information that the computer uses. RAM is random access memory and is used for readable or writable memory that is completely wiped when the computer shuts off. The instructions that a computer chip follows is called programming. There are different languages that computers can be 'taught' to read where the chip simply takes the programming language and translates it into action. Because of what we are attempting, we are writing our own operational language that is spatial instead of linear, meaning that it can communicate with numerous adjacent components at the same time."

"In other words, like SIMON?" I inquired.

"Exactly" Peter replied.

"In other words, a microscopic quantum computer?" I asked.

"George, you're catching on!" Peter added. "Most computer chips can only handle so many different instructions on their transistors and it takes about five cycles of the transistors before a command can be executed. Because the limit has been based on the number of transistors and the addition of transistors results in greater size, heat and energy consumption, the challenge has been to create chips out of materials that will allow for smaller, more efficient transistors and we are to the point where we have moved beyond those that are molecular in size to those that are the size of an atom. Our goal is to see if we can get smaller and go to the sub-atomic level."

"Do you mean the God particle?" I asked, surprising the boys by my question.

Peter responded. "No, we don't think we can get to Higgs Boson because first, we don't have the equipment unless you want to dump in a few billion to build another Large Hadron collider particle accelerator like the one in Switzerland. And second, even if we did have the equipment, we can't do something that's never been done in terms of determining the different subatomic particles that are responsible for giving matter different properties.

Tad added. "We're trying to integrate computer technology into physiology and can't even fathom how you would go about determining the particle which gives mass to matter."

Being the smart ass, I asked whether Father Paul would know, to which both guys gave me a strange look and so I continued. "Well, Father Paul does say mass every day and twice on Sundays and for many that does matter."

As usual, I asked Peter what time it was and the group told me how to build a watch! Adding a little levity to the discussion seemed to bring things back to what prevailed, which was what we could actually do with the time, materials and technology we had. Time was of the essence!

It wasn't long before the brain group, that we began calling the 'Brainiacs', concluded they needed to develop specific holographic Nanochips that better emulated the cellular structure of the neurons in their bionic neighborhood. In other words, chips that replicated cells within the organs and those in the brain, by creating artificial versions of the cells themselves.

Tad added. "By using this system, each Nanochip could store and process millions of bits of information in tandem, enabling data transfer rates that matched or even exceeded the transmission rate of the human nervous system."

I was amazed! The team had reached basic neural transfer speed, but knew the real challenge would be within the brain itself, as the fastest any computer had ever worked was at .02% of the speed of the brain. The boys thought they could speed things up. We hoped so.

I had guessed right! The Brainiacs surmised that, because each chip was, in fact, a microscopic computer, the only way they could accomplish our objectives was to incorporate quantum designs that could solve multiple calculations at once. By using a principal called 'superposition' that not only looked at zeroes and ones, like old-fashioned binary computers, but also all the states in between and do so simultaneously, just as SIMON did so that the speed would increase and response time would go down. The challenge became creating different molecular computers that would integrate automatically with the part of the body it was supposed to work with and do so without rejection or damage to the host cells that surrounded it.

Chips falling As They May:

If creating a computer chip to be inserted in the human body sounds difficult you are right. In fact, it's nearly impossible. Yet it is what dreamers dream and that's what allowed mankind to move ahead, simply by pushing farther and farther and farther into what was once considered impossible.

The first question became chip structure. Everyone agreed that using traditional "flat chips" made of silicon, would mean much more invasive implants that could possibly do damage to surrounding tissue. It was decided that the team would develop spherical chips.

I asked, "Why spheres?"

"Because spheres are the most efficient of all solid objects." Peter pointed out. "Rain drops or bubbles of any kind are always a spherical shape. This is because the liquid tries to minimize the surface area while maintaining the same internal volume, resulting in a higher potential energy level than any solid figure with the same surface area."

Tad, our mathematician, added. " This is called the surface-area-to-volume ratio and is the amount of surface area per unit of volume of an object or collection of objects. In chemical reactions involving a solid material, the surface-area-to-volume ratio is an important factor for the reactivity, that is, the rate at which the reaction will proceed.

Peter confirmed. "For a given volume, the object with the smallest surface area is the sphere which is the consequence of the isoperimetric inequality in three dimensions."

I must have looked befuddled as Tad added. "Isoperimetric inequality in three dimensions simply means having the same perimeter."

Back to Peter. "The ratio of the surface area and volume of each cell and organism has an enormous impact on their biology, including not only their physiology and behavior but their function and so we are examining all the options to create the least intrusive design possible."

Tad added. "An increased surface-area-to-volume ratio also means increased exposure to the surrounding environment and that can lead to biological problems, but also greater possibilities. The greater the contact with the environment through the surface of a cell or an organ, relative to its volume, the greater the loss of water and dissolved substances, which would mean lower efficiency."

"High surface-to-volume ratios can also present problems in terms of temperature control which could also result in greater fuel consumption. The heat build-up could actually damage surrounding nerve cells, whose damaged axions would then impede the transfer of the electrical signal to the dendrites we want the signal to be transferred to. However, higher surface-to-volume ratios will also mean faster response time and a more three-dimensional communication path that replicates the structure of cells.

Peter added. "In other words, by developing spherical chips, we can pack in more computational capability than we could with a cube. This will result in a less-invasive device with the same capability while increasing the speed and transfer purity of the signal. Then, taking the principles from the holographic design team, we can make the sphere more efficient and have greater computational speed. Our goal is to see how small we can make either a petabyte or zettabyte chip. We feel that creating a yottabyte chip would create too much heat."

I thought of Amy's and my walk on Orient beach and how it all seemed so simple and pure as I asked. "How big of chip are you designing?"

Tad replied. "Externally, we feel we can increase SIMON's capacity to the zettabyte level and reduce the amount of heat, thereby reducing the cooling requirements while increasing not only his computational speed, but his self-learning capabilities, as well. Internally, our goal is to develop a series of holographic

Nanospheres with varying degrees of capacity ranging from one gigabyte to ten terabytes."

I knew that a terabyte is 1,024 times bigger than one gigabyte and to convert terabytes to gigabytes you multiplied by 1024 and vice versa. I wanted to know why ten terabytes and asked, "Why such a broad range?"

Tad responded, each size would have a different application. "The single gigabyte Nanospheres are the ones that could be placed in a serum and injected into the blood stream. Due to their plasticity, the small Nanospheres would also have a pre-programmed identity where they would float through the body. Then, by using the electro-magnet guide the boys in San Diego are developing, the Nanospheres could be directed to any location we wanted. When they were in place, you would simply turn off the electro-magnet and lock the Nanospheres in place in the appropriate organ."

"How small will these Nanospheres be?" I asked.

"One gigabyte Nanospheres would be about one-tenth the size of the end of a ballpoint pen." Peter replied. "This is why they would need to be put into a serum consisting primarily of glucose and injected similar to a vaccine."

I was amazed. Flooding the body with tiny computers.

Mark added. "The brain is different and will require larger Nanospheres. Most computational neuroscientists tend to estimate human brain storage capacity somewhere between one and one-hundred terabytes, with the full spectrum of guesses ranging from one terabyte to 2.5 petabytes, where a petabyte is 1,024 terabytes."

Peter added, "At 2.5 petabytes, we believe you are talking about all the functions - autonomic and emotional, plus long-and-short term memory."

"In other words, you want the capacity of the human brain?" I concluded.

"As our first threshold, we feel our nanosphere could cover either the autonomic aspects or long-and-short term memory, but not both. If possible, we would like to continue working towards developing a holographic nanosphere with a one petabyte capacity. This would allow for the storage and retrieval of all short and long-term memories." Peter replied.

"What are the challenges?" I asked.

Peter paused, looked out the window and responded. "There are a several. First, is the size of the nanosphere. It can't be too large or it would be too invasive. Second, is heat. We can't have a nanosphere that would destroy the tissue around it. Heat would detrimentally affect the neurons it's supposed to communicate with. Third, is the question of what material the chip would be made of. Finally, is the functional duration or life of the nanosphere. The nanosphere will need to be powered by something within the body and we will need to determine some sort of chemical reaction that will allow it to work for an extended period of time."

Peter continued. "To address these concerns and work on an atomic level, we are developing 'multiferroic' crystals that are capable of expanding the capacity of storage devices by one-thousand to a million times while, at the same time, minimizing chip size to what we believe will be the sub-atomic level."

"What is a multiferroic crystal? I asked.

Peter responded. "Multiferroic materials are a class of crystalline materials which exhibit a number of unique properties, in which at least two different parameters exist at the same time. These can be ferro or anti-ferro magnetic, ferro-electric and ferro-elastic degrees of freedom."

Now Peter really had me bewildered and so he continued. "In physics, several different types of magnetism are distinguished that are based on the atomic structure of the material, which are then classified accordingly. Ferro-magnetism is the basic mechanism by which atoms within materials, such as iron, either are modified and become permanent magnets or are attracted to magnets."

"In anti-ferro magnetism, the atoms align in a regular pattern, but point in opposite directions. Ferro-electricity is simply a characteristic of certain materials that have an inherent electric polarization that can be reversed simply by applying an electric field. Finally, ferro-elasticity is a phenomenon in which a material may exhibit a spontaneous strain and can therefore be modified. A crystal is ferro-elastic if it has two or more stable states of orientation in the absence of an electric field, and if it can be reproducibly transformed from one to another state by the application of any form of stress. If you were to examine it, it would look like liquid Jell-O that would be impregnated in a semi-pliable sphere.

Tad added, "We feel we need to use this type of material, not only for its efficiency, but also for safety, in that it won't rely on lead, as regular chips now do."

Peter added. "In addition, since the data will be written both electrically and magnetically, it will also be far more secure."

Tad added. "Like driving a car, the faster you go, the more energy it takes as the car becomes less efficient. This is the same thing with Nanospheres and that's why we want to use the multiferroic crystals."

Peter continued, "You remember when we budgeted for the 3D laser printer?" I nodded in the affirmative, remembering the 'you want to spend how much on what?' moment, as he continued. "Our printer has 12,000 nozzles and we've used it to create about three billion layers of multiferroic crystals in what we are calling a heliosphere. Under an electron microscope, the holo-sphere looks like a sponge with millions of sub-atomic holes in it. In so doing, we've literally created a series with not only memory and computational capability such that each individual cell acts as a microscopic antenna that emits signals to the surrounding cells."

I shook my head. These guys were off the chart when it came to intellect and passion and I quietly thanked God for their existence.

Tad added. "Because we know which chemicals are needed for the different responses and also know the neuro-transmissions needed to stimulate different adjacent cells, we can program each cell group within the holo-sphere to function as the dendrite, or receptor for the chip, activated by the neuro chemicals it receives. The Nanochip would then replicate the neuro-chemicals it receives and serve as the transmitter, or axon, for the chip, that will then transfer the right amount of neurochemicals to the adjacent brain cell's dendrites, as well."

I must have had yet another puzzled look on my face and so Peter explained. "Dendrites are projections of a nerve cell that receive information from other neurons, while an axon, is a long slender projection of a nerve cell that conducts electrical impulses away from the neuron's cell body."

I took my left hand and pointed to my brain - "Dendrite in" - then took my right hand and pointed towards space and said - "Axon out". The two wizards looked at me with sheepish grins and realized I figured it out.

Tad continued. "Once the holo-sphere transfer has taken place, the body's normal neural response would happen as the body would naturally replicate the process by stimulating the dendrites of the next layer of adjacent live cells and then the next and next and next until we have the necessary thought, action or response."

Peter added. "The challenge right now is called 'beam steering' which is developing a way to efficiently channel the signals so that they are only transferred to the correct cells. We don't want someone to be stimulated and think or respond to or about one thing, only to have the chip activate a different thought process in their brain. We think we can program the cells and also control what they are activated by. If we can do what we think we can, only the correct cells would be affected."

"So you would take a bunch of holo-spheres and combine them into one nanosphere?" I asked.

"Yes" both said in unison. I asked. "How many Nanospheres are you talking about?"

Tad replied. "It will depend upon capacity and function. From a functional perspective, we believe we can develop three different types of cerebral Nanospheres. In the Primary Nanosphere, the objective is one-way function. Here, we would have SIMON harvest topical data on specific subjects and download the information into a small nanosphere that would be implanted to provide a particular area of knowledge. As an example, SIMON could harvest all the world's knowledge on Anatomy, Physiology and Biochemistry. With that implant, the recipient would instantaneously have all the medical knowledge as a resource and could then invest the necessary 10,000 hours to become a physician."

I shook my head in disbelief.

Peter added. "This could be done with any field - law, chemistry, physics, music, you name it. SIMON can harvest the information and we can download it in a matter of minutes."

"In addition, if someone had a seizure, stroke or subdural hematoma that impeded part of their mental functions, we could provide a Primary Nanosphere that worked with, or bypassed, the affected part of the brain to compensate for its damage, such as rebuilding their entire vocabulary."

"In other words, you could implant knowledge and bypass the rudimentary process of learning?" I asked.

"Correct and do so while providing the entire spectrum of knowledge on a specific field."

"What happens when the chip loses power?" I asked.

"With the Primary Nanosphere, all the information will have been transferred to the person's area of the brain where that knowledge would have been stored anyway and so the chip would simply cease to function with, what we believe to be, no detrimental effects."

"How do we make sure?" I asked.

"We will ask Hsu for her help in evaluating a test protocol and possible subjects," Tad added.

"You said there were others," I noted.

Peter responded. "In the second type of chip, which we call Compensatory Nanospheres, we believe that integrating these devices with satellite Nanochips implanted in selected locations in the body would allow us to have an internal form of medicine. Here the brain would work with the different organs to provide increased or decreased levels of neurochemicals such as insulin or dopamine that would control everything from diabetes to alcoholism and drug abuse. As a second function, the Compensatory Nanosphere could also be downloaded with information that would remain functional and not transferred to damaged areas of the brain, unless it had been absorbed in other non-damaged areas. At this point in time, we simply don't know if the human brain would adapt to the Compensatory Nanosphere or not."

"Would this help The Duke?" I asked.

"Neither of these structures would help anyone with Alzheimer's or dementia." Peter replied. "Both the Primary and Compensatory Nanospheres are one-way devices that only input data into the human brain and would be a reference source. When it comes to dementia, Parkinson's, Alzheimer's and ALS, we feel that the degradation of the brain, due to plaque build-up, low dopamine or cellular death, is such that we will need to develop a storage medium for information that harvests the information stored in the functioning cells. It will also attempt to retrieve the information in the dysfunctional or impeded cells, but this is a big challenge and is why we are moving forward with a larger device called a Dynamic Nanosphere. Our goal would be to harvest all short-term and long-term memories in a person we can and have the chip function as a supplemental internal hard drive, so to speak."

My mind was simply overwhelmed! Nanospheres? Primary? Compensatory? Dynamic? Wow! I continued with my interrogation. "How big would these holographic Nanospheres be?"

Mark responded. "As Tad noted, the Primary Nanosphere would be approximately the size of the end of a ball point pen and have a one terabyte capacity. The Compensatory Nanosphere would simply be a compilation of Primary Nanospheres, all packed within one holo-sphere. Here, because of the omni-directional transfer of data, we believe it would be about the size of a pencil eraser and have a four-terabyte capacity."

"The Dynamic Nanosphere is still in theoretical development. However, we believe it can consist of a series of Dynamic Nanosphere crystals packed into one housing that will be also about the diameter of a pencil eraser but one and one-half times as long and have a capacity of one petabyte. We feel that, at this time, going any larger would be too invasive for the brain."

I concluded, "In other words, you're telling me, you believe you can develop a chip the size of a pencil eraser that has the same capacity as an IBM Watson computer?" I asked.

The boys all smiled and nodded in the affirmative.

Water, Water Everywhere:

"How are you going to power the chip?" I asked.

Peter looked at Tad and then at me and responded. "That's where the real challenge was".

I liked the word "was" as it meant they had a hypothesis.

Matt noted. "We know that the brain is about 73% water. And so, we looked at chemicals that could be affected by water in the body and then the chemicals in that water."

Peter added. "We know that in a healthy adult, all cells have sodium potassium and chloride. All we needed to do was create some sort of coating for the nanosphere that would react with these chemicals in water and create the electric current we need.

"And you have a solution? I asked.

Tad offered. "We believe, we can use what is called osmotic power, which is energy generated by a natural phenomenon occurring when fresh water comes into contact with seawater, when passed through a membrane."

"Seawater? "A membrane?" I asked incredulously, shaking my head and believing the boys had found some funny looking weeds in the alfalfa field.

Mark added. "It's actually quite simple. You take an inert liquid, namely purified water and surround it with a membrane, then you add salt water and the chemical interaction between the inert liquid and the salt water could create enough electricity to power the chip."

I must have had another one of those "looks" on my face that said "bullshit" as the boys decided to dumb it down, so that I would understand and so Peter continued. "A healthy human body must have a certain percentage of sodium, or salt in it. If you remember back to Doctor Brockett, who spoke about nutrition, she said that sodium is an essential electrolyte that helps maintain the balance of water in and around our cells and is important for proper muscle and nerve function while maintaining stable blood pressure levels."

I shook my head in agreement, as Peter continued. "All we need to do is pair it to an inert liquid that doesn't have any sodium in it and control the interaction between the two by limiting the access of the chemicals ions to each other. Since an ion is simply an atom with an electrical charge, the movement of the salt ions would be harnessed to generate electricity and you could power the chip."

"Really?" I asked, in disbelief. "You mean, simply having purified water on one side of a membrane and then the water in our body on the other, will create enough electricity to power the chip?"

Peter nodded in the affirmative and continued. "The secret is controlling the interaction between the two liquids and this is where the membrane comes in. If our calculations are correct, we believe we can create one that is only three-atoms thick and made of molybdenum disulfide that would have tiny holes, called nanopores in it."

"Molybdenum?" I asked with my nose scrunched up. "Didn't Doctor Brockett talk about that, too?"

Peter affirmed my question and continued. "Thanks to its properties, the membrane would only allow positively-charged ions to pass through, while pushing away most of the negatively-charged ones, thereby creating the voltage between the two liquids as one builds up a positive charge and the other a negative charge. The interaction would result in current being generated which would result in the flow of ions and therefore the energy needed to power the chip."

"How long will it take to create the membrane?" I asked.

"It's already done!" Peter replied. "It wasn't that easy, because we had to first fabricate and then investigate the optimal size of the nanopore. If it was too big, negative ions could pass through and the resulting voltage would be too low. If the nanopore was too small, not enough ions would pass through and the current would be too weak."

Mark added, "Slowly, the saline solution's ions would pass into the inert fluid and continue to do so until the salt concentrations of both liquids were equal."

I was incredulous. The brilliance of these guys was overwhelming and yet, they made it all sound so simple and easy to do.

Tad, the math wizard chimed in. "Even though the membrane was created, we still needed to calculate the relative ratio between the two liquids and the nanopore. To do this, we realized we had three variables…the nanopore, which could be increased or decreased in diameter, and then both liquids."

"Fortunately, we can easily measure the sodium level of the receptor person, which meant we could simply adjust the chemical composition of the inert liquid to calibrate the attrition level and therefor the energy flow. This will not only stabilize the electron flow, but maximize the duration of the assimilation process."

Back to Peter. "Structurally, after measuring the coefficients of the person's sodium level and the inert liquid, we developed the membrane to allow us to load the inert chemical (purified water in my terms) into the space between the chip and the membrane before inserting it into the hippocampus. Then, because the body contains the sodium solution around the cells, the process would begin in a matter of minutes."

"How do you get a person's sodium level?" I asked.

Peter replied. "It's simple. All you need is a drop of sweat and you can acquire the sodium composition, based on their genetic profile."

"That's it?" I asked.

Mark nodded and continued. "That's it, and other than times of strenuous exercise or stress, the body has a somewhat constant level of sodium in it. However, if there was reduction in the person's level, they would easily sense it and all they would need to do is drink electrolyte-infused liquids, calibrated to their genetic profile."

"So you guys figured out how to power the chip?" I asked.

"Yup," they said in unison, with great big, shit-eating grins on their faces.

Peter cautioned, "We need to remember, we are talking about microvolts and we need to be really careful, because all we are trying to do is change the nerve cell potential by simply opening a single acetylcholine receptor channel of the adjacent cells."

I must have had yet another bewildered look on my face as Peter instantly added. "A single acetylcholine receptor channel is the integral membrane protein that responds to the binding of acetylcholine, which is the neurotransmitter."

I must have had another blank look on my face as Matt added. "Neurotransmitters are relatively small and simple molecules that serve as the messengers of the brain which allow the electric signal from one neuron to be transferred to the next."

I still didn't get it until Matt added. "Think of a draw bridge between two sides of a river. When the bridge is up, you obviously can't drive across. When the bridge is down - in other words, serving as the neurotransmitter, you get to cross."

Ta! Dah! The light went on above my head and I understood. Chalk one up for me, even though it took three different explanations to get it.

Peter interjected. "Different types of cells secrete different neurotransmitters, or bridges in your case. Each of these brain chemicals work in widely spread, but fairly specific brain locations and may have different effects according to where the brain is activated."

Tad added. "Neuro-scientists have identified sixty different neurotransmitters that fall mainly into one of four classes that control everything we think and do."

The boys were willing to summarize all sixty, I didn't want to know how they built the clock. I only wanted to make sure that it ran and so the boys stopped digging deeper, only providing the following information apropos to our discussion. I must admit though, it was fun watching the three of them talk about what they were involved in and excited about.

Peter started. "Dopamine controls arousal levels and motor control in many parts of the brain. When levels are severely depleted, such as with Parkinson's Disease, patients are unable to move voluntarily. LSD and other hallucinogenic drugs, are thought to work on the dopamine system. Improper levels of dopamine in either direction may be a root cause of chemical dependency such as alcoholism, gambling, sex and drug abuse" to which I immediately thought of Rodney and the challenges the Hochunk nation faced and remembered his oratory on the subject.

Matt was up next and said. "Serotonin is the neurotransmitter enhanced by many anti-depressants, such as Prozac and has thus become known as the 'feel-good' neurotransmitter. It has a profound effect on mood, anxiety and aggression."

Next Tad offered. "Acetylcholine (ACh) controls activity in brain areas connected with attention, learning and memory. People with Alzheimer's Disease typically have low levels of ACh in the cerebral cortex and drugs that boost the level within the brain may also improve memory in some patients."

The boys never ceased to impress me with their knowledge and their passion.

The Study:

The conversation was treading into deep water as Peter added. "Noradrenaline is mainly an excitatory chemical that induces physical and mental arousal and elevated mood. Production is centered in an area of the brain called the *'locus coeruleus'*, which is one of several of the brain's 'pleasure' centers. Medical science has proven that the chemical mediates the heart rate, blood pressure and the rate of glucose conversion for energy, as well as other physical benefits."

Back to Matt. "Glutamate is the brain's major excitatory neurotransmitter, and is vital for forging the links between neurons that are the basis of learning and long-term memory."

Finally, back to Tad, "Enkephalins and Endorphins are opioids which, like heroin and morphine, modulate pain, reduce stress, etc. and may be involved in the mechanisms of physical dependence."

I had no idea what they just said, but they all looked at each other with satisfied grins on their faces. The computer nerds had gone through the medical summary and done so with flying colors.

Matt offered. "We believe that our primary Nanochip has the ability of not only measuring these chemicals, but stimulating the brain to increase or decrease their production, until a position of homeostasis, or balance is achieved. However, we have one challenge".

"What's that," I asked.

Peter responded, "The volume of inert chemical surrounding the nanosphere can only be so much or the membrane will be too large, which would inhibit the flow of information into and away from the Nanochip."

"OK" I responded, "what does that mean?"

"It means that the duration of time relating to the chemical assimilation between the body's sodium and the inert fluid is limited and therefore, the operating life of the cell will also be limited."

"English, please!" I requested.

"We believe that the calculated life of the power source for the chip is between seven and ten years."

"Then what?" I asked.

"The chip stops working!" Mark added with a forlorn look on his face.

I lurched back and asked the obvious, "what are the consequences?'

Peter looked me in the eye and I knew what he was about to say was really important. "That depends on the chip type. If we are simply transferring data to the appropriate areas of the brain, that has been downloaded onto the chip, there should be no consequence and this, we believe, will be the case with the Primary Nanosphere."

"With the Compensatory Nanosphere, where we are alleviating symptoms, we believe the symptoms will return, but can't predict to what degree. However, with the Dynamic Nanosphere, where we have actually harvested thoughts and emotions, our projection is that, when the cell stops functioning, the brain will also stop functioning, as well."

I tilted back in my chair as stark reality slammed into my face.

"In other words, with the Dynamic Nanosphere, we would be pre-determining the life span of the recipient?"

"Correct." Peter stoically, affirmed.

"So, we are playing God."

All three quietly nodded their heads in the affirmative.

"Insert the chip to alleviate symptoms, but establish a life span?"

"Yes!" Peter replied, looking down at the floor.

"Anything we can do about this?"

"Not that we can see." Tad answered.

I sat back and took a deep breath. "Whew!"

"How long would the chip operate?" I asked again, hoping for a different number.

"Our forecasting model tells us seven-to-ten years, with the number seven being the most likely." Peter replied.

"Can't we just take the old chip out and replace it with a new one?"

"These implants are one-way streets." Matt replied.

The choice then became, if - and that was a big if, we could actually develop the chip and have it run, we would be giving the Dynamic Nanosphere recipient suffering from Alzheimer's Disease the choice - "Would you rather have seven-to-ten years of normal mental acuity and then abruptly expire or face the slow decline into the abyss of the mental quagmire called Alzheimer's Disease?"

The boys all nodded.

"Do you think that in seven years you could come up with a procedure that would allow for either replacing the inert fluid around the nanosphere to give it more operational life or replace the entire device?" I asked. There was no response.

I phrased the question a different way. "If someone else came up with a different method of storing thoughts and memories, could you remove the chip?"

Peter looked at me and said they were working on those alternatives, but it didn't look probable while confirming, "Right now, it's a one-way street."

I looked at them and said. "In terms of the Primary Nanochip, it's a no-brainer. "Go for it!" as my mind was flush with ideas and applications. I could only imagine a computer the size of a pencil eraser, that could be implemented in thousands, if not tens-of-thousands of products, including humans.

As for the Compensatory Nanochip, my question became, would you be willing to take the risks of surgery to mitigate challenging symptoms for a period of time knowing that, when the chip died, the symptoms would return? Needless to say, I had a tendency to equivocate the options and the consequences over and over and over again.

Once again, I made an affirmative decision and told the team to go for it rationalizing that symptomatic relief, for any period of time, albeit temporary, was better than no relief at all.

Then the big question. "Would you look at life from a qualitative, instead of a quantitative perspective and choose surgical risk and seven-to-ten years of existing mental acuity over a potentially longer life span, consisting of a debilitating malady, not knowing if, during that time, an alternative treatment could take place that would return your mental state and provide a longer life?"

I knew which one I would take, but then, I wasn't the one who had to make the decision and tabled further discussion until I had other opinions. I wanted to keep this 'in-house' as much as possible and wanted to speak with Luke regarding bioethics, Amy regarding her thoughts, Melia concerning the medical consequences and Derrick concerning the legal ramifications. I told the boys I needed a week before addressing further expenditures on the Dynamic Nanosphere. This was a big decision and I needed some time, knowing that if I approved and the process could be administered to The Duke, I was determining his fate.

It was getting late and I was tired. Time to head home. Instead there was one place I needed to go, where I hadn't been in a long time. The ride into Mineral Point took about ten minutes, even though I went up High Street and out to the cemetery. Sunset was just about upon me and yet I felt I needed to go there. I pulled in next to the little building where the directory was, but knew exactly where I was headed and walked east to where Grandma and Grandpa were buried and looked at the headstone and simply nodded my head, hoping they were together in heaven and looking down on me as I made one of the biggest decisions of my life.

Dad had been gone for a while and yet, the memories and emotions I had were still so strong from the entire funeral debacle, I had shied away from visiting his grave. The wounds of his death and how it divided Tommie and me were still fresh, even though there had been resolution. Perhaps that's why it had been so long and I simply didn't feel I could go there.

A strong urge came across me and I walked to where he was buried. I looked down at the granite marker and nodded out of respect. It was then that the answer came to me regarding the Dynamic Nanosphere as I looked at the headstone. Upon the headstone was my mother's name. The year of birth had already been etched in stone as had 20. Everything was set for the time when she went to be with dad and they would simply add the last two digits to define her year of passing.

There was no drama! There was no question! All they needed to do was add the year when she was gone. It was then, I finally realized that life and death were normal quantitative events. I was not playing God with the chip. All I was doing was giving people an option as to when and how they chose to live the qualitative aspect of their lives. Nothing was being forced! Nothing was absolute! This was just an option. Quantity versus quality, where the quantitative aspect probably meant intellectual oblivion along the way.

I bowed my head and said 'thanks dad' and walked away. I had my answer and thanked him for his opinion. I got back in the SUV and headed for home, calling Amy on the way to tell her I loved her and what time I would be home.

When I got to Pine Lake, Amy was still up and we talked. The whole issue of quantity versus quality was put on the table. The discussion began with the entire concept of life and death. The stark reality was that we were talking about her father, someone we both loved and respected, who was the last person I wanted to create a death sentence for.

The question kept coming back - quantity versus quality? Seven years of normalcy, while knowing it would then be over, or the long, slow decline that had already begun? We both agreed this was not to be our decision and something we would have to live with the rest of our lives. This would be The Duke's decision, where we would lay out the surgical risks, the probabilities of maintenance and then demise or the option of simply waiting to see what happens. My God, what a decision!

Mom:

It can only happen once in a man's life and that's certainly more than enough. Before it happens, one cannot fathom the depth of feeling, the sense of loss or the massive hole it puts in your heart. The loss of a man's mother is unlike any other feeling there ever is. She bore you! She nurtured you! She cared for you and then she's gone!

Mom continued to run the Dodgeville Chevy dealership long after she needed to and yet she did. Every morning, she would be there. Everyday day, there would be homemade something-or-others for those who came to visit. The employees became her extended family, her customers her friends as we implemented programs and ideas that we took chain-wide. The first was free oil changes for life on any vehicle purchased from her, along with the directive and mandated training that there would be no sales pressure when returning customers came back for the service. Those who had purchased from her were to be treated as guests.

Dale, the Service Manager was to learn their names. The salesmen were to greet their former customers as family and friends and never pressure them into considering a new vehicle when they only came for service. Mary, the receptionist was to treat them as visitors and offer them coffee and mom's homemade what-evers, while making certain they had a newspaper and a computer that was working if they wanted to use it. Charlie, head of facilities, was to ensure that the showroom and bathrooms were spotless and copies of children's books and pages to color were readily available in their play area with completed pictures hung with pride along the wall.

Each month, mom would have an 'art fair' of the coloring and a winner chosen. Their artwork would be mailed to them along with a gift certificate for a Culvers custard cone. No one knew that all the kids were winners and everyone received the same letter and the same award. When there were two kids from the same family, it was designated by age. There's always something special to a little kid who believes they were the best.

All customers with extended service needs were given a loaner car or a ride to wherever they wanted to go and the lot boys were never allowed to take a tip for doing what they were being paid to do. The sales team was given the latitude to make any deal they needed as they were paid on profit and never had to go to the sales manager for approval who was mom. None of that dickering back and forth was ever allowed.

When the customer came in to pick up their new car, all the paperwork was completed and the goal was to have them "out the door" in fifteen minutes, with all employees from all departments lined up, applauding as the customer drove their new vehicle down the dealership's "street of fame" making them feel appreciated by all those whose purchase they supported. Within a week, a small package would arrive with a local gift made at Shake Rag pottery and a hand-written note from mom. Dodgeville Chevy was involved in virtually every local event from high school sports to the farmers market and even the book fair at the library, along with spring and fall cleaning of the cemeteries in Mineral Point, Dodgeville and Spring Green. They were to be a good citizen, giving back to those who supported them.

Mom decorated the dealership for the seasons and it was never a cold, impersonal showroom. Instead, everything centered around a small waterfall in the middle of the floor that had live fish in it, whose sounds compensated from the those of business.

Mom was "getting up there" and I would ask her if she wanted to retire and the response was always the same – "And then what, sit home and die? This is my extended family."

Mom was also a very private, very proper person and when she found out she had stage four pancreatic cancer, she kept it to herself, knowing that it was a one-way street. She was losing weight and getting tired, yet she worked until a week before she died. When her time came, she asked to be cremated and her funeral held at the dealership. We followed her wishes, removing all the vehicles and having a luncheon in the facility for family, friends and customers. Dodgeville is a little town and yet nearly 700 people including Rodney and Ann came with dozens of floral arrangements placed everywhere. There was no talk of cars or sales as they had been put out of sight. There was no talk of service or business. All people wanted to do was talk about the kindness and dignity of Mrs. Terrill and pay their respects and so mom got her wish.

Tommie and I worked together on the plans. Unlike dad's funeral, there was no animosity. Unlike before, we were brothers bonded together by the love of our mother. When the celebration was over, Tommie and Hsu, Amy and I quietly rode to Graceland cemetery and saw the small round hole that had been dug next to dad. I looked at Tommie and he at me and we held each other before slowing lowering the urn in the ground. Kneeling, all four of us scooped the rich Wisconsin soil and refilled what had once been the future with what had become forever. "Goodbye mom. I love you!"

Black River Falls:

One day, I called Rodney and asked how he was doing. He said things were great, business was booming with the new facility in Beloit really doing well.

"I've got a favor, Big Brother" I asked.

"Sure, anything, you know that." Rodney replied in a totally different and more serious tone.

"I want to send 'V' up to work with Ann's team and learn more about what all you are doing."

I could almost hear the "Holy shit, anything but that" in Rodney's mind as his tone changed again and he politely replied. "OK". Rodney had not only heard of, but repeatedly seen 'V's" jocund façade where everything was intended to generate a laugh, regardless of who it hurt. I also knew that Rodney considered 'V' to be knavish and that the perceived level of untrustworthiness, dishonesty and mischievous acts were so great that the willingness to help was only being absolved by the depth of our friendship.

I also finally knew there would be reticence towards the old 'V'. As was the case with so many others, 'V' had burned the bridge and good, honest, conservative people like Rodney didn't appreciate his 'style' of living. I added. "I think you're going to see a change in my son and I want him to begin to mend bridges with those who are the most important in our lives and that means starting with you."

Rodney's tone was serious as he asked, "You know he's got quite the reputation?"

"I know, but I think you're going to see a different person. If he isn't better, let me know and I'll bring him home." I responded.

Arrangements were made and I called 'V' and asked him when it would be convenient for him to go to Black River Falls and work with Ann's team for a week. He would be oriented into the Ho-Chunk history, the social challenges and finally, ways that we could work together to improve everything for all sides. I had a plan, but needed to make sure everyone was on board before sharing it with anyone.

'V' checked with Peter and asked if he could get a different vehicle. He didn't think driving a red Ferrari would make the best impression. I remembered the parking lot at the Ho-Chunk offices was always filled with pick-up trucks and suggested a Silverado. 'V' thought that would be cool and went to our Oconomowoc Chevy dealership and picked out a black Silverado, Off-Road, LTZ, just like The Duke's.

The week was set and 'V' elected to drive up Sunday night instead of Monday morning. He wanted to make a good first impression and that meant being there when the offices opened Monday morning.

About 2:00 PM, Monday afternoon the phone rang and it was Rodney. "Who in hell did you send up here?" Rodney asked.

"'V' why?" I inquired, quite concerned.

"This isn't the same, spoiled brat, my kids talked about, behind his back."

"Good or bad?" I inquired.

"Are you kidding me?" Rodney responded. "He was here when the office opened and everything has been 'Yes, sir! No sir! All day long'".

"He's grown up! He's become a man!" I replied.

"There's more, Little Brother! Ann says she can feel the aura."

"What aura?" I asked, not having a clue what Rodney was talking about.

"You know - the energy field around all living things."

"OK!" I said, remembering what Great Grandfather had said.

"Ann says that the field around 'V' is one of the strongest she's ever felt. She said it reminded her of Great Grandfather."

I didn't want to spill the beans about what happened in The Forest and so I brushed the whole thing off by saying, "Why don't we wait until the week is done and then you tell me what you think?"

"Ok, Little Brother. Good idea." Rodney replied, promising to call me on Friday with an update.

With everything going on, the days flew by and Friday arrived. As promised, Rodney called in the afternoon. "He's still here and everyone is mesmerized by him." Were the first words out of Rodney's mouth. "He went with our Amelia to the health care center and when they left, the director called and asked when 'V' could come back. In a matter of minutes, everyone was taken aback by him and one old man asked if the Great Spirit sent him. 'V' replied that, indeed the Great Spirit had called and asked that he work with us to make this a better world."

"Q, I don't know what's going on, but whatever it is you've done to your son, congratulations."

"You said he was still there?" I asked.

"Yah, he said he didn't have any weekend plans and after working with our Amelia all week long, they're going up to Minneapolis tomorrow morning to Mall of America for the three-on-three basketball tournament. They're coming back tomorrow night."

"'V' was a gentleman and asked me if that was all right. I said, 'sure.' These kids have known each other their entire lives and this past week they've been inseparable."

"Did 'V' say when he was coming home?"

"He said he would give you a call." Rodney replied

"OK, Big Brother. Thanks for everything." I answered.

"No, thank you Little Brother."

About twenty minutes later the phone rang and it was 'V'. He explained that he and Amelia had worked all week at the health center and social services and had really gotten along. He told me, he asked Amelia to go with him to Mall of America and she said yes.

I played dumb, which wasn't too difficult an acting job and said OK. I pointed out that these were members of our family and asked that he please act like a gentleman. 'V' assured me that he understood and everything was way above board. I could tell by the sound of his voice that things were a lot more 'serious' than anyone else could perceive. I hoped this infatuation wasn't because of what the Great Spirit had shared with 'V' and the attraction wasn't simply because of the increased energy field that was emanating from him.

I asked when he would be coming home and he said he planned on Sunday and then going back in a week. With it being a five-hour drive each way, I suggested he park the truck at the Ho-Chunk office and I'd have one of the choppers pick him up and he could drive the Ferrari when he got home. I told him to ask Rodney if that was OK and text me what time he wanted the chopper there.

About twenty minutes later, I got the text. *"Been invited to Uncle Rodney's for dinner Sunday. Was told that it won't be porcupine and rattle snake. Can the chopper pick me up at 8:00 PM at the Ho-Chunk office?"*

I called Dennis and arrangements were made and texted 'V' back and confirmed the time. Dennis sent two guys over to the house to pick up the Ferrari and one of them got the cheap thrill of driving it back to the helipad next to the office, then I sent a message to Amy telling her that her youngest son got bit.

She asked, "By what?"

I answered, " The Love Bug," and put a smiley face after it.

That night Amy and I went to the Five O'Clock club on Pewaukee Lake for their fabulous Friday fish fry and I filled her in on the entire week and how things were transpiring.

Amy said, "I hope he's not rushing into anything."

"Gee, not in your family!" I said sarcastically, to which she kicked me under the table.

After fish, I said, "Let's go to LeDuc's and get some custard."

Amy nodded in agreement and we drove to Wales and stood in the long line for some of the richest frozen custard you could imagine. The owner recognized Amy and asked if she wanted the usual … *chocolate custard with marshmallow topping.* This was Derrick's favorite, but I was surprised the owner recognized Amy and asked her how many times she'd been there without me as I went into my awful rendition of what she said the first time we had Chocolate Shoppe Ice Cream. "You'z don wanna get no fat butt, doos yah?" This got a swift set of knuckles to my shoulder. "Ouch!".

Sunday night, I heard the Ferrari roar into the driveway and waited for 'V' and then waited some more and then some more. Finally, after about a half-hour 'V' came walking in with a frown on his face.

"What were you doing?" I asked.

"Talking"

"To who?" I asked. "You were sitting out there for a long time."

"Oh, just getting caught up on some things," 'V' replied.

"With whom, might I ask?"

"Amelia." 'V' answered.

"But didn't you just have dinner with her?"

"Yup, but we needed to talk."

I just shrugged my shoulders.

"Dad, when you and mom were going out did you get 'the stares'?"

"You mean the racial thing?" I asked.

"Yes" 'V' replied.

"Every now and then, why?"

"When we were at Mall of America, a few people gave us the stare as Amelia called it. You know like they didn't think it was right for us to be together because we are of different races."

"It comes with the territory, son." I replied. "It's something your Grandma and Grandpa really had bad. One time, when Grandma and Grandpa were first married and The Duke took Grandma Marie to his 'beginners club' as he called it, there was a real raucous when someone thought Grandma Marie was one of the hired help and told her to go back to the kitchen."

"I can only imagine what Grandpa did," 'V' responded.

"No, you can't." I replied with a smirk on my face.

"Grandpa was so pissed, he bought out the guy's membership and the clown wasn't allowed back in the club again." I answered.

"Wow!"

"Remember, money means power and you never want to cross grandpa."

"What about you and mom?" 'V' asked.

It was something your mother and I had periodically, but never really that bad. It's something you'll find no matter where you and whom you are with. Some people still judge others by what they are instead of who they are. It's a terrible thing that is incredibly unfair and yet it happens. Don't let it get under your skin."

"That's what Amelia said, too. She said it happens to her all the time. She also said that her own people do the same thing to other races. Isn't there anything that we can do about it?"

I was proud of 'V' for asking, but felt that only time could remove some of the vestiges of racial prejudice in America. I didn't share the story of Rodney and I when we got pulled over for speeding. That was a long time ago and he had heard enough stories. Instead, I offered "Son, just be careful and don't react. Normally those who are incredibly biased are from a different spectrum and are biased towards everyone else. You just have to learn to ignore it."

"At what point do you say enough is enough?" 'V' asked.

"When they are offending the person you are with." I replied.

"Then what?" 'V' asked.

"Then be careful." I answered, thinking not only of the legal aspects but the litigious ones as well. Have someone taunt you to the point of anger and then they sue you because you've got money. It's one of the first lessons you learn when wealth comes your way.

"It isn't right, dad!"

"And who said there was equity in the world?" I inquired.

I wanted to change the subject but realized that 'V' was already sizing up the situation on the challenges of a long-term relationship.

Fortunately, 'V' changed the subject when he added that they were talking about what they were going to do the week after next.

"You mean the health center and social services?" I inquired.

"Well that and going out with some of her friends."

I just shook my head. I knew the bait has been put on the hook and this kid had chomped down - hook, line and sinker.

"Be cool" I instructed. "Let me tell you what Great Grandfather told me."

"I know, a good relationship is like a rose."

"How do you know that?" I asked.

"Remember, I'm the one who talked to Great Grandfather last," 'V' snickered.

'V' took a deep breath and smiled a contented smile, as my Amy came out of her office.

"Hi, mom!" 'V' said.

"Hi, son!" Amy replied

"Good week?"

"Awesome! What great people and I really think I can work with them on some of their social issues."

"Like dating you father's best friend's daughter?" Amy asked.

There was a shy smile on "V's" face. "She's special mom. I can't believe I didn't see it before."

"Perhaps your eyes weren't open," Amy replied.

"They are now and I like what I see."

"Take it slow!" Amy responded.

"I know, like a rose."

"You tell him that?" Amy asked, looking at me.

"No, some florist did," I replied, being the smart ass.

It was nearly eleven and I was tired. Amy and I went to bed and heard 'V' on the phone. It had been an entire hour without talking to Amelia and so he just had to call her. Ain't, love grand?

Permutations:

The week flew by and my conversations with Luke, Amy, Melia and Derrick all led to the same conclusions - proceed with the project, but let it take an evolutionary course. There was no need making a decision when the chip hadn't even been developed yet. To me, it felt like a stay of execution.

I choppered down to the farm still enamored like a kid at Christmas with the XH. I wasn't at all surprise to find the MadCity Boys hard at work on the Primary Nanosphere design who reported they had an idea. I was surprised that Luke was in the meeting, as his responsibilities included both facilities and bio-ethics and not computer programs. I should have known that the boys had something blockbuster up their sleeves.

While everyone thought the project would work in inanimate objects to help move mankind one-step further away from using our brains, the concern was implementation in humans and whether the chip would be functional.

How could you test an implanted chip? We also knew it would be difficult, if not impossible, to get government approval for implanting test chips in humans and so the idea of using animals came about.

Luke asked me. "Do you remember, Koko, the gorilla?"

I did.

Peter added. "Koko had a vocabulary of 2,000 words that she understood and could sign 1,000 of them. She had emotions and a concept of life and death. If we worked with someone of Koko's intellect and taught them different permutations, I believe they could have a vocabulary exceeding 5,000 words."

"But that took decades of work and we don't have time. Also, where would we buy a gorilla?" I countered. "They're not selling them on Amazon! Or, anyway, I didn't think they were."

"First, Gorillas are indigenous to Africa and not South America and, we have another option." Tad added.

"What's that?"

"How about an animal that is compatible where we already use valves for human hearts because they aren't rejected?"

"Pigs?" I asked.

They responded in the affirmative.

"You're saying we could use a pig for testing?" I asked incredulously.

"Yes!" Matt interjected. "Pigs and humans are very much alike genetically."

I looked at the MadCity Boys and smiled. They knew what I was thinking.

Matt added. "Animal geneticists created a side-by-side comparison of human and pig genomes. They took the human genome and cut it into 173 puzzle pieces and rearranged it. When they were done 'moving the furniture' they had the genome sequence of a pig. Using a pig would take out a couple of steps regarding rejection and give us a better perspective of whether the chip could be implanted or not."

"A pig?" I was in disbelief. "If we're that much alike, why the difference between pigs and humans?" I joked.

Matt seriously answered, "The same gene in the pig may work in combination with other genes to control something very different than it does in humans."

"But we're interested in getting the pig to communicate." I noted.

Luke added. "Scientists have studied pig brains and found they are similar to human brains in several respects. First, they have many of the same structural features. Second, they are quite large. Finally, like humans, the cortical neurons appear to be fully developed at birth, with the number at approximately 425 million neurons compared to 82 billion in the human brain."

Peter interjected, "This means that a domestic pig has the capability to think, reason and have emotions."

"What about dexterity" I asked, thinking of those on the farm.

Matt replied, "Pigs can play video games with joysticks and are capable of abstract representation. They love video games and one has even been turned into an iPhone app called Pig Chase, that gamers use to play against pigs on Dutch farms."

"Can they be trained?" I inquired.

Luke answered, "Pigs can be taught to sit and jump as well as fetch a ball, play Frisbee and lift a dumbbell on command. Even after years, trained pigs were still able to identify the objects they were previously taught and are brilliant at remembering where food is stored, while being able to distinguish between different-size stashes of treats."

Matt smiled and said, "If we are allowed to proceed, we need to always remember that pigs are sneaky. They learn to follow other pigs to find food and will even use evasive tactics to try to throw a pursuing pig off the trail, so that they can keep their trove to themselves."

"Sounds to me like they could be members of the MadCity Boys." I replied.

Luke offered. "If approved, we're going to need someplace to keep our pig and we're hoping that Hsu would allow us to use some of her lab space."

"Indoors?" I inquired.

Matt responded. "Not only do pigs have temperature preferences, where they can learn how to turn on the heat in a cold barn and off again when they get too warm, they are actually clean animals, who can be taught to turn on and off a shower by themselves."

My frown just motivated them to continue.

Luke added, "In a scientific study carried out at the University of Cambridge, pigs were found to be highly sensitive animals who become aware of their own existence. Moreover, their skills help them to gain knowledge that can be used later to solve complex problems, which is why the team feels we can teach a pig to communicate."

Peter added. "In one study, a plate of food was shown to pigs who were already familiarized with a mirror and the test was to see what would happen when they were only be able to access the food by sight and not by smell."

Matt added. "In order to get there, the pigs had to understand what they were seeing was only a reflection and, therefore, the food was not behind the mirror and they had to memorize the entire space in which they found themselves. Only a handful of other species, such as dolphins, elephants, and chimpanzees, have ever passed the 'mirror test' or have been documented to understand that mirrors are reflections, not windows. In so doing, the pigs repeatedly passed the test, which leads us to conclude we can teach the pig permutations, if they are given a reward for their efforts."

My first thought was 'just like the MadCity Boys. However, I politely I shook my head in disbelief. This just motivated the boys even more with Luke adding, "Several studies have shown that pigs are smarter than dogs and cats and are able to solve problems quicker than many primates. Their cognitive abilities can be compared to those of a three-year-old human."

Peter chimed in. "When given the opportunity, pigs are curious animals who form affinity groups, just as humans do and sows are very protective and loving with their little ones, who love to play constantly".

Luke looked at a piece of paper and read, "In his book '*The Whole Hog*', naturalist Lyall Watson writes, *'I know of no other animals that are more consistently curious, more willing to explore new experiences and more ready to meet the world with open-mouthed enthusiasm. Pigs, I have discovered, are incurable optimists and get a big kick out of just being.'*"

Peter added. "As you can hopefully see, pigs possess high intelligence, emotional complexity, a sense of time and other attributes that are beyond the scope of companion animals such as dogs and cats. Like Koko the gorilla, all they need is to have the ability to communicate, but you obviously can't do that with sign language when you have four hoofs."

"But they're pigs." I countered having been raised with them on the farm, I had a somewhat jaded opinion.

Matt added. "You're right, pigs are pigs. However, there is a reason why and it has to do with the fact that they have more unique olfactory genes than humans or dogs and can therefore smell things humans and other animals can't. The reason they act the way they do is because their sense of taste doesn't keep up with other animals and so they end up eating everything."

Once again, I looked at the group in front of me with a wicked smile on my face as they put down their bags of Fritos, Cheetos and Doritos.

Matt continued. "Anatomically is where things get real interesting in that, most of the neurons in a human brain are created before the person is born and there are only a few small areas that continue to make new neurons after birth through a process called postnatal neurogenesis. Pigs also have a great majority of their established neurons at birth. However, pigs also have a much greater postnatal neurogenesis than humans."

I scratched my head and wondered what this meant.

Peter saw my concern and added. "George, what this means is that, even though pig's brains are smaller than humans, they have the ability to learn more, if given the opportunity to do so."

Matt added. "Some scientists also believe the addition of new neurons in the hippocampus may enhance learning and memory because new neurons are more plastic than older neurons. This means pigs can more easily modify their connections to form and store memories."

Peter added. "Interestingly, the hippocampus is not only involved in learning, but in forming memories of events and experiences. Because of this, we have been zeroing in on this area in our chip design and feel confident that placing a Primary Nanosphere there would allow us to reach our objectives."

"Would this area be the right place for humans as well? I asked.

"We think so," Tad added.

The lights were on and I **was** home. The boys not only felt that they could teach a pig to 'talk', but determined where to place the chip, not only in the pig's brain, but in humans as well.

Matt continued. "It's not as simple as it sounds." (Gee, brain surgery sounding simple, I don't think so!) "What makes chip placement complex deals with two factors, potential damage to tissue during chip insertion with the neurons adjacent to the chip and finally, the fact that neurons aren't the only cells that make up the brain."

Peter added. "The brain's other cells, which are called glia, maintain the blood-brain barrier, protect neurons from pathogens and control neuron function. The glia make up about half of the human brain's mass and are renewed and replaced on a continuing basis. Placing a chip in the glia would have no positive effect that we can foresee. With these two challenges, we estimated that inserting a chip in the hippocampus would require profound accuracy so that it was placed exactly at the right location."

"What about reaching our ultimate goal?" I asked.

Matt stepped in and added. "What's interesting is that the researchers have identified 112 positions in the genome where pig protein has the same amino acid as humans. With the same amino acid, pigs are also susceptible to protein aberrations associated with obesity, diabetes, dyslexia, Parkinson's disease and Alzheimer's Disease."

We were getting too serious and so I had to break it up with an old joke. "Did you hear about the dyslexic agnostic who didn't believe in dogs?" Zoom, that one sailed right over their heads as they were too intent in convincing me of something I'd already agreed on and only I laughed at my own bad joke. Fortunately, Peter saw my smile and realized they had hit the nail on the head.

"In other words, we might have a test sample right in our own backyard that could help us reach our final objective?" I included.

The MadCity Boys nodded in the affirmative again.

"But how would you get the pig to talk? You mentioned they can't do sign language like Koko did." I commented.

Peter added, "Steven Hawking"

"Steven Hawking, the astrophysicist? I thought he died?" I inquired.

"He did, but the technology that allowed him to 'speak' lives on." Peter responded. "Dr. Hawking had ALS and was totally incapacitated. He used a form of cuneiforms and a basic form of artificial intelligence that allowed the computer to speak for him.

"Explain, please!"

Peter continued, "The boys think they can download Oxford's English Dictionary onto the Primary Nanosphere as a good place to start. The dictionary contains 171,476 words of which the average American uses about 20,000 and really, really smart people around 42,000."

"In other words, people like you guys," I added, as a compliment, trying to make up for the bad joke.

I was impressed, but asked how can you put all those words on one chip and how would they be used? The boys looked at me as if I was some sort of dummy, which in their world I was.

Tad asked. "Do you know anything about permutations and combinations?"

I responded that they consisted of a bunch of numbers that Rodney told me about long ago, when we went through gambling 101.

Tad explained. "There is a difference between combinations and permutations. As example two-times-six equals twelve. When it is taken as two-times-six or six-times-two, and there is no consequence to the sequence, it is a combination. When the sequence becomes important, where two-times-six has a different meaning than six-times-two, you have a permutation."

I shook my head in the affirmative. I remembered and understood, but didn't understand how this would make a pig talk.

Tad asked. "Do you know anything about powers?"

"Teach me," I replied, thinking of Amy and the power she reigned around the house.

He responded. "The power of a number says how many times to use the number in a multiplication of itself. So, two-to-the-fourth power means 2x2x2x2 which would equal 16."

"OK!"

"If we take two to the 16th power, you would have a number of 131,072 and we could represent over 75% of all words in the English language and do so with just sixteen cuneiforms. If we wanted to represent the typical American vocabulary, we could do so with only fourteen, but your grid could not be factored. By creating a 3x3 grid, you would only have 512 permutations which would limit the vocabulary. However, by going to a 4x4 grid, you would have sixteen and therefore 131,072 permutations, by simply touching two different squares in the correct sequence."

Peter added, "If we also include some artificial intelligence in the Primary Nanosphere that kept track of trends, such as word use and phrases the user has, it wouldn't be too long until pressing just a few squares could result in faster dialogue."

"OK" I said, not seeing where they were going, asking, "You could create a grid and press some buttons and create words the computer would pronounce?"

"Yes," Tad replied excitedly. "What's really cool is we can also give the computer an accent so that we could have a southern drawl, a British accent, even your Wisconsin accent, George."

I never knew I had an accent, asking "All right! Then what?"

"We think we can implant a chip in a pig and teach them to use a grid to talk to us!"

I shook my head. "Crazy!"

Matt added. "Tommie's got a whole bunch of pigs and some of them are really smart. All we need to do is pick one that is smarter than the rest, implant the chip and see if it works."

"Talking pigs?" I just shook my head in disbelief.

Melia:

The boys had flabbergasted me – again. Talking pigs! Next, they would tell me they could get one to fly and one would be flying my chopper! I somewhat understood what they were talking about, but went to our resident medical expert for clarification by calling Melia and asking if we could have lunch. I told her I needed information about the hippocampus of the brain.

We met in the cafeteria of Children's Hospital in Milwaukee, where Melia showed up in her white coat with the stethoscope hanging out of her pocket. Above her left coat pocket was her nametag with Dr. Amelia Terrill, MD, which made me very proud. I glanced over Melia's shoulder at a new plaque on the wall denoting the fact that the hospital had been named one of the *World's Ten Best* by *Newsweek Magazine* and looked at 'my little girl' with a tremendous amount of pride."

"Melia's grandmother Marie, helped lay the foundation of greatness and our daughter was carrying on the tradition of commitment to excellence above and beyond what anyone could ever expect. If people only knew the dedication and personal sacrifice people make to become the best.

Melia had her mother's deep brown eyes and infectious smile, with the same white glistening teeth that radiated a sense of warmth and goodness. We sat in the corner and after the usual, what's going on and what's new dad stuff, Melia got right to the point. Time was never in great supply and so the small talk had to come in blurbs between bites of her salad.

After explaining what it was, I added, "The MadCity Boys think they can implant a Primary Nanosphere in the hippocampus of a pig and teach it to talk."

Melia's head jerked back, first thinking it was another one of my corny jokes before realizing I was serious.

"A Nanochip in the hippocampus?" Melia questioned.

"Yup! And I don't have a clue what a hippocampus is and why they think it will work." I added.

"Let's see if I can explain what the hippocampus is and what it does and then give me a few minutes to decipher whether I agree with them," Melia said, pausing to collect her thoughts.

Melia began. "The hippocampus is part of the brain responsible for encoding long-term memories and helping with spatial navigation. It is one of the oldest parts of the brain where, by oldest, I don't mean the individual's brain, but one of the first parts to develop in mammalian evolution and did so to the point that the hippocampus is basically the same across all mammals. This is why the MadCity Boys are thinking they can implant a chip in a pig and replicate how it would work in humans."

Melia had met all the gang many times and always got a kick out of them - a bunch of profoundly intelligent nerds, who had low social skills, liked to have fun but, periodically, like Mediglove and the new Kaleidoscope, knocked the socks off the world with their insight and achievements.

I took a sip of my coffee as Melia added, "The hippocampus is known to be associated with the consolidation of episodic memories."

"What?" I asked.

Melia continued, "Episodic memories are those consisting of personally experienced events and their associated emotions and are in contrast to semantic memories which consist of abstract facts and their associations."

I must have had 'that' look on my face as Melia added, "The best way to separate the two is through analogies. Episodic memories can be represented as stories. Semantic memories are not and consist of things like formulas and most medical information that need to be memorized, which is why I wonder if what the boys want to do, will work."

'Thanks kid for throwing ice water on the party,' I thought. But then Melia was like her mother - always the pragmatist.

"My concern, dad, would be potential damage to the hippocampus from the insertion of the chip. Any damage could result in the inability to form new long-term episodic memories.

However, even with slight damage, new procedural memories, such as motor sequences, for everyday tasks, could still be learned."

In other words, the implant might impede further memory, but not affect motor skills?" I asked.

"Correct," Melia replied.

Ding! Ding! Ding! Dad got one right.

Melia continued. "However, there's another function of the hippocampus that deals with spatial orientation that is really critical and if this was damaged there could be major problems. You see, for navigation, the hippocampus contains what are called 'place cells' which will activate depending on the perceived location of the individual or animal. Researchers believe that these cells exist in the hippocampus because memories must be employed to determine current location from more fundamental variables like orientation and speed. This is why most of our memories start with a description of where or when the event took place."

"Activation of the place cells has been observed in humans who are navigating in virtual reality towns. As you can see, the place cells are really important and require an intact hippocampus to accomplish the spatial navigation tasks. Without the spatial information, the episodic memories would be disjointed or not exist at all."

"What are the risks?" I asked in all seriousness, thinking not so much of the pig, but of The Duke.

Melia added. "In terms of the pig, it could result in a big picnic," which formerly would have got a smile but, in learning that pigs had emotions, only a sense of guilt. "People with certain conditions that lead to lower function of the hippocampus have harder times retaining and remembering memories and why the hippocampus is considered a major link to Alzheimer's, where both severe memory issues and changes in the hippocampus occur."

I inquired, "In other words, the boys are spot-on, when it comes to the location of placement of a chip that might help grandpa?"

"Precisely!" Melia added very seriously. "The boys will need to do risk/reward analysis and then someone/somewhere is going to have to determine not only the type of chip, but where to place it in the hippocampus and finally the procedure for placing it there, while minimizing potential damage."

I shook my head as Melia continued, "The challenge will not only be developing the chip, but how to power it so that it doesn't interfere with or damage adjacent tissue and then comes the entire process of implanting."

Melia looked me in the eyes and said in all earnest. "Being one of the base components of the brain, the hippocampus is surrounded by the Occipital lobe of the Cerebral Cortex, which controls vision; the cerebellum which coordinates voluntary movements such as posture, balance, coordination, and speech. If that isn't enough, there's also the Amygdala, which is responsible for emotions, survival instincts, and memory and finally the Brainstem which controls the flow of autonomic messages between the brain and the rest of the body, controlling basic bodily functions such as breathing, swallowing, heart rate, blood pressure, consciousness and even whether someone is awake or not."

Melia took a deep breath to emphasize what she was about to say, "One false move that causes damage, could be paralyzing, if not fatal, especially to the brain stem as it acts as the primary source of all activity concerning motor and sensory function, hearing and taste and reflexes and functions such as breathing, heartbeat and blinking."

Wow! Melia had said all that without any notes. This kid really knew her stuff!

"In other words, it's in a tough neighborhood to get into without doing damage," I stated.

Melia responded. "I'm not a neurosurgeon, but the best way I could see would be to try and go between the cerebral cortex and the cerebellum from the back of the skull. Insertion anywhere else could be catastrophic. As it is, even going in where I suggest, will cause some degree of degradation, depending on the size of the incision. Any time you're going into the brain, you're taking a huge risk there will be changes."

"We know that to do nothing will mean grandpa will be leaving us. But what are the risks if there is a successful implant?" I asked.

Melia added. "After brain damage, the chip could result in a lot of psychological changes. As an example, in schizophrenia and certain types of severe depression, the hippocampus shrinks. Because what you're trying to do has never been done before, no one can give you answers regarding what the prognosis will be."

"What about a talking pig?" I asked.

Melia smiled. "Leave it to the MadCity Boys to think they can get a pig to talk. Anatomically, there's no way."

I took time to explain how the boys thought they could use the 16 squares and the Hawking Talking Machine, while downloading the Oxford dictionary and saw the gleam in Melia's eyes and the realization that maybe, just maybe, it could work. However, like all medical personnel, she had been taught to eliminate absolutes from her vernacular with words like 'maybe' and 'perhaps'. I was just grateful it wasn't an absolute 'no'.

With the hippocampus dissertation over, the conversation shifted to Amy, Derrick and 'V'. Mom was mom and Freud was so right when he said that those of the same gender within a family, normally would not be as close as those of the opposite gender. Amy and Melia were close, but not nearly as close as I was to her.

Melia just shook her head when she referenced Derrick. Behind his back, Melia called Derrick, Mom-The-Second, as Derrick and Amy were two peas-in-a-pod, in terms of intelligence, demeanor and drive. Derrick was working at the Wilco law offices and was on track to take over the whole shooting match someday, when my Amy decided she'd had enough and wanted to retire.

"I heard, I have a new brother?" Melia inquired.

"What?" I asked, incredulously.

"I heard that 'V's' a changed person. What happened to him?" Melia asked.

"I think he saw a ghost!" I added, to which, Melia smiled. Amy had told her all about me taking him to The Forest and leaving him there.

"What's going on with him wanting to spend all his time in Black River Falls?" Melia asked.

"You know about that, too?" I replied with a smile on my face, knowing that Amy, Melia and Derrick were on a party-line, when it came to texting each other.

"What about you?" I asked.

Melia smiled and looked at her watch to politely indicate she needed to go. We stood and I hugged her. I was so proud of her! It was an honor to have her as my daughter.

"You make me so proud!" I announced.

"Thanks, dad. The feelings are quite mutual."

That made me feel good.

"Talking pigs!" Melia said shaking her head as she was about to leave. "Knowing the boys, if anyone can do it, it will be them."

D.C.:

'V' and The Duke were becoming good buddies and The Duke wanted to introduce him to all his cronies in New York and Washington. 'V' wanted to go back to Black River Falls, but realized the trip was important to The Duke and agonizingly deferred seeing Amelia for an additional week, explaining why it was so important to go with Grandpa.

The Duke and 'V' hit all the high spots, with all the right people in New York, staying at the Ritz Carlton, where they each had suites and people falling all over them. 'V' said the two of them made their way down to Wall Street and met with all the financiers that The Duke had made wealthy and visited our New York office, where everyone first bowed to The Duke and then to 'V'.

Wilco PR contracted with a photographer who went with 'V' and The Duke to every meeting and took photos of the two of them with whomever it was they were meeting with. 'V' thought it strange until The Duke outlined that it was part of the transition strategy. Every person in every meeting would receive a photo of them with 'V' and The Duke as a remined that The Duke had personally selected 'V' to be his successor.

When they returned, 'V' and my conversation discussed subjects ranging from people to events and circumstances and then to the musings of The Duke, who had relayed to 'V' his mantra that, 'With wealth, comes power, but it's never a constant and never to be taken for granted.' 'V' added that The Duke noted 'properly managed money can last forever, but power is a fleeting thing.'" The Duke also told 'V', "Business-is-business and friendship-is-friendship and rarely did the two ever meet. Never assume, because you are doing business with someone, they are your friend and never, ever believe that you have to do business with a friend."

'V' thought New York was cool and it helped him have a better understanding of Wilco and the Foundation. The Duke also introduced 'V' to a lot of people he thought the Foundation could hit up for donations if the time came and we needed to call in some favors. My thought was to save those chips for the time when I hoped 'V' would run for public office and needed some real money.

'V' noted that Washington was phony and quite transparent in nature. He said it wasn't what he expected and was alarmed that it was so insubstantial and vague and he didn't like it at all. He said it was all just egos on Red Bull. I responded that egos on Red Bull lead to one result – bullshit, and he laughed. I also told him to get used to it and remember that everything said and promised were done to get people what they want.

The Duke and 'V' visited both Wisconsin Senators and 'V' took an instant disliking to Senator Fitzgerald, proving to me that some things do run in the family. He reported back that he felt Fitzgerald believed he was some sort of demagogue who pandered to the voters by supporting popular opinion regardless of his own true feelings or the good of the nation and that his aloof demeanor not only insulted 'V' but created an instant sense of dislike, distrust and degradation.

'V's' level of disapproval represented a side of him I hadn't witnessed in a very long time. At first, I was concerned and then realized that his level of disdain was one based on his inherent values that paralleled mine and simply amplified his goal of trying to help mankind for their benefit and not his own. I could see that 'V' sensed the bullshit that permeated Fitzgerald's entire demeanor, carefully buried beneath a façade of public duty.

'V' said that the most profound thing The Duke said on the entire trip was "Secrets are only scary when they are secrets. Once you let them out, they're not so scary anymore." I thought of Amy and Sydney and realized it was probably true, realizing the Washington was full of "secrets" that needed to be told.

The most discerning thing 'V' reported was The Duke was choosing the wrong words when trying to communicate and forgetting some people's names. I'd hoped that it was ephemeral, but concluded it was another step in the wrong direction in terms of The Duke's mental capacity. Regardless, I checked with Melia about the word usage and she indicated that it was a sign of the progressing malady where the wrong word choice is called 'semantic paraphasia'. As for the forgotten names, The Duke had always been like that and even though there was no genealogical connection between us, it certainly was like-father-like-son-in-law, as I am terrible at names, too. The meter was ticking and the sound of the clock just put more pressure on us to resolve the technical questions regarding the Nanospheres.

The two amigos were only gone for four days and yet 'V' said The Duke broke open a bottle of expensive scotch on the plane on the way home and 'V' tasted some and said it was terrible. He asked me if I drank that stuff. I replied, "You have to acquire a taste for it and you were drinking $3,000 scotch. You can imagine what the cheap stuff tastes like."

I knew where "V's" heart was and thanked him for going with Grandpa, who called Amy and told her they had a good time and enjoyed being with our son, not mentioning his name or nickname for that matter. What had Amy most concerned was The Duke's disordered speech pattern that saw him jump from one subject to the next, sometimes in mid-sentence and, at times, substituting a word with a non-word that preserved half of the syllables of the first word, which Melia indicated was called phonetic paraphasia and another sign the Alzheimer's was progressing.

After a family visit, we realized that people The Duke had known for years were being erased from his memory. Then there were the small things like hiding the keys of his nurses' cars so they couldn't leave without his permission. When they confronted him, he would get angry and tell them they were holding him captive and he needed to get to the office. He would argue that it was a conspiracy and the company would pay the ransom.

While always grateful for the rewards of his efforts, he began to worry about money and was constantly concerned that his fortune was disappearing. He hadn't been poor for decades and there was enough money to last a millennium, yet poverty became his sole preoccupation and he was tortured by the prospect of it, accusing anyone and everyone of theft, fraud and attempts to cheat him out of everything he and Dr. Williams had acquired. While Badger football had always been one of his passions, he lost total interest as he no longer could differentiate between the teams and his cribbage games became impossible as he could no longer count his cards.

We decided to have a family meeting and determine when we should tell Grandpa what was wrong. God, what a terrible thing to have to tell someone! It was voted that we wait a few weeks to see if there was a leveling of the deterioration, as sometimes the changes came in plateaus instead of a linear slide.

We set the meeting and all of us went to the house. It was the most heartbreaking thing I'd ever witnessed as The Duke didn't recognize any of the kids. He smiled at Melia and said it was nice to meet her. He looked at Derrick and asked if he was Melia's husband. He looked at 'V' and a slight glimmer flickered in his eyes and noted "We've met somewhere before. Do you work at the club?".

The male nurse of duty reported that The Duke had entered the repetition phase where he would do the same thing over and over including eating then asking when was lunch after he'd just finished forcing us to realize we'd waited too long. There was no sense telling someone something they didn't understand. As we left the house, there wasn't a dry eye on anyone. I hoped and prayed that the chip would bring him back, but my confidence was quickly waning.

Tic-Tac-Toe:

We met in the silo where the Madcity boys showed me a rudimentary 16 position "keyboard" noting that the squares were large enough to fit a pig's hoof, yet small enough to allow for maximum dexterity. Of course, the boys had to give me a tutorial on pig's feet first.

Matt indicated that a pig's foot was called a trotter and each trotter consisted of four toes that all pointed down, where he added, "This is because a pig walks on the tips of his toes, rather than the whole foot and only walks on the two, somewhat-webbed, center toes as the outer toes are used only for balance."

This was why the 'verbal squares,' as the boys began calling them, could be smaller, simply because the pig would actually be 'pointing' at the appropriate key instead of stomping on it with his entire foot.

I just shook my head. Talking pigs? Trotters? 'Verbal Squares?' Yet, once again, I was incredibly impressed by how much thought was going into the project. Nothing was being left to chance and that was good.

Tad then summarized square placement, as it applied to pig mobility and dexterity. He noted that because pigs are the smartest land animals next to humans and had an intelligence level that exceeded elephants, dogs and even chimpanzees, it was necessary to make certain that the motions needed to communicate through the keyboard were fluid and not constraining. There was a concern that if the grid was too complicated, it would be too confusing, while one that was too spread out had the potential to make the pig frustrated and stop attempting to 'talk' to us.

I shook my head again. What started out as a joke, was getting really serious, really fast and I was beginning to feel guilty about eating the bacon and lettuce, cheeseburger from Culvers for lunch on my way down to the farm.

The boys all had wicked smiles on their faces as Peter announced the name of the pig. They wanted to call it Francis. I shook my head and asked why.

Matt looked and me and said, "First, Francis can be of either gender, but second, we want the pig named after Sir Francis Bacon."

Sir Francis Bacon? I thought it just sounded too cute until SIMON justified the name with a brief biography of the real guy by saying, "Sir Francis Bacon discovered and popularized what is called 'the scientific method' of research, whereby the laws of science are discovered by gathering and analyzing data from experiments and observations, rather than by using logic-based arguments."

SIMON added, "Bacon championed the inductive method of research, where you move from specific facts to a general rule, which was the opposite of Aristotle's method of starting with a hypothesis or theory and working backwards to garner proof of the conclusion. With an IQ estimated to be at 190, Sir Francis Bacon was also one of the most intelligent men in history."

Leave it to the MadCity Boys to not only be creative, but have a logical reason for what they wanted to do.

Tad took over and outlined the importance of word placement on the keyboard. Because there were going to be sixteen squares with different permutations, it was determined it was critical that each square contain related parts of speech. Of course, Tad had to summarize the different structure of nouns, verbs, adjectives, propositions and others which included pronouns, possessives, articles, adverbs and conjunctions, all of which reminded me of Mrs. Landini's eighth grade English and the courses I had to take for my world-shaking, at least I thought at the time, degree in Journalism.

Peter added. "The first twenty-five words people use make up about one-third of all printed material in English and the first one-hundred words make up about half. With a two square permutation, it means the two-to-the-fifth power, or 32 permutations, need to be the easiest for the future Francis to tap, with two-to-the seventh or 128 permutations required to cover half of all words used."

Tad included. "As an example, the word, 'the' is the most common word and we   would place it at 1-1. When Francis stepped on the word square 1 twice, the computer says 'the'. The normal logic would be to then place the second most common word, which is 'be' by pressing 1-2. Then third word is 'to' in 1-3."

"So, you would keep going all the way to 1-12?" I replied, thinking I was ahead of the game.

"No, because Francis would have to move too far to go to the twelfth most common word which is 'for'. Instead, we asked SIMON to look at all written English on the internet and determine word adjacencies so that we could place words found normally with others, closer together. We then asked SIMON to break the common pairs into blocks of four so that 1-1, 1-2, 1-3 and 1-4 are words normally found in conversation together. When we did this 1-1 remains as 'I', 1-2 becomes 'am', 1-3 is will, 1-4 'can' and so forth. "

I quickly saw the logic and, once again, it was brilliant. By word pairing, the future Sir Francis Bacon, could speed up the communication process and, with the addition of artificial intelligence, learn his verbal patterns, smooth out the communication and make it flow in a more natural sequence.

"Does this system have an application for those who have suffered a stroke and cannot speak?" I asked.

The boys smiled as they punched a series of squares so that the computer spoke and said, "We think so, George."

This was amazing. We were taking the Hawking Talking Machine to the next level and everyone agreed that the Wizard of the Universe would have thought it was great. May he rest in peace!

The Beauty Pageant:

Most people, including me, look at a pig pen and only see pigs and little else. We knew we wanted the most intelligent juvenile pig in Tommie's pen who had the greatest social skills. We had no idea how to determine the top candidate and so we turned to the UW School of Agriculture and asked how we would go about determining the smartest pig in the brood. Instead, they elected to send Dr. Richard Maas, a pig expert, to assist us in our decision making.

Dr. Maas was a big dude and a body builder on top of that. He had long blond hair and wasn't at all what I expected when he parked his battered truck in the farmhouse yard. The MadCity Boys were all there, along with Tommie, Luke and me. I had asked Hsu to join us, but she had a conflict.

Dr. Maas told us it was important to have whomever it was who fed the pigs available and that was Tommie, even though he, like me, initially thought it was a big joke, which we justified by one of the basic rules of farming being, never get emotionally attached to the animals. Tommie and I both looked at the pigs as nothing more than an investment. Boy were we in for a shock.

First off, what I thought would be a short 'that one', took all day and had several different criteria. It was like watching the Miss America pageant without the bathing suits. The contest looked at comparative psychology, including nonsocial and social cognition, self-awareness, emotion and personality. By looking at the juvenile porkers, Dr. Maas told us he would be able to determine which were alpha males and who had the greatest social skills. From that, he was able to narrow the contestants from all twenty-five of Tommie's finest to twelve quarter-finalists where we spray-painted washable numbers on their butts, ranging from one-to-twelve, simply to make life easier.

Next, Dr. Maas put the quarter-finalists through what he called a Sensory Abilities Assessment to determine their cognitive capacity, which I learned later was their smelling power. The test was based on stimuli within the setting, which happened to be a fenced in area next to the milk house. To do this, Maas hid pig treats in the pen and released each pig alone, where they had to find the treat in the least possible time. The good doctor used a stop watch to measure how long it took for each one to determine the location of the prize while Tad our mathematician, kept score. It was like going to Arlington Park in Chicago and watching the horse races.

Dr. Maas said, "Pigs use a wide range of stimuli, both in their physical and social environments to develop not only their personalities, but also the social pecking of the group."

Except for the MadCity Boys who we called the boys, we called pigs, well pigs. Dr. Maas noted that a group of young pigs was called a drift, drove or litter and older pigs are called a sounder of swine, a team or passel of hogs, a singular of boars or a herd of pigs."

This guy was really serious, but then, when you're considered one of the world's top pig experts, you'd better be. I wanted to ask him if he ate bacon, lettuce and tomato sandwiches, but thought I'd better not. This guy was way too serious and also much, much larger than me - almost to Rodney's size.

Dr. Maas continued by explaining. "It shouldn't come as a surprise, considering the gregarious nature of their wild counterparts, that pigs are highly social animals and tactile information plays an important role in their behavior. The highest density of their tactile receptors are found in the pig's snout, which they use to engage in highly manipulative behaviors such as rooting, carrying and pushing in their social interactions."

We all knew from the MadCity Boys report that olfaction, or smelling, in farm talk, was the pig's keenest sense. Thus, pigs learn olfactory discriminations more easily than others, relying heavily on odors to find appropriate food items when foraging. What we didn't know until the doctor told us, was the olfactory sensitivity wasn't limited to foraging for food, but also used in their social domain in a wide range of subjects including discriminating social identity, sexual state and the emotional state of other pigs, as well as in creating and sustaining dominance hierarchies.

After testing social interactions, Dr. Maas was able to remove four pigs from the beauty contest as they were too passive and we were down to the elite-eight semi-finalists. And people thought it was only exciting during March Madness!

Dr. Maas noted that sound, which we called grunting, is also used by pigs in many social contexts, including communication and determining identity, where an arousal state could be conveyed through vocalizations. We also didn't know that pigs have an incredibly high frequency hearing range that allow them to hear sounds even dogs can't hear. To make this point, the doctor blew into what I was always thought to be a dog whistle and three of the pigs came running.

To validate his test, Dr. Maas pulled out what looked like and old fashion ray gun and turned the dial. At first all the pigs stood still. However, as the good Doctor turned the dial further, noting that pigs were sensitive to ultrasonic sound, things began to change. At around 40,000 Hz, we watched as each one began to shy away, until there were only six standing. Dr. Maas noted that we needed to have a pig who was less excitable to alien noise, as it would affect their level of concentration and so two more pigs left the pageant.

Next, it was time to see which of the group had the social skills necessary to participate in hours of daily training. Dr. Maas began with a dissertation on what he called "nonsocial cognition" that refers to how animals perceive and mentally represent and process physical components of their environment, including problem-solving in the physical realm, object discrimination, spatial cognition and other elements of learning and memory in the physical/object domain, including time perception. All I wanted was a talking pig and this guy wanted to create a social dynamo.

Here the key was observing the individual contestants to determine what they would do on their own. To evaluate this, each candidate was herded into an obstacle course we were instructed to build prior to Dr. Maas's arrival. Dr. Maas noted that object discrimination made categorization and concept formation possible. These capacities, in turn, provided cognitive scaffolding for other complex capacities. Whatever that meant, it sure sounded 'official'.

Maas noted, "All animals possess some ability to discriminate objects ranging from discriminations of simple concrete stimuli to complex and even abstract concepts."

I had no idea what this meant, but a PHD in Pigology put him way above me, as he continued. "Normally, we like to expose pigs to both novel and familiar objects and assess their responses to each exposure for two days. Because this is a one-day trial, I brought along some unique items and we will place them in the holding area and observe the different pig's level of interest. In the lab, we know that pigs can remember an object for at least five days and those who show a preference for novel objects over familiar ones are demonstrating their capacity for long term memory."

Amazing!

We put all six pigs through the test and three pigs could have cared less about the new objects and were politely told they wouldn't be getting the tiara and a dozen roses.

After the novel test, Dr. Maas noted. "Pigs have the ability to prioritize important memories, such as the requirements of food searching. When given the opportunity to access only one of two food sources, the pigs regularly preferred the one with the greatest amount of food and remembered that site, using either or both their visual and olfactory cues while foraging." This sounded like the MadCity Boys in the research refrigerator.

The doctor continued, "Rather than rely on the spatial placement of a location that previously contained food, pigs can follow both certain colors and food odors to find a food source, thereby, showing that they can make discriminations in both modalities."

It was getting to be the middle of the afternoon when the pigs were normally fed and, per the doctor's instructions, Tommie prepared their normal meal where time perception and the ability to detect the passage of time was measured while still anticipating the future would take place. Once again, the entire concept was simply amazing to me.

Dr. Maas said, "Basic time perception is not entirely synonymous with, but is arguably, a basis for more sophisticated mental time travel. The conscious ability to represent the past and future reflects a level of intellectual capability and, therefore, the more intelligent the pig, the greater the level of comprehension."

I just shook my head in disbelief. The doctor continued, "Taking it one step further, when coupled with an episodic memory system, time perception may become part of a sense-of-self, regarding the past, present and future."

In other words, pigs had a self-concept, along with a relative perception of not only where they fit in the group, but when and how. Now, I was beginning to feel a little guilty about loading them in a truck and sending them to Oscar Mayer.

The doctor continued. "There is substantial evidence that other animals have internal timing mechanisms that help them know the time of day and predict when events will occur and are also able to anticipate future events and act accordingly, such as during feeding. Pigs can remember highly-specific contextual elements, that is, the what, where and when of events, even when weeks and even years have passed." Geez, now I was feeling really guilty about loving BBQ ribs!

The semi-finalists were herded back into the holding pen. At approximately the time they would have been normally fed, three made their way to the feeding trough and automatically entered the realm of finalist, while the other three just roamed around wondering what all the attention was about.

Instead of pouring the food into the trough, Dr. Maas had three lever machines in place that would dispense the food. Tommie was instructed to fill each hopper and then press the lever to show the pigs how the food would be dispensed. After watching three passes, the pigs were allowed next to the levers. Two went immediately to the levers. I thought it was unfortunate that their hooves slipped off and the pigs tried to respond with their snouts instead of feet. On the contrary, Dr. Maas noted that it showed they understood the cognitive requirements of the task, despite the physical limitations.

Dr. Maas looked and smiled and said we had our two finalists. Tad, the wise guy was polishing the tiara as the doctor spoke. "Spatial cognition (learning and memory) refers to the ability to acquire knowledge and remember, organize and utilize information about spatial aspects of one's environment, including navigation and learning and then be able to discriminate and prioritize the locations of objects. It is highly dependent upon mental representations in both short and long-term memory and often forms the basis of complex cognitive maps of the environment, thereby providing the Foundation for many other social and non-social strategic behaviors during such tasks as foraging and traveling."

Maas continued. "Pigs, as foraging animals, are especially good at using spatial information. They are highly competent at learning to navigate mazes and other spatial arrangements, although many of these tests are done in highly artificial settings."

For this test, a small maze was set up where the pigs would be walked on a leash through the maze and when they got to the other end, given a treat. Both finalists were, at first, uncomfortable on leashes, as they had never been on one before. When they calmed down, they were led through the maze three times. After the three trials, they were told to go get the treat they could see Tommie was holding at the other end. It was amazing watching the two pigs run the course and never get it wrong with each pass getting a little faster than the time before.

Dr. Maas continued. "Pigs rapidly learn spatial discriminations that depend upon working and reference memory. Pigs also remember the location, content, and relative value of previously discovered sites that contain stimuli of interest and do so using spatial memory to search areas for food and avoid areas previously found to be empty. As you can see the smarter the pig, the faster they adapt."

Maas added, "Studies have shown that pigs can use what is called 'flexible spatial memory' where they can be trained to either return to a location where they previously found food or use the memory of a previously discovered food site to forage elsewhere."

"In another particularly interesting experiment, pigs were presented with two different food sites that were baited with unequal amounts of food. When made to choose between one of the two locations in a foraging context, pigs showed a preference for visiting the site containing the larger amount of food, suggesting that pigs are able to discriminate between and remember the locations of food sites with different relative values."

We were down to our last two contestants and it was nip-and-tuck with one ahead of the other by a nose. (Sorry, I couldn't resist). We explained to Dr. Maas that we wanted to train the pig, but didn't tell him to what degree or for what purpose and never discussed that we wanted to have a talking pig.

In our discussion Dr. Maas noted that, to a pig, there was little difference between training and playing, if it was done right. We needed to find a pig who wanted to continue to learn and not get bored and also a pig who could handle intense training, as it was a lot more complex than we initially thought.

Dr. Maas had rapt attention of the entire ensemble. What started out as a lark in terms of determining pig intelligence, became an eye-opening experience for all of us. Dr. Maas continued. "Play in all animals, is related to creativity and innovation and therefore forms the basis for complex, object-related and social abilities. Exposure to novelty enhances learning experiences and responses can have an impact on performance in other cognitive tasks, as well."

He added. "Social play, which involves creating new interactions and situations, plays an important role in the development of all social mammals. Therefore, curiosity and the preference for novelty are, arguably, related to cognitive complexity and certain personality traits."

The doctor put down his clip board and looked at the team and said. "Play is found most predominantly in the most cognitively complex and adaptable humans and nonhuman species. Therefore, play appears to be a marker of cognitive complexity. While many people would never perceive them to be so, pigs are playful animals. A recent study of play behavior in pigs showed that they readily engage in quite complex types of play that include social and object play that involves shaking or carrying an object such as a ball or stick or tossing straw. Locomotor play includes waving/tossing of the head, scampering, jumping, hopping, pawing, pivoting and gamboling - which is energetic running - flopping on the ground and hopping around."

"Social play in pigs includes play fighting, pushing and running after each other. Many of these categories of play are combined and the behaviors are similar to play behavior in dogs and other mammals. Play in pigs not only satisfies a need for exploration and discovery, it also is critical for healthy development."

"Play is best stimulated by diverse, complex, hands-on and renewable objects and materials. So important is the need to play that insufficient opportunity to explore leads to behavioral abnormalities."

Thank God we were recording the entire session as Dr. Maas's dissertation would have left a great deal on the table, if we hadn't been and it only got more complicated as the 'final exam" began that consisted of having the four of us positioned about twenty feet apart where we were told to toss a ball between us. If the pig came to us, we were to give the pig a treat and then throw the ball to one of the others. If the pig went to that person, they would be given another treat. It only took two throws until both pigs caught on and as soon as the ball was thrown the pig ran to the other person. The pigs had correlated the ball toss to the treat and it was a tie.

Dr. Maas noted that we were at the final test phase, which was social cognition and complexity. He noted, "Social cognition is the use of skills within the social domain and forms the basis for cognitive complexity and intelligence, including culture, across a wide range of species. There is an abundance of empirical evidence showing a positive correlation between various high-level cognitive capacities and measures of social complexity in groups as wide-ranging as primates."

"Whereas domestic and wild pigs are social animals, relatively little is known about how these capacities manifest in their natural lives and what cognitive and emotional abilities underwrite their sociality. What is known, points to the possibility that pigs are as socially complex as many other highly intelligent animals, possibly sharing a number of cognitive capacities related to social complexity. The ability to discriminate among individuals forms the basis for social relationships, hierarchies and reactions to familiar versus unfamiliar individuals." And I thought this guy was just going to look at twenty-five pigs and say – 'that one!'

The doctor continued. "To determine who is the most socially complex of our two finalists is quite simple. All we need do is open the gate and first see if the remainder of the group comes in and then who they go to. Because it's dinner time, they might pass by, but normally the pig with the highest level of social complexity will attract the greatest number of followers to the trough."

Sure enough, of the twenty-three other contestants, fifteen made their way immediately to candidate number six and we had our winner, who was immediately crowned - Sir Francis Bacon, to which Dr. Maas let out a loud guffaw saying, "I thought it was going to be number eight!" while totally missing our play on words.

Even though our winner was a boar, Tad turned on his phone and played the 1955 Bert Parks theme song from the Miss America Pageant "There She is Miss America" to which we all applauded and roared with laughter as all the contestants were provided with a special mix of their favorite treats including vegetarian dog biscuits, fresh and dried fruit, unsalted popcorn and peanuts, uncooked pasta and fresh vegetables and were allowed to eat to their heart's content.

We thought we needed a back-up in case something happened to Francis and, because the test scores were so close and there would be a need for social interaction, we deemed the second pig and named him Aristotle, who would go through the same training. This would be the last night Francis and Aristotle would be sleeping outdoors. Little did Francis realize how his life was going to change. Little did we realize how he was going to change our lives as well. The doctor did not come cheap and yet, at day's end, his knowledge and wisdom was considered an investment and not an expenditure.

Mary:

As Dr. Maas was about to leave, we asked for the names of individuals he thought could work with us to train Francis and he gave us three. I had Wilco personnel interview and screen all three and a week later a young woman named Mary Magdaleno showed up ready, willing and more than able to take on the task.

I learned that Mary's family had been circus people who trained all kinds of different animals and when public opinion shut down the major circuses, she realized, after four generations, the circus life she had known and loved, had come to an end. To simply have a job was one thing. To have a well-paying job was another. To have a job that included a residence and benefits was almost beyond her imagination and finally, to spend her time with Aristotle and Francis was going to be something she would never forget.

All Mary knew when she arrived was that she was being hired to train a pig. Was she in for a surprise! After a couple of days, Mary called and indicated she thought the boys, Aristotle and Francis that is, and not the MadCity Boys – well, maybe some of them, too, needed to be 'fixed' or neutered. She said the testosterone in their systems was already beginning to impede her training as they were becoming quite competitive.

I called Hsu, who indicated she too was in favor of the boys losing the 'boys.' She noted it would not only reduce any potential aggression, but greatly reduce the probability of them suffering from prostate cancer as they got older. I had no idea that the reproductive systems of pigs were virtually identical to that of humans. However, reflecting on the MadCity Boys and some of their conversations, I began to see the parallel.

Tommie volunteered to do the deed, but we had too much at stake and called the vet who came out and gave the boys a sedative. It was interesting hearing them snore as the Vet did his procedure.

When the vet was done, both Aristotle and Francis were given warm blankets which quickly became their sources of security. There were video cameras already installed in their holding area and it was fun to watch them take their respective blankets and cover up when they were going to sleep. Both knew which blanket was theirs and were extremely protective of their prized possessions.

As I watched them sleep, my mind wandered back to my beloved Jake as he would slide under the covers and snuggle. I also found it heartwarming to watch, as first one and then the other, would put their chin on the others rump as both snoozed. Aristotle and Francis were buddies and they seemed to enjoy each other's company and companionship. I was certainly glad the MadCity Boys talked me into having the two of them, even though they were being trained apart.

Within a week, Mary had both boys identifying and coming when their names were called. They also quickly learned to respond to the tone of Mary's voice. When it was calm and soothing, they were happy little pigs. When they were naughty or uncooperative, you could actually see it in their demeanor with their ears not quite as pointed, their heads not quite as high and what appeared to be, their little smile, gone.

It took a month until I was asked to come down and see the progress. I wasn't expecting much. As we entered "pig heaven" as the MadCity Boys were calling it, I saw the toys and barricades that were used for the daily training and didn't expect much more. Tad was allowed in the training area with Mary and they were going through the routine. The rest of us were behind one-way glass so Aristotle and Francis wouldn't be distracted. Both little piggy's went through their paces and you could tell they were enjoying the mental stimulation. Mary asked Francis what his name was and Francis went to a board with nine different squares on it and pushed the block that represented his name so that a small treat came out. Next, Mary asked Francis what his friend's name was. Francis went to the panel, this time pressing Aristotle's name.

To make certain we didn't think it was based simply on learning the right block on the board, Mary asked which slot I would like the names to be placed in. I selected the upper left hand for Aristotle and the lower right for Francis. I was then asked which pig I wanted first. Amazingly, in both instances both pigs went to the correct squares and pressed their name and then that of their buddy.

Needless to say, I was impressed. Both pigs had acquired a concept of 'self' which was critical for communication and meant that we were on our way. As I was flying home, I called Amy and told her the good news. "The pigs had degrees of self-concept". Amy asked which pigs, Aristotle and Francis or the MadCity Boys? I said both!

Derrick:

Amy had arranged dinner with our son, Derrick. It had been months since the three of us had been together. Amy saw him at work and they, along with Melia, were always texting and so, 'V' and I were left out of the day-to-day stuff.

We agreed to meet at Sanford Restaurant for dinner. As was always the case, Derrick was running late, which drove me crazy. Seven o'clock meant seven o'clock. If we wanted to meet at seven-thirty, I would have made the reservations then.

Derrick knew it irritated me and was always apologetic when he arrived. The big surprise was the young lady he had with him. I wasn't expecting to meet anyone and, yet, I guess they had been dating for a while and Derrick thought it was time for us to meet.

The young lady's name was Andrea who was from Germany. First off, she was drop-dead gorgeous with long blond hair, light blue eyes and a sparkling smile. Derrick announced she was getting her MBA at Marquette and they met through a mutual friend. Milwaukee was always famous for its German heritage and many residents still have relatives in the 'old country'.

Fortunately for Derrick, he took after his mother and was a handsome young man with light almond skin and piercing brown eyes and the two of them made quite the couple. To say Derrick had been raised "properly" would be an understatement. Thanks to his mother, Derrick was sophisticated beyond his years and between Cornell and the University of Chicago law school, the kid had everything going for him - looks, smarts, social graces and of course, money.

As Andrea began talking, I could see she was a match for Derrick as her English was impeccable, her manners pristine and like Derrick, she was extremely well-dressed.

Because of our wealth, we were always cautious about who our kids were involved with. 'V' was dating my best friend's daughter and so that was certainly OK. Melia was too busy and we only hoped she would find someone. This was the first time

Derrick ever brought a young lady to meet us and I didn't know what level the relationship was in.

We had a pleasant dinner and watched as Derrick said all the right things and made all the right moves to ensure us that Andrea was in the proper social realm. Little did she realize, the day before our dinner, I was down on the farm watching a pig find his name on an electronic keyboard.

Andrea asked me what I did for a living. While we were always quite reticent about telling people what we did. I mentioned that I was involved in a research foundation.

Andrea asked which one and I told her the Derrick Williams Foundation.

"You mean, Medigloves?" Andrea inquired.

"Yes, you've heard of the Foundation?"

"Certainly, everyone in Germany knows about Mediglove and the fact it is owned by a non-profit foundation here in the States. We've studied it in Business School at Marquette. Germans think it's wonderful, because all we ever hear about at home when it comes to American health-related industries, are the big pharmaceutical companies and how they are trying to make such exorbitant profits on the illness of others." Andrea responded.

It was a very nice, very formal evening and I was impressed. On the way home all I could think about was spending one day on the farm watching a pig run a maze and the next day having dinner with my son and his beautiful girlfriend.

"They're pretty serious, George." Amy announced as I was thinking of Francis and Aristotle.

"They're pretty young!" I responded.

"Older than we were!" was the reply.

Two days later, Derick called and asked me what I thought. Now any father who wasn't a total doofus would simply say that she was wonderful - I mean gorgeous and intelligent and yet something was bothering me and I didn't know what.

"Can Andrea and I go to House-On-The-Hill?" Derrick asked.

"That's up to your mother." I replied. "It's her house, not mine" - but then everything was hers.

I didn't know what to think and so I called Andrew and asked him to run a little, non-intrusive check on Andrea Mueller. I outlined what she told me and he thought it wouldn't be a big deal.

"Andrew, one thing." I noted.

"Yes, sir!" Andrew replied.

"Only between the two of us, Ok?"

"Certainly, George."

The next day, the report came back I learned that Andrea's father was a butcher who owned a small butcher shop they lived above in Wiesbaden. I called Amy and told her the news. The question became, what to do about it, if anything. Amy noted that her family had money and she married the son of a dairy farmer and it turned out all right, adding that love is blind. I said I knew that and reminded her who she married. Amy, being closer to Derrick than me, offered to let Derrick know we were aware of Andrea's family background and that it didn't matter. I asked her not to. I had a different idea.

With Andrea's positive response to the Derrick Williams Foundation, I called Derrick and asked if he and Andrea would like to visit the facility. Derrick hadn't been there in a long time and I thought they would be interested.

At first there was reluctance and then reserved agreement. The day was set and I told Derrick to meet me at the office. He assumed we would take the chopper. My plan was to take the truck.

The day arrived and Derrick and Andrea were actually on time. Perhaps this girl wasn't so bad after all. Derrick looked for the chopper and I told him it was in for maintenance and we were taking my truck. I got in the front and the two of them were in back. From Pewaukee to Madison, we talked about the Foundation and what we were doing, while Andrea discussed Marquette University versus schools in Germany.

From Madison to Mineral Point, I talked family history. First, we discussed The Duke and Dr. Williams and how they met and the challenges in Milwaukee of a white man with an African-American wife. Then, I outlined Amy and our love story. Finally, I began telling Andrea about Waldwick and the Terrill family history. I explained that when I met Amy, I owned one sportscoat and two pairs of pants and wanted to be a writer. I outlined that my dad had been a dairy farmer who milked 250 head of Holsteins twice a day, every day and died of a heart attack because he couldn't afford to go to the doctor!

As we pulled in the farmhouse driveway, I asked the couple to follow me and took them to the ridge where my ancestors were buried within the limestone walls. I outlined their honesty, dignity and how they dedicated their lives to one thing, making the world a little better for everyone else.

We walked to the research center which was now called Pig Heaven, and I introduced Andrea and Derrick to Mary and asked her to show them our latest project and have her put Aristotle and Francis through their paces. Andrea was impressed and Derrick just shook his head.

As we walked to the research compound, I stopped and said I wanted to show them a very special place and followed the cinder path into The Forest. We stopped at the remains of the school house foundation and I outlined the history of why the school was so important. We went to Grandfather's obelisk and I explained who he was and how we fought to save the land, showing Andrea where George the First saved Rodney's ancestor and why the land was so precious to us.

As we were walking to the springs, Andrea stopped me.

"Mr. Terrill, a profound feeling has come over me. It's unlike anything I've ever felt before in my life. I feel goodness and charity and above all else honor and dignity and beyond that truth - deep-seated truth. There is something I must tell you."

"What's that?"

"Derrick was afraid of my not being accepted because I am a butcher's daughter."

"Is your father an honest man?" I asked, looking straight in her eyes.

"Most certainly!" was the response.

"Has he shown you love and kindness?" I asked in all seriousness.

"He has sacrificed everything so that I could come to school here." Andrea answered.

"And what are you feeling right now?" I inquired.

"I feel goodness and a profound sense of decency, unlike anything I've ever felt in my life." Andrea said, with tears welling in her eyes.

I looked at her and then at Derrick who stood mute and afraid.

"Follow me, just a little further," I beckoned.

We made it to the springs and I took the small tin cup and placed it in the cold water until it was full. I then offered the cup to Andrea who took it and placed it to her lips. I watched as her eyes closed and then opened and then closed again. I watched her body tremble and then recover with tears streaming down her face.

"Oh my God!" was her response. "Oh my God!" she repeated as she began crying in earnest. Andrea's head tilted upward and then back down. Her mouth opened and then her head turned from side-to-side. Derrick stood with mouth agape. He had been here. However, like Amy, The Forest never affected him and he had never seen The Forest's inextricable effects on anyone else before.

Andrea looked at me and a slight smile crossed her lips. "You knew, didn't you?"

"You knew!"

I had no idea what she was talking about and so I stood and waited.

Andrea continued. "When my mother died, I couldn't handle the pain and I became a rebel against everyone and everything. My father, my dear father, had no idea what to do with me. He thought he had been too strict, too difficult, too demanding - as all he ever wanted was for me to be more than a butcher's daughter. And yet, today, you have accepted me! You have shown me that there is more to life than being something or someone you're not. You brought me here to cleanse my soul and I am so profoundly thankful." Andrea began to sob again, turning into Derrick's arms for consolation.

I took a deep breath. The goodness that the Medicine Man once said would come was beginning as I touched a life and hopefully made it better as Andrea calmed down emoting a sense of relief about her.

The Duke had instructed 'V'. "secrets are only scary when they are secrets. Once you let them out, they're not so scary anymore." We spent the next two hours touring the research facility, where I outlined the projects and showed the couple the first prototype of the Medigolve and how the design had progressed. I pointed to the Mediglove digital display that indicated over one billion participants who had provided personal medical information from around the world; I introduced her to SIMON and then the IMVR glasses, explaining how we had people working with us all over the world and could interact with them in any language at any time.

As we stood there, I zoomed in on Germany and touched Wiesbaden on the map. Slowly, the two of them toured the city as they worked the joystick, finally ending up standing out front of a small butcher shop.

"That's my father's shop and above it is where we call home," Andrea said with pride.

"Just a minute, there's someone who wants to say hello," I said, as I used the joystick to walk through the front door, to where her father was standing.

"*Hallo Andrea, ich vermisse dich,*" Andrea's father said, which SIMON whispered meant ‚*Hello Andrea, I miss you*' before

I switched on SIMON'S auto-translator and everything came out in English.

For the next half-hour we got to know each other with both Derrick and Andrea's father, Hans smiling from ear-to-ear.

I turned off the translater and said ,*Danke Shon*' or ,*thank you*' to Hans, which represented the entire extent of my German. Andrea giggled, as my pronunciation of Danke came out Donkey instead of Dahnkah! thinking that once again, I'd made an ass out of myself.

Hans just smiled and nodded. We made everyone's day a little more special, hoping that I sent the right message to Andrea and to my son that his father didn't judge people by the amount of money they had, but by the wealth of goodness in their heart.

We turned off the screen, as Derrick put his hand in Andrea's and looked at me and said. "Thank you, dad!"

We walked back to the truck and began the drive home. For a bit, there was a reflection on the day and then total silence until we were back to the office. I felt as if the day had been a moving experience and more words would simply dilute the feelings that permeated Andrea and Derrick's soul and so my mouth remained shut as I kept checking the rearview mirror and both parties simply were looking forward - not at me, but tomorrow.

As we entered the parking lot and got out of the truck, I turned to Andrea and Derrick and said, "Derrick's mother told me you were going to House-On-The-Hill. I hope you enjoy it. It is filled with many fond memories."

There was no more need for explanations. Derrick knew I approved. I hugged both of them and they departed. I walked into my office and sat on the chest, looking at the two feathers and simply whispered, "Thank you."

Simoni and The Head Lock:

Michelangelo di Lodovico Buonarroti Simoni, commonly known as Michelangelo, was an Italian sculptor, painter, architect, poet, and engineer more than a few folks have heard of. If not, perhaps, the mention of the statue of David, Creation of Adam, Sistine Chapel ceiling, Pietà and Bacchus would make them aware of his greatness.

I'm certain you are wondering how Michelangelo got into the picture? Well, he didn't, but we needed to name the new device we wanted to create that would insert Nanospheres into the brain and with da Vinci already taken by another incredible medical robot, the boys looked at alternatives. I had been down the naming road before and found the passion and bullshit, at times too much to handle. Instead, I let the MadCity Boys come up with ideas and some of them thought Michelangelo was cool because he and da Vinci are always mentioned in the same breath, as the two greatest artists of all time. The problem with the Michelangelo name was, it was a tongue twister and took me five tries before I could spell it correctly.

The discussion, no, make that argument, over the naming of a machine reached epic proportions until I put my foot down. How could adult - well somewhat adult - men be so passionate about naming a machine? To make everyone happy and due to the fact the machine was going to work with SIMON, we went with Michelangelo's last name - Simoni and made him, a her, as women always have more dexterous hands.

With naming rights settled, the performance criteria for Simoni was established by the bioengineering team who developed incredibly finite parameters concerning incision length, width and depth and Simoni's ability to maneuver within the brain and deposit the Nanosphere where it needed to go.

Linked to an MRI, Simoni had a micro-camera that was controlled by SIMON. As the visual data was fed from the electron microscope, Simoni was capable of making the minute incisions at the perfect place to insert the Nanosphere and do so with minimal invasive damage in the desired location within the hippocampus.

The engineers took Simoni one step further and added a microscopic laser which would seal each phase of the operation, using an incredibly small amount of heat to cauterize the incision. If the machine worked, there would be no skin damage, minimal invasive damage and virtually no recovery time, other than the sedative.

After extensive discussions concerning accuracy, the bioengineers also determined that the patient's head would need to be completely immobilized and secured in such a way that it could not move during the procedure. In order to do this, the bioengineers wanted to develop a frame that went around the head of the recipient that 'locked' the head in place, which, without any discussion - no make that any argument - became known as the 'headlock'.

"Simoni and the Head Lock" sounded like a grunge band, but the name stuck and designs began to be developed. To create the accuracy needed, increments needed were to be measured in nanometers. Dealing with something that small meant the team wanted to build a monster version first and then miniaturize it. The budget for jumbo Simoni alone was set at three million dollars. Yikes!

Within Simoni, the engineers first needed to develop the scalpel. Traditional surgical knives were too broad and would probably do too much damage internally and so the engineers turned to lasers for cutting and cauterizing the incision. By using the laser, the incision width was reduced by 90% and the engineers were confident their system would create a cleaner and more accurate incision than anything ever developed. By using a laser and then a sensor that measured the laser's distance and reflection, the idea of a camera gave way to a three-dimensional outline of the area Simoni was working in, so that the actual size of the incision could be even less.

The question became, how do we get the laser to move in and out of the brain? The engineers knew they couldn't use typical drive belts, as the connectors between the links would be too large and therefore the incisional incrementation too great. Once again, I needed an explanation and the response was that a belt-drive system would be like taking giant steps, when baby steps were needed. It didn't take long for the team to come up with an answer - hydraulics and the use of a piston that could be moved in nanometer increments.

The nanometer requirement meant the environment would need to be totally secure and devoid of any vibration and the cost of our "operating room" quintupled. The MadCity Boys started working on the software that would link Simoni-to-SIMON via the electron microscope (which quickly became known as Bubba for some reason).

To explain it to me, the guys said. "The MRI would be active at all times and send locational data to Simoni, who would then correlate her location with the MRI and send the electronic data to Bubba, where it would be scanned and sent to SIMON. SIMON would review it, double check for accuracy and send the information back to Bubba, who would then instruct Simoni regarding insertion or retraction, laser or cauterizing activity and Nanosphere insertion and Simoni would do her thing. All the time, the Head Lock would not only be sustaining the patient's head in a locked position, but sending MRI data to SIMON so that he could double check it against the information Simoni was sending to him.

While it sounds complicated it really wasn't. If the process sounds slow, I was assured it wouldn't be. The boys noted that the entire procedure would be as fast as you could possibly get, because all the data would be transmitted at the speed of light using fiber optic cables instead of traditional transmission lines. There would also be incredible accuracy because SIMON and Simoni were going to do the actual procedure without the need of hands-on neurosurgeons being involved, which left no room for human error.

The team got to work and within a month they had drawings completed and materials ordered to build the prototype. All that was needed were items to test the equipment on. Luke got involved as head of bioethics and indicated he was against using any live animals for the initial tests. Even though we ran all the protocols through SIMON and came back with a 99.4% success rate, everyone was concerned.

Instead, people started thinking about alternatives and the idea of running tests on fruits and vegetables came about. The edibles could be fixed in place by Head Lock and we could see inside the item to determine our success rate. The team tried grapefruit, apples, watermelon and all types of fruit without the success they felt they needed. The biggest challenge was keeping the MadCity Boys away from eating the test materials.

We were all just about to give up when someone suggested the eggplant. Eggplants are soft on the outside and have a fibrous interior, which closely parallels the brain. The inside of an eggplant has a white flesh with soft small seeds that are barely visible, but would show up really well on our MRI and, therefore, provide tests for Simoni to see if she would go around them.

We learned that some eggplants have their center filled with larger seeds which, Tad learned, was usually due to improper harvesting before they were ripe. Being in Waldwick and only having a small grocery store in Mineral Point that didn't handle egg plants, meant our only option was to come to Madison, where I think someone in the produce department at the Verona Piggly Wiggly, must have thought Tad was nuts when he purchased their entire inventory.

We had the design for the machine! We had the software developed for communication and we had the fruit. Now all we needed to do was put the entire system together to see if it would work. After several miscues and a lot of tinkering, which is a polite way of saying, a lot of profanity, the boys decided that I should see the process.

When I asked how long the test would take, I was told four hours.

"Four hours! Why so long?" I asked.

The boys confirmed it would be a long process because we were moving everything in MPH which stood for molecules per hour, instead of miles per hour.

The afternoon was set and the chosen eggplant was affixed with the Head Lock, even though no one thought it was going to move or go anywhere. Slowly, ever so slowly, Simoni made her way towards the purple fruit. I really thought it was faster and more exciting watching paint dry.

As Simoni reached the surface of the eggplant and the first incision began, we could see inside the plant on the video board, and do so from a hole so small it couldn't be seen with the naked eye. Simoni was doing her job!

Gradually, Simoni made her way towards the prescribed depth, where she encountered a seed. Instead of going around it, she increased the laser power for a microburst that split the seed in two and proceeded. At the programmed depth, Simoni's second arm began slowly inserting a non-working replica of the Nanosphere, that was slid through the same hole, making its way to the probing end. Upon reaching the same depth, a small set of arms opened and the insertion arm pulled back. In so doing, the nanosphere slid off and was put in place, at which point there was a tremendous round of cheers from those of us in the audience.

Carefully, the insertion arm reversed direction and the probe began the process of cauterizing the tiny hole, to ensure no bleeding or loss of brain matter, or in this case eggplant fluid as Simoni's arm reached the outer surface and she administered one last blast of energy to close the insertion hole and we were done. In doing so, Simoni had done exactly what we wanted. She made the incision and placed the nanosphere precisely where it was supposed to go and then sealed the deal so the incision was closed.

As we looked at the MRI, we could see the nanosphere where it had been designed to go and when the engineers examined Simoni's arm, they realized there was no eggplant juice on it at all, meaning the cells around Simoni were still intact. The team had created a machine that could successfully do micro surgery and there were high fives all around the lab. Mission accomplished, at least on the eggplant.

It was time to celebrate! You guessed it! Eggplant Parmesan as the boys removed the nano-chip, cleaned it off and put it into a hard drive to see if it retained the data they had programmed, which turned out to be a series of off-color cartoons, some old Beatles songs, a copy of the Bible - compliments of Peter - along with a test created by SIMON that tested its functional capabilities.

Twenty minutes later, the report came back - fully functional - the chip had survived. Now it was time to really celebrate and out came some really good Terrill booze that Tommie had fermented and hidden from the Feds. 160 proof? That was for children! This stuff was almost 100% alcohol and was like good German schnapps except Tommie had added a raspberry flavor so that it wouldn't taste like we were drinking gasoline.

Hello, it's 'V' Again:

The time spent in Black River Falls was increasing and I needed an update and called Big Brother saying, " Heh, Rod, how's my son doing?"

Rodney laughed, as he knew that I knew that 'V' was doing well and answered. "He's doing fine. He didn't realize that this would be a complex job that included not only the challenges of keeping one generation off drugs and losing their ethnic identity, but everyone being overcome by the financial windfall that was coming their way."

"Is he learning anything?" I asked.

"Sure! He's learned that we've got our hands full and it isn't as easy as he thought it was going to be."

"Is he still working with your Amelia?" I asked.

Another chuckle from the big guy. "They're inseparable."

"What do you think?" I asked.

"I think they need to slow down." Rodney said in all seriousness.

"You want to tell them that?" I countered.

"Why me? Why do I have to be the bad guy?" he asked.

"Well, I can't do it." I responded. "Every time I see him, all he talks about is going back to work with you. By the way, what is he doing?"

"He's working on the social outreach program where we're trying to show our members that not all white guys are assholes." Big Brother said with a huge guffaw that put a smile on my face.

"Well most aren't," I responded.

My best friend countered, "At the same time, your son is getting a lesson in racial prejudice and how it can affect how a person perceives the world."

"Is it helping him?" I asked.

"Yes, very much so," Rodney answered in a very serious tone.

I always thought having a mixed-race mother would have taught him something about how people judge others until I realized he grew up in a white bread world and only identified with those of the same socio-economic class.

"Good old ethnocentrism!" Rodney responded.

"Do you want me to talk to him?" I asked.

"About what? About not falling in love with my daughter, when she's falling in love with him? About understanding minorities and tolerance? What can you teach these kids?"

"About what our parents taught us?" I asked, to which we both said in unison. Nothing!"

We needed to cool things down and Peter needed help at the farm. I called Peter and outlined what was transpiring and requested that he call 'V' and tell him he was needed for a two-week project in Waldwick. I knew 'V' wouldn't like it, but there was no other way to expand 'V's perspective on what we were working on.

Peter called back about an hour later and said that 'V' would come home on Friday and report to Waldwick on Monday. I asked if there was any complaining and Peter said, "No", noting that 'V' agreed he needed to work there for a better understanding of the social issues involved in our project and not just the Ho-Chunk. Now I was worried that he and Amelia were having problems.

I felt like I couldn't win! First, I worried that the twosome was getting too close and then I worried that they weren't close enough. I said to myself 'Come on 'Q' stop micromanaging.' Little did I know that Rodney had talked with Amelia and indicated he thought things were getting a little too hot and heavy, too fast and the two of them needed to come up for air. The Big man said his Amelia wasn't very happy with the observation, but understood. Ahh! Parenthood!

Soul:

Mary had both Aristotle and Francis doing multiple tasks in a few weeks as she was preparing them for the eventual incision. Both buys had been exposed to the 'checkerboard', as we began to call the sixteen-square board they would use to communicate. While the idea was to get them ready to communicate, Mary believed that hooking up the checkerboard first and seeing if she could get answers before the implant might speed up the post-operative learning cycle.

Slowly Francis was being accustomed to stepping on the different squares and receiving a treat. At first, his reward came with each square pushed, then Mary began to make it more complex in that Francis needed to step on two squares to get a treat and then in the proper sequence. Mary said Francis was one smart pig and it wasn't long until she had him identifying different objects that were printed on the squares with numbers in the corner. The objects were for Francis, while the numbers were for the MadCity Boys, as they needed to program the different permutations to create specific words.

After testing the images, the group realized that they were doing it all wrong and changed the images to different scents thereby adapting the grid to the pig's greatest asset, their sense of smell. Mary determined that even though they changed the location of the scents, both Aristotle and Francis would go to the correct scent combination time-after-time.

I walked by the compound and watched Mary through the one-way glass, working first with Francis and then Aristotle. She had the patience of a saint! As the training session ended, I stuck my head in the door and applauded.

"I didn't know anyone was there," Mary said.

"I didn't want to interrupt," I responded.

"There's something I'd like to show you." Mary said and went and opened the gate and allowed Francis back into the training room.

"What is your name?" Mary asked.

Francis went to the checkerboard and pressed 1-1 and the word "Francis" was spoken by the Hawking Talking machine.

"Who is your best friend?" Mary asked to which Francis pressed 1-2 and the word "Aristotle" was spoken.

"Who am I?" Mary asked.

Francis pressed 1-3 and "Mary" was spoken.

I stood mystified. Francis knew his own name, who Aristotle was, not only by name but emotional bond and Mary's name. He had a self-concept.

"One more," Mary said, turning to Francis and asking. "What is your favorite thing?"

Francis stepped on 1-4 and the word "blanket" was spoken, as I shook my head in disbelief.

"Why Francis? Why your blanket?"

Francis stepped on 8-6 and the speaker said. "Warm".

My God, Francis not only knew people and objects, but was beginning to learn adjectives as well.

"Where is your father, Francis?" Mary asked.

12-12 was stepped on and the word "Heaven" was spoken.

How did Francis know about heaven? Was it just a guess? My God, were we doing ethical things? My mind was in a tizzy.

"Mary, can you train Francis to walk on a leash?" I asked.

"Sure, why not?" Mary replied.

"How long will it take?" I asked.

"Can I have a week?" she inquired.

"Sure" I replied.

One week later, I went back to the farm and Mary hooked Francis into a collar.

"Francis, would you like to go for a walk?" I asked.

Francis let out a squeal and ran to the opposite end of the training area where he relieved himself. Mary was shocked! He had never acted like this before.

I stood in disbelief, as Mary attempted to coax Francis out of his fear.

"Come on little buddy. What's wrong?" Mary asked.

Francis looked at her and snorted. Mary put the leash on and began pulling him towards me. Instead, Francis broke loose and went to the checkerboard and began punching 12-12, 12-12, 12-12. A concerned look came over Mary's face.

Francis was typing, "Heaven. Heaven. Heaven".

"My God he thinks you're going to take him to be slaughtered" Mary concluded.

"Oh my God!" I said, and continued speaking directly to Francis. "No little buddy, I want to take you for a walk into The Forest. No one's going to hurt you!"

There was real concern in my eyes. Was I setting all that Mary had accomplished back, when time was so critical?

I looked at Mary and asked if she would come along. She agreed, as Mary was the only one Francis really trusted.

We put the leash on the profoundly-scared Francis and walked out the back door. Other than his outdoor pen, Francis hadn't been outside in over six months, nor away from Aristotle. At first, Francis was reluctant and then, when we reached the loading chute, he froze. It was as if he was visiting the scene of an accident, where loved ones had been killed. I let him pause and watched as his ears flattened and his head dipped. I sincerely believe he was saying a prayer for the departed and it made me feel profoundly guilty.

After what seemed like an eternity and Francis' realization he wasn't going 'up the chute', he began to relax. The further we walked, the more relaxed he was becoming, as he was beginning to enjoy the outdoors and the sunshine and was becoming his old self again.

Slowly, we made our way to The Forest allowing Francis to explore the route. When we got to where the old apples trees were, we knew there would be no stopping him as Francis made a bee-line for the fallen apples. Mary and I sat and watched him eat for a while and then Mary said, "Francis, you're making a pig out of yourself."

We coaxed Francis - actually pulled him - out of the orchard and continued our walk to The Forest. We must have been quite the sight, two humans with a pig on a leash. As we entered The Forest, Francis stopped and raised his snout in the air and let out a loud grunt and began pulling Mary toward the clearing where Great Grandfather's obelisk stood.

Mary had never been to The Forest and so I explained its importance, as we quick-paced our way to the obelisk. Francis stopped at the monument and raised his head to the sky and, by God, it looked as if he was smiling. He stood for a moment and we watched his entire body quake.

The three of us were so mesmerized I hadn't noticed. In the distance 'he' was there. The big buck stood and looked at us and nodded in the affirmative. I got the chills. My God, it was Grandfather's way of indicating his approval of Francis and what we were doing.

Francis rubbed his jaw against the obelisk. Mary attempted to pull him back but I shook my head 'no' and then did something she never expected - I released the leash from Francis collar. Francis turned and looked at me and there were tears in his eyes. Mary had informed me that pigs cry real tears when they are hurt or grieving, but this was totally different. Like their distant cousins, the elephant, pigs don't forget things, events, or people, but I wondered about the transfer of thoughts and emotions. Was Francis receiving the pain and misery I had, when I met with Great Grandfather? Mary read that pet pigs can grieve themselves into death, but we were seeing much more than that. I believed we were seeing the transfer of Great Grandfather's soul into Francis and stood in awe.

We were frozen in time, watching Francis at the obelisk. Then the spell was over. Francis looked at Mary and me and began slowly walking down the path. Mary wanted to stop him, but I shook my head 'no'. I already knew where he was going.

Francis walked slowly and carefully, all thirty yards to the springs as if on hallowed grounds. He never stopped and never looked back. As we approached the rocks where the water cascaded from the ground, Francis let out a loud squeal and dipped his mouth in the cold, clear water and raised his head towards the sky. It was then he looked back at Mary and, once again, we saw tears in his eyes.

Mary was one of those who didn't feel the effects of The Forest and I felt sorry for her. The sensations I got, were always of such magnitude as to cleanse my soul and refresh my spirit. The gleam of the old tin cup caught Francis' eye and I thought he wanted to play. Instead, our little porcine friend picked the cup up with his mouth and brought it to Mary, dropping it at her feet. Mary looked at me and I nodded. Francis wanted her to drink the water. Francis was telling her to join him - be baptized in its purity.

Mary took the cup and dipped it in the water and as she drank the clear, clean liquid, I could see the change come over her. I was witness to her baptism and confirmation! I stood in awe as this woman became one of us, affected by the purity that surrounded us. Tears welled in her eyes as her head tilted towards the light blue Wisconsin summer sky.

Mary set the cup down and Francis picked it up and dropped it at my feet. Francis was telling me to do the same. I dipped the cup in the water and took a swallow. As the cold water entered my body, I realized that God was with us.

I reached down and petted Francis. His head turned and compressed my hand between his head and my leg. This was his way of telling me, 'Thank you' for allowing him to come to The Forest and be saved.

Slowly, normalcy returned and Mary looked at me in wonder.

"Did you know this was going to happen?" she asked.

I shook my head, "no" but deep within my soul I had a feeling something profound was going to transpire.

We slowly began our walk back towards the compound. Mary wanted to put the leash on Francis. I told her it wasn't necessary, he would know the way. Just like my dog, Jake, who had been one of the loves of my life, never needed a leash, I knew that

Francis was the same. We bonded and would carry that special friendship for the rest of our lives.

As we arrived at the training center, Francis waited for the gate to be opened and walked in and nuzzled Aristotle as if to say, "It's OK! We're amongst friends." Mary inquired whether we should take Aristotle to The Forest, but I already knew it wouldn't be the same. The power and glory of Great Grandfather had already been transferred and Aristotle would never sense the emotions that Francis had received.

I thought the day was over. I couldn't have been more wrong!

After the trip, I had concluded that Francis would take his blanket and take a nap. Instead, he went to the checkerboard and began punching keys. The MadCity Boys had installed a permutation recorder that translated the digits into words and the words into sentences, if it all made sense. What I saw will never leave me. What I felt cannot be completely shared. The guilt still pervades my soul.

Pressing on the keys, the screen came alive and Francis began writing. "Francis went to meet his father, but he was not there. Francis went to where the stone (obelisk) sticks from the ground and a human with white eyes appeared. Francis was afraid, but the human with white eyes only smiled and made Francis feel life. The human spoke to Francis and told Francis that many people were happy and his heart should be filled with joy."

"The human with the white eyes, told Francis that George the First, Elizabeth, Sarah, Henry, Baby Henry and Morning Star were at peace and said that Old Ed and Jake play together and Old Ed eats apples and mom, dad and Dr. Williams are looking down upon life with joy in their hearts."

By his actions, you could tell that Francis was getting tired. He looked up at Mary and then at me and typed a few more words. "The human with the white eyes said 'all living beings have a soul' and to say, 'Little Spirit, the time has come.'"

I sat with Mary and told her about Great Grandfather. I shared with her all the times we met and how he had spoken to me and how my mind was filled with the sadness and turmoil my Indian brothers had suffered. It seemed crazy and yet, I now believed those thoughts, emotions and recollections had been shared with another and it wasn't a human, it was Francis the pig.

When I was done, I walked out of the compound stunned. God had sent me a message that all living beings have a soul and it was our responsibility to nurture and protect that soul at all costs. I had never been much of an environmentalist until that day. Yet, I saw with my own eyes that humans were not alone and we needed to do everything we could to protect those who can't protect themselves.

I stood for a moment to reflect on what had transpired and thanked God for the few moments of respite before the pressures of the day bore down upon me again. The Duke was fading and we needed to move at a faster pace. The boys told me that what he was losing could not be restored. All the chip would do was stop the degradation and not retrieve what had been lost. We weren't ready! Yet, I didn't know if we ever would be. My God! The pressure pounded in my head as I looked skyward for any sort of sign that we were traveling down the right path.

<u>Good News:</u>

Wisconsin is home to eleven federally recognized Native American tribes: Bad River Band of Lake Superior Chippewa, Ho-Chunk Nation, Lac Courte Oreilles Band of Lake Superior Chippewa, Lac du Flambeau Band of Lake Superior Chippewa, Menominee Tribe of Wisconsin, plus the Oneida Nation, Forest County Potawatomi, and the Red Cliff Band of Lake Superior. Normally, they function as independent nations, yet periodically, they would come together to discuss issues common to all such as the medical and social challenges, government intervention, education or finances.

The work 'V" and Amelia were doing was showing demonstrable increases in every possible venue and Rodney had asked 'V' if he would possibly speak at the next roundtable and 'V' agreed to do it. Not being there, I can only imagine what transpired. What I can share are the results reported to me by Big Brother who indicated that 'V' had mesmerized the leaders until they had tears in their eyes and received a standing ovation when he was done. The coalition was so moved by the speech and also by the progress reported, that they asked if it could be standardized and implemented throughout all eleven nations. So my son became somewhat of an ambassador who traveled with Amelia to the different communities to assist in setting up the social program they had developed.

As the program was implemented, word spread to other communities, not only within the Native American realm, but within the State. What started out as a youth program to help establish personal pride, reduce drug use and minimize violence had gained momentum until city mayors began contacting 'V' to see if his program would work with other minorities. It wasn't long until Amelia and 'V' were deeply involved with African-American and Hispanic groups throughout Wisconsin and with each other, I might add.

One day, the phone rang and it was ABC news calling. They wanted to do a piece on the pride program as a feel-good segment on the Nightly News. While 'V' and Amelia weren't in it for the notoriety, it was agreed that it might help extend the program beyond their realm and help others throughout the country. The camera crew arrived and within a few minutes, they, too, were mesmerized by the dynamism of 'V' as they recorded the interview and then experienced one of his speeches.

A few days after the article was broadcast, the telephone rang again and it was CBS who said they wanted to do a segment for 60 Minutes. The crew arrived and the same results transpired. 'V' had taken a somewhat indifferent set of newscasters and made them feel the passion he carried with him as he shared the story and the steps he and Amelia were taking to create a group of young men and women who had been lost and given them direction. He noted that, subsequent to attending the sessions, not a single individual had been incarcerated and a great majority, who had never finished high school had not only received their G.E.D., but in many cases, were attending either a community college or university.

The days were long! The amount of travel incredible and yet 'V' and Amelia were working as a team that was making Wisconsin a better place to live for everyone. While never mentioned, word spread that these two were not paid and covered their own expenses. With that knowledge, they stopped staying in hotels as people opened their homes and welcomed them to stay there as honored guests.

A few months after the media hype had cooled, Ceclia came into my office with a huge smile on her face.

"There's someone on the phone who wants to say 'hi', was all she said.

It was the Governor! "George, I just called to personally commend your group for what you have instituted with both the HoChunk Nation and your foundation. I was attending a session with several of the State's mayors who explained all that your son and Amelia Whitehorse had done and how, through their efforts people who once had nothing, now have something to look forward to and the profound changes in attitude and behavior they have created."

"Thank you, Governor," I replied.

The Governor continued, "I would also like to inform you that both George and Amelia have been chosen to represent your foundation and receive the State Medal of Honor for acts of courage and self-sacrifice based on service to others."

"I am also pleased to inform you that both will represent your foundation as candidates for the national Citizen Honor award as well. I'm not certain you're aware George, but each year a nationwide search is conducted which selects five US citizens and one organization to receive the national awards. The honorees are chosen by and receive the award from, living members of the Congressional Medal of Honor Society."

I was in tears. The kid, I threatened to disown, had become a man of honor.

The Governor added. "Members of the Congressional Medal of Honor Society have all received the recognition for their acts of valor performed during wartime. They are the ones who will review the credentials of the State recipients and choose this year's winner and present the Citizen Honors Award to those who are showing courage and dedicating themselves to service here at home."

"I wish we could have all your team recognized, but the awards are limited to just two people and there is no guarantee that George and Amelia will be chosen. However, to be held in such high esteem, is an honor itself."

"George, this is the highest civilian honor we have and I don't ever remember it being nominated to men as young as your son and a member of an Indian nation."

"Thank you, Governor," I politely said.

"No, thank you George, for your institution's dedication and commitment to the betterment of the citizens of Wisconsin. We have decided to have a special plaque made for you to hang in your offices that commemorates all that the Derrick Williams Foundation is doing. When it is completed, I would like the honor of presenting it to your team personally, if you don't mind. Please let them know we are grateful for their efforts and achievements."

"Thank you, sir. However, we cannot take all of the credit and I will only accept the recognition for our foundation after you have presented the same recognition to the eleven Native American nations, as they are the ones whose idea it was to go beyond their realm and include other minorities with whom we are sharing the costs of the endeavor."

"George, I cannot say how impressed I am with the generosity you are showing concerning the well-deserved recognition. I will try to make plans to visit the different nations myself to make the presentation or have someone represent me there."

"Governor, I sincerely believe that it is important that you personally make the presentations to all groups as a sign of respect. To that end, I would like to offer to have 'V' and Amelia go with you and use one of Wilco's helicopters to make the trips as efficient as possible, as I know your time is valuable. I also believe that making a personal statement to all the different nations will go a long way to showing them that you really care."

With that, the conversation was over. I sighed a deep sigh and smiled a broad smile as Ceclia walked in the room. I didn't need to say a word. She knew it was a pleasant conversation. I looked at her and simply said. "The Governor called to tell me to thank all the members of our team and so, Cecelia, I say thank you to you!"

With the satisfaction of a cat who ate a bird, I leaned back and wondered, how do you tell my wife what her kid just did? My only regret was not being able to explain to his grandpa that all we hoped could happen was only a small part of the dignity and grace that our son had achieved. How do I share the news with Great Grandfather that Two Feathers was already becoming the great warrior Great Grandfather knew he would become? All I knew is that everyone, and I mean everyone, would be proud. My son, potential recipient of the Citizen's Honor Award. My God!

Aristotle:

With everything going on, it seemed the time had come to see if all the aspects of what the boys had been working on for nearly three years actually worked in conjunction with each other.

Peter consulted with Mary and Dr. Harris, the vet. A timetable was developed to make certain that Aristotle was in peak physical shape which meant no illnesses and maximum nutrition. While the procedure had been simplified and practiced dozens of times, they wanted to make certain that the risk factor was zero.

For the seven days leading up to surgery, Aristotle was placed on a high protein diet consisting of all his favorite foods. As 'D' day arrived, the 'surgical area' was scrubbed one last time and all outside exposure was reduced. The primary nanosphere that was going to be inserted had been programmed with a combination of the entire English language and basic knowledge of math, science and philosophy due to the belief that simply adding language wouldn't allow for its maximization and we could see whether the chip worked or not.

It had been months since Aristotle had been anywhere expect the training facility and he appeared somewhat confused and then excited to have a different environment to explore. Mary allowed him to walk around and get comfortable and brought his blanket so that he felt secure.

Dr. Harris was to be assisted by Mary and Hsu and all three were in surgical attire. The insertion was scheduled for 10:00 AM and the entire research team congregated to watch the procedure while we broadcast it globally to all the team members who had been part of the process. Quite honestly, it was a lot like watching paint dry in terms of excitement as we all knew what steps were being taken and how slow the process would be. However, we were still excited to see the fruition of our labor, as were all the researchers around the world who had contributed so much to this event.

The night before, Aristotle had been given a bowl of his favorite meal that had been laced with just the right amount of sedative and, of course, he made a pig of himself. When it was time for the sedative, he was as mellow as possible and the injection went without incident. A few minutes later, with what appeared to be a smile of contentment on his face, he simply lay down and fell into a deep sleep. At this point, he was lifted onto the surgical table and his head was affixed with Simoni and the Headlock.

I guess everyone thought the pre-insertion speed could have been a little faster, but we were told that having an increased speed would increase the probability of errors and so we watched as the laser got closer and closer and closer to the back of Aristotle's skull.

As Simoni reached the tiny spot on the back of Aristotle's head, the monitors came on and we began seeing images of the process as it happened. All of Aristotle's vitals were projected on the bottom of the screen and everything was going as planned. For the next two hours, we watched as Simoni slowly made her way into Aristotle's brain and placed the nanosphere in precisely the pre-determined spot.

As Simoni was making her way out of Aristotle's head and cauterizing the incision, we watched as the process concluded. I looked at Peter and said, "Now what?"

"We wait" was the answer.

"For what?"

"The sedative to wear off."

"How long?" I impatiently asked.

"Dr. Harris thought it would be between one and two hours until he wakes up, but not until tomorrow until he is lucid."

The question then became, do we sit and watch a pig sleep for two hours or go do some work? It was decided that we could go back to the research center and SIMON would contact us with any changes.

A little over 90 minutes later SIMON announced that Aristotle was coming out of the sedative. We all rushed back to the operating room to see Aristotle still sleeping and then beginning to move. It was funny watching his eyes open and then close and, with each minute, regain a little more lucidity. I can only imagine what was going on in Aristotle's head, 'what in hell happened?' The sedative had really whacked him a good one him as he was both weak and quite sickly. I was assured it was the medication and that he would be back to being himself in a matter of hours.

When Aristotle attempted to get up and realized he was tethered to the operating table, he appeared confused and yet, with each passing moment, he was becoming more alert and attuned to where he was. Mary began stroking his head and scratching behind his ears and there seemed to be a smile on his face.

After what seemed like an eternity, he was 'back' and the boys lifted him down and Aristotle sort of wobbled, grabbing his blanket to make certain it was still there. Spotting a corner, Aristotle went and lay down. He was going to sleep and wanted someplace where he felt secure. The boys had put a remote collar on him that broadcast his vitals and so we felt confident everything was going to be all right.

Dr. Harris came in and noted that Aristotle would be groggy for the rest of the day and the doctor wanted him sequestered until he was 'back to normal'.

"In other words, tomorrow?" I inquired.

Dr. Harris nodded in the affirmative.

With so much going on, I opted out and told the boys to contact me if there were any major developments. One of Dennis's pilots had been on call and the chopper arrived in twenty minutes to take me home.

A little less than an hour later, I walked in the house and Amy asked how the day went. My response was, "I don't know, surgically, everything went as planned. Now all we need do is wait to see if the Nanosphere has made any changes." Little did I understand the magnitude of what was about to take place.

Pandemonium:

At 5:30 the next morning, the phone rang and it was Peter. "George, we've got a problem!"

"What?" I thought as the probabilities ran through my head. Bleeding? Paralysis? Death?

"Aristotle has gone berserk!"

"What do you mean?" I shuddered.

"He's gotten really aggressive and attempted to bite Dr. Harris and Mary."

"What?" I asked incredulously.

"He's so wound up, they had to give him a sedative to calm him down."

'Shit!' I thought to myself and asked, "Do I need to come down there?" I knew there was absolutely nothing I could do.

"Not really!" But I thought you should know.

"Thanks! Call me if there is any change."

Around two the phone rang again and it was Peter. "George, they got him calmed down."

Whew! Is he back with Francis?

"Not yet! He's still really agitated and they don't want to make too many changes too fast."

"Makes sense! Keep me in the loop."

At five, the phone rang again. "George, they're afraid Aristotle has had a nervous breakdown."

"What?"

"He's acting really strange - very aggressive - and attacking anything and everything."

"Now what?"

"They don't know if it's temporary or permanent and they've called Dr. Maas to ask for his assistance. Dennis is having him picked up and he's coming right away."

So much for our cover. I thought.

At nine that night the phone rang again. "George, Aristotle seems to be calming down. Dr. Maas recommended getting him back in his area, but removing Francis for safety reasons. He said that agitated pigs are very unpredictable and he's concerned that Aristotle might attack Francis."

A few minutes later the phone rang again. It was Mary informing me they had transferred Francis out of the lab. He was spending the night with Tommie and Hsu, sleeping on their screen porch, which brought back memories of my Jake, who I could actually envision the two little buddies snuggling and enjoying life.

I realized that sleep would not come and so I packed a change of clothes, got in my truck and drove to Waldwick, calling Mary and Peter on the way. Amy understood.

Arriving just after midnight, I went to the lab and it was a disheveled mess. Anything that wasn't bolted down had been tipped over and there was pig poop in the middle of the floor. I looked at Mary and saw the forlorn look on her face. I'm certain she felt that this was her problem.

I did something I'd never done before, I hugged her. "It's not your fault! It's not!" I whispered.

"I'm so sorry!" was all she could say.

"Again, it's not your fault!"

I took a deep breath and inquired about what all had transpired. Mary outlined the day and the transfer and the aggression. I asked about the verbal matrix and Peter indicated the day had simply been too chaotic to even try.

"Let's try," I suggested.

Mary was concerned about entering the lab with a crazy pig and so I told one of the assistants to go to the barn and get a cattle prod. If Aristotle was going crazy, at least Mary had some form of protection.

We all took a deep breath as we watched from behind the one-way glass and slowly exhaled as Mary opened the door and walked into the maelstrom.

"Aristotle, what's the problem?" Mary inquired in a soft, gentle voice.

Dr. Maas appeared and saw the mess and was filled in on what was going on from the initial training - to the surgery - to the disaster and responded. "In general, while you simplified the procedure, you must realize and accept that a process may have numerous causes, which are also said to be *causal factors* that may lie in the pig's past. Subsequent to this, an effect can itself turn into a causal factor for many other effects, which will all lie in the future."

Maas was beyond our realm and I was both impressed and afraid as he continued. "As an example, placement of the primary nanosphere in Aristotle's brain constituted the cause, where the effect has been an expansion of not only his mental capabilities, but potentially his ability to take the concepts and create new and different thought processes that are leading to a myriad of patterns heretofore impeded."

Mary just stood as we all watched Aristotle challenge her without any violence as Dr. Maas continued explaining to me. "If it was your intent to determine if you could transcend the communication barrier, I think you have a totally different set of problems in that you have upset the normal intellectual, emotional and social balance that existed in Aristotle. The consequence is that Aristotle is both reticent and angry and perhaps feeling as if you have been demeaning, degrading and now, quite honestly, somewhat below his level of intellect."

Maas paused for a moment and continued. "You must realize that changing one event or process may contribute to the production of another event or process where the cause is partly responsible for the effect and the effect is partly dependent on the cause. When you do this, there is a high probability that the logical pattern of cause-and-effect can be changed and can have serious consequences."

Peter looked at me and simply shrugged his shoulders. He was both profoundly impressed and incredibly scared. Had we created a monster as Aristotle began punching the keys on the keyboard, but nothing made sense.

Maas continued. "While you have attempted to increase the communication capability of Aristotle, in fact, you have over-stimulated his brain and the neural responses, as such and he has had a traumatic experience that led to a mental breakdown."

I looked at Peter and he at me as Maas concluded, "it is my belief that Aristotle has gone insane."

Until the last comment, I had no idea what Maas said. I knew we had a problem and looked at Peter and shook my head as Peter whispered. "We've opened Pandora's box and there's only one way to dig deep enough and that would be to re-program the chip for the next insertion."

"What about Aristotle?" I asked. Peter took a deep breath and closed his eyes. He was in deep thought before looking up at me while shaking his head and shrugging his shoulders, saying. "Let's see what happens."

A few days later Mary called with the news. Aristotle continued completely out of control and had intentionally rammed his head into the concrete wall and died.

"In other words, suicide?" I inquired.

"Yes," was the response. "My God!" was the reply.

Aristotle was buried in our family plot next to my little buddy, Jake.

The Ticking Clock:

We knew that we were running short on time to save The Duke. Each day, some more of his memories were being lost and soon, it wouldn't matter if the chip was perfect as there wouldn't be anything to harvest. We also felt that the situation with Aristotle meant that the system needed a software change, but still might work. I called the boys together and asked them if they were ready to implant the chip in The Duke which got a very concerned response about everything from programming, to the medical aspect, to the consequences such as those we saw in Aristotle. The final question became, was it legal? Were we following federal guidelines concerning FDA approval?

After all the issues in the past, I knew that government delays and paperwork would mean that by the time we were ready for the implant, The Duke would be so far gone there wouldn't be much to harvest. I felt we needed to act fast and inquired theoretically about moving Simoni and the Head Lock to Hochunk land to see if that couldn't provide some protection from federal law. I sent an encrypted note to our Atlanta lawyers knowing that all of our email was being intercepted and I didn't want the Wilco legal, and especially Derrick, to have knowledge of or participation in what I felt needed to be done.

Two days later, I received the following letter via certified mail.

Dear Mr. Terrill:

The following summary reflects our opinion regarding the rights of Native Americans pursuant with contemporary federal laws.

The original inhabitants of North America quickly became a minority as European settlers arrived and treated them as hostile foreigners in their own land, where they were eventually rounded up and sent to reservations and done so against their free will. Eventually, these abuses mitigated and Native Americans were granted rights and citizenship like other Americans. However, the Native Americans also retained their own unique cultures and national identities, which had been forcefully taken from them instead of given up freely, as part of the acculturation process of European immigrants.

In recognition of this fact, the United States government created a unique status for American Indian tribes, recognizing them as sovereign nations, while still existing under the laws of the U.S. government and the state in which the tribal nation is located. In so doing, they are considered "domestic dependent nations," retaining certain elements of tribal sovereignty, while still remaining subordinate to the U.S. and state governments.

"Tribal sovereignty" was granted consisting primarily of the right of a tribal nation to limited self-government by defining its own membership, managing tribal property and regulating tribal business and domestic relations. It also refers to the recognition by the US government of a governmental body that affords it the freedom to carry on relations related to the rights and interests of its people. In turn, the federal government has certain "special trust obligations" to protect tribal lands and resources, the right to self-government and to provide services necessary for tribal survival and advancement, thereby creating a very unique situation for Native Americans who are both beholden to the U.S. government and independent of it.

This status exists because Native Americans are subject to many of the same social and economic problems as other victims of long-term bigotry and discrimination in the United States, where Native Americans suffer disproportionately high rates of poverty, infant mortality, unemployment and high school dropout rates. But beyond attempting to level the playing field, these federal laws are also geared toward preserving Native American culture, including passing on traditional religious beliefs, languages and social practices without fear of discrimination.

As a result, reservation areas and tribal lands are often subject to the varying jurisdictional laws of the tribes that own or control them, such as allowing for Casinos and their own police forces. While still treated as indigenous Americans, their unique struggles since the arrival of European settlers has entitled them to certain accommodations in order to restore their sovereignty, preserve their culture, and grant them a better chance at equal opportunity.

The FDA considers Indian Reservations to be possessions of the United States within the meaning of section 201(a)(2) of the Federal Food, Drug, and Cosmetic Act. Consequently, FDA has complete jurisdiction over products within the purview of the Act that are manufactured on an Indian reservation. The products are in interstate commerce within the meaning of section 201(b) of the Act at all times. However, whereas no product is being developed, sold or transported from Indian land, it is our opinion that the acts within the confines of the land are not limited by those applicable to non-Indian property.

J. Ronald Perkins

Based on the letter, I called Rodney and tried to outline what all was going on. After the problems we'd experienced with the NSA and their 'concern' over all the data we had that we refused to give to them, I always felt as if we were being watched or at least listened to and that the data collected or transmitted by SIMON was being intercepted. Information relayed to Big Brother, who was my best friend, regarding my concerns about Big Brother in Washington, required that we spoke in code.

Whereas the HoChunk were part owners of The Forest, my initial thought was that because the land was part of their splintered Wisconsin reservation, it would therefore be a place where we could perform the chip implant without legal consequence. To ensure secrecy, I called it an engagement party, as if referring to 'V' and Amelia.

Rodney responded by stating he was concerned with modifications to The Forest in terms of creating a spot where the 'party' could take place. Instead, he offered the use of facilities – namely their clinic - in the Dells, which put a smile on my face. We both knew we were sitting on the edge of legality, but I also felt that any delay was worth the risk both medically and legally.

The legal part dealt with not only not having FDA approval, but taking a non-Indian and doing the procedure on Indian land. So far, our conversations were innocuous and generalized as we both feared the government was listening. With so many calls between the two of us regarding 'V' and his Amelia, we hoped no one would be suspect of the real reason concerning yet another call.

A few minutes later, I got a text from an unknown number. It was Rodney asking how sophisticated SIMON was. My mind was spinning. Why would he want to know that?

Instead of e-mail or a text that could be traced, I wrote and told him that we needed to 'talk about the kids' and I would call him at exactly 10:00 AM the next day. In the meantime, I purchased a burner phone and awaited for the time to call.

The next morning at exactly 10:00, I called the number and found out it was his administrative assistant's phone. After the normal pleasantries, Rodney asked what SIMON could do. I replied, virtually anything.

"Could he break into Ancestry.com?" Rodney inquired.

"Sure," I replied.

"Great! If we're going to have the engagement party and its reserved only for members of the Hochunk nation, The Duke is going to need some Indian blood in him."

I smiled and thought that this dude had it all figured out asking, "How much blood does he need?' referring to generational splits.

Rodney, being his normal affable self said, just enough to get him into the tribe, but not so much that he will be hungry for possum and rattle snake, referring back to when we were roommates.

The conversation ended and on my way home, I stopped at The Five O'Clock Club, walked down the hill to their pier and inadvertently dropped the burner phone with the SIM card removed, into the lake. 'Oh my, the evidence is gone'!

The next day, I drove to Madison where Peter and I had lunch. I explained what was going on and asked him to program SIMON to break into Ancestry.com and replace one of The Duke's grandmothers with an Indian name, which would thereby make him twenty-five percent Hochunk.

Peter shrugged and smiled and said, "Consider it done!"

That night, in less than fifteen seconds, SIMON scanned our medical records for an unused name and entered the Ancestry database, adding the name Morning Star Two Feathers as The Duke's maternal grandmother, denoting that she had never married his real grandfather so that his mother was born out of wedlock. Whereas The Duke never knew his real father and his mother was long gone, there would be no way for anyone to double check in case the situation arose. Over breakfast the next morning, I shared the results with Amy and asked her how it felt to now be part Native American. She just smiled and then laughed and went 'Woo! Woo! Woo!' as if on the warpath.

Two days later, a letter was delivered with the formal application for membership into the Hochunk nation in it. With 'V' planning on working in Black River Falls the next week, we completed the document and he hand-carried it, giving it to Rodney. In less than one week, The Duke became one-fourth Native American and therefore a recognized citizen of the Hochunk Nation.

The Duke's 'citizenship' provided access to the clinic. Now all we needed to do was transfer Simoni and the Headlock, get the chip ready, convince The Duke to go to the Dells, sneak in one of the examining rooms, install the chip, wait for the sedative to wear off and see what happened. That's all! That's all? Holy shit!

I sent Amelia IX and Rodney flew to Madison and we met, sitting at the State Street entrance to the Capitol, eating our Teddywedgers. The leaves had turned and it was a bit chilly to be eating pasty on the capitol steps. Yet, it was always good to see him.

"Nice ride," he commented.

"Thanks! Quiet." I said

We talked about 'V' and Rodney and Ann's Amelia that we were calling the love birds and I told him that 'V' was thinking about popping the question.

"What if I say no?" Rodney inquired.

"Do you remember the last time your ancestors were 'asked' to leave the State?"

A huge guffaw emanated from my best friend as he looked at me and simply shook his head and mumbled 'touché' to which I put an elbow in his ribs and smiled.

We discussed logistics and how to get The Duke settled. He was slipping fast and the thought was to have him admitted under an alias. No one in the Dells had a clue who he actually was and so we could clandestinely admit him, allow him to settle in and then perform the procedure.

The name George Carlson was agreed to for some unknown reason and Rodney called back to his office and directed his administrative assistant to clear a room for Mr. Carlson at the center. With that, it was done. We finished our pasties and both stood, never noticing the man on the roof of the Teddywedger's building with the camera and long angle lens.

Arrangements were made to take The Duke to the Dells by car. The windows were tinted and the Chevy looked like every other car on the road. When they arrived, The Duke was taken to

Great Grandfather's old room. After he was settled, the security detail began their twenty-four-hour watch. Dressed as orderlies, no one except the general manager suspected anything, and all the manager knew was that whomever Mr. Carlson was, he was important.

After three days, our physicians were flown in and examined The Duke to make sure he was comfortable and healthy. The Neurologist gave one final exam and deemed The Duke stable enough for the procedure.

The following day, four men in HVAC uniforms scoured the facility to check on the heating and ventilation, bringing with them a cart loaded with equipment marked air conditioner compressors. Room number four was selected and the lock on the door was changed. Inside, lights were added, an operating table was assembled and seismic sensors put in place. One slight tremor could be fatal.

For the next twenty-four hours, the room was guarded and constant surveillance of the seismic meter took place. With no vibrations, it was determined that the room was secure and Simoni and the Headlock calibrated.

Like all nursing homes, it got real quiet a little after eight when the medical team arrived. Dressed as locals, no one would have guessed that they were some of the greatest brains in Wisconsin. At nine, The Duke was given a sedative and within five minutes was sound asleep. Quietly, he was rolled into room four and the door locked as the team positioned a portable MRI and then Simoni and connected the 5G transmitter so that SIMON could take over.

At ten, the process began, the chip was loaded and slowly began its progression towards the back of The Duke's skull. It took nearly thirty minutes before it reached the point of incision and then another thirty to reach the selected spot in The Duke's hippocampus. As the minutes ticked away, Amy and I watched from home, holding each other's hand, waiting, hoping, praying that the procedure would be a success.

A whispered voice announced that the implant was in place and the insertion rod was cauterizing its exit. We breathed a sigh of relief when the end of the rod appeared and the incision sealed. No stitches! No bandage! Nothing more than a tiny one-eighth inch red line on the back of The Duke's neck at the base of his skull.

Quietly, Simoni was shut down and The Duke was returned to Great Grandfather's former bed. The boys packed up all the equipment and changed into technician clothes. The night 'guard' was the anesthesiologist who kept track of The Duke's vitals as the rest of the crew got into their vans and headed home. As they neared the Wisconsin River, the vans stopped and peeled the decals off the sides of the vans, placing them in a weighted canvas bag that was conveniently dropped into the waters below. The vans hit the merger of I-90 and I-39 and split up – one to Milwaukee, one to Madison and one to Mineral Point.

As the night progressed we wondered if what we had done was the right thing to do. We had risked The Duke's life in an attempt to provide a little more quality time with us. Were we being selfish? Were we being cruel to a man who had given us so much? We didn't know. For the first time in a very long time, I opened the Bible and read Romans 14:8 - *For if we live, we live to the Lord, and if we die, we die to the Lord. So then, whether we live or whether we die, we are the Lord's.*

Amy and I fell asleep on the couch and when the phone rang it was nearly sunrise. On the other end was a familiar voice, "Where in hell am I and when can I come home?" I looked at Amy and she at me and we both wept for joy. The Duke had survived!

"Dad, you were having a rough night and we thought it best you get checked out. They kept you overnight just to make sure."

"I'm hungry, when do these people eat around here?"

I smiled at Amy and said, "Your dad's hungry," to which I received a reflective grin.

It had been agreed that he should stay another day, just to make sure and so arrangements were made to have one of his male nurses work a shift and play cribbage with him. The nurse reported that The Duke whipped his ass every game and was more alert than he ever seen him. This obviously put joy in our hearts.

The next day, the entourage, headed by Dennis, was scheduled to pick up The Duke and bring him home. He wanted nothing to do with a wheelchair and walked out the door. The last person leaving was one of The Duke's security personnel who handed the manager an envelope with $10,000 inside as our token of appreciation, also to make certain that what happened stayed within the group who knew, as we violated several FDA laws and several people could have been in deep shit.

The Duke said he wanted to drive, but the answer was 'no'. Instead Dennis allowed him to sit up front with two 'security' people in the back seat who happened to be doctors, just in case something happened. Little did The Duke know that the trunk was filled with every type of emergency equipment you could think of. Again, just in case.

Dennis reported that as they were driving, The Duke asked what day it was. When he was told he seemed surprised. Then he asked what year it was and when that was shared, he was shocked. He had been 'gone' for over two years.

As the car hit the split and headed towards Milwaukee, The Duke began complaining of a headache. At first it was a little thing and then, as they progressed, he mentioned it was getting worse. Soon his arms began shaking and he was going into convulsions. The doctor in the back seat, pulled out a syringe and through The Duke's shirt injected him with a sedative. Within two minutes, the shaking stopped and The Duke was sound asleep. Later, I learned that brain operations can cause things like that, as the brain adjusts to being invaded.

When they arrived at The Duke's house, he was helped into bed and the nurses took over. They were directed to watch his vitals and contact the doctors if there was any problem.

The next morning, The Duke awoke and went to the kitchen and asked the crew what in hell they were doing in his house, threatening to call the police if they didn't leave. Dennis was called and came immediately to a ranting, raving madman demanding to see Dr. Williams and wanting to know where she was and why she hadn't come home the night before.

Dennis called the physicians and they explained that, with a brain injury caused by even a small incision, there might be a chemical imbalance that could take a few days to stabilize. As The Duke calmed down, he wandered into the living room and saw the empty red vase and that's when it hit him. Falling to his knees, he began to sob, begging Marie to come back. Realizing that she was gone, he was finally allowing all the pain and suffering kept inside with her death to explode onto the living room carpet in a torrent of tears.

"Why, why did you do this to me?" The Duke cried.

"Why did you leave me? I loved you more than anything!"

Dennis tried to console The Duke, but to no avail. Once again, the doctor was called, this time instructing Dennis to give The Duke a sedative.

For the next few days, it was nothing but hell. When awake, he was in anguish about Dr. Williams not being there. Then it turned to anger, not at her, but at us. He had realized what we had done and wanted to know why. Why hadn't we let him simply live in peace? Why did we bring him back?

After the fifth day, The Duke began to settle down and life became less tumultuous. Amy, the kids and I went to visit and he was glad to see us, sharing stories of his childhood and that of Amy. There were missing pieces, but most of the pieces of the puzzle of life were still there and fit together as they should.

After two weeks, everything seemed normal except that The Duke seemed so distant, so different than ever before. There was no joy! There was no laughter! While normal humans experience happiness, sadness, surprise, fear, anger, disgust, and contempt and about 20 more emotions, for The Duke, they were missing from the man I once knew and loved to the point that all there was consisted of him living the day and thinking about yesterday.

We continued having someone with him at all times. He was ambulatory and even taking care of himself and yet there was something different in his personality, demeanor and outlook on life. I thought back to Aristotle and shuddered.

After six weeks, normalcy seemed to settle in and I called and asked if he wanted to go to the club. He said no, he wasn't ready for that. He did say that he missed Nicole and Charles and did want to see them, though.

As the days progressed, we all began to feel a little more comfortable. Instead of The Duke driving to the florist, arrangements were made for one white rose to be delivered every Wednesday morning and that seemed to calm him down. It wasn't long until we began to feel comfortable, believing we had made the right decision. The Duke was alert and stabilized but still 'different'. Sadly, the fire that had burned in his belly was gone, as was the gleam in his eyes. He no longer commanded attention nor respect. He no longer laughed or frowned, was angry or even frustrated and his passion for his beloved Badgers had evaporated leaving an old man, living, existing, wondering, waiting for the next event which would be his demise.

The toughest part was the dynamic personality going "flat". There simply wasn't any emotion. I knew that when we are happy, we have better mental health and normally we feel better and are more satisfied with life. I also knew all about depression. What I didn't know was what happened when there were no emotions at all and this really concerned me as it applied to Amy's dad.

The Duke had always been dynamic and one reason was his over-abundance of pleasant emotions that drew people to him simply because his personality was wider and richer than almost everyone else and people liked that. Before everything started falling apart, The Duke had a tremendous level of satisfaction with life. Sure! Money and success was part of it. However, so was the sense of quality of life the also existed, where little things like looking out at Lake Monona in Madison that we took for granted gave him much joy.

With the insertion, we were able to save The Duke's thoughts and memories, but not his emotions and this had affected his personality which in-turn, affected the man we all loved.

Jermaine at Wilco once said. "The Duke had been a self-constructing person who would always score high on positive components that brought him joy and low on those factors that normally detrimentally affected his life, thereby eliciting a higher level of happiness and sense of well-being."

Amy and I recognized that the transition had changed The Duke into what could be called a 'neutral affective' personality where there was minimal affect towards either the positive or negative extremes and therefore little happiness or sadness, along with limited awareness of the "small things" that formerly brought a smile to his face all of which had all been replaced by a mundane existence where there were no peaks or valleys at all.

One Friday afternoon I had to go to Wilco and decided to drop by and see The Duke. Formerly, you just never did that. Now it was different. I entered the house and he was sitting on the couch looking out at Lake Michigan.

"Hi, son," he said. "Is Amelia with you?"

"No dad, I just thought I'd stop by and say hello."

He offered to take me out on the patio to look at Lake Michigan and I agreed. As we reached the railing and concluded our pleasantries, The Duke stopped peering at the lake and looked at me and asked, "Why did you do it?"

"Do what dad?"

"Bring me back. I wasn't hurting anyone and I was at peace. Now all the problems have returned."

"You mean you would have preferred staying – away?"

"Son, I was at peace, simply waiting to go and be with Marie. We all have to go sometime and my time was coming. Now I don't know if or when it will happen and there's really nothing for me 'here'."

"What about us?" I asked.

"You and Amelia and the kids have your lives to live. I've lived mine and now I'm a burden. You once told me about the qualitative and quantitative aspects of life. I'm beyond that point of intersection. My life has been wonderful and when God decided it was time for me to go, I was doing it in a very slow way, but I was leaving and I was ready. Now, now – I really don't know anymore."

With that, The Duke buried his face in his hands and then looked up at me. "I've been everywhere and done everything and now what? I have a babysitter and you and Amy's world centers around taking care of me. That's not how I wanted it to be."

"But dad!' I countered.

"No son! I hate to say this, but you and Amy were selfish. Instead of letting me go, you made me stay, not because I wanted to, but because you felt you needed me. I was ready and now I'm here, not for me, but for you."

A profound sense of guilt permeated my mind. We had messed with nature, not for his sake, but ours. Perhaps what we wanted to do wasn't what should have been done. There is a rhyme and reason to the Hayflick limit and we were playing God! I had come to see how he was doing and learned a profound lesson about leaving well enough alone.

I didn't stay long as I felt as if I was intruding and my drive home was silent. My thoughts were of The Duke and what we had done.

Panic:

A few weeks transpired since my visit with The Duke and even though I was feeling guilty, like everything else, the sharp point of regret was being smoothed away by the day-to-day events of this thing called life. It was five AM when the phone rang. Sleep left me! I breathed deep as my shoulders folded to cover the pain, pressure and discomfort that invaded my body. Four words were spoken – *"The Duke is missing!"*

How can one explain panic? The incredible response to something unknown, where your body goes through a whole series of changes - heart pumping, faster breathing, sweating, all in order to respond to the perceived danger in front of you. Amy almost retched, as nausea overtook her body and dizziness permeated her brain, informing me that she felt faint.

I closed my eyes and attempted to eradicate the tingling and numbness in my body. My brain went into overdrive as things around me seemed strange, unreal, unfamiliar and detached from body. The norm became a slow-motion evolution, thoughts blurred and words became stretched before me. Our greatest fear was upon us and thoughts of losing control pounded in my head. The Duke was gone!

While his male nurse slept, The Duke slipped out, leaving a packet next to the white rose that had been purchased on Wednesday with the wavering scribbled inscription - *"I've gone to be with Marie"* written across a large brown envelope.

"Oh my God!" I looked at Amy and she at me and we didn't know what to do or whom to call. Dennis? Andrew? Where and how had he left and why?

Unbeknownst to us, in the past few weeks The Duke had begun to marginally deteriorate and it appeared that, for some reason, the chip had begun to fail. All the symptoms were slowly coming back.

I hung up the phone and looked at Amy who said, "Call Dennis".

"It's only five in the morning." I replied, knowing that she was right as I picked up my cellphone and pressed Dennis's number.

The other end came to life as a sleepy voice answered, "Hello".

"Dennis, it's George. I hate to call you this early, but The Duke's gone!"

"What?" the now fully-awake friend elicited.

"He's gone and left some sort of envelope."

"Where was the night nurse?"

"I don't know! Sleeping I guess!" After the period of normalcy began to wane, we set up the night nurse with a room next to The Duke's, never thinking there would be a problem.

"Oh my God!" Dennis exclaimed. "I'm on my way to the house right now!"

"Should we stay here or come there?" I asked, knowing we would be of no use at the house.

Dennis didn't answer, as I heard his car start and then inquired, "Was there any message?"

"Yes, The Duke said he was going to be with Marie!"

"Holy shit!" Dennis exclaimed, as I could sense the fear and panic. The man who was Dennis's best friend and mentor and the man who made him wealthy. The Duke was like a second, no make that, a first father, was gone!

I looked at Amy and shrugged my shoulders. What could we do? Where would he have gone? Do we call the police? Knowing the rules about missing persons, being gone a few hours would mean that they would tell us to wait, as they had so many other issues to take care of.

Instead, I called Andrew and relayed the message. After virtually the same response, Andrew announced he was on his way. Living closer than Dennis, I knew he would be the first one there.

For twenty minutes, Amy and I stood motionless in the kitchen, frozen in time and space. We were hoping and praying that this was something minor, but fearing the worst.

The phone rang and both of us jumped. It was Andrew. "There's a large Manila envelope addressed to the two of you. Can I open it?"

"Of course!"

We heard the sound of the phone being set on the table and envisioned Andrew standing in the living room next to the red vase with the one white rose and the photo of Amy's mom.

Andrew picked up the phone and there was a deep breath. "There are five envelopes in here. Each one is addressed separately to you and the kids. Then there is a sheet of paper. It's in The Duke's handwriting of the past and not the way it is right now." I knew that Alzheimer's makes one unsteady and can quickly show in their penmanship.

I put the phone on speaker and told Dennis to read the letter. Again, there was a deep breath and I knew there was trouble.

"Read it Andrew, please!" Amy said with a degree of urgency.

Again, a deep breath and then Andrew began reading the letter.

Dear Amy and George

This letter was written after one of my first visits with the doctor when knew there was something wrong. I saved it, knowing that, as time went y, my ability to communicate would become a greater challenge.

I know I have Alzheimer's Disease! I know what the consequences ·e! I know that you have done everything you possibly could to slow down ıy regression and yet, like all others, the time has come when my quality of fe has intersected with its quantity and now, before I can no longer function : all, I am doing what I want to do and that's make certain I'm no longer a ırden to you, anyone or myself.

My life has been a wonderful journey. It has been filled with joy and appiness, love and a sense of achievement and I have sincerely felt wanted, ɔeded and loved. Amy, you have been the light of my life. You have filled ıy heart with the beauty of knowing that my greatest accomplishment has been you. You are honest, sincere, loving, compassionate and have been a wonderful daughter and mother, just as I hoped you would be.

George, you filled the saddest day of my life with joy and became the son I always dreamed about. You have shown me respect and honor and a sense of decency that I cannot fathom. You have filled my life with happiness, simply because I know that you love Amy and she loves you. While my journey is about to end, yours still has a long way to go and I hope and pray that your days are filled with the profound pride that mine have been. Thank you for being my son! Thank you for being my friend! Thank you for the honor and dignity you have always expressed towards my Amelia.

While right now, I am certain you are in shock. Please don't be! Plans and arrangements have been made to ensure that my departure is done with honor and dignity. We must all accept that when the quality of life is no longer there, it is better to go with head held high, than to linger, unable to enjoy all that God has given us, reliant on others as nothing more than a burden – a stark shadow of yesterday.

While some might think this is selfish, I do not. I cannot imagine what it is like to linger, with no hope for a better tomorrow. I cannot accept dying as the last step. My only wish is that I am fondly remembered and truly missed and that I have touched the lives of others and made them better. I hope that tomorrow when reality strikes, you, too, will realize that what I have done, was not only for me, but for everyone.

Within this envelope are letters to each of you and to Derrick, 'V' and Melia, expressing my pride in all that you have accomplished. In addition, you will find a thumb drive that includes a video that I would like you to play at the next annual Wilco meeting, because without those who will be in attendance, my life would have never been the same.

We all must go someday. It's not a question of if, but of when and how. I am one of the lucky ones. I got to choose my way. I hope that my life has been worthwhile. I hope that tomorrow, when I reach the gates of heaven, Marie is standing there with Derrick, waiting for me with arms open and a great big smile as once again, we will be together.

Love - Dad

Tears roiled in Amy's and my eyes as she collapsed into my arms, sobbing. We knew the day would come, as it does for us all and yet, like everyone else, we didn't want it to be that day.

"What now?" I whispered to Andrew.

There was silence and then Dennis's voice could be heard in the background as he picked up the phone and said, "George, Amy, we don't know what to do. The statement that your dad wanted to be with Marie could have meant anything. Did it mean The Forest, heaven or St. Martin? I called flight ops and was informed that The Duke had not taken Amelia X, as it's still in the hangar."

Did this mean he might be was somewhere in Milwaukee or Wisconsin? I thought. Andrew came on and said, "The real challenge is that we don't know how much of a head start he has and what his level of mental acuity is like. I hope he's not alone."

The one thing that stuck in my mind was the comment, *'plans and arrangements were made to ensure that my departure is done with honor and dignity.'* This meant to me, that someone was with him. He knew that, as his mind deteriorated, he would need help. The question then became, 'who?'

"We're coming over there!" I announced to Andrew. Stay there, but begin calling anyone and everyone you can think of who would help him."

Amy and I quickly got dressed and drove to the house. Dennis and Andrew were both on their phones as we walked into the living room and both shook their heads and shrugged their shoulders indicating we were no further along than before.

"What about the security cameras?" I asked.

"Someone turned them off," Andrew replied.

"When?" I asked.

"Yesterday."

"Now what?" Amy pondered.

I shook my head trying to come up with an answer.

At 8:00 AM, Amy called Sissy, who had been The Duke's personal assistant and dear friend for over thirty years and she could tell by the tone of her voice, we were in a panic mode. I asked Sissy if The Duke had acted strange lately and realized that she hadn't seen him in months. Even after the implant, he was reticent about going to the office. Afraid! Embarrassed! Reluctant for anyone to see this little old man, all stooped over, who once commanded the attention and respect of anyone and everyone. I asked her if there was ever any weird questions he had asked her.

Sissy paused and said she didn't think so and then responded that there was one thing. I asked what it was. Sissy noted that The Duke had called several weeks before and inquired about Uber and Lyft and how they worked. She noted that it seemed strange, when he always had a driver.

"Uber and Lyft?" I questioned out loud.

"Yes!" was Sissy's reply.

I thanked Sissy and told her we would keep her in the loop and looked at Andrew. "Don't those two keep records of all rides?"

"Yes!" Andrew answered as he punched in buttons to our security division, instructing them to contact both companies and that it was urgent. We had no other clue and the time we waited was excruciating. When Andrew's phone rang, we all jumped.

Andrew was nodding and then shook his head. "Neither company sent a driver here this morning."

"Have they ever sent a driver to this address, I asked?"

Andrew frowned and understood my inquiry, calling back whomever had called him and instructing them to check all records. Another hour went by. It was now nearly ten o'clock and we were no further along than when we started. The phone rang and Andrew answered. "OK, thanks, " he said. Putting the phone down, he looked at me and said that over 20 times drivers had been to the house.

"Twenty times?" I challenged with Andrew nodding in the affirmative.

Then it came to me, some of the people taking care of The Duke were using the services, as they didn't have cars and we provided the service for free.

I shook my head and tried to correlate the nurses and directed Andrew, "Call security and find out where they went after picking up their passenger."

Andrew frowned for a moment and then realized I was onto something as he called back again. Another 30 minutes went by until Andrew's phone rang and he was instructed to turn on his laptop as there was a report from both companies regarding days and destinations.

"With Andrew running the computer, we looked at all the activity and nothing seemed out of the ordinary until one popped up. The driver had come to the house and then left with no passenger. Could it be that The Duke wanted to see how the system worked? Could it be that he then wanted to hire the driver without using the service? Could it be that last night, the driver came and took The Duke somewhere?

"Zero in on that one!" I directed. "We need to find out who the driver was."

Andrew sent a text and we waited. Before long we were informed that it was private information and could not be shared. I said "Bullshit, get it done!"

As Andrew went in through the *'front door',* I went in through the back, calling Todd Franklin, head of Wilco Purchasing, telling him to put the squeeze on Lyft. We were doing hundreds-of-thousands of dollars of business with them each year for both our employees and our customers through our corporate account at the dealerships and we either got the name or they lost the business.

Another hour went by and I received a call from legal. They had contacted Lyft and were told the information was confidential. Once again, I said, 'bullshit' and demanded the name and number of who they talked to. As my Minnie Point badass mentality came into play, I called Sissy and asked her to find out who the CEO of Lyft was. Ten minutes later, Sissy called back and reported that Lyft was actually a division of General Motors. It was all she needed to say! With over 100 GM Dealerships, Wilco had some clout!

I picked up the phone and called GM Corporate. I explained who I was and demanded speaking to someone immediately. I was told they were in a meeting and I said I didn't give a damn. Within a minute, another call was coming into my cellphone and it was the Vice President of Dealer Development.

"Mr. Terrill, so nice of you to call."

I thanked him for taking my call and explained what was going on. I told him that all we needed was the name of the driver who came to the house on the specific date and why I needed it.

"George, I'll do my best!" was the response.

"No, you don't understand, this is a fucking emergency and I need it NOW!"

Mr. V.P. must have been taken aback by my insistence as his tone changed and he responded. "Yes, Mr. Terrill. Can I call this number?"

"Please do and as quickly as possible, Doug Williams' life may be at stake."

"I'll do my best, sir!"

Thirty minutes later the phone rang and we had our answer - Casey Banks and his phone number. I scribbled it on a piece of paper and handed it to Andrew who punched in the numbers.

On the fourth ring, Andrew began. "Mr. Banks, I represent Wilco Security, a Division of Wilco Corporation. A few months ago, you were called to the residence of Douglas Williams, CEO Emeritus of the company - Mr. Banks, I know that you have made hundreds of trips, I have your records in my hand. It is our belief that, while here, you had a conversation with Mr. Williams and departed. The house is a very large colonial with an electric gate - Yes, that's the house."

"Mr. Banks, where were you early this morning? You say you weren't working and yet you had six trips last night, is that right? No, Mr. Banks, I am not trying to cause any trouble. All I'm trying to do is find out what happened to Mr. Williams. No, I will not communicate with anyone at Lyft, **if** you cooperate."

"You have a void in your manifest between two and three this morning. At that time, did you come to the Williams' residence? Sir, we have security cameras and if you want me to, I can play them back and see if you were here. Mr. Banks, if you keep this up, we are going to call the police, report Mr. Williams missing, show them the security tape and you will become a prime suspect in his disappearance. However, if you simply confirm you were here and where you took Mr. Williams, our conversation will end."

"Where?" Andrew asked incredulously. "At three in the morning? Thank you. Yes, I know he's a nice man and quite generous. Thank you, Mr. Banks."

Andrew turned to us and announced, "The Lyft driver took him to the Milwaukee Club."

I was flabbergasted, "At three in the morning?"

Andrew nodded in the affirmative.

It was now nearly noon as we drove to the Club. Pulling up in front, I jumped out and went in the front door, asking the Maître'd, "Is Duke Williams here?"

He shook his head and looked at the frazzled man in front of him, replying "Sir, Mr. Williams hasn't been here in months."

"We have information that he was driven here at three this morning."

"Sir the building was closed!"

"Well, he's got to be around here somewhere or someone has to know where he is," I replied as I began walking into the bar.

People began staring, as I was a stranger on an urgent mission and they didn't like their decorum broken.

"I need to talk to the servers!" I announced, to which no one moved. At that moment, Mr., Larson appeared, who was General Manager.

"Can I help you, Mr. Terrill?"

"Douglas Williams is missing. We have a witness who says he was dropped off here around three this morning."

We are closed then, sir!" (*No shit Sherlock*, I thought).

"I know, but why in hell would he come here at three this morning? I need to talk to your servers."

"Sir!"

"Please, don't sir me now!" Time is really important! Mr. Williams' life may be in danger."

With that, Mr. Larson raised his hands as if to tell me to calm down and then motioned to follow him. In minutes, we were in the kitchen. I looked at the kitchen staff and then the servers. I recognized Nicole and motioned to her. "Mr. Williams is missing. It was reported that he was here this morning. Do you know anything?"

Nicole shook her head and I could tell she was telling the truth.

"What about Charles?" I asked.

The manager said that he had called in sick. Right away, we had our suspect.

"What's wrong with him?" I asked.

"I don't know, his wife called us," was all the manager said.

"I need to call him," I replied.

The manager could tell I was serious and responded, "Follow me!" as we went to his office.

He took out his small directory and called the number from his desk phone. There was no video screen with the number for me to see and write down.

"Mrs. Waters, this is Mr. Larson. Is it possible for Charles to come to the phone?" The manager inquired. "I see, he went to the doctor. Does he have his cellphone with him? - He doesn't have one? - Do you have the name of his doctor? - He went to immediate care? - You wouldn't happen to know which one? This is very important! - You don't, OK thank you. If he should come home, would you have him call me as soon as possible?"

With that Larson hung up and shrugged his shoulders. He had done all he could.

I went back to the car and shared the information with Andrew saying, "I smell a skunk in the woodpile!" The words – *'Be with Marie'* kept rolling over in my mind. *'Be with Marie', 'Be with Marie!'*

I looked at Andrew and posed the question. "Let's say that The Duke wanted to go to St. Martin. Let's say he knew Dennis would never take him. Let's say he knew he wasn't stable enough to go alone. Let's say he asked Charles from the Club to escort him there. What would he do next?"

Andrew looked at me and said, "buy two tickets to St. Martin!"

"From?"

"Milwaukee?" Andrew asked.

"Nope!" O'Hare!". I replied. "They have a non-stop flight."

I called Sissy and instructed her to look on-line for flights from Chicago to St. Martin. She panned the schedule and reported, "One left at 7:45 on United Airlines."

"Non-stop?"

"Yes!"

I called the house and asked Amy to check the safe to see if The Duke's passport was there. She did. It was not!

Holy shit! I felt that The Duke had met Charles, who was accompanying him to Princess Juliana Airport. Andrew called his office and they ran a check. Sure enough John Douglas Williams and Charles Waters had first class seats on United flight number 1671 departing at 7:45 AM and arriving at 2:45 PM.

I looked at my watch. It was now 1:30. Perhaps we could stop the insanity. It was then that I realized that 2:45 PM was St. Martin time and two hours ahead. It was already 3:30 there, and they were probably gone.

Andrew looked at me with a forlorn look on his face. "George, Charles never got off the plane, it departed a few minutes ago for Washington Dulles."

I knew that The Duke was in no condition to be alone and the only person he would trust would be Uncle Frank. I quickly called Amy and asked for Aunt Julia's phone number, knowing that Uncle

Frank hated cellphones. Amy gave me the number and I called the jewelry store. Aunt Julia answered in her soft voice.

"Aunt Julia, this is George! I need to speak with Uncle Frank. It's urgent."

Aunt Julia was perplexed by my insistence. "George, Frank isn't here. He said he had an important errand to run."

I was reluctant to tell her what I knew. "How do I contact him? This is important!" I pleaded.

"I'm sorry, George, but you know Frank hates cellphones when he's fishing !"

I had to tell her what was going on and outlined the entire day, to which I got, "Oh, my God, no!"

In her Pigeon English, I heard Aunt Julia direct one of the employees to do something before responding to me., "George, Frank said he had some clients and was going fishing."

"The client is The Duke and we think he wants to commit suicide" I murmured.

"Oh, my God!" was all Aunt Julia could say before offering to call the police.

Within ten minutes, the St. Martin shore patrol was en-route to Bai Maria.

Twenty minutes later, the phone rang and it was Uncle Frank on someone's cellphone and he was crying. "George! George! I am so sorry! He, he had these pills and said that either I took him to where we spread Marie's ashes or he would take all the pills and die in the boat. Honest to God, George, I tried to talk him out of it, but with each word, he took another pill and told me to shut up. I am so sorry!"

"What happened?" I inquired.

"I was told to meet him at the airport. I asked him why he was flying on a regular plane and not Amelia X and he said she was in for maintenance. I didn't think anything of it, especially when he said he had a fishing buddy with him. I asked him where his friend was and he said he got sick and couldn't come."

"I had the boat and we left from the airport. We got to Bai Marie and Doug thanked me for bringing him home. He took a handful of pills out of his pocket and put them in his mouth. Then took a bottle of his favorite scotch that he told me to bring from the house and drank it. The whole thing George! He drank the whole damn bottle!"

Uncle Frank continued, "George, I looked at him and he at me and there was a wry smile on his face. He stood up, grabbed the anchor and fell overboard. His last words were, 'Tell Amy I love her' - He just fell in the water! I wanted to save him, but he disappeared. I'll never forget the look on his face, George. Never! I am so sorry!"

Uncle Frank was sobbing and his words were staccato as he gulped for air. After what seemed like an eternity, he continued, "A few minutes later, the police boat came and we tried to look, but it was too late. He was gone George! He was gone!"

The sobbing on the other end was sincere. The Duke did what he wanted to do. He wanted to go his way! He wanted to be with Marie!

I hung up, knowing that he was gone. All I needed to do was tell my wife. How in hell do you tell your wife that her father just committed suicide?

We drove back to the Williams' house and I looked at Amy and she already knew, as tears welled in her eyes and I whispered. "It's what he wanted. He never wanted to be a burden."

"But I didn't get to say goodbye!" Amy cried.

I wondered why today? Then realized that it was the anniversary of Dr. Williams' death and he just wanted to be with Marie.

There was profound silence. Dennis sitting in one chair. Andrew in another. Amy in the kitchen. All simply sitting thinking about the woulda's, coulda's, shoulda's of life.

The next day, I called the St. Martin police. They had taken the time to determine who John Douglas Williams was and all that he had done for the Island of St. Martin and ruled his death accidental. They also indicated that, in all likelihood his body was pulled out to sea by the current and was gone forever. I told them, if it didn't happen that way, please quietly have his remains cremated and spread his ashes in the ocean.

I requested they not tell us. It had already been a traumatic experience and we needed closure. I told them that, should he be found and procedures followed, simply send Wilco the bill and it would be paid. No bill ever came and I knew The Duke got what he wanted - to be with Marie, forever!

There is a stillness in death that can't be described. There is a profound emptiness to one's soul and yet, like all else, time marches on, not stopping, not pausing, not relinquishing one second for anyone. Then there are the firsts – the first moment we knew! The first moment we walked into that empty house and felt all alone, with nothing but memories. The white rose already wilting and yet we let it lie within the vase. Memories flooded Amy as she went through everything personal and there are the lasts – the last time we saw him, the last time was said goodbye, the last time for everything in his thing called life.

Time brought on reality and we accepted that we needed to move on. We had a family meeting and then added those so close to the family – Dennis, Andrew, Ceclia and Sissy, who knew more about us than we probably knew about ourselves. It was decided that we would sell the house, as we had no need for it and the memories were too strong to have any of the kids live in it. With its location, it didn't take long. We divided up the furniture to whomever wanted whatever and donated the rest. The most cherished possession – the little red vase came home to our house and sits on our mantle. Every Wednesday, two white roses are delivered and placed where one had resided for so many years.

When it was time to read the last will and testament, we met in the board room along with the family's financial entourage of accountants, lawyers and consultants. The will was quite straight forward. Everything was bequeathed to Amelia Williams Terrill except for one million dollars each to Dennis, Sissy and Charles Waters and one-hundred thousand dollars to Nicole at the club. In less than an hour, I went from being married to a multi-millionaire to a multi-billionaire, who would have given it all for one more day, one more hour, one more moment with her mom and dad.

How can one express the profound sadness that comes with death? How can one amplify that feeling when, deep down, the circumstances were something that was preventable? How can one travel on, and yet we did?

We are all wired to fight to live and yet, what about those who want to die? What about those who feel that tomorrow will be no better than today and are ready to go?" What should we feel when someone departs – especially when they go on their own terms?

Our first reaction was denial, believing the news was somehow mistaken, as we grasped a falsehood - a preferable reality to what was true?

We fought like hell to believe it wasn't true and then all the facts came in and we had to accept that he was gone! Amy and I normally had few disagreements and yet, this time, she became frustrated, especially at me, by accusing me that this was all my fault. She looked at me and asked "Why me? It's not fair!"; "How can this happen to me?"; "Who is to blame?"; "Why would this happen?".

I saw the pain in her eyes. She was the only one left in her family. Through what we had done, we had created hope that Amy could avoid or defer the eventual grief and give her a few more years with her dad –and we failed. When Amy realized there was nothing we could do, she began trying to negotiate with God, but it didn't matter. One more minute! One more hour! One more day!

Amy finally accepted The Duke's mortality, but it was pure hell. At first, she shut me out - becoming silent, refusing visitors and spending much of her time mournful and sullen. As time passed and wounds healed, she began her journey back to reality as she realized the permanence of death and said "It's going to be okay!" "I can't fight it"- finally embracing mortality as the end result of all of our inevitable future.

What does one say? What does one do? What can one feel? I loved the Duke as a second father. It was my decision to try to extend his life. In the end, it was me who elected to try something, anything that would give us more time, more memories and more emotions with a man who simply asked "Why have you done this to me when all I want to be is with the one I love."

I remember is words "I'm ready to go and you won't let me! All I want to do is be with Marie!" My God, what had I done?

Warning:

The attorneys provided envelopes with messages from The Duke and also Dr. Marie. The contents were personal and we never asked what was said. Likewise, what The Duke had written to Amy was between the two of them. My letter was simply profound and I can only assume that its contents paralleled those of the others, detailing our relationship and his love and pride for all that we had accomplished.

My letter was different because The Duke's included a warning regarding what was probably going to transpire with him gone. He knew we had enemies and with him out of the picture, they would attack. He outlined those he thought would come after the Foundation and me and how it would probably transpire. I took a deep breath and realized that without his shield, we were in for a tremendous challenge that would take all my efforts simply to sustain what we had built.

Little did I realize the depth of the tentacles of those who were about to attack. It was then I realized just how powerful this man had been and how he had used his power and connections to shield me from the ravages that lurked behind every CEO who wanted nothing more than the Derrick Williams Foundation gone.

The Medicine Man:

We all have our own ways to mourn. At first, I blamed myself for foolishly thinking I could repair what was broken. When I finally accepted The Duke's demise, I turned to Amy for guidance and support. She knew I was embarrassed by my own enthusiasm and frustrated that I had spent valuable time and resources on what became a dead end. She sadly watched my dream of helping even more people than we already were evaporate in a cloud of sadness. Mediglove was thriving and yet, because I had been with it so long, it no longer filled me with the excitement it once provided.

I asked her if she minded if I went to The Forest. With the research compound next door, I had been to Waldwick dozens of times. Sadly, even my friends the trees had become somewhat commonplace. She said she understood, but then she always did. She was getting more like her mother every day.

The next afternoon, I wanted to be alone with my thoughts and quietly drove to Madison, turned south on I90 & 39 towards the 18&51 West exit. Instead, my mind took me east and I turned into the parking lot of the Ho-Chunk casino where it had all started - meeting Rodney, working and growing up.

I entered and all the memories came rushing back. The sounds! The smells! They were all still there frozen in time, simply waiting for me to return! I stood for a moment in the entry to allow my eyes to adjust to the dim lights and then I saw him. The Medicine Man stood before me. His face wasn't painted and he wore a traditional navy-blue business suit with a white shirt and beautiful striped red-and-silver tie. I looked down and he was wearing highly polished black boots.

I smiled. He smiled and beckoned me over.

"I've been waiting for you," he said.

"How did you know?" I asked.

I closed my eyes for an instant to see if I was dreaming. I was not!

"Follow me. We need to talk!" The Medicine Man beckoned me to come back to one of the empty rooms and I followed.

He stood by the door and said, "You might think this is a coincidence that we are both here. Great Grandfather came to me in a dream and called me and said you needed to speak to him."

The Medicine Man continued. "I can feel your sadness and frustration. You feel betrayed by a system you thought you could beat and now you think everything you have done is wrong. It's not, and your world is not the mess you think it is. We all have innate needs to create order out of chaos and right now, Little Spirit, I sense chaos in your life."

The Medicine Man closed the door and beckoned me to sit down, "Let me see if I can't help put your mind at rest and your heart at ease."

With that I sat and he began. "Many times, you heard from Rodney and Great Grandfather our belief that we are all connected. The world today has a term for this concept that my people have believed in since the beginning of time and it is called 'synchronicity', which is the invisible network that connects everyone and everything, no matter where it or they are in the universe."

He looked at me with his deep brown eyes and smiled. "The Forest is a classic example, where the positive energy is so great that the synchronicity can be felt and transmitted, processed into both emotions and behavior. For some, like you, the feelings are profound because that energy is positively linked to your soul. For others, there is little or no feeling and, therefore, no emotion. No matter how strong the feelings, the connections are still there and that is why we must respect all that there is."

I looked at the Medicine Man and realized he had validated what Melia had told me and, yet, he still sensed my apprehension - not about The Forest and the feelings, but about my lack of success as he continued. "Just as sharks have ampullae in their skin that can detect small electromagnetic changes that help them identify their prey, Indians believe that humans have similar mechanisms that can detect energy." Once again, he was validating what Melia said. "The Indian people are not alone in these beliefs. Many biologists, such as Austrian biologist Paul Kammerer and theoretical psychologist Carl Jung believed the same things. They would not have been surprised by the coincidences, such as you coming here today, arise from unknown forces called 'seriality' by Dr. Kammerer in 1919 and 'synchronicity' by Dr. Jung nearly fifty years later."

With his head cocked, the Medicine Man continued, "Little Spirit, you are confused and that is quite normal for someone as dedicated and passionate as you are. You are looking for answers to many questions, which is an inevitable consequence of your mind searching for a causal structure to your own reality that will provide the answers you need and allow you to learn and adapt to your environment."

My head bowed in thought as he continued. "You have been blessed with a wife and children. You have the joy of good health and immense wealth and yet you ask yourself, '*which is worse to have nothing or everything?*' What makes things work for you is your spiritual belief. This is what makes you care for my people and be more connected to the world around you, thereby providing an opportunity to find the meaning you seek."

The Medicine Man looked at me with his dark eyes and continued on. "What you have achieved is not by coincidence. In fact, it's only when you begin to recognize the pattern that has been drawn, that your coincidences will take on the spiritual meaning that you desire. Someday, there will be a point where solace and clarification will focus and there will be total peace in your heart regarding all that has happened and all that lies ahead."

As we sat, he asked if I wanted anything to drink. I thanked him and said no.

"May I continue?" he asked.

I nodded in agreement as he continued on. "You are sad because your dreams did not come true. Yet, you have only looked at the big picture and not at what lies beneath."

It was good to have him there, as he was someone I could confide in, lowering my guard, as I nodded in the affirmative. "When you are a husband and father, perceived by so many to be successful, it is difficult to hide your fears and frustrations. To have someone, anyone, who will listen and let you open your heart is always good. Do you every wonder, Little Spirit, about that first night when you and your friends visited here?"

I shrugged my shoulders and nodded in affirmation.

"Rock, paper, scissors?"

I nodded again, wondering how he knew about our silly game, but afraid to ask.

"Do you remember Rodney standing over there?" as he pointed to the spot where Rodney was the night we met.

Again, I nodded in the affirmative.

"Have you ever wondered why the five dollars you had went so fast in the slot machines you played?"

Now I was getting spooked.

"And why you walked over to Rodney and there was an instant bond?"

"I thought it was because of our ancestors," I replied.

"Yes, that's correct, but that is only part of the reason. You see Little Spirit, you were chosen long before that night to take the journey you are on. Our world is not one of cause-and-effect as much as one called 'entanglement', where one particle can instantaneously influence another, even if the two particles are on opposite sides of the universe. These are the synchronicities that someday you will understand and there will be peace in your soul."

He leaned forward and asked, "Do you ever wonder why it is that so many of my people and those of other Indian nations, continue to live on reservations when they could afford to live wherever they wanted? It is because of the synchronicity we feel."

"Do you ever wonder why, when so many people have given up on their heritage and traditions, we fight to keep ours?" It is because of the synchronicity we feel."

"Do you ever wonder why, even when times were so bad for so many of our people, we remained proud and independent? Again, it is because of the synchronicity that we feel."

"These are the reasons we are what we are, because we accept that we are all connected with every other atom in the universe - no greater, no smaller - no more or less important."

Goose bumps were on my arms.

"George, what about your accident and all that time in the hospital? Do you think it was something that just happened?"

I shook my head as my mouth dropped open.

"Let me explain," he added.

With that the Medicine Man sat down across the table from me and opened a new deck of playing cards. I thought this was strange, but said nothing. Carefully he spread the cards out in a fan shape and flipped one end as I watched them all become face-up.

"The freedom my people have begun to enjoy come from these," pointing at the cards, as he spoke into the quiet casino air, caring a great deal to make certain I was paying attention.

"These playing cards can make one rich or poor, happy or sad and make life good or bad, just like your dreams. But let's look at the playing cards and see if there isn't greater meaning for you, just as there was, a long time ago, for me."

With that, the Medicine Man pointed at the deck and said. "The deck is a unit and thereby represents the oneness of God. There are four different suits to the cards, just like there are four seasons to our life. Not only in terms of the weather, but in terms of people themselves - babies, children, adults and elderly, each with a different perspective on today, tomorrow and yesterday."

This gentle man with the quiet voice continued. "The cards also represent the Quadrature of the Great Pyramid of Gizeh and when you leave here and go to The Forest, stop and look at Great Grandfather's memorial. You will see the four sides that you chose where the sides represent Iminium, Nour, Ruach, and Iebschah, which mean water, fire, air and earth."

I looked at the Medicine Man and saw the deep focus that was burrowed around his eyes as he continued. "There are 52 cards to the deck, just as there are 52 weeks in a year and yet some of the cards have more value, while others less, as time goes on, just like life."

"There are 13 cards in each suit representing the total number of people in the Golden Circle of Christ and his 12 disciples. The thirteen plus the joker represents the number of generations from Abraham-to-David in the Bible. Sometimes, you will find two jokers. Why? Because there were fourteen generations from David to the deportation to Babylon and fourteen from the deportation to Christ. The total face value of the complete deck is 365, which parallels the days of the year."

I sat profoundly mesmerized. Something I had never thought about had so much more meaning than I could have imagined.

The Medicine Man spread the deck further and pulled out the face cards saying, "The Triads are three in number - king, queen, jack - representing the ancient thought of mind, matter and product and also the Trinity of Father, Son, and Holy Spirit."

Once again, as he had done before, the Medicine Man was making me see things I had looked at before but had never really seen as he continued, "While there are four Aces and suits of cards, there are actually five, as the Joker can stand with any one or all suits," as he pulled the joker from the beginning of the non-face cards. "Called the 'odd card,' the Joker represents the missing link in life. As there is a point to Great Grandfather's memorial, the Joker is the 'capstone' of the temple, the head stone of the corner, as symbolized by the coni al ha associated with the Joker. Once again, you can see that there are five and not four suits, just as in the first five days of creation, all things of the air and sea had been created the heavens, sun & fire, the seas and water, air and fowl!

The Medicine Man continued, pulling the tens from the remaining cards. "There are four tens that represents the ten expressions or emanations of God in the creations of the heavens, earth and all that dwells therein. These are found in the first chapter of Genesis in which 'God said'. Thereby, He spoke the world into existence. There were also ten generations from Adam-to-Noah and ten from Noah-to-Abraham. In addition, in the Bible, Abraham was proven with ten trials and there were ten plagues in Egypt."

"As you can see Little Spirit, a simple deck of playing cards can mean so much more when you look at them carefully. The deck has components where each individual card gives the full deck its meaning. Remove just one component and the remaining cards mean nothing."

His dark, piercing eyes met mine as he continued. "Your attempt to deliver medicine to people throughout the world does not mean you have failed, only that you have opened the deck of life and chosen the wrong card. Worry not, Little Spirit, the right card will come to you soon. You see, all things are destined and we have no control over them. Your accident! Meeting Rodney, Ann and Amelia were planned by the Great Spirit so that you would become the leader you are about to be."

"But I have failed!" I interjected.

"Perhaps you have been dreaming the wrong dream," was the Medicine Man's reply, shaking his head and repeating, "simply the wrong dream."

The Medicine Man rose and looked down at me saying. "Little Spirit, there will always be things that don't work out. You must never give up. There are great things ahead you will achieve."

I stood and looked into his calm face and deep within his soul. This was a man of peace who was sent to make certain I realized there was more and that I shouldn't give up.

I wanted to express my gratitude and did something I had never done before, I reached out to shake his hand. There had always been a wall between us - invisible and yet there, a barrier that had always existed and yet, for the first time, I felt it had evaporated and that he was truly on my side. No longer was I intruding! No longer was I an adversary! No longer did he reject the belief that I was the chosen one and I was profoundly glad.

As I went to shake his hand, I felt a small gold ring on his right pinkie finger. I looked down and realized the embossed emblem was that of a square with two compasses with the letter 'G' in the middle. My head bowed and all that he had been saying was put into perspective.

As we stood in the otherwise quiet, room, the Medicine Man gave me a hug. For the first time ever, he spoke as if he were my contemporary. "Hang in there, Little Spirit." With that he was gone walking out amongst the flashing lights, disappearing into the darkness of brightness and the abyss from which I had come.

Slowly, I made my way toward the front door and peered out at the first vestiges of a Wisconsin sunset pointing its crooked fingers across the western sky. I got into my car. Enveloped in thought, I made my way past all the small towns that had become bedroom communities to Madison, now called by many, the metroplex.

As I skirted the edge of Mount Horeb, I wondered how many people knew that Mount Horeb was the Greek name for the mountain on which Moses received the Ten Commandments where the first five dealt with man's relationship with God and the last five, with each other. I also wondered how many people could recite those Commandments. My head bowed in remorse as I concluded how trivial, so many Commandments had become as mankind justified their actions by reactions where goodness and honor are replaced by the concept called 'me,' satisfied only by the thing called greed, and right and wrong are compensated by rationalization and denial.

I arrived at the farm. Tommie and Hsu were living in the house and I didn't want to bother them. I needed to be alone and reflect on where I was in life and what needed to be done. I parked the car in the complex and walked into The Forest. The sense of energy I needed engulfed me immediately as if to say hello and welcome home. I walked to where Great Grandfather's obelisk was placed established in an honorific mode that required all those who came across it to stand in stoic silence, including me as I stood and listened to the breeze rustle the leaves. I closed my eyes and took a deep breath. I looked at the capstone and reflected on all the Medicine Man had outlined and it made sense. I looked at the dark sun-dial and realized that, it too, had much more meaning than I ever thought.

I made my way to the springs and took one of the little tin cups and filled it with water. As I slowly sipped the cool freshness, I closed my eyes and felt as if Great Grandfather was there. I opened my eyes and all the pain and frustration of failure were gone. They had evaporated and I knew that it was time to move on, but where?

I turned back towards the obelisk and there, within the woods, stood the buck. I hadn't seen him in decades, but he was there. His big brown eyes caught mine and for a moment we were one. I blinked and when my eyes opened again, he was gone.

"I knew you would come tonight," I heard from a soft whisper. I turned but there was no one there. Only the slight breeze in the trees comforting me, caressing me, letting me relieve the sadness and frustration that filled my heart.

I sat on the bench besides the obelisk and let my mind wander. When would the answer come to the riddles before me? Life had become a conundrum and I needed to solve one riddle before moving on to the next.

Passion:

Needless to say, there was a great deal of anxiety and depression permeating the psyche of the MadCity Boys. They felt they had failed and, in some ways, believed that they had killed The Duke. I knew we needed to right the course and regain our direction.

I spoke with Luke and asked for his guidance and then addressed the subject with Peter. Whereas, it was time for the annual foundation meeting, it was decided that it would be two days long. Day one was to be a general meeting and day two would include a motivational keynote speaker. 'V' had come to me regarding who was to speak and asked if I thought it would be all right to ask my friend James to speak to the group. Everyone in the Foundation knew about James and were aware that he taught psychology, but only a few had met him and I don't think anyone knew how profound he was. This scholarly gentleman had all the qualifications one could ever ask for in a college professor – well educated, deeply learned, knowledgeable and scholarly and then the one ingredient that made him stand out above all the rest – humility, to the point of composure so that no matter how tense the situation was, he could keep his cool during times of stress, conflict or trouble.

I called James and asked if he could possibly share his wisdom with the MadCity Boys. James inquired on what subject and I said 'Passion'. There was a pause on the other end and then the comment that he would do anything for me, for which I was both humbled and honored. We both checked our schedules and the meeting was set with the entire Foundation board being assembled including Big Brother and the Medicine Man, as the Hochunk had a vested interest in what we were developing and still owned half The Forest.

I arranged for a chopper to pick up Big Brother and bring him to The Forest. It had been a long time since he had been there and even though we had met in Madison, I truly missed his friendship. James flew in with me and we arrived about 30 minutes early. I was in a sports coat and James in his doctoral splendor of jeans and Wisconsin t-shirt that said "drink Wisconsinably" ablaze across his chest that made him immediately blend in with the Madcity Gang as good-natured laughter echoed throughout the compound.

About five minutes before 'kickoff' as 'V' liked to call it, the global LED's began blinking as researchers around the world who had been invited 'clicked in' to hear the words of a renowned psychologist. It would take over an hour to enumerate all the attendees and so, we did it in percentages that allowed us to track the overall popularity of any meeting and its impact on what we were doing.

The first part of the meeting was pretty dry and looked at financials and market penetration. Everyone was commended for their efforts and cheered for their accomplishments.

As the first part came to a break, Big Brother and I walked into The Forest and looked at Great Grandfather's obelisk. As he knelt down, Big Brother picked up a handful of dirt and put it in his pocket. He was taking some of Great Grandfather's soul with him to give him the strength he needed to continue on.

We returned and the second section dealt with technology and the different projects and where we were regarding achieving our goals. It was here that I made the announcement that we were suspending development of the chip that would be placed in the hippocampus of the brain. I could see the disappointment and frustration in the eyes of everyone. Luke stood up and indicated that we had accomplished an incredible amount, but our goal was not met, not because of lack of effort, but because we had taken an empirical process that wouldn't allow for emotions to prevail.

Luke spoke and said. "Ladies and gentlemen, you haven't failed at all, you have created a device that can be implanted into a myriad of products and services that will make the world better, more efficient and more concise. Look at what you have done! You took what formerly required a machine the size of an entire office and reduced its size to that of a marble. The only thing we could not program, the only thing we could not capture, the only thing that is missing is emotion and those can only come from God. You did not fail! We were able to harvest thoughts and memories, but emotions are so complex no one machine could ever duplicate them."

"In the period of a few years you did so much, but human emotions emerged over a much longer evolutionary history and we simply cannot program a chip to develop or store emotions in the brain. Along the way, emotions developed considerable complexity that can easily confound social interactions. Emotions readily form associations with each other, such that the experience of one emotion elicits a combination of other emotions."

Luke stopped for a moment and looked at me and I nodded for him to continue. "By adulthood, most of our emotional responses are conditioned "scripts" that the brain follows automatically and sadly, these could not be retrieved. While you valiantly tried, we learned that some emotions act as inhibitors of others and there is nothing we can do to program a chip to compensate for this."

Luke looked at the audience and then at the camera lens and continued. "Shame and fear are the most potent and universal emotional inhibitors. One cannot experience love if it smacks of the probability of rejection or foretells a person's inability to sustain it. One cannot experience sufficient interest to achieve their fullest potential if they sense the shame of failure or the risk of harm, deprivation, or isolation. Fear if failure slams on the brakes, freezing motivation in its tracks and these are things we simply could not program."

Luke looked down at the floor and a soft frown pursed his lips. "Think back to Aristotle and you can quickly see a particularly tragic form of emotional constriction that occurred simply because Aristotle could see beyond his realm and suffered the sense of shame the feelings of inadequacy and unworthiness and when he couldn't do what his brain wanted, which was simply have the feelings he had before and he simply couldn't handle it."

"We all felt the rush when we believed we had a successful solution with Mr. Williams, but that rush was dependent entirely on the realization that there was a possibility of failure. You did not fail! You took it as far as we can go. You have created an incredible achievement. It's just that we cannot continue trying to play God when only He has the ability to create emotions."

There was total silence in the room. Not of defeat, but of acceptance, where each person looked inward and justified their limits, while accepting the reality that they had really accomplished a lot.

Lunch was Tommie's venue and he was never going to be upstaged by any meeting, and did so by making arrangements for the first vestiges of the Wagyu beef to be offered as grilled ribeye sandwiches, accompanied by fresh garden salad and asparagus from mom's garden and homemade lemonade, all topped off by some of his famous homemade ice cream that, once again, Tommie made with fresh cream and liquid helium.

With everyone's belly full, 'V' announced it was time to restart the meeting and we went through all the budgetary financials and what was planned for the upcoming year, with goals presented by each team and recognition for what had been accomplished. With the business part of the meeting completed 'V' introduced James to those who didn't know who he was.

James smiled in a somewhat embarrassed manner and began. "I want to thank you for your time and attention today. I was asked to present my thoughts on passion".

For effect he paused and then James' eyes went round the room and finally at the camera. He was about to start and wanted everyone's attention as he began. "Passion! What an incredible topic to discuss, as it can rage throughout all living species affecting, infecting, correcting, dissecting who, what and where we exist. It has affected history and lies beneath all of the greatest achievements and failures of mankind."

James paused for a moment and looked at the audience before continuing. "I thought long and hard about where to begin and how to end. I realized I needed to start at the beginning. In other words, the physiological aspect of how humans are different from other species. In so doing, I hope that the ideas shared motivate you to go beyond my words in both thought and deed so that you feel the passion that exists in this room." James hands opened as he expressed the thought that he was talking to everyone. "Within this group and you have the ability to change the world, simply because of your dedication to such a noble deed."

There was a hushed silence amongst the audience as James continued, "Passion is not an emotion but the culmination of emotions and so to understand passion, we first need to ask, what is an emotion? The human species actually elicits 27 different emotions, both good and bad, that affect all we do and how we act, react and interact in the world in which we live."

"Emotions are the things that add spice to our life and enhance our existence. But where do they come from? Some of my fellow psychologists believe that emotions start in the sub-cortex or older region of our brain, that we share with other species and this is why they too share many of our responses. Other researchers believe just the opposite! They believe emotions begin at the top of the brain, called the Cortex, where humans reason regarding such topics as context, memories and categories within a culture, better known as acculturation and language as stored."

"Recently new theories have been proposed that purport that emotions actually come from both sources in humans, such as the Prefrontal Cortex and Subcortical level, where the top provides the emotions that are learned and the lower provides preprogrammed emotions, such as those dealing with threats which can affect, but do not actually develop, our emotions."

"If that isn't enough disparity in thought, there is yet another theory that states that emotions are not hard wired, but dynamic in that they can change based on socialization, repetition or imitation."

"Things like as opinions towards others, such as racial or sexual prejudice, that once resulted in one set of emotions, have been eroded and minimized and elicit different emotions today. Concurrent with this is the concept of awe, where what was once something that took our breath away, becomes less exciting due to what is called the theory of acclimation, where repetition removes an emotion simply because the brain has seen, heard, smelled or done it all before."

"The important point is that regardless of how an emotion is triggered, it affects who you are, what you feel and how you respond. What's interesting is that the same stimuli can affect different people in different ways. This can be caused by anything from one's DNA to how much sleep we had the night before."

James walked to the window and paused for a moment to create effect before continuing. "We all refer to emotions when talking about others. We say so-in-so is in a bad mood today where moods are just one form of generalized emotions that can last for days, weeks or months and are the Foundation of an entire division of the drug industry. The key is that emotions are normally short lived and can be described specifically - happy, sad, ornery, obstinate. These are all moods."

"Finally, there are personality traits which are enduring dispositions that can cause a person to actually feel more or less emotion. Here the range can be extreme, where people more exposed to positive emotions are usually extroverted and experience the joy of socializing."

The entire audience turned and looked at me.

"Taken to the extreme, emotions can also result in bi-polar disorder, which is a chemical imbalance in the brain, that allows for tectonic shifts in emotions from one end of the spectrum to the other and do so with devastating consequences along the way. The important thing to remember is that emotions are not the enemy of reason, they work with reason to help us organize our thoughts."

"What then is passion?" James continued. "Passion is a feeling of intense enthusiasm towards or a compelling desire for something or someone and is the culmination of several emotions all blended together in a form of emotional soup. It can range from eager interest to enthusiastic enjoyment, to strong attraction, excitement or emotion towards a person, project, goal or event."

"Passion can actually have a feel to it, but it encompasses much more than just an emotional feeing including a direction, drive, commitment to a purpose or a cause. Passion is a slow fire that consistently burns inside a person, which is why it is different from an emotion, which is temporary and transient and requires reaction to external stimulus. The trouble is that people confuse passion with strong emotion and once the emotion fades they start to lose interest or question themselves if it was really a passion at all that was worth following in the first place. If you look at failed marriages, it's the realization that it wasn't passion that put two people together but emotions that were temporary and transient."

"The key here is that passion involves the mind, while emotions exclude mental judgements. Passion drives you to action to make something better while emotions themselves may make it difficult for you to describe why you feel the way you do."

"A passionate person will likely give you the specific reasons why they are excited about the subject. Please, don't think I'm denigrating the importance of emotions, as they distinguish us from many animals and bring in some beautiful moments in our life. However, passion is what drives people to greater heights and is what has allowed our species to progress in both good and bad directions."

"Those who are passionate are the lucky ones as they are excited about what they do or with whom they do it. The challenge is, was and will always be, maintaining passion towards the goal to which you aspire. How do you do that, you ask?"

"First, you must realize that achievement comes in small increments and that one needs to constantly look at where they came from before evaluating where they are."

"Second, you must truly enjoy what it is that you are doing and with whom you are doing it and this means a spirit of teamwork based on three criteria -mutual trust, mutual respect and mutual reward. When all three components are in place, then the goals are more manageable and there will be a bond between you that will be synergistic in nature."

"Finally, you need to have measured goals that will allow you to see your progress along the way. To begin and only see the end is not natural and will eliminate passion as one cannot see the progress being made and the reward process is an all or none affair that many lose interest in."

"While passion is not an emotion, but a consequence of emotions, never minimize the importance of being passionate towards who you are, what you are doing and what you believe in. I have a wonderful friend who is the most passionate person I have ever had the honor of knowing. His passion is infectious and so appealing because it takes the valleys and rearranges them so that he believes they are only smaller mountains."

James took off his glasses for effect and looked at the audience in a more personal manner. "You are in the cusp of world-changing discoveries and developments and have the opportunity to one day be considered great, held in awe by those who didn't have the ability, desire or dedication that you have. What you have accomplished probably seems uncertain to many. Yet, so many of what we discover is unplanned, rather than deliberately thought out or carefully considered. Some call it luck. I call it perseverance, for which the odds of success become greater and greater and greater."

"Never give up! Never stop dreaming and believing and never, ever stop being passionate about what you are doing, as it is simply profound to which I have the honor of meeting people like you who have dedicated your life to both excellence and humanity, for which I simply say that I am honored to be in your presence."

"In conclusion, passion is the exuberance you bring to your work. Emotion is the attachment to the outcome of that work. The two, particularly in your endeavors, should never be confused with one another because both will impact not only how you perform, but how you feel about what you accomplish. Passion is sparked by your love, interest, creative abilities and the possibilities for greater opportunities for growth around your work."

"Never forget that your greatest challenges can fuel a dynamic outcome as your passion brings an all-encompassing satisfaction, while emotion, even when it is well guarded, and especially when it is internalized, brings frustration, increased stress and sometimes defeat"

Ouch! James was talking to me.

"When you are emotional you lose sight of the issue, the problem and what has been achieved and concentrate on what hasn't been done. If so, you will lose sight on all that has been accomplished and that is why I am honored to speak to you today."

"You, all of you here in this room and those across the world, are leaders. You are noble in your cause, honorable in your integrity and exceptional in your decency and are in the process of making the world a better place for all living beings and for that I say thank you. Thank you for your dedication! Thank you for your commitment! And, above all else, thank you for your passion!"

"Recently, we lost a friend, a mentor, and a loved one who made this world a better place for many. We all feel his loss, but in leaving, he also donated the one gift that he had and that was a passion for life and for that, we will all be eternally grateful."

Wow!

The room was quiet and then one sole clap began as the room realized that the message given was a message received. Greatness starts from within! I looked at the man who started the applause. I looked at his long, black, pony tail with the small feather in the end and the broad smile upon his face. It was my friend and my Big Brother who understood what the message was all about - persistence and never, ever giving up.

Day Two:

As for the second day, it was for my 'inner circle' as I concluded I needed to share the confidential warning part of the letter from The Duke with my most trusted advisors consisting of Peter, James and Luke. My rationale was quite simple. Peter was my 'brains' who knew more about what was going on than anyone else in terms of the technology and where we came close to the edge in terms of patent infringement. Luke was and remains my ethicist, telling me right-from-wrong, good-from-bad and making certain that what we did was the right thing to do. James and I had grown so close that, in many ways, he had replaced Rodney as my most trusted friend. This was not because anything had happened between Rodney and me, but simply because James and I were working together on a daily basis, while my interaction with Rodney had become more social and infrequent.

We addressed what was called our SWOT analysis which stood for **S**trengths, **W**eaknesses, **O**pportunities and **T**hreats. Then concluded that the urgency that had been in place when we were trying to beat the clock for The Duke, was simply gone, but we still needed to continue on.

We all agreed that our strengths revolved around SIMON and the MadCity Boys and their commitment to betterment. They were all wealthy and the work environment was conducive to their personalities. We also felt that the global network of researchers was such that they would remain loyal to us if enticed by other companies.

The question then became do we have the same priorities, now that The Duke was gone? There was very little discussion. The answer was yes! However, we realized the urgency that once pervaded all decisions was gone. We agreed that we were going to continue down the research path we had created and complete the project. In other words, find a way to reduce or minimize the crushing reality of Alzheimer's disease.

We understood what our weaknesses were. We also realized that we didn't have the capital or size to compete against Big Pharma and felt they would do everything they could to impede, limit and control any form of progress that detrimentally affected their bottom line.

We agreed that our opportunities remained with Mediglove and the new Kaleidoscope eye exam that Matt and the boys had engineered to the point that it could be sold for under $100 and provide the same services as Mediglove.

The challenge became, what are our threats? We narrowed these down into different classes - economic, technical and political. While we had initially jumped profoundly ahead of all other institutions in terms of computational capability, these institutions were rapidly closing the gap regarding structures similar to ours where they purported to offer like services at a lower cost.

As day two wore on, it became very apparent that we were in a for some real legal battles. To this end, it was agreed that we needed to add a full-time legal expert to our team. We needed someone who could defend and protect us from the probable onslaught that was about to take place.

The team agreed that we needed to find someone to join our group. I raised my hands and inquired, "Where do we find someone like that?" Peter smiled and noted that he believed he had just the person. His name was Philip Actman. Philip had grown up with Peter and Andrew and was not only a legal genius, but understood the realities of law and the use of technology in maximizing legal thought. He had a reputation of being a bit capricious by changing his opinion as things around him changed. I knew that if he was the right fit, we needed to ensure a forward plan that would not allow for much deviation.

I asked Peter where Philip was working and he noted that he was living in Milwaukee and working for social services.

"You believe he's the right man?" I inquired.

"Wait until you meet him!" was Peter's response.

I called Andrew and inquired about Philip and was surprised by Andrew's answer. "He's a brilliant man with a warm heart, but a pessimistic head. He's always been a person who was willing to do something for others, but never could see how it could be done. Having said that, he's going to give you all he's got, every single time."

Philip:

I called Jermaine Washington at Wilco and asked him to look into Philip and see if we couldn't have dinner. Jermaine called a few hours later and indicated that Philip wanted to know why I wanted to meet with him. Jermaine noted that to assuage Philip, he outlined who we were and what we were trying to do and there was still reticence. He indicated that Philip wanted to know how Jermaine got his name and when Jermaine mentioned Peter and Andrew, the entire tone of the meeting changed with the conversation set at Carnevor, one of Milwaukee's finest and The Duke's favorite.

I arrived five minutes early and was shown to my table, which had been the one always reserved for The Duke. I guess, I was assuming a new role in the company and what had been a gradual transition was beginning to speed up.

At precisely 7:00 PM, Philip showed up. He was wearing jeans and a golf shirt and a navy-blue sports coat. His hair had begun to salt-and-pepper and his dark rimmed glasses hid his piercing eyes. Simply by his demeanor, I could tell that I was about to have a conversation with yet another brilliant man.

For the next two hours, Philip filled me in on his life, career and why he was working in social services by noting that the public legal world wasn't at all what he thought it was going to be when he graduated Magna Cum Laude from the University of Chicago law school before getting his PHD at Oxford.

I shared with him that Derrick had attended the University of Chicago law school and was working in our company and asked how he knew Peter and Andrew and he noted they all went to the same high school. He noted that Peter had always been brilliant and that it got him into a lot of trouble. He noted that Peter was the most profound autodidact he had ever met. I feigned understanding until Philips said, "Peter is always able to self-educate to the point of brilliance on any subject he chose to learn.

I inquired about his hobbies and interests and Philip indicated that he loved to fish, which put another big smile on my face, as I thought of my friend James, and how we met.

Peter looked at me and inquired, "Why am I here?" I guess that after two hours, three drinks and a hundred-dollar porterhouse steak, it was a good question. I took it upon myself to explain who we were, what our goals were and then, almost verbatim the SWOT analysis, concluding that we needed to add a legal mind to our team to protect and defend now that The Duke was gone. There was a nod of understanding as he had researched the Foundation and The Duke, and had spoken with both Peter and Andrew.

"I'd like to invite you to come and see our facility." I offered. "It will provide more insight into what we are all about."

Philip nodded and the following Saturday was arranged. I told him to meet me at my offices and we would go from there. Once again, Philip was right on time. I smiled and nodded towards the chopper.

"Cool!" Philip responded, as we boarded and began our journey. For me the flight was just another one. For Philip, it was something he had never done before and so I let him peer out the window and marvel at the land below.

Upon landing at the farm, we made our way to the facility and Philip was shown what we were all about. With a slacked jaw, I could tell that he was impressed by the facilities and capabilities.

As the tour was winding down, I offered to take him into The Forest, explaining why it meant so much to me. As had been the case with Peter, Luke and James, Philip's response was exactly the same, as feelings overwhelmed him and I could tell he was profoundly moved.

"Peter told me about this, but I thought it was hyperbole," Philip shared. "There is a sense of purity and tranquility here I've never felt before. I can honestly feel the goodness and compassion. Just as Peter said the chimera didn't seem logical and that it wasn't an illusion.

We made our way to the springs and took out the tin cups that I filled with water. We toasted and then I saw the man in front me change before my eyes. Gone was any reservation! Gone was any sense of doubt! Gone was any reluctance!

Philip smiled and said. "George, I don't know if you are a man of religion, but I am. Not your sequestered religion that is segmented based on the teachings of others that follow the teachings of one great prophet, but on a comprehensive collection of thoughts and ideas, beliefs and values that transcend all religions. As an example, Buddha taught his followers that to realize enlightenment, a person must develop two qualities: wisdom and compassion, which are sometimes compared to the two wings of a bird that must work together to enable flying or two eyes that must work together to see deeply."

"When I am affected by a place like this, I turn inward and ask why? Is it me or the fact that I have found a very special location that adds to my values and beliefs. George, I am a man who prides himself on his compassion which literally means 'to suffer together'. I have spent my career being confronted by another's suffering and I have been motivated to relieve that suffering. This has been my purpose!"

Philip continued. "I have always practiced enlightenment, where many people delineate and build walls based on the 'individual me' and 'the individual you' which limits one's ability to ever be wise. What you have shown me today is an entire organization that doesn't ask those questions and, an entire team of people who never ask, 'What's in it for me?'"

"Do you want to join our team?" I inquired.

Philip responded, "I already have! If you want me."

Arrangements were made to have him work out of my office, which made all the sense in the world, as it was initially designed and decorated in early law firm.

Francis:

I would have been totally remiss in many ways if I didn't report what happened to Francis. With Aristotle gone and that part of the program disbanded, we had no idea what to do with Francis. He was a family member and we all loved him, but at 500 pounds, he certainly wasn't a lap dog. The second question became, what about Mary.

The idea came to me one day. We had a pig whose ability would amaze people and a woman who grew up in the circus and taught him everything. Why not find a place where they could continue to explore the possibilities and yet teach the world a little bit about humanity?

I contacted the State of Wisconsin historical society and asked about the Circus World Museum in Baraboo. For those unfamiliar, the museum honors and celebrates a time gone by when the circus came to town. It is filled with artifacts from those days including many from Ringling Brothers Circus, which was founded and wintered in Baraboo, reflecting a time of innocence of days gone by.

The museum was only 60 miles from Waldwick and drew hundreds of thousands of people each year. I inquired about their Big Top program that featured all types of acts and events. I asked how it was funded and made them an offer they could not refuse. The Derrick Williams Foundation would pay the Big Top entertainment costs each year, and would continue to do so until Francis could no longer be on the program.

We sent them a demo tape and they were astounded and the board of governors agreed. We drew yup a contract where we had no control of anything but Francis, concerning other acts and it was agreed that Francis would join the team. We also agreed to build a training and medical facility on circus grounds that could be used by all animal acts where visitors could observe through one-way glass how the animals were trained and cared for before going into the Big Top to perform.

Little did anyone realize what the consequence would be. "Francis the Talking Pig" became the biggest draw in the history of the museum. Tens of thousands came to see Mary put Francis through his workout of pressing buttons and "talking to the audience". They were shocked during the Q&A segment when Francis answered questions about life and God and people walked away with heads shaking in disbelief. Soon word spread and the networks picked up the feel-good story and Francis was featured on all the morning news programs, 20/20 and 60 minutes. Francis was a star!

As promised, the Foundation built the training facility on museum grounds and arranged for lodging in Baraboo for Mary. It was there she met a man named Jon. They fell in love and she lives there today working as an employee for the museum. Francis performed for several years and then retired to the profound sadness of millions who had marveled at his ability, insight and love. Upon his death from old age, Francis came back to Waldwick to be buried next to his friend Aristotle and my little buddy Jake. I loved Francis. He was kind, generous and sensitive and proved to me that all living things have a soul.

Urgency:

With the pendulum no longer swinging at such a frenetic pace, the MadCity Boys asked how things were changing. I informed them that, while the initial goal had been to ameliorate the insipient malady pervading The Duke, his departure meant that the timetable no longer had the urgency it once had. In fact, I announced that it was my belief that we should scrap the idea of implanting the chip in the hippocampus for mental acuity and focus on chips that would allow for modifications of chemical balances such that the body would rectify itself physically, but not mentally. I guess some of the big words from college slipped out as the boys looked at me as if I was from Mars and so I said "OK guys, we are still on course to develop the chips, we just don't need to be in such a big hurry."

I knew when I got to the research center that the MadCity Boys had something they wanted to show me and I felt it must be a biggie because they were all gussied up with big shit-eating grins on their faces.

Mark and Peter were in the front of the room while all but Luke were standing along the outside walls, too excited to sit down. I took my normal position and Mark smiled at Peter and Peter replied with a big smile on his own.

"George, we've been doing a little work and have something new and exciting to show you," Peter began.

"We've been working on it for the past year in our spare time and think you're going to like what you are about to see," Mark added.

"We thought that the Mediglove needed to be updated, and hope you don't mind, but we began developing a new product based on what we thought were the shortcomings of Medi One," Peter said.

"In order to show you what we've done, we need to outline a little technology." Mark added and with that turned to Tad who began. "We wanted to make Mediglove more durable, more functional and easier to use and first turned to the batteries with the goal of eliminating the battery pack on the back of the glove altogether. We examined all types of composites and decided that we wanted to incorporate a lithium polymer technology."

A slide came up that showed all the different types of batteries and the advantages and disadvantages of each chemical composition and Tad added. "Lithium polymer cells have evolved from lithium-ion and lithium-metal batteries. The primary difference is that instead of using a liquid lithium-salt electrolyte held in an organic solvent, the battery uses a solid polymer electrolyte which can typically be classified as one of three types: dry SPE, gelled SPE and porous SPE."

Peter noted. "If you remember the coronavirus masks, you probably also remember that the most effective material was the inner liner called melt-blown fabric. To create melt-blown requires a machine that melts plastic and blows it out in strands, much like cotton candy, which is then placed between two standard cloth materials to create the mask, creating an extremely fine mesh of synthetic polymer fiber."

Tad continued, "We got the idea of experimenting with melt-blown fabric to see if we couldn't use it to create a polymer so that we could virtually 'layer' and create a cloth battery. At first, it didn't seem possible. However, we began working with it and created a positive electrode by using lithium-transition-metal-oxide as the conductive additive spun with a polymer binder and then a carbon-based melt-blown polymer for the negative electrode."

I shook my head as if I understood what Tad had said. Once again it shot right over my head.

Tad continued. "In between the two layers we then developed a melt-blown microporous separator to prevent the electrodes from touching. This allows only the ions and not the electrode particles to move from one side to the other."

"In other words, you created battery cloth? I inquired.

There was a huge smile on everyone's face and they replied in unison. "Yes!"

"Is it effective?" I asked

Mark replied. "Our fiber works on what is called the principle of intercalation which is the reversible inclusion or insertion of a molecule into materials within the layered structures and de-intercalation of lithium ions from a positive electrode material and a negative electrode material. Graphite is the most common and least expensive intercalation host, which not only saves money, but expands the van der Waals gap, which is the distance-dependent interaction between the atoms or molecules, thereby, making the battery more efficient."

Again, I had no idea what Mark just said, but knew the MadCity Boys were on to something as Mark added. "Unlike lithium-ion cylindrical and prismatic cells that have rigid metal cases, our cells have a flexible body so they are not only relatively unconstrained but lightweight and can easily be produced in almost any desired shape. In addition, our fiber has a low self-discharge rate of about 5% per month, which means that after a full charge you would have nearly two years of non-use before the fiber would need to be recharged before operating efficiently."

"While a typical Li-ion battery cell has a life cycle of about 1000 recharges, we also added a silicon–graphene additive that helps to preserve the positive terminal during discharging, thus increasing the cell longevity and cycle-life to an estimated 2000 cycles."

"In other words, over five years if used daily?" I asked.

"Yes"

"So, you've developed a layered fabric which is actually the battery, that can be made into anything from gloves to clothes to carpeting, to you name it?"

"Peter nodded while adding. "Yes! Then, if we want to, by adding a simple layer of thin carbon fibers that can be printed onto the substrate and temperature sensors, we can not only make clothing, but bedding as well that is designed to keep a person at the optimum temperature at all times."

"But won't it be thick and heavy?" I asked.

"About the thickness of a sheet of paper, yet virtually indestructible."

"As good as Kevlar?"

"Virtually equal in terms of tensile strength, yet half the thickness."

"OK." I replied, realizing the boys were off on one of their tangents. "How does this apply to Mediglove?"

Mark added. "It allowed us to reduce the thickness of the glove and increase the length of time it can operate, while also enhancing its durability. We've been able to eliminate the battery completely and actually build in a blue tooth transponder simply by adding one more layer of fabric on just the finger tips. Because of this, we have also been able to add another feature where we now can measure a person's pulse and oxygen levels. In terms of oxygen, SIMON will know whether a person is in a healthy range, which is typically around 95% to 100%."

Peter replied, "To do this we simply have small beams of light pass through your finger where a sensor measures the amount of light absorbed by oxygenated and deoxygenated blood."

Back to Mark: "With this, we now see Mediglove moving beyond a diagnostic tool to also incorporate athletic training and those involved in any form of high stress activities such as pilots, divers and also those who are exposed to demands on their body."

My turn. "So, the next Mediglove measures your fingerprint, DNA, pulse, blood pressure, heart rate, body temperature and oxygen level?" I asked, shaking my head in amazement. "And you've incorporated blue tooth so that it doesn't need to be connected by wires to anything?" The boys were all smiling.

"There's one more thing that we've added." Mark responded. "Mediglove is now bi-directional. This means that SIMON can communicate with Mediglove and even do greater diagnostics including an EKG to determine if a person has had or is at risk of having a heart attack and even send automated warning messages concerning potential risks such as heart attacks or strokes to a physician."

My mind was swirling. I remember being in the hospital and having all the wires connected to different machines and sensors taped to my chest. With Mediglove, the patient would simply put on the glove and have all the data broadcast to a panel without wires and connectors and no 'beep, beep, beep'. Not only was this good for patients, we were also opening up a totally new market. I simply shook my head as reality struck and I asked, "How much more will the new glove cost?"

Peter smiled and replied, "With mass production, the cost will go up about thirty-" I was waiting for the word dollars when he added, "cents."

"What?" I said incredulously.

"Yes, we've eliminated the battery pack and on/off button and there is no more charging. Manufacturing the fibers and laminating them can be done in volume and Mark believes we can even pre-charge the fiber before lamination to save time and reduce costs. In addition, the gloves will be completely impervious to dirt and moisture, as they are totally sealed."

"What happens is someone rips or cuts the glove?"

"The circuits all go dead!" Tad replied.

"In other words, the product doesn't need UL approval?

"It's no longer electrical." Peter responded, looking at Phillip.

"How does the user know the unit is failing?" I asked.

Mark smiled and replied, "We re-designed all the sensors to be static when there is power and begin vibrating when inadequate current is applied."

"How long will they vibrate?" I asked, thinking they could be laying on a shelf and go off on their own.

Mark saw my concern. "There is a primary sensor built into the back of the glove that actually begins the entire process by using your own electrical energy to complete the circuit."

In other words, the 2000 hours isn't shelf-life, it's operating time?"

The boys all nodded in the affirmative.

"Once a month for two thousand times? That's over 150 years. That means buy it once and use it forever!" I just shook my head in amazement.

"What about cleanliness and multiple users?" Phillip asked.

Peter responded, looking directly at Phillip. "First of all, each glove remains designed for only one person's use and once the fingerprint and DNA is recorded, it becomes inert. Second, all a person need do is use a hand sanitizer or any alcohol wipe on their hand before putting it into the glove and it should kill any virus or bacteria. Because the glove is not intrusive other than the surface of one's skin, there is no greater risk than any other glove."

I looked at the glass topped pedestal that had Mediglove #1 in it and it looked like a 1958 Buick and simply shook my head. We were progressing and the gravy train that supported the entire Foundation just added a whole bunch of new cars.

"One more question," I asked.

"What?" Mark inquired.

"Does it come in Badger red?"

There were smiles all around the room as Phillip sat shaking his head. I don't think he had any idea the brilliance or passion of the group he was joining, nor how much beer they could drink.

That night, I called 'V' and asked him to set up a follow-up team meeting as we needed to review where we were on both Kaleidoscope and the Nanochips. The full team meeting was set and everyone was there. The weeks between The Duke's departure and this meeting had allowed some of the pain to go away, and yet, I knew it would never all be gone.

The meeting was scheduled and 'V' began by formally introducing Philip to the boys and Mary. I think there was some question as to why a lawyer was being added to the team, but I knew that we would soon be in deep water and having a bio-ethicist in Luke and a formal lawyer in Philip, we had the internal core we needed to fend off the anticipated onslaught.

As 'V' transitioned to Peter, the original Gannt Charts came into play and it was agreed that the initial plan had been too aggressive and optimistic. Mary reported that Francis was fine, but getting bored. Very few people ever knew about The Duke and what had transpired in the Dells. We did that intentionally, to protect them in case of a federal investigation.

With Simoni and the Headlock working perfectly, it was concluded that, if the chip was ready, we should proceed with the experiment and see what transpired if we inserted a chip. While the chip implanted in The Duke had "brought him back" it did so with repercussions and the boys felt there were some areas that needed re-programming. It was agreed that when they were confident they had made the right changes, it was time for Francis to have the chip inserted.

A date was set for the implant into Francis and we all thought that we were good to go. Two days before the planned procedure, we received a Certified Letter from the A.S.P.C.A. indicating that they were filing for an injunction to stop the 'torture' of Francis. I was incredulous. First, how did they get the information? Second, did anyone really feel and that a virtually non-intrusive insert was torture?

I turned to Philip and said, "the war has begun. Can you get this overturned?"

Philip assured me that it was a nuisance action and he could get it thrown out.

I asked how long would it take and he said two weeks.

For the next fourteen days, we had media trucks and protestors at the research facility. The world watched as a simple procedure was blown out of proportion and we went from being good guys to villains using the system to make ourselves rich at the expense of innocent animals.

At first, I tolerated the intrusion. However, when damage was done to our facility and the MadCity Boys were being harassed, I knew it was time to put my foot down. I called Andrew and told him to get some of the larger crowd control guys down to the facility and throw the tree huggers off our property and make a really big impression.

For some reason, this all seemed to coincidental. Why us? Why now? Who were these people?

A second call to Andrew got the wheels rolling. I wanted to know who was behind what was going on. Once again, the odoriferous emanation of a Mephitis-Mephitis situated in our stacked lignis, got my dander up. In Cheese head language. The goddamn skunk was in the fuc- - ng woodpile and I wanted to know who put him there.

I think the tree huggers got the shit scared out them when all four of our corporate choppers landed in the field and out jumped 20 of the biggest musclemen you could imagine. The big boys were dressed in skin-tight, black t-shirts, black cargo pants and military style stomping boots. Anyone not intimidated, would need to be crazy.

As the last of "big guys" got out, next came Andrew. He knew this was really important and even though he had been "out of practice" in terms of hand-to-hand combat, he wanted to be the spokesperson.

It took all of five minutes to round up the entire protestor ensemble and read a formal letter concerning trespassing, criminal damage to property and all kinds of other legal-speak meant to let these folks know we weren't messing around.

Andrew politely asked them to leave and was told, *"fuck you!"* to which he nodded and handed out cattle prods. Now, if you don't know what a cattle prod is, think of a cane with electrodes on the end which is used to make **cattle** move by providing a relatively high-voltage, low-current electric shock.

The twenty "enforcers" slowly surrounded the thirty or so demonstrators while Andrew offered, one last time, to let them leave peacefully, to which, he received the same response as before. With 50 people involved, Andrew knew he needed to break things down and asked who was leading the demonstration. At first, no one responded and then a woman in her late forties indicated she was.

"Your name, please," Andrew asked.

"Why do you need that?" was her response.

"All I want is your first name so that we can have a more personal conversation. My name is Andrew. Is that too much to ask?"

"Sheryl," was the response, as she began to soften.

"Tell you what Sheryl, why don't you and I go into the research center and you can see what it's all about. If, after you see what we are attempting to do, you still feel that we are wrong, we can have further discussions. If not, your group will agree to leave.

Luke gave Sheryl the full tour, showing her all that we had accomplished and what our goals were for the future, along with how our environmental footprint was zero. Forty minutes later, Andrew and Sheryl came out and Sheryl looked at the ground and then at the group and then at Andrew. "Sir, we were instructed to come here and were told you were abusing animals. We owe you an apology. There is nothing in this facility that is doing harm. In fact, I feel guilty in saying that it is one of the most noble gestures I have ever seen."

As the tensions waned, I radioed Andrew and asked him to take the group on a tour of The Forest and explain its history and offer them a drink from the springs. I thought that if we got just a few to feel what we felt, they would become our allies.

Thirty minutes later, the twenty big guys and the demonstrators returned and I could see a totally different set of expressions. For some, it had been an epiphany, for others, simply witnessing how good can prevail and affect those around them.

As the groups were about to disband, Sheryl took Andrew by the side and confessed that they had been 'instructed' to visit the center and wreak havoc. They were assured that any and all fines, penalties or bonds needed would be covered. Someone had paid these folks to protest, just like the picketers when small businesses are faced with a strike.

We now knew what The Duke had warned about was beginning to happen. There were people out there who wanted us stopped, no matter what the cost. Our goal was simply to build a protective perimeter around all that we had created, physically, intellectually and legally.

Andrew asked who was paying them and Sheryl indicated that per diems were arranged and deposited in checking accounts on a daily basis and no one knew where the money was coming from, inquiring whether they all were going to the same bank and Sheryl indicated "yes". We knew what we needed to do and sent our representatives to First City Bank in Madison. Philip was lead person and was accompanied by Wilco PR and Wilco operations. Philip met with one of the Vice Presidents who notified the group that the business of the bank was private.

Philip said he understood and indicated that his goal was only to find out where the funds were coming from. The banker remained reticent. So did Philip. Because the bank was part of a publicly traded corporation, Philip did a little research and found out that First City had branches in Madison, the Dells and several other small towns including Black River Falls. It didn't take a genius to quickly realize who their biggest customer was.

Philip called me and I called Big Brother. I explained what happened and Rodney said "holy shit! consider it handled."

Twenty minutes later Philip's phone rang and the V.P. exclaimed there must have been a misunderstanding and that the requested information would be available the next morning. What had been a stonewall quickly turned into a pile of rubble as we learned that funds were transferred from a lobbying group in Washington D.C. closely associated with Big Pharma and also working closely with none other than Senator Russ Fitzgerald. We'd had our run-ins with him periodically and yet we also pledged to ourselves that there would be no capitulation to his style of dominance.

Rodney called to make sure we had the information we needed. I thanked him and realized that, once again, money talked. I found it particularly interesting that the Senator's denigration bordered on libel or slander. He had besmirched me so often, to so many people that he thought he could get away with it simply to weaken me through false statements and rumors to the point that 'V' would never consider running against him for his Senate seat when the time came. Those who knew me, also knew better. I wasn't the greedy monger he portrayed me as. I was simply a man whose quest was the satisfaction that comes from helping another and I always felt rewarded when the gift was me instead of my money.

The Hurricane:

The demonstrators were but the first salvo. We knew the storm was brewing. We just didn't believe it would be a category five hurricane like the one that had destroyed St. Martin and was now trying to destroy us. To have the full Judiciary Committee command the defense of your company and its operation is an almost anti-altruistic experience where one sits and wonders if it's all really worth it.

The initial demand was that we turn over all documents regarding the technology and database of SIMON. The Atlanta boys refused using the Fourth Amendment that protects Americans from 'unreasonable searches and seizures'. We were told that the Supreme Court's interpretation of 'unreasonable' has varied over time. Philip explained that some searches require warrants, but others do not. In general, the Fourth Amendment protects a person and their property from searches by the government wherever there is a 'reasonable expectation of privacy'. We knew that the government was attempting to infiltrate SIMON. We also believed that every message coming in or going out of the Foundation was being intercepted.

After the 9-11 attacks, Congress passed laws making it easier for the government to use information when investigating terrorism. We were informed that SIMON was a risk to national security. We challenged the assertion, denoting the Fifth Amendment protects the right to private property in two ways. First, it states that a person may not be deprived of property by the government without 'due process of law,' or fair procedures. In addition, it sets limits on the traditional practice of eminent domain.

Under the Fifth Amendment, such takings must be for a 'public use' and require 'just compensation' at market value for the property seized. However, in *Kelo v. City of New London*, which we used when we defended The Forest from becoming a county park, the Supreme Court interpreted public use broadly to include a 'public purpose' of economic development that might directly benefit private parties. In response, many state legislatures passed laws limiting the scope of eminent domain for public use.

I was stunned! All we wanted to do was help people and make life better and the government wanted it as yet another weapon of war. While we talk in millions and watch our pennies, they talk in trillions and watch nothing – it's not their money. While we saw our virtual existence at stake, they saw it as just another day at the office. While our hopes and dreams, aspirations and accomplishments were put in harm's way, to the twelve Senators who would sit before us, it was nothing more than a way to be on national television and build their brand awareness amongst their constituents so that they could retain the power, prestige and perks they coveted so much.

The order mandated that we address both antitrust and competition policies including the Sherman, Clayton and Trade Commission Acts as the Senators purported that selling Medigloves for the cost we did and with such success, was being detrimental to the entire health care industry and went further in terms of looking into our proprietary software that limited competition and also at alleged violations of FDA regulations.

In other words, the overt claim was that the US Government believed that the Foundation was impeding competition and was falsely representing itself as a non-profit entity because we made all of the MadCity Boys wealthy. The government also stated that we had violated FDA rules by injecting The Duke with the Nanochip and that, had they so desired, they could have charged us with third-degree murder, due to his suicide. Finally, the government contended that the Foundation was in violation of national security by incorporating a secured database that maintained confidential records of over one billion people throughout the world, which we refused to share with the NSA or any other security branches of the government.

I Zoomed Peter and Luke and asked them what was going on and they concurred that this wasn't about Mediglove, it was about the power we had with SIMON. We knew more than the government did about more people and their health and wellbeing all over the world. We had data they coveted, that we would not share, based on our protection under the Constitution.

It was then that Luke really hit home when he said that man had always been at war and that it would continue. "George, war is evolving from a face-to-face, person-to-person battle where the victor represented took control of the mindset of the defeated, to where we are today. In addition to those deaths caused directly by violence – for instance those from gunshot or explosions – a significant proportion of lives lost in conflict are *indirect*, due to disease, starvation or exposure. This is particularly true where conflicts lead to famine or outbreaks of disease among the civilian population. But historically, such indirect deaths were also a major cause of military fatalities."

Peter added. "SIMON has data on over one-billion people. This means he knows more than any security agency of the US government. More than the NSA! More than the CIA! More than anyone! This is what the government wants. Because SIMON is a two-way street, it has the ability to 'communicate' all forms of propaganda to one-seventh of the world's population. Because everyone checks in, SIMON knows the location and time the person checked in. He also has some behavioral data where, using algorithms SIMON can determine what people love, what they hate and what directions people will ignore. Because of the massive amount of data SIMON has, we could easily program him to predict, with astounding accuracy, what people are or are not likely to do, including propaganda and even war."

I was appalled! All I wanted to do was help people and never thought of what the 'other side' could use SIMON to do.

Peter continued. "George, war has three general purposes. First, to conquer and destroy the armed power of the enemy. Second, to take possession of an enemy's sources of strength and third, to gain public support at home and the opinion of the citizenry of the defeated.

There wasn't a smile on Luke's face as he added in earnest. "In the past, war was 'inter-personal' as I call it, that was sustained through all the battles from Caesar until World War I. In these wars, it was man-vs-man, sword-vs-sword, knife-vs-knife and then gun-vs-gun. The methodology of war evolved, but it was primarily face-to-face where you saw who it was you killed and watched them die. World War I changed everything! It started with men on horseback and digging trenches, still fighting face-to-face. It ended with poison gas and men in airplanes and tanks anonymously creating death."

"Every war since has seen increased killing sophistication to the point where today, war has become impersonal. An unmanned drone flies over a target and someone, somewhere pushes a button that eliminates someone they never saw or felt and would not watch them die. They do so without remorse or consideration for the loss of a husband, father, son or friend with no risk or consequence to themselves while eating lunch and thinking nothing of what they just did."

"Today, war is not about destruction, but about capturing the hearts and minds of those who are affected and right now SIMON has the potential to be the most powerful weapon on earth. While we have built in safeguards, the concern within the government is that either someone will break in and take all of SIMON's data and programming and use it against our country, or we will. That's why we are being called in front of the Judiciary Committee and why, to circumvent any negative attacks by the citizenry, they are doing it under the Federal Trade Commission. The goal is not to stop us, but to make us share all the data and programming with the government so that they have the ability to use it for their purposes."

"George, I sincerely believe that 'bullet wars' are over. Our country has experienced a dress rehearsal of one form of tomorrow's wars, where an enemy creates a deadly virus and inoculates their own citizens and then lets the virus run rampant everywhere else, thereby creating a pandemic that only kills people and does so to the degree that all resources, other than humans, are retained intact with no physical or collateral damage. Imagine being able to walk into any country and simply remove the dead and take over the infrastructure and populate it with people who were loyal to you. It would be an incredibly efficient form of domination."

Luke leaned back in his chair and asked, "Do you see why the information SIMON has is so valuable? In the wrong hands, the enemy would know what people they could "select" to kill simply by manipulating prescription dosages or knowing what to include or limit in their chemical arsenal."

I shuddered to think of the power we had and now realized why the government wanted us eliminated.

Peter added, "I believe that soon there will be more sophisticated electronic wars capable of shutting down entire economies simply by infiltrating and infecting software for things such as the financial, communication and medical networks and we will have reached our social, political, technical and ethical Hayflick Limit. We have had around twenty-one generations since the Constitution and we all know that our country is now about one thing – money! What would happen if all of sudden money was erased? No more 401K's or stock portfolios! No more bank accounts or credit cards! Our economy and our world would come to a standstill. What about our power grids that could bring our nation to its knees?"

Peter opened his hands and said. "All of our hydroelectric dams are now computer controlled. Imagine breaking in and opening the floodgates on all of them simultaneously! It would kill millions of people and destroy cities and towns without a single missile being fired. Imagine wiping away all the medical software so that there were no medical records or controls of medical robots. Cars have become mobile computers that are all connected to the manufacturers. Imagine infecting their software so that engines would either destroy themselves or take control of moving vehicles, creating thousands of accidents all over the country! Imagine controlling all flight operations to the point that no one, including our military, could safely take off and land. As you can see, we are vulnerable and right now, the government believes SIMON has the capability to do any or all of the above."

I thought of how easy it was for us to break into the FDA and change the rules to try and save Dr. Williams and how, within fifteen seconds, SIMON had infiltrated Ancestry.com and changed The Duke's heritage to make him part Native American.

Luke continued. "I agree with Peter. War isn't about killing, it's about control of the mind - about opinions, attitudes and beliefs, where changing those can result in the total collapse of a society and its political structure. The misinformation program used during World War II by the Germans, Japanese and Americans were classic examples of a rudimentary form of persuasion."

"The 2016 US Presidential election was a classic form of electronic warfare, where an outside source meddled in our election to get the individual or individuals they wanted elected. They did so simply by planting misinformation about the opponent and doing it with such sophistication and verve that our simplistic protection system was unable to stop them. In a period of two weeks, they were able to change attitudes of voters and subsequently the entire course of history of our country without invading, nor having a single shot fired and without anyone even knowing what happened until it was too late."

"George, the reason we are being called into Washington is not about what we have done, it's about what SIMON **could do** that's equal to the power and might of the US Government. They're afraid! They don't like it when someone or something is equal to them in power or capability! All we have on our side is goodness and decency and yet those in power, who have seen what power can do, fear that we will unleash our power to control more than they want us to. This is why we are called to Washington. All the other stuff is just camouflage to their real purpose which is shutting SIMON down.

I was aghast! I felt so stupid, so innocent, so naïve. All I wanted to do was help people, not hurt them, control them or affect them and I hadn't accepted what The Duke had warned me before he died.

Luke looked into the computer camera and said. "George, you are a good man. You've done things no one else has ever done. You've accomplished more, helped more and did more than any one man could ever can to do. Yet, this is all about power – power to control. Because the capability is there to do what we could do, those in Washington, who currently have the power, simply want to take it away – to neutralize us – to minimize our ability to challenge them at any time. You've heard of the Golden Rule, he who has the gold rules. They have trillions of dollars behind them and powerful industries who feel threatened by us and all we can do is play the game their way."

I leaned back in my chair and thought for a moment of Amy and how she fought back from near death and realized that in one sense, this was a battle to the death as well – not physically, thank God – but ethically, and I wasn't going to allow the government to stop us by giving them every single thing we had. I needed to make certain that we could continue to help those who couldn't help themselves.

"How do we fight?" I inquired.

Luke eyes pierced the screen as he said, "We have one thing they don't have and if we use it properly, we can win."

"What's that?" I asked.

"The fifth estate," Luke replied.

I had a frown on my face as Luke added, "Only 17% of Americans today say they trust the government in Washington to do what is right. Incredibly only 3% put their total trust in our leaders and 14% believe in them some of the time. This means that 83% of all Americans are cynical. At the same time, 90% of all Americans still believe in God. No matter what religion or no religion at all, it still boils down to the same criteria – humility, generosity, compassion and forgiveness. If our testimony focuses on those four factors, we will have America and American voters on our side and the media will support us. If we have that, those in power who want to stay there, will realize that hurting us will result in diminishing their own chances of staying in power. You need to realize, power is narcotizing. Once you have it, you don't want to let go. The money! The perks! The sense of entitlement that comes with power is addictive and those who have it will do anything to keep it."

Philip had his work cut out for him, explaining that Congressional hearings represent the principal formal method by which committees collect and analyze information during the legislative policymaking process that can then be used to write laws or turned over to the justice department for prosecution.

Philip added, "the Senate implemented Rule XXVI which sets forth many of the hearing regulations that the committees must conform to, including the quorum requirement, advance submission of witness statements, the opportunity for minority party Senators to call witnesses of their choosing and also procedures for closing a hearing to the public."

"Senate committees, are guided mainly by their chairperson, who has broad discretion in how they conduct a hearing, in part because the committees adopt their own rules of procedure. These rules may supplement Senate rules. However the committee can't supersede those rules, which could be to our favor."

We knew that the committee members and their staff usually prepared extensively for any hearing and that they would include collected background information on everyone that was going to be called, while preparing a preliminary hearing memorandum for the chair and members. We told the boys to prepare a short autobiography and then have Wilco Marketing work with them on smoothing it out. They all refused, saying they'd rather do it themselves.

We were certain that the twelve Senate amigos would discuss the scope of the hearing before we arrived and what they felt the outcome would be. The Senators would all have input into selecting witnesses and determining the order and format of the witness's testimony. Finally, because we had the fifth estate on our side, the Senators would all probably prepare questions or talking points to make sure they looked good in front of the camera.

Philip told us that, on the day of the hearing, the committee would need to have a quorum to proceed with testimony. He also explained that Senators typically made opening statements, then witnesses would be introduced and sworn-in by the chair. The witnesses would be called and they were to present oral testimony in accordance with an arranged format submitted in advance. The question-and-answer period that followed would be an opportunity for the committee to expand upon a witness's statement and gather information to support future actions.

Philip added that, following the hearings, the committee staff normally prepared a summary of testimony and drafted additional questions for the day's witnesses, which meant that day two could be pretty tough. He also felt that day one would be easy, with just each subpoenaed person telling the Senators who they were and the real battle would start of day two when it could get nasty.

There were so many challenges, so much data, so many nuances that needed to be covered, I thought it would be impossible. 'V' volunteered to be spokesperson, as everyone knew that my Minnie Point Badass temper would get us all in trouble. I asked Peter to work with the crew and he suggested allowing SIMON to do the research. Within two weeks, then entire defense had been outlined, summarized and researched to the point that it included references to specific court cases defending our position and, in every instance, the 'four pillars' as we called them were referenced. Little did we know that our friend, Senator Fitzgerald had an ace up his sleeve that he thought would destroy our credibility.

We were given a date and the docket was set. Every member of the Foundation was served a subpoena and this had me worried. I couldn't fathom why they wanted everyone there. Arrangements were made and each member was given an outline of our position. We then had a 'dress rehearsal' so that everyone was comfortable with what we believed the questions would be. The boys from Atlanta had posters made of the photos of each of the Senators so that when we were in their presence there would be a level of familiarity, thereby minimizing the intimidation. Wilco Security ran personal checks on all the Senators and we knew more about them than they did about us and found it quite interesting to see the level of their integrity.

We had been informed what the structure would be - five minutes of questioning by each Senator plus interrogation by whomever the committee wanted to have us grilled by. As the days counted down, productivity at the farm slowed to a crawl. Cecelia made reservations for thirty people and we reserved a conference room at the hotel where Andrew's team would be stationed to not only make certain there were no intruders, but ensure there were no recording devices present. If the Senators wanted a pissing match, they were going to get one and it was their shoes that were going to get wet.

The night before we were to travel I couldn't sleep. I wanted the battle to begin. I wanted to show these folks they had met their match. We weren't going to knuckle under to their might and would go down swinging if it meant the end of all that we worked so hard to build. Amelia, the kids and I took Amelia X. Philip, Andrew and Dennis met with the MadCity Boys along with Rodney, Ann and members of all the Native American nations of Wisconsin who came in the Badger Bus, as we called our largest regional jet. That night we had a dinner and I stood before those who came and raised a glass first to them and then to humility, generosity, compassion and forgiveness.

The Hearing:

The hearing was to start at 10:00 AM. We were told to be there at 9:30. At precisely 9:30, all thirty of us walked in. The first row had been reserved, which constituted only twelve chairs. Philips went to the clerk and demanded an additional row. When the clerk balked, Philip threatened to have the meeting postponed until our requirements were met. This wasn't about who sat where, but who had power and, after a phone call, the second and third rows were cleared. Using Wilco leverage, we made arrangements for all the national media to be there. If there was going to be a war, it was going to be brought into America's homes in living color. Using our leverage, we made certain that the hearing was not only going to be on the government channel, but segments would be broadcast on every major cable news network and the network and local news as well.

At precisely 10:00 AM, the doors opened and the twelve Senators proceeded to their seats each with aides behind them. The meeting was called to order and the war was about to begin. I looked at the twelve and wondered what they were thinking. They had been informed there was going to be a large group, but I don't think they were expecting Rodney and the fellow presidents of the different nations to be there. Not a single smile crossed anyone's faces. You don't smile when you go to war.

We had been informed that day one would consist of verbal presentations by each individual regarding who they were and their association with the Foundation. I was told that normally, the Senators would be quite pleasant and amenable, but not to infer that this was how the meeting would go. All they were doing was sizing up the opposition. Day two would be when the fireworks started.

Sitting at the primary table was Philip and two of the Atlanta boys we hired as well. In between was a single chair. As a person was called, they had been instructed to sit in the empty chair after swearing to tell the truth and nothing but the whole truth. It was interesting to see the MadCity Boys all in suits with hair combed, shoes shined and ties straightened. None of them had forgotten to shave. All of them knew we were there with one purpose – to show the Senators and America that we were professionals whose commitment was to the betterment of all living species.

The Wilco PR team had each member of our group wearing dark suits highlighted by either a red or blue tie on a white shirt. In everyone's label was a small pin. It was an emblem of the flag of the United States of America. As a sign of their disdain, the MadCity boys decided that on the second day they would wear the flag upside down as a signal of dire distress which is only done in instances of extreme danger to life or property.

The meeting was called to order with the least senior Senators sitting on the outside edges that graduated with tenure, towards the center where none other than Wisconsin's own Senator Fitzgerald sat. This was his meeting and it was his time to get even, or at least that was his goal. The Duke was dead and gone and he felt our power base had eroded. You could see it in his eyes and the smug look upon his face.

Matthew Chapman:

"Dr. Matthew Chapman please take your seat."

After being sworn in, Matt joined Philip and the questions began. Everything from where he got the idea for Mediglove to his compensation was asked. Not once did Matt flinch. When the Senators asked him why he worked for so little pay, Matt answered. "Ladies and Gentlemen, my career began with a national medical equipment company where I was in product development. In working there, I created a device that cost a few dollars to make that would save thousands of lives. That company took a concept I created and began selling it for nearly one thousand dollars each. To justify the mark-up, they began advertising it on television so that they could report the 'investment' as research costs."

"I was naïve and realized that the business of health is just that - a business, designed to capture customers and sustain them, not cure them, until they could no longer afford the product and then I believe simply let them die. I could not justify my talents and contributions and simply resigned. As a going away present, I was served with a non-disclosure statement and told that I could not work for another medical device company for a period of five years and that, should I do so, or created products similar to what I had developed came to light, I would be sued."

"For five years, I was harassed, belittled and periodically threatened. Fortunately, during that time, my family and friends supported me, as I lived with my parents and worked at McDonalds, simply afraid to take my education and my talent elsewhere. One day, a friend called and asked me to meet with Mr. George Terrill and show him my idea that was totally different from what I had developed previously. Needless to say, I was reticent until I met Mr. Terrill and learned that his family had founded a non-profit foundation whose only goal was and remains the betterment of all living beings. I asked for and received compensation of one-dollar per unit. When I reached a point of self-sufficiency, I stopped taking the compensation and began my own foundation that is involved in sponsoring children with terminal illnesses and am proud to say that I have sponsored over one-thousand children and their families to make certain that they have a lasting memory."

"In addition, I have purchased three condominiums in Orlando, Florida that are adjacent to Disney World and work with the Disney Foundation to make certain that my guests are given VIP treatment at the park with private dinners with the characters that I pay for."

"Finally, I work with the University of Wisconsin Athletic Department and fund a portion of the handicapped section at Camp Randall Stadium where I purchase seats for football games that are given to children at the University of Wisconsin Hospital and their families."

"I am blessed that, because of the Derrick Williams Foundation, I am giving back to those in need, while also saving tens of thousands of lives around the world by allowing people in underdeveloped countries, along with developed nations, to have regular check-ups they would otherwise never have received."

"For our efforts, we have been recognized by the World Health Organization, where the Derrick Williams Foundation was named an honorary member. We have also been recognized by the United Nations for our achievements in bringing world health to all people. While the Medi-Glove has a cost of $50.00, the Foundation has developed a reserve to make certain that no person in the world who needs one of our products is ever denied. For me, my goal has been to help all living beings lead a better life."

"If Senators, you feel that I am remiss in helping others, in donating my net proceeds to satisfy one wish for a dying child or putting a smile on a sick kid's face by allowing him to not only attend a University of Wisconsin football game, but receive a football autographed by all the players, I am open to suggestions as to how I can do more to help make the world a better place for everyone."

"In conclusion, the Derrick Williams foundation does not judge by age, gender, race, religion, nationality or orientation. Our goal has always been to help **all people** and in so doing, bring peace and comfort to those who believe that America can be more than greed at the expense of others."

There was stunned silence. The first Senator was speechless. This was not what she was expecting. How could she possibly chastise a man who was giving so much to so many, particularly when the world was watching? The Senator spoke. "Thank you, Mr. Chapman for your explanation, your humility and above all else, your generosity. I commend you for your service to our country and mankind."

Mark Stevenson:

"The committee calls Mark Stevenson."

Mark took the seat vacated by Matt and the question from the second Senator was the same. Mark looked at the Senator and responded. "Senator, I was a juvenile delinquent who was sentenced to five years in prison at the Ethan Allen School for Boys in Wales, Wisconsin. One day a man by the name of Peter Washburn visited the school and talked about computers. The more he talked, the more interested I became. Upon being released from the school, the Derrick Williams Foundation provided a scholarship and paid for my education, along with living expenses."

"Upon graduating from the University of Wisconsin with a double major in computer science and electrical engineering, I was offered a position with the Foundation at a salary of $35,000 per year or half of what I could have earned elsewhere. I was told that after one year, I would begin earning ten cents for every glove placed anywhere in the world."

"My role in the Foundation deals with bio-electronics and my team is responsible for creating the sensors used to measure all the bodily functions that Mediglove entails. Like Matt, I have earned a decent living and also like Matt, I have established my own foundation and today provide scholarships to those graduating from the school in Wales."

"To date I have paid the full tuition and expenses for seventeen students, of which I am proud to say, all have graduated from college and I have the honor of saying that I sponsored two physicians, one dentist and one lawyer, along with five individuals who have turned to public service in either social services or working with troubled youth, to keep them out of my alma mater."

"Senator, like Matt, I look to you for any suggestions you might have that will allow me to better either myself or those that I assist. I am proud of the Derrick Williams Foundation and most proud of the freedom we have to choose how we personally give back to the communities in which we live. In a world, so rife with problems, where people are judged by what they are instead of what they can be, if given the dignity of respect, I hope that my small contribution to society is worthy of the gifts I received from Mr. Terrill and Mr. Washburn in terms of trust in me."

The Senator sat back in his chair, simply overwhelmed. This was not what they were expecting as he said, "Mr. Stevenson, it is an honor to have you speak to me today. I can only say that you, sir, represent what America can be, when people are given a chance."

Dr. Luke Arnold:

"The committee calls Doctor Lucas Arnold."

Luke arose and quietly made his way to the chair. He paused for a moment, took a deep breath and sat down. Philip's hand touched Luke's forearm as assurance that what he was about to say would go well.

"Ladies and gentlemen. I am honored to stand before you today to share my role in the Derrick Williams Foundation and be associated with the men and women who make up our team. While older than the rest of the team, I have had the blessing of being involved almost since its inception."

"I received my PHD is astrophysics from Stanford University. While there, I was a member of the Navy ROTC program and enjoyed the opportunity to serve our country for twenty years, first as a Navy pilot and then as a flight instructor at the Naval Air Station in Pensacola, Florida, where I taught advanced avionics and re-certification of Navy pilots to fly the F-15E Strike Eagle."

"Whereas my career goal was to be an astronaut, I unfortunately was not chosen for the program. After twenty years in the Navy, I retired with the rank of Captain. With an interest in space, I was able to gain employment with the 'Stratospheric Flight Company' commonly known as World View, where I initially ferried supplies to the space station."

"Periodically individuals interested in space flight would accompany me. In one such instance, Mr. and Mrs. George Terrill were my passengers. Unless you have never been in space, you cannot fathom the effect it can have on a person and their beliefs. In the book '*To Touch the Face of God: The Sacred, the Profane, and the American Space Program*' it's reported that a handful of the astronauts reported feelings of divinity while on the moon, including a feeling of 'universal connectedness'."

"Apollo 15 astronaut James Irwin reported that when he stood on the moon he felt God all around him. Indeed, Irwin was so overcome by his experience on the lunar surface, he asked his colleague, David Scott, if they could hold a religious service atop some nearby hills before they departed. The request was denied by Mission Control and Irwin made do by quoting Psalm 121, *"I will lift up mine eyes unto the hills, from whence cometh my help."* Irwin later reported, it was the beginning of some sort of deep change taking place inside him, marked by a profound belief in the power of God."

"I, too, have had the epiphany! I too have the profound belief in the power of God and in so doing, I joined the Derrick Williams Foundation, where I serve as both facilities manager and Bio-ethicist, whose responsibility it is to ensure that all products, actions and results sustain the same objective - the betterment of all living species."

"As facilities manager, I was involved in developing and am currently responsible for maintaining our research center that was created in such a way as it provides an absolute zero carbon footprint in terms of both energy and natural resource consumption. For our efforts, we have been nominated for the Pritzker Architecture Prize and were recently honored by being recognized as a contributor to the creative genius of the Frank Lloyd Wright Foundation. Currently we are also under consideration as for the UIA gold medal which is awarded every three years for outstanding contributions to architecture. Beyond that, we have been recognized by the Sierra Club and numerous State, local and regional environmental groups for our efforts."

"Beyond our facilities, I have been involved in developing the hyponic greenhouses on the adjacent farmland to help improve the productivity of agricultural facilities throughout America.

Currently, obtaining one pound of animal protein uses about 7.5 pounds of plant protein and 80% of all US agricultural land is used to feed livestock. By developing and building hyponic greenhouses, we have not only increased the amount of protein per square meter of land, but shifted the focus away from relying on beef, pork and chicken for protein to more efficient forms of food sourcing for humans and did so in virtually any climate in the world."

"As head of the bio-ethics team, I work with all aspects of product development, testing and implementation to ensure that our products are not only safe and for the betterment of all living beings, but incorporate recyclable materials, so that no item increases the amount of waste or refuse on our planet. It is also my responsibility to retain all communication with social, political and religious groups pertaining to our role in the community at large, addressing a broad swathe of human inquiry, ranging from debates over the boundaries of life, such as abortion and assisted suicide, to the allocation of scarce health care resources, such as organ donation, to the right to refuse medical care for religious or cultural reasons."

"As part of my bioethics role, I work with Doctor Johnson to examine the scope of bioethics including cloning, gene therapy, life extension, human genetic engineering, astro-ethics and life in space, along with the manipulation of basic biology through altered DNA, XNA and proteins which may affect future evolution and require new principles that address life at its core."

"From a medical perspective I work with numerous researchers globally to study moral values and judgments as they apply to medicine in respect to autonomy, beneficence, nonmaleficence and justice. In so doing, we address the consequence encompassing its practical application in clinical settings as well as working on our projects history, philosophy, theology, and sociology to ensure we are addressing all moral issues involved in our understanding of life and death, while continuing to resolve ethical dilemmas concerning medicine and science."

"My challenge is to address all religious communities who have their own histories of inquiry into bioethical issues who have developed rules and guidelines on how to deal with these issues from within the viewpoint of their respective faiths. Because we are a global entity, it is therefore my responsibility to understand

and implement guidelines that honor non-Western cultures, where a strict separation of religion from philosophy does not exist and ensure we create a compromised program that meets the criteria of all researchers and not just those within our facility or the Western Hemisphere."

"Personally, I have the honor of being married to Doctor Indira Patel, whose global research in immunology has allowed for breakthroughs in infectious diseases that has saved or enhanced millions of lives. In addition, I also am the public liaison for the Derrick Williams Foundation and provide presentations on space flight and how it affects mankind's belief in humanity, government and equality that is provided to school-age children anywhere in the United States at no cost to the schools, organizations or institutions I visit. Finally, I am a 32nd degree mason and am proud to have joined the ranks of sixteen former presidents including George Washington, FDR, President Truman and President Ford and work with fellow Masonic members in achieving the goals of our organization."

Luke paused for a moment and looked at the Senators. He took a deep breath and, for effect, slid his prepared speech to the side. Looking down at the carpet and then up, I could tell he was about to begin to speak from the heart. "Ladies and gentlemen, I am here today as a humble man who has served his country and continues to serve its citizens. Each day, I ask God for directions on how I can make the world a better place for those who reside here. I have been profoundly blessed that my passion for life, liberty and the pursuit of happiness is totally supported by the Derrick Williams Foundation. Not once have my beliefs been challenged! Not once has my objective of helping others ever been questioned! Not once has the belief in the Almighty, who so profoundly influenced by my experiences, ever been minimized, denigrated or criticized."

"I began with a goal of traveling into space. It took a while, but I made it and, in those journeys, I was able to look down on the majesty that God created and ask myself, what can I do to make it better? What can I do to help those who cannot make the journey I have taken? What can I do so that others can at least reach for the stars to make our world a better place for everyone. We are not perfect! We are not without fault! We are not a group who seeks rewards for ourselves, but for everyone."

"Because of the honor and dignity of one man – George Terrill the Fourth – I sit before you. Because of the Derrick Williams Foundation, my hopes, dreams and goals of helping others is allowed to take place, for which I am eternally grateful."

Again, there was total silence as Luke wiped the tears from his eyes and took a deep breath of satisfaction.

John Williams:

"There was a pause and then, "The committee calls John Douglas Williams"

I looked at Philip with a degree of both shock and disdain. Everyone knew the The Duke was dead. Philip looked at the group and said, "Ladies and gentlemen, Mr. Williams is deceased and has been for nearly a year. Why have you included him in the docket?"

Fitzgerald knew what had happened and this was his way of sticking it to us and he inquired. "Mr. Williams is deceased? You wouldn't happen to have a way of verifying that would you?"

Philip was ready, "Senator, Mr. Williams died in a boating accident in St. Martin. Extensive search and rescue activities took place. After two days, a recovery team was incorporated but Mr. Williams could not be found."

"Boating accident?"

"Yes, Senator, a boating accident."

"We're there any mitigating circumstances?"

"Not to my knowledge."

"Who was Mr. Williams boating with?"

"A family friend, Senator."

"Did he perish too?"

"No, sir."

"Did he attempt to rescue Mr. Williams?"

"Yes sir, he did."

Fitzgerald took off his glasses and rubbed the bridge of his nose. "A boating accident" he said, shaking his head. "Proceed!"

Fitzgerald's irascibility was famous and he wasn't going to change, simply because one of his largest, former supporters sat in front of him. You could see the anger in his eyes! You could sense his irritability in the perpetual frown. As always, his reputation of being short-tempered and impatient shone through in laser-like focus during the formal proceedings in which we were incarcerated. When the great Senator spoke, it was always pompous, wordy and redundant to the point that you could see that his only love was for himself. Nothing had changed!

Peter Washburn:

"The committee calls Peter Washburn."

Peter rose and walked to the podium. Unlike the others, he had no notes. I also knew that, what he was about to say would be profound. His level of expertise paralleled his inherent, cogent manner. Whatever the subject, Peter would study it until he could talk on the same plane as those with whom he was having a dialogue. I remember one particular time when we were being sued and Peter studied tort law until he was able to understand and argue a level of State and Federal law that was profoundly superior to the lawyer representing the plaintiff. If you didn't know better, you would have simply assumed that Peter was a law professor because of his innate ability to present references to cases that paralleled our defense.

That didn't mean that Peter considered himself superior to the rest of us, as he had the ability to talk in such a manner that we all could understand what he was communicating. It was when he "took the gloves off" as he so adroitly called it, that his intellect became apparent.

Peter began. "Senators, my name is Peter Washburn. Unlike my esteemed colleagues, I have no formal education, never graduated from high school and was a convicted felon, until receiving a full pardon by the President of the United States."

"During my adolescence, I was repeatedly in trouble and in my early adult years looked down on society, government and people with disdain. I admit that I was a rogue even though the compurgation of twelve jurors said otherwise." Peter brought some of his five-dollar words with him to toss at the Senators. From the looks on their faces, they had no idea that compurgation meant 'the clearing of an accused person who swear to his innocence'. Tee hee!

Peter continued, "I paid my dues, and it was during the incarceration that I looked within and realized the gifts God had given me were being squandered. To look at my records without any further investigation would lead anyone and everyone to the same conclusion - I was not a model citizen, which would be an understatement. To show my contempt for society I did everything possible to socially and politically distance myself from virtually anything and everything that was good."

"While incarcerated at Waupun State Prison, I had a chance meeting with a man of the cloth. I was angry, frustrated and lashing out at anything or anybody that I believed was holding me back from what now appears to be the ultimate goal of my own self-destruction. This man of the cloth who has since passed away, didn't judge me by my attitude, nor my tattoos, thoughts and provocations. Instead, he looked inside and saw a frightened, insecure, bitter, young man who thought the world owed him everything."

"At first, our meetings consisted of him talking and me rebelling. One day, he brought a chess board and asked me to play one match with him. I had never played and had no idea of the complexity or dynamics of the game. He taught me the moves and left the board with me. At first, I simply placed it on a shelf in my cell and he would visit and ask if I had any questions about the game. After three months of the same questions every week, I took the board down and began examining the pieces and what their roles were and realized that chess is like life, full of options, where each move has a consequence."

"One week, this man of cloth asked if I was ready to play and I said yes. He came into my cell and took out a blindfold and told me to put it on. I thought, how could I possibly play a game I could not see. With each move, he would call out the position of the piece that had been relocated. With each move, I would counter. For the first few times, I was soundly beaten and then, as I began to understand the nuances of the game and the ultimate goal, I began to win."

"As I became proficient, I began to understand the majesty of chess, as the man who became my friend, began talking about how it reflects life, where the king was not of royalty, but represented God and for some reason, it all began to make sense and I became a believer."

"As my proficiency grew, my belief in God did, too. It was then, that my friend took it one step further and asked if I could play two games simultaneously blindfolded. Being young and brash, I thought I could and so I competed against not only him, but a fellow inmate who had been touched as well. Needless to say, at first, I was beaten badly. Then, with time, I mastered the ability to play two games simultaneously blindfolded and then three, then four and finally five."

"One visitation day, my friend appeared and asked if we could go for a walk. I was incredulous, as I was an inmate. He said that I had been given an afternoon pass and for the first time in over two years, I went outside and saw life from a different perspective. The world was not my enemy, it was a place filled with chessmen, each moving in different directions, yet everyone was working to serve God."

"That night, I returned to my cell and on my pillow was a Bible. I'd never read it and stayed awake and read all 783,137 words and was deeply moved, as it talked of men like me sharing stories of turbulence and frustration, greed and hypocrisy and the ultimate transgression. As the morning bell rang, I proceeded to breakfast and did something I had never done before, I said grace and thanked God for the opportunity afforded me. I asked a guard if I could see a counselor and arrangements were made. Instead of the rebel, I wanted to be a leader, not of avarice, but of goodness."

"I had been incarcerated for committing computer hacking and asked if I could begin teaching fellow inmates first how to play chess and then how to either program or repair computers and was given the opportunity to do so. Because of my 'change', my socialization began and I became a model prisoner and was paroled early."

"Unfortunately, the stigma of being an ex-convict, not only limited where I could work, but who would even consider hiring me. After numerous rejections, I began slipping back into the world from whence I came – angry, bitter and confused – when my brother Andrew, told me a of great man who would not judge me by what I had done, but what I could do for the betterment of man. That man was George Terrill, who looked beyond my past and envisioned my future, who had a dream he shared with me – simply to make the world a better place for everyone."

"Today, I head up the research and development of all projects at the Derrick Williams Foundation. I am proud of the people who work with me! I am proud of our diversity! I am proud of our honesty and integrity and respect for each other and most of all, I am proud of what we have given and continue to give back to mankind."

Peter opened his hand and placed the chess king on the podium, saying, " I go nowhere without my king, for he guides me through the darkest hours and gives me light that shall forever shine within my heart."

Without notes in front of him, Peter continued, "I would like quote Marcel Proust, a French novelist who said it more adroitly than I ever could, *'There is no man, however wise, who has not at some period of his life said things, or lived in a way the consciousness of which is so unpleasant to him later in life that we would gladly expunge it from his memory.'*"

With that, Peter turned and returned to his seat. As I reflect back on that moment, tears still roil within my eyes. Tears of pride, tears of love and tears of respect for a man who walks besides me where I know that within his heart is goodness.

Andrew Washburn:

After another long pause, punctuated by total silence throughout the hearing room, "The committee calls Andrew Washburn"
Andrew made his way to the hot seat as we began calling it and opened his statement. As always, Andrew only sat on the front three inches of the chair with straight back and a military look and began. "My name is Andrew Washburn. I am a college graduate from Purdue University with majors in mechanical engineering and aeronautics. Upon graduation, I joined the United States Army and was assigned to the 3rd Infantry Regiment where I applied and was accepted, as a member of the Honor Guard at the Tomb of the Unknown Soldier. I maintain my Tomb Guard Identification Badge that I hold in highest regard as do the other six-hundred plus soldiers honored to serve those who gave their lives for our country who also strictly abide by the criteria of integrity that goes beyond Army regulation to one of personal conduct throughout life."

Andrew paused for a moment, took a small sip of water and continued, "Upon completing my tour of duty, I was employed as a pilot for a regional airline based in Milwaukee, Wisconsin. While I was completely happy with my employer and responsibilities as a pilot, I was urged to meet with Mr. Terrill and became his personal assistant at Wilco for three years, prior to the inception of the Derrick Williams Foundation."

"My current duties include providing protection and security for the facilities and personnel of both organizations. I am not an employee of the Foundation, but an employee of Wilco. This was structured by Mr. Douglas Williams so that all costs are incurred by Wilco, allowing the Foundation to use those resources to provide more services to those in need."

"Beyond the protection and security aspect, my wife and I manage the Wilco Personal Defense offices where we teach the art of Brazilian Jujitsu. Under this umbrella, we provide basic self-defense training to anyone interested and take particular pride in the fact that no one has ever been turned away if they couldn't afford the classes. In fact, we actively recruit women in high risk areas so that they can have a greater peace of mind that comes from self-defense and the mental aspect of Brazilian Jujitsu. While many people think of martial arts as a form of physical altercation, our goal is to teach a smaller, weaker person how so successfully defend themselves against bigger, stronger, heavier opponents by using leverage and weight distribution along with emotional control.

Our training program embodies a system of both physical skills and moral values such as respect of property, being faithful and sincere and exerting oneself in the perfection of character. When combined, these can instill physical and mental relaxation, control of mind and body and increase self-confidence. In addition, we incorporate principles of emotional control such that our students are trained to remain in a defensive mindset and never serve as the aggressor. In so doing, we teach honor, humility and respect, for not only the opponent, but all forms of life."

With that Andrew was done. He had shown the Senators what dignity was all about. The Senators politely nodded as they called Doctor James Johnson.

James Johnson:

James was impeccably dressed in a dark pinstripe suit, white shirt and red and white tie. As he reached the chair, he pulled out his glasses and slipped them on his nose. "Ladies and gentlemen, my name is Dr. James Johnson. My background includes a bachelor's degree in psychology from the University of Wisconsin with a Master's Degree from Johns Hopkins and a PHD from Princeton University. Currently, I am employed by the University of Wisconsin – Milwaukee and serve as head of the psychology department. In addition, I work with Milwaukee County Social Services Division concerning troubled youth and also donate my time to serve as a board member of the bio-ethics team headed up by Mr. Luke Arnold, who spoke to you earlier."

"My association with the Derrick Williams Foundation came about because I wanted to go fishing with a bunch of my buddies and we had chartered a boat owned by Wilco Corporation. Whereas it conflicted with Mr. Terrill's personal schedule, the easiest thing for Wilco to do would have been to say the boat had mechanical problems. Instead, Mr. Terrill took it upon himself to make arrangements for all parties to have a great time, including me."

"During that fishing trip, I found a man of impeccable character, who had a passion for decency and compassion for others – a man with power and prestige – a man with incredible wealth and resources, who was willing to give it all away, simply because he felt he needed to help mankind. Imagine if you will, relegating your seat as a United States Senator and moving back home and beginning again. No job! No income! No connections! Imagine starting with nothing and building it into one of the finest, non-profit foundations in the world. That's what Mr. Terrill has done."

"In America today, the average charity spends 36.9% of all of its donations on themselves. The Derrick Williams Foundation spends only 19.4% of which 11% or 56.7% of the entire overhead, is used simply defend the patents they have on the incredible products they have developed. How do they do it? The teammates exchange passion for pride and work together without avarice or greed, without petty squabbles and certainly without envy of each other. While they have become financially comfortable, solely based on the sale of their products and without any donations whatsoever, Mr. Terrill earns a salary of one dollar per year and those on the board of governors receive the same amount.

The Derrick Williams Foundation's goal is to help people and not help themselves, for which they are recognized globally. How do they do it? By having the right people on the team – people who want to give more than they receive. You have heard from several of them already, who are giving not only their time and talent, but their treasure as well, simply to help others."

"My role with Dr. Arnold is to ensure that the path upon which the Foundation travels does not veer off the course. We examine the consequence of each action to make sure that it sustains the core value of the Derrick Williams Foundation, which is to help all living beings – not some – but all living beings, in every way possible."

"Isaac Newton once said that for every action, there is an opposite and equal reaction. If this hypothesis is to remain true in a world so rife with takers, it's the people who stand before you today who are giving all they have to make this world a better place for everyone - including you!"

There were nods along the bench with eleven of twelve Senators affirming the words and passion that James had spoken as they called Tad to the chair.

Thaddeus Johnson:

Tad was called to the table and quietly made his way. As he sat, he took a moment to look each Senator in the eye, slowly took a sip of water and began. "My name is Dr. Thaddaeus Johnson. I was a classmate of Mark Stevenson, who spoke previously. Like Mark, I was incarcerated. Like Mark, I was a punk who thought he knew everything, until one day a man arrived and challenged me to a game of chess. This man said that if I beat him, he would work to see about early release. If he beat me, I would agree to meet with him every week for three months to talk about anything I wanted to discuss."

"While incarcerated, I too had learned to love the game of chess as it takes passion, concentration, anticipation and thought and it had been a long time since anyone beat me. My voracious nature was such that my incarcerated life revolved around the game as it both symbolized my internal turmoil while allowing me to strive for something that would eradicate the pain of the past and embarrassment of my regrets."

My opponent relayed data, as a wry smile came across his face, as he pointed out that chess is infinite and therefore not an easily conquered game. This stranger noted that, there are 400 different positions after each player makes one move, 72,084 positions after two moves apiece, over nine million positions after three moves apiece and over 288 billion different possible positions after just four moves each. He noted that, in a 40-move game, the number of potential moves is greater than the number of electrons in our universe."

"I wasn't that impressed and the game went on. I hadn't been beaten in several years and my fellow inmates believed this would be a great lesson for the interloper who invaded my domain as the room grew silent. At the 40th move, the stranger attacked with an offense developed by Mikhail Tal in 1960, when he won the world chess championship. I made a blunder and he attacked with a move of Queen's-Knight four to block my advance and then checkmate – I lost, but also won!" "

While I was in a position of checkmate in the game, my soul was ebullient with the concept of meeting an individual with the same background and temperament as me to whom I could look up. In the end, one chess game had been efficacious by giving me my freedom from the throes of uncompromised singularity which had smothered me and turned me inward instead of out at a world filled with the majesty of goodness that can prevail if one gives on himself instead of always taking from others."

"That man was Peter Washburn. He had been directed to come to our school and meet with people like me – intelligent, yet belligerent, gifted yet selfish – winning the small battles, but losing the war of life!"

"For three months we talked and played chess. For three months, no matter how hard I tried, I could not beat him. In the end, he asked me what I wanted to do and I shrugged my shoulders, to which he took the entire chessboard with all the pieces and threw it on the floor. I sat shocked and appalled and it was then I realized I was losing at more than chess. I was losing at life. We had reached the peak where no more could be gained and, for the first time in a very, very long time, I regretted who I was, what I was and where I was, and made it my goal to simply change. I vowed there would be no more egregious acts on my part. My goal was to become a better person and follow in Peter's footsteps, to give of oneself and not expect to receive."

There was a pause in Tad's delivery and then a more somber tone as he added. "Mr. Washburn and the Derrick Williams Foundation made arrangements for me to get early parole. They had me tutored to complete my GED, then take the ACT and SAT tests, where I earned admission to Marquette University and received my bachelor's degree in physics from which I was then accepted into MIT, where I received both my master's and PHD."

"As I walked across the stage to get my diploma, I looked out in the audience and there sat my entire family – my mother, brother and best friend, Peter Washburn. Sitting next to them were Mr. and Mrs. George Terrill, who had made arrangements for my family to be there and it was then that I realized the joy of giving of oneself to help others and vowed that I would pay it all back - every dime they had invested in me."

"If it weren't for Mr. and Mrs. Terrill and the Derrick Williams Foundation, I would have been just another black statistic who met an early death. Instead, I joined 'the team' and became a member of the Derrick Williams Foundation, serving on the projects including not only Mediglove, but the new Kaleidoscope that detects Alzheimer's disease in its infancy and also the chips we are developing to help with other neurological disorders."

"My wife wanted to be here today to show her support, but we are expecting our first child in the next two weeks. We know it's going to be a boy and his name will be Peter George Johnson and will be named after the two men who saved my life. By the way, Mr. Washburn and I still play chess and these days, he still wins most of the time, but not much as he did in the past. Thank you for your time"

Bartholomew Price:

While everyone else had the composure needed to speak to the group, Bart was my biggest worry. Wearing a suit that was probably one size too small, having a crooked tie and his hair pulled back in a pony tail, I was concerned. Social skills were not one of Bart's many assets. I could tell by his demeanor that he was nervous and yet, he had been subpoenaed and required to speak.

Bart was confined to a wheel chair and slowly made his way to where the hot seat previously had been placed. As he tried to open his mouth, nothing came out. Philip whispered in his ear and a slight smile came across Bart's face.

"Ladies and Gentlemen, my name is Dr. Bartholomew Nathaniel Price. I am a computer programmer and chip designer. I work for the Derrick Williams Foundation and am responsible for the software for our computers, including not only our quantum computer, but the six binary computers that are linked into who we call SIMON. This is the first time in my life, I've ever spoken to a group of people. It's just not my nature and I apologize for my nervousness."

"Like those who came before me, I too, have an advanced degree. And, like Tad, earned a Masters and PHD from MIT. My problem was that, due to my physical and social limitations, when I graduated I wasn't capable of teaching and those companies I did interview with, didn't feel that I would fit in their corporate structure. Being from a little town in Wisconsin called Merrimack, my thought was returning home and opening a computer repair shop."

"Like many of my contemporaries, I am what is called a 'gamer'. In other words someone who enjoys video games, especially competitive video games, you play on the internet. One night, I was playing and it was brutal. The person I was competing against had developed a strategy I'd never seen before and in doing so challenged me. I asked for a 'time out' and in an hour returned and not only thwarted their offense, but reversed the outcome of the game and won. It was four in the morning and our marathon had gone on for ten hours."

"As I was about to turn off my computer, a message popped up asking my location." I responded 'Wisconsin'. The opponent asked what was the most popular brandy sold in the State and I replied 'Korbel'". They asked what was the fastest growing type of cheese and I replied 'curds'". They asked what was the fastest growing beer and I responded 'Spotted Cow'. Finally, they asked what students did at the beginning of the fourth quarter in Camp Randall and I replied 'Jump Around' and then named the band and the year the song was released. The person then asked me when I could come to work, indicating the job required long hours and lousy pay. I told the them, I needed to take a shower and would be ready in an hour."

Bart paused for a moment and then said, "that fellow gamer was Peter Washburn and that's how I got my job at the Derrick Williams Foundation."

Bart paused for a moment and then looked at the group in front of him as he spoke. "For the first time in my life, I was not handicapped! For the first time in my life, I was not judged and considered limited! For the first time in my life, I was accepted as a man! For the very first time, I got to be me!"

"I know what it's like to be judged! I know what it's like to be left out! I know what it's like to be all alone and wishing you were dead! However, because of the Derrick Williams Foundation, I am no longer judged, no longer left out and no longer alone. When I started at the Foundation, I thought I wouldn't be able to attend meetings in what we call the Silo because it only had stairs leading up to the top floor. My fellow workers took care of that by first carrying me and then developing a special lift that I simply drive my wheelchair onto and push a button."

"I am a member of a team – a team that is helping people around the world – a team whose only mission is goodness – whose only passion is life, where I fit in and am judged by my thoughts and actions and not my physical limitations. I can only thank Mr. and Mrs. Terrill and Peter for giving me the opportunity to live a life I thought would never happen. Because of them and our location, I met a woman, who is also confined to a wheelchair and we married. Because of them, my wife and I have two children. Because of them, I am alive and look forward to each any every day as a new tomorrow, filled not with frustrations, but with hope that we will make our world a little better for all of us."

There wasn't a dry eye in the place!

Heads were down as Bart made his way back up the aisle. I looked at him and mouthed, "you are my brother!" as I placed my clenched fist to my heart.

Thomas Terrill:

Speaking of brothers, mine was next as they called out Thomas Terrill. Tommie was as nervous as my dad would have said, *'a whore in church'*. He had a hard time talking to three farmers, let alone a dozen Senators, one of which he despised. As Tommie reached the hot seat, he looked down at the script that was written, pushed it to the side and walked to the podium. Like Bart, this was to be a speech from the heart.

After a long pause and a deep breath Tommie began. "Ladies and gentlemen, my name is Thomas Terrill and I am a farmer. I did not go to college, nor do I have any advanced degree, except perhaps from the school of hard knocks. Instead, I get up every morning and milk 400 cows and then, in the afternoon, those same cows come back and we start all over again. These are grazing cows. We do not keep them confined all day and provide a life for them that's worth living. They are not machines, but animals, that are nurtured and cared for, looked after and respected for what they are – one of God's creations."

"Several years ago, my farm was nearing bankruptcy. Costs were high, milk prices low and the expense of being an independent dairy farmer excruciating. Like my fellow dairy farmers, I looked at the numbers and felt I would join the ranks of those who were giving up what they loved, where on average, in Wisconsin - America's Dairyland, three family farms cease to exist every single day.

My next-door neighbor is the Derrick Williams Foundation founded by my brother, in honor of the deceased brother-in-law he never knew. At first, I took offense to the Foundation's existence and doubted its merit. As I learned more about what their goals were, I realized that what they are doing is something noble that can help humanity."

"As my farm languished, I turned to my brother and the gentlemen who have come before you for guidance. Because of their knowledge and resources, we began open discussions, first on survival and then prosperity. I can honestly say that it was their wisdom that changed me from being a dairy farmer into an agri-businessman and also from a bitter man who thought the world owed him something, to someone who relishes the majesty of giving. Everything from our hyponic greenhouses that allow us to grow high protein cattle feed year-round, to grazing, to shifting to beef production and distilling our own world-class Bourbon, has taken what was about to die and made it live."

"While the investment was substantial and the risk far too great for any bank to consider, my neighbor, the Derrick Williams Foundation loaned me the money to begin. I signed a twenty-year note at the prevailing rate of interest and am proud to say that my wife and I were able to pay back every dime owed in seven years."

"While many organizations would have taken the profits and split them amongst the shareholders, the Board of Governors of the Foundation asked for my guidance as we took the money and set up a trust fund that offers low-interest loans to struggling farmers throughout Wisconsin, thereby, allowing them to diversify and continue to exist. In addition, we have developed a group health insurance program that allows farmers to protect their families in times of medical need and the risks involved with today's health care situation and it is our belief that we have saved over 200 family farms from going out of business."

"None of this would have happened without the understanding and generosity of the Derrick Williams Foundation. None of this could have taken place without their belief and resources that there was a better way to do things than were done before. While many might think all of this has taken place because the Foundation's founder is my brother, that is not the case at all. My brother excused himself from all dealings concerning the farm, including the loans and the insurance program to make absolutely certain there was no bias nor favoritism and above all else, no nepotism."

"There were many times when two brothers disagreed. There were times when two brothers fought! And yes, there were times when two brothers did not speak to each other! Yet, in the end, because of the humility, generosity, compassion and forgiveness of one of the brothers, the other can stand before you today and simply say thank you."

I looked at Tommie and quenched my teeth, not out of anger, but out of love and pride for, in his own way, he had thanked me and made me eternally grateful that he was my brother.

Rodney Whitehorse:

The moderator noted that, in addition to those who had spoken, a special request had been granted to allow Mr. Rodney Whitehorse to speak to the Committee representing the eleven indigenous nations of Wisconsin. My dear friend came forth with all the confidence acquired through years of leadership.

Tipping his head to the committee, Rodney began. "My name is Rodney Whitehorse. I am president of the Hochunk Nation and am here, along with members of all Wisconsin Native American nations to show our support for the Derrick Williams Foundation. With that, I would like the tribal leaders of my fellow nations to please stand and be recognized."

Ten gentlemen stood and each identified himself, providing his title and the nation he represented and then sat down as Rodney continued. "I have had the honor of witnessing the dignity of the men who have stood before you today first hand. I have the honor of knowing Mr. George Terrill for over 30 years. I have the honor of witnessing his passion, generosity and sincere goodness, while sharing his compassion for others and consider him my little brother."

"While we are here to defend the role of the Derrick Williams Foundation, as it applies to medical research and development, we are also here to provide insight into what else the Foundation has done. A few years ago, I received a call from Mr. Terrill requesting that his son be allowed to witness the challenges of our nation and Native Americans in general regarding the social and physical issues that we face."

"At first, I was reluctant, then reconsidered and thank God every day for my change of heart. A young man appeared one Monday morning from the Foundation. He said his job was to see how he could help. After nearly 150 years of pain, I thought it would be a waste of time. Instead, this young man took it upon himself to identify our challenges from a white man's perspective and develop social programs aimed at curtailing the drug and alcohol perspectives afflicting our people, while assisting in creating a sense of worth amongst the young people of our nation."

"As the program took hold, we began to see incredible results in terms of academic achievement and reduction in use of illegal drugs and unwanted pregnancies. For the first time in many generations, there was a sense of pride instilled in our people and a sense of enthusiasm about tomorrow, based on hope and commitment towards making their world and subsequently our world a better place. Concurrent with this evolution, we began to see pride restored in our heritage – pride that had been missing – pride that has resulted in a restoration of traditions that had been eroded by the pervasive role that depression can take socially, financially and emotionally."

"As our nation began to see results, this one man asked if it would be all right to expand beyond the Hochunk to the ten other nations in Wisconsin. It was agreed and the results for our brothers matched those that we enjoyed. While, today our nations are more financially secure than ever before, when the issue of cost for the program was addressed, we were told that there was no fee. There were no costs! The entire program was funded by the Derrick Williams Foundation. All that was asked is that we continue the program and share it with other nations under the same set of conditions. Today over 50% of all 574 recognized Native American nations are involved in the program developed by one young man. Today, there are over five million Native Americans residing in the United States. For the 22% who continue to live on reservations and the 78% outside, the program implemented has allowed everyone to hold their heads up high knowing that tomorrow will be better than today, which was better than yesterday."

"With the committee's permission, we would like to recognize the young man who has done so much to help our nations. Will George Terrill the Fifth please stand up?"

With that 'V' arose and was about to begin his elocution when Rodney nodded towards the chamber doors and four gentlemen walked in. As they walked past Rodney, all ten Presidents of the Wisconsin Nations rose and stood at attention.

The first new gentleman announced. "Mr. Terrill, I am pleased to inform you that you are the recipient of the National Citizen Honor Award, as is the Derrick Williams Foundation. You and your Foundation were chosen to receive this award by living members of the Congressional Medal of Honor Society."

The second gentlemen continued. "The members of the Congressional Medal of Honor Society received their recognition for their acts of valor performed during wartime and are the only ones who reviewed your credentials regarding courage and the dedication you have provided to serve here at home."

The third gentleman opened a small navy-blue velvet case and removed a special commendation medal with a red, white and blue lavalier. 'V' bent down as the medal was hung around his neck and he straightened up with tears in his eyes as the gentlemen said, "It is an honor and a privilege to finally meet you."

The fourth gentleman added, "George Terrill we, the members of the Congressional Medal of Honor Society, salute and welcome you to our ranks. From this day forth, you are a member of a small group of men and women and we thank you for your service."

All four men came to attention and saluted 'V' and then proceeded out the door to the resounding applause that echoed throughout the chamber.

While normally, the Senior Senator would have called the room to order, Fitzgerald knew to do so would be politically incorrect, he allowed for a moment of celebration as 'V' looked at the medal and then at Amy and me and smiled.

Amy whispered, "Our parents would have been so proud!"

I squeezed Amy's hand and looked at Rodney and then the Senators and then the MadCity Boys and back again at 'V' as I stood and gave 'V' a hug of gratitude as did Derrick and Melia, for they too were proud of their little brother.

Fitzgerald rapped his gavel and called the meeting to order and announced that the committee would adjourn for the day and reconvene the following morning at 10:00 AM. Day one was over and I felt that we had made our point. I looked at Philip and smiled. His return look caught me by surprise. There was little joy to be seen.

As others were leaving, I caught Philip and asked what the problem was. His response floored me, "they didn't ask you to speak!"

That night we had a group dinner and there was relief on the part of the MadCity Boys as they thought the war was over. Philip quietly reminded everyone that all they did was verbalize what the Senators already knew and the challenge had just begun. "Tomorrow, the gloves will come off and we will quickly see where this is going," Philip said.

The Testimony:

We arrived the next morning and discovered that the room had be rearranged. Instead of one small table with three chairs, there were a series of tables with names of each of us on placards facing the Senators. I moved in front and looked - Mathew Chapman, Mark Stevenson, Luke Arnold, John Williams, Peter Washburn, George Terrill, Philip Actman, James Johnson, Thaddeus Johnson, Bartholomew Price and Thomas Terrill.

I asked Rodney, if he wanted to sit at the table and he politely declined. Instead, he and the ten heads of the Indian nations took seats in the first row. I looked at the space reserved for The Duke and knew right away who should be sitting there and asked 'V' to take his place.

At precisely ten the doors opened and the Senators walked in. There was a concerned look upon their faces. The meeting was called to order and the Senators began their questions. The initial questions dealt with Mediglove and how it worked and what level accuracy it provided. After each Senator had a chance to ask questions about Mediglove, the second round began which dealt with SIMON. Again, the questions dealt with operations, computation speed and programming. The MadCity Boys did their best to dumb it down so that the Senators had a more logical understanding of what SIMON was all about.

The third round of questioning began and examined the network of researchers we had around the world. Specific questions were asked about those located in countries considered adversarial to the United States with concerns that we were sharing valuable research with potential enemies, who could use the information against our country. Peter outlined the fact that no researcher was provided more information than that in his own category and each researcher was linked to two others to allow for the seamless transfer of research data to those who resided in countries considered allies of the United States. Peter noted that all researchers had been vetted and their credentials were such that they were considered part of a unified team and not competitors with each other.

The fourth round began and examined our objectives. The 'situation' with the FDA was mentioned as the government was well aware we had penetrated their website and changed the parameters to allow for the experimental treatments for Dr. Williams. We were challenged on our integrity and Luke asked what harm had been done. Luke noted, that the two federal bills, Trickett Wendler Right to Try Act of 2017 and a companion act in the House that claim to give terminally ill patients the "right to try" experimental drugs outside of a clinical trial really don't and all that had happened was to give one person the opportunity to try an experimental drug when we had been ignored for months and that, within a matter of minutes, we had reversed the parameters back to their original state.

The fifth round focused on the Nanochips and what we were attempting to create. Halfway through, the subject of The Duke arose and we quickly learned that the Derrick Williams Foundation had been under close scrutiny for a long time and they knew about the change in The Duke's ancestry, the surgical procedure and where it was done. It became apparent they knew more than we thought they did. The subject of The Duke's demise came up and Luke again addressed it by noting that our research had moved from focusing on a mental aspect to assisting in developing chips and software that would assist the body in compensating for its own physiological shortcomings. We never mentioned the new battery fiber, as we were only partially through the patent application process and knew that upon receipt, we would have a product that could revolutionize the world.

After five rounds and sixty questions, 'V' and I were the only ones who had not been called on. There was a fifteen-minute break and I asked Philip what was going on. He said he didn't know. As we returned from the break, a new face appeared on the panel, sitting next to our buddy, Senator Fitzgerald. The gloves were about to come off and I could sense it wasn't going to be pleasant.

The first set of questions came from Fitzgerald.

"Mr. Terrill, are you head of the Derrick Williams Foundation?"

"Yes."

"Mr. Terrill, do you control investments, expenditures and all capitol?"

I looked at Philip who nodded and I replied, "Our family does"

"Mr. Terrill, was it your decision to purchase the quantum computer you have in your possession?"

Again I looked at Philip who nodded in the affirmative and replied, "Yes".

"Mr. Terrill, does your quantum computer scan the global internet four times each day seeking out information that would assist your foundation?"

I responded, "Yes".

"Mr. Terrill, if you are scanning the entire global internet, does that mean you are scanning all correspondence, communication and information of all American citizens, companies and organizations, including the government of the United States, involving both classified and highly classified data?"

I looked at Peter and he arose and came over and whispered to me and I explained to Fitzgerald, "We have specific, medically-oriented terms and phrases that we scan and do not scan other public, private or sensitive information."

"But you have the capacity to do so, if you so desire?" Fitzgerald replied.

I looked at Peter who nodded in the affirmative and I said, "Yes".

"In other words, your foundation, that has generated millions of dollars in revenue and made many of your employees wealthy, has the ability to invade the privacy of anyone it wants to, whenever it wants to?"

My Minnie Point badass temper was quickly rising. "Senator, that has not, is not, nor will it ever be our objective."

"But you have the capacity to do so?"

Before I could answer, Fitzgerald added, "In other words, you have the ability to be a threat to the security of the United States of America!"

I shook my head and stared at the loud-mouth, clown who was center-stage.

I replied. "Senator, if I happened to own a gun, which I do not, would that mean I had the capacity to shoot someone and should therefore be considered a threat?"

Fitzgerald ignored me, as he continued. "Our records indicate that a few years ago, you broke through one of the most sophisticated computer security systems in the world and breached the database of the FDA. Is this true?"

I looked at Philip and realized that a denial would be perjury. I looked at Peter as his eyes got big and he came to my side again, leaned into the microphone and said. "Senator, the FDA's *'sophisticated security system'* as you call it, is so rudimentary that it doesn't match that of many high schools in America. It's probably breached dozens of times each day and we previously confirmed that we had done so, why we did so and the extent of our incursion and the fact that, within seconds, we returned the program to its original parameters, such that only one person, the terminally ill mother-in-law of Mr. Terrill who was a renowned pediatric cancer physician was given one last chance at survival."

Fitzgerald ignored Peter and continued drilling down. "Mr. Terrill, yesterday, we called John Douglas Williams to the stand and you indicated that he was deceased, is that correct?"

"Yes!"

"You indicated that he drowned in a boating accident?"

"That is correct."

"Can you explain why no death certificate was filed?"

"The accident happened in St. Martin."

"Is it true that you personally contacted the St. Martin police and indicated that, should Mr. Williams remains be found, he be cremated and no one notified?"

"Yes, that's true."

"In other words, you weren't interested in the cause of death?"

"He drowned!" I replied.

"Could it be, that you didn't want certain things determined?"

"No, the intent was to protect my family from further grief."

"Do you know what Mr. Williams family lineage entails?"

"English and Scottish," I replied.

"Can you tell me why, one day it magically included Native American?"

I realized that the government had been intercepting all of our communication and had been building the case against us for years as I replied, "I really don't know."

"Could it be so that Mr. Williams could be admitted to the Hochunk assisted living center in Wisconsin Dells?"

Before I could answer, Fitzgerald came at me again, "Who is Rodney Whitehorse?"

I looked at the Senator and replied, "The gentleman you met yesterday."

"What is your relationship with Mr. Whitehorse?"

"He is my best friend."

"Do you believe that the Constitution of the United States denotes Native Americans as separate and unique and yet, their recognition requires that they abide to all aspects of law?"

I looked at Philip and he whispered, "No," which I reiterated.

"In other words, they are above the laws of the United States?"

"No, Senator. However, it is our interpretation based on other agreements and rulings between the federal government that what happened on Indian property was their business, as long as it didn't violate the Constitution."

Fitzgerald ignored my response. "Do you believe that the rules and regulations implemented by the FDA are designed to protect people from unscrupulous and sometimes dangerous products or procedures that could risk the health, wellbeing or even life of citizens of the United States?"

"Yes"

"Do you feel that Native Americans are exempt from these rules?"

I knew where this was going and replied, "I am neither a lawyer, nor a person with medical knowledge and, therefore, cannot answer that question."

"Mr. Terrill, is it not true that your computer modified the heritage of John Douglas Williams to include Native American ancestry, such that you could usurp the rules and regulations of the FDA?"

My answer was "No, sir, that was not the case at all."

"Why did you do it?"

"Senator, I didn't!"

"Did you authorize it?"

"We had discussions."

"Including one between you and Mr. Whitehorse as you sat on the Capitol grounds in Madison, Wisconsin?

They were spying on us, as I replied. "Senator, Mr. Whitehorse is head of the Hochunk Nation and together we own sacred land that is held in perpetuity for the good of all people. As my friend, we discussed several things including the demise of the mental acuity of Mr. Williams, due to the onset of Alzheimer's disease and what could possibly be done to minimize its effects and make the last days of Mr. Williams life more beneficial for him."

"With his condition worsening and his generosity to the Hochunk nation, the idea of Mr. Williams residing in the Wisconsin Dells facility was discussed and done to the point that Mr. Williams did spend one night at the assisted living center during which it was determined that the location would be inconvenient for the rest of his family."

Fitzgerald came right back at me. "Is it not true, that you ran experiments on farm animals that included implanting computer chips in their brains that allowed you to control not only their thoughts, but emotions?"

I thought for a moment and replied, "That's incorrect, Senator. We could not control emotions and therefore determined that the chip was not a viable replacement for the human brain."

"Did you, implant one of your chips in the brain of Mr. Williams?"

"Yes, we did!" I responded, as a surprised rush permeated the Senate chambers.

"Even though you had no FDA approval. Even though the chip had no certification, you proceeded?" the Senator said incredulously.

"Yes, we did and I don't regret what we did for a single moment. We had a man, whom I loved, who was mentally deteriorating literally before our eyes. A man you knew, who was intelligent, dynamic and powerful, yet kind, considerate and generous beyond all comprehension. A man who was wasting away for whom I would have done anything I could to save him from the ravages in place before him."

"For a short period of time, that man was given the opportunity to regain his life so that **he** could make decisions regarding his own wellbeing. If providing a human being the opportunity to choose their own destiny is wrong, then I am admittedly wrong. If, however, there is the opportunity to modify an existence to the point that a few more days, a few more weeks, a few more months are added, along with the dignity that can only come when a person has the right to choose, Senator, I will take that choice every chance I'm given."

"We did not act out of avarice! We did not act out of disrespect! We acted out of compassion, knowing that the speed of degradation was such that, further delays would have resulted in catastrophic circumstances."

Borgwardt:

With my expose, I thought we were done, but the second barrel of the gun was aimed at my heart as Fitzgerald introduced Dr. Robert Borgwardt and I looked at Philip with a questioning look that inferred, 'Who in hell is this guy?". Philip shook his head and shrugged his shoulders, indicating he didn't know who he was. Fitzgerald then expounded on Dr. Borgwardt's education and experience and that he had a PHD in religion and was considered an expert on the Bible and bio-ethics. My mind raced, wondering why would he be here?

Borgwardt began by asking me my name, to which I again responded, "George Terrill the Fourth".

"Do you have any other name you go by?"

I thought for a moment and then said "No".

"What about the name, 'Q'?"

"That was a nickname I used growing up," I responded.

"Q?"

"Yes sir, 'Q'."

"And why the letter 'Q'?"

"Because I am the fourth person named George in our family and the 'Q" stood for quad."

"Do you know anyone else who uses the letter 'Q' as a name?"

"No, I do not?"

"You don't and yet, is it not true that you have surrounded yourself with individuals whose names all can be correlated to another person?"

I shook my head and then realized why the chairs were set the way they were and the names pasted on the fronts. It had never crossed my mind until that very moment. It was a coincidence. The MadCity Boys and members of the Board all had formal names of the twelve disciples.

"Do you have a Messiah complex?" Borgwardt inquired.

I looked at Borgwardt and incredulously responded "No".

Borgwardt continued, "Q is the designation for a gospel that no longer exists, but many think it must have existed at one time. In fact, even though no copy of this gospel has survived independently, some nineteenth-century scholars found fragments of such an early Christian composition embedded in the gospels of Matthew and Luke."

Borgwardt looked at me with disdain, slowly shook his head from side-to-side and continued. "By putting these two gospels beside that of Mark, scholars realized that the gospels Matthew and Luke are telling the story about Jesus, for the most part, because they both follow the same order and often, even the same wording of Mark. But, into this common narrative, Matthew and Luke each inserted extra sayings and teachings of Jesus. Although Matthew and Luke do not put these sayings in the same order, nevertheless they each repeat many of the same sayings, sometimes word-for-word."

I had no idea how this reflected on me and allowed Dr. Borgwardt to continue, "Since, for other reasons, it seems unlikely that Matthew or Luke could have copied from the other, how can this sort of agreement be explained? The answer appears to be that Matthew and Luke each had two sources in common: the Gospel of Mark and another gospel, which is now lost, that contained a collection of sayings known only as 'Q' which comes from the German word for "source".

Again, I saw no correlation as the doctor continued. "Although no actual copy of Q has ever been found, many scholars are convinced that such a document once circulated in early Christian communities. Since it was difficult to get excited about something that did not exist, Q remained a hypothesis that lingered on the edges of scholarly research. But in 1945, a chance discovery in Egypt provided surprisingly new evidence that rekindled interest in the possible existence of Q and sir, it is my belief that you have this self-concept that you are the author of that chapter of the Bible."

I was so deep in thought, I was oblivious to what was happening behind me, as the entire MadCity group along with 'V' stood, arranged themselves behind me and linked arms.

Borgwardt added, "It seems apparent to me Mr. Terrill, that you feel that you are the next messiah! While the names might be a coincidence, there's more – much, much, more - that leads me to believe you have created a following similar to Jim Jones where, instead of a few followers who drink poison Kool Aid, you have accumulated over one billion followers and you and your followers have the potential to control their minds under the auspices of providing health care."

I sat in shock.

"Mr. Terrill, or should I call you 'Q', the image of the historical Jesus is older than the traditional Gospels themselves and was written by Jesus' contemporaries. 'Q' preserves Jesus' original words — the Sermon on the Mount, Beatitudes, the Lord's Prayer, parables, and his counsel for a compassionate life. Sadly, your acts and deeds are contrary to the very foundation of our society and government."

Borgwardt was drilling down. "For some reason Mr. Terrill, it appears that you believe your wealth has elevated you to a level above the rest of us. And yet, according to scholars, the Synoptic Gospels did not view Jesus as "the Christ or 'the anointed one' or the promised Messiah, nor as the redeemer who had atoned for their sins by his crucifixion. In fact they also did not consider him the son of God who rose from the dead and, sir, it appears neither do you!"

There were whispers throughout the room and Fitzgerald pounded his gavel for silence as Borgwardt continued. "Instead, these contemporaries say, 'Q's' authors esteemed Jesus as simply a roving sage who preached a life of wandering, with full acceptance of one's fellow human beings. No matter how disreputable or marginal these teachings are, you, Mr. Terrill appear to believe that you are a reincarnation. Examining the history and pedigree of those you have brought with you, I completely see a parallel association. In that respect, religious scholars say Jesus would wait for America in the third millennium, which is now, and sir, I sincerely believe you think that it is you - a Jesus with supernatural power, who preaches respect for cultural, ethnic and gender diversity, which you have repeatedly purported throughout your adult life."

I was angry! I was frustrated! I wanted to simply stand up and challenge this clown. Instead, Philip's hand rested on my forearm signaling me to calm down and keep my mouth shut.

Borgwardt continued. "Mr. Terrill, the roughly parallel verses in Luke and Matthew that scholars have identified as written by the source named 'Q' do **not** include the Gospel narratives of Jesus' passion and resurrection, which seem to have come from other sources, written or oral. Therefore it appears that the authors of 'Q' knew nothing about the way Jesus died or the stories of an empty tomb – or, if they did know, did not care. Hence, there was no atonement doctrine in 'Q' theology and yet you and your 'team' have attempted to create a Nanochip that would bring a person back from the abyss of Alzheimer's disease in a form of atonement never before conceived."

I sat shaking my head in disbelief, looking in the eyes of Fitzgerald as Borgwardt continued. "Because belief in Jesus' resurrection is the core belief of Christianity, the people who wrote 'Q' must have been adherents of Jesus' in Palestine and were not Christians, unless one stretches the word to include anyone who admires Jesus to such a degree that they would lie for him, violate social laws and finally sacrifice themselves for his existence, such as those with you today."

My mouth was agape. I couldn't believe what I was hearing. My only goal was to help people, not be some sort of religious zealot.

Borgwardt continued. "I've learned about this place you call The Forest. I've been told that you have taken people there and baptized them yourself and yet, you are not a member of the cloth. I've been told that you expound upon the purity of the water and its soul-cleansing action as it applies to a person's existence and yet, you do not expound to the teachings of John the Baptist, let alone Jesus Christ."

"How can it be, Mr. Terrill, that you feel that you have the right to pontificate on God and have a physical representation of heaven, when you have never been educated in either subject? How can it be that you have taken good men and made them your disciples? How can it be that you have used your massive personal wealth to create a system that has the potential to brainwash one-in-seven people on earth and do so in a clandestine manner that would elevate you above anyone and everyone in either the religious or political realm? As you can see, Mr. Terrill, your power over others to create a force so strong, has this panel gravely concerned regarding the wellbeing of the American people and, subsequently, its system of jurisprudence."

Fitzgerald was sitting with a smug look on his face. He felt that he had torn me apart, shredded me and destroyed me, eliminating me as any form of threat to his existence. I sat for a moment in order to collect my thoughts and took a deep breath.

It was my turn to respond. However, as I was about to reply, Fitzgerald banged his gavel and indicated time was of the neigh and further discussions would need to take place the next day. He had won the skirmish! We knew the newspapers and cable news networks would have a field day replaying the allegations, to which I had no chance to defend myself, thereby positioning me as a self-conceived Messiah and a threat to American democracy.

I looked at Philip and he at me and we realized the power of the government. They had created a montage of alternative facts woven together to create a very compelling argument that was not only untrue, but incredibly defamatory and they timed it so that the acquisitions were set forth to the media when I could not respond, let alone reply.

As the hearing room cleared, I realized we had but a few hours to establish my defense. The MadCity Boys were in shock. My family just shook their heads. Rodney came and gave me a big hug and whispered, "We know who you are, and who you will always be – Little Spirit."

The Response:

We spent the next several hours strategizing and while I wanted to roll up my sleeves and go at it, I was told to simply calm down. The next morning, the room had been re-set to the original one-table design. The MadCity Boys were supposedly done and the room was just me against them – or anyway that's what they thought. Instead we had a little surprise. There was only one person who could command the attention of the audience and exculpate me from their allegations and that was 'V' who stood before the Senate subcommittee and looked all twelve directly in the eyes. He wasn't afraid, intimidated, nor in any way demeaned by this powerful group.

Senator Fitzgerald called the meeting to order and looked at me with disdain. He hadn't forgotten his visit to Waldwick, nor the fact that we had a dossier on him that, at one time, could have easily destroyed his career. Carefully, he had slithered away from the legal aspects. Seven years was up on the car accident. He'd purchased a different residence and his own car. I knew that, of the twelve, he would be the most challenging. I understood what The Duke had once said, "Great friends make worst enemies."

Philip reviewed the complaints against us and said, "The most difficult charge against us was one of sedition."

I went huh?

Philip detailed that sedition was...the overt conduct, such as speech and organization, that tends towards insurrection against the established order.

I cringed as Philip continued. "The charge of sedition often includes subversion of the Constitution. and potential incitement of discontent toward or resistance against the government."

This really had me scared.

This was serious shit as Philip added, "Sedition may include any commotion, though not aimed at direct and open violence against the laws." Peter added that seditious words in writing were called seditious libel and this is where he thought the committee was going.

I was somewhat relieved when Philip added, "Typically, sedition is not considered a subversive act and the overt acts that may be prosecutable under sedition laws vary from one legal code to another". Yet, I was really concerned for my son whose job it was to defend our foundation and potentially had its future in his hands.

'V' took a deep breath and was about to begin his testimony when the Senator tried cutting his legs out from beneath him by saying, "Son, what is your legal background and why have you been chosen to speak for your family?"

With no formal education, we knew that having 'V' speak would be a risk and, yet, there was something different, something more profound and there was an aura about 'V' that was growing each and every day.

'V' paused and looked at the Senator and began. "Senator, first of all, I am not your son. My father is sitting to my left and I would appreciate it if you referred to me as Mr. Terrill."

Fitzgerald slapped back in his chair. He wasn't expecting 'V' to come back swinging. The other eleven Senators and their aides all had small smirks on their faces. The kid had put the illustrious Senator in his place.

Fitzgerald took a deep breath and looked at 'V' and responded, "Mr. Terrill, what is your legal background and why have you been chosen to speak for your family?"

'V' countered. "Senator, unless I am mistaken, formal legal education is not a requirement to speak before a Senate subcommittee. In fact, it's not a condition for election to the seat you or your peers currently hold. The guiding document for our government specifically spells out the requirements to be a Senator which state that you must be at least thirty years old, a U.S. citizen for at least nine years and a resident of the state you want to represent. Nowhere does it require that you need to be a lawyer to either be a Senator or give testimony to a Senate subcommittee."

With that, the MadCity Boys commenced to smile as 'V' continued, "Whereas I'm not quite thirty years old, I'm not eligible to hold your office. However, I have been a citizen of the United States and resident of Wisconsin my entire life, something Senator, you no longer seem to be." The gloves were off.

"Excuse me!" Fitzgerald bellowed.

'V' continued. "Senator, your only legal residence is in Virginia. You haven't had a home, apartment or condo in Wisconsin for the past seven years when you sold your house in Milwaukee. If there's anyone who shouldn't be here, Senator - someone who does not qualify - it's you!"

Holy shit!

Fitzgerald glared at 'V' and responded, "With the cost of housing, I simply can't afford to maintain two residences, but I do represent the people of Wisconsin and am attuned to their needs."

'V' countered. "Senator, travel records obtained through the 'Freedom of Information Act' indicate that in the last twelve months, you have only visited your Madison offices once and were there for less than two hours before boarding Delta Flight 7673 back to Washington. How can you say you represent people you don't live with? People, you don't talk with? People you don't communicate with on a regular basis?"

Fitzgerald was flustered as his Irish face got beet red as he responded, "I am not on trial here; you and your company are. My choice and my voting history speak for themselves and I would appreciate it if you would stick to the agenda at hand."

'V' responded. "That's precisely what I intend to do and do so without the formal legal training you indicated I needed to be worthy of your time." Touché!

'V' took a long drink of water. Paused and, taking a deep breath, leaned forward into the microphone and added, "In order to put everything in perspective, I need to provide a summary of the principles of our family foundation - our **non-profit,** family foundation, begun by my father at the behest of my grandfather - a foundation for which my father takes the princely sum on one dollar per year in salary and my grandfather - who was his employee, the total of seventy-five cents per year – both of whom did so in such a manner that neither of them received reimbursement for expenses. That's a total sum of one dollar and seventy-five cents per year, for which there is no pension program, health insurance, private gymnasium or swimming pool, administrative assistants, per diem and Senator, no added perks."

The Senate aides all smiled as they knew who 'V' was targeting. With that, Rodney turned to the rest of our entire enclave and they all nodded. The Senate and Senator Fitzgerald realized they were now face-to-face with the entire contingent of spectators, reporters and those in our group.

'V' added. "Several years ago, what would have been my uncle, perished from a drug overdose. Concurrent with that, my mother was diagnosed with leukemia, to which she was admitted into an experimental program that saved her life that a cost nearly one million dollars just for her."

"Subsequent to that, my grandmother was also diagnosed with leukemia, from which she perished. Sadly, one of the reasons for her demise was because the Federal Drug Administration placed limits on who could and who could not participate in experimental drug treatments that might, and I emphasize the word **might**, have saved her life. Sadly, our family never got to know."

"Finally, my grandfather was diagnosed with Alzheimer's disease and our family bore the burden of watching a powerful, dynamic, man slip away into the abyss of isolation this profound disease causes."

"As you are aware, Senator, our family is of means to such point that my father established the Foundation to do medical research that would bring medical treatment to **everyone**, at costs they could afford. My father does **NOT** have a Messiah complex and is a humble man. My father's goal is **not** to make more money, nor to alter the minds of those who enjoy the benefits of his generosity. My father's goal is **not** to supersede the rights of commercial entities to generate a return on their investments. My father's goal **is** simply to help people and yet, we have been called before your committee because **you** feel that we have exceeded the legal rights to provide products and services that might improve the quality of life for others."

'V' looked down at the floor as if to regain his thought process. Instead what he was about to say caught everyone including me, by surprise. "Ronald Regan, the actor, who never went to law school, once said, 'freedom is never more than one generation from extinction. It cannot simply be mechanically transmitted to our kids in the bloodstream. Instead, it must be fought for, protected and handed on, for them to do the same. If we are allowed an existential existence that supports the belief in free will and the freedom of the individual, we cannot, should not and will not fear the power of the government.'"

Eleven Senators sat in rapt attention as 'V' continued, not realizing that their own aides had begun standing behind them to the point that the only people sitting in the front of the crowded room were the twelve Senators who sat alone as cameras rolled. Fitzgerald knew that any admonishment would be political suicide and so he simply ignored the silent demonstration.

'V' continued. "You have called us here because of the concerns you and those with more money and more power than we have, instructed you to do so, people who provide huge political donations to elected officials from companies who feel threatened by what we have accomplished. Yet, it is us who feel threatened by you! Through your inquiry, you appear to be attempting to expropriate what we have developed and allow those who did not have the ability, desire or dedication to replicate our technology and do so in the name of free enterprise. Yet we stand before you innocent of the claims levied against us and non-sullied by your assertions of monopolistic and egregious actions against the sovereignty of the United States and humankind."

'V' walked to the right and paused. No one dared interrupt as he had the rapt attention of everyone in the room as he added, "**Not once** have we proposed a doctrine that did **not** have as its ultimate goal the betterment of **all** living species and, yet, you consider us a threat. **Not once** have we usurped the honor and dignity of life nor, in any way denigrated the belief that freedom starts and ends with the human soul. **Not once** have we attempted to monitor, change or alter the thoughts and beliefs of those whose commitment has been the betterment of man!" 'V' stopped for a moment for effect and to allow those words – betterment, honor and dignity settle in.

He looked at the panel and then at me, then back at the panel. "You have alleged that my father has a Messiah complex and yet, his name has never appeared in any form of communication from the Foundation. While our family financially supports the enterprise, my father isn't even the head. Leadership is done by the committee of men you have heard from over the past three days. These honest, noble men all have an equal vote. These are men who are donating their lives to make the world a better place for **all** of us to live."

'V' stopped for a moment to gather his thoughts and continued. "When my father began the Derrick Williams Foundation, he had a dream – a dream to build a community for the betterment of man – a family – a family of brilliant individuals who trust each other – believe in each other and honor each other every single day. Those people are in this chamber today! They care for each other, like brothers who have extended global network based on mutual trust, mutual respect and mutual reward, which appears to be the antithesis of our society and culture today."

"Instead of singular individuals isolated in their own world, reliant on the support of strangers on the internet for social interaction, we have a team of scholars who are respected for what they do. We do not know their race! We do not care about the religion! We do not ask about their political thoughts or even their orientation. What we ask, and the only thing we ask, is whether they will join our team as an equal, someone whose ideas are of the same value as everyone else."

With that, the entire audience stood and linked arms. Fitzgerald raised his gavel and then realized, he was about to be skewered if he stopped the quiet, peaceful sign of unity. This was a message from the people to those who governed. This was a statement that these Americans had enough of special interest groups, cronyism and favors. They were saying 'enough is enough!'

'V' added, "I am a young man, and yet I am afraid Senator. Afraid of what I see, which is profound loneliness consisting of people moving about in their own little bubbles, simply doing what they need to do just to get by. Sadly, these lonely people once had support groups of family and community. Sadly, these support mechanisms have eroded and dissipated and people are lonely and afraid. Instead of looking in, they reach out through the internet to other lonely strangers, who fill their minds and their worlds with vitriolic nonsense that is demeaning and degrading the concept of community and the founding beliefs this country was based on."

Once again, 'V' stopped. This time slowly shaking his head. "If this isn't bad enough, we have people in power, who expound the hypothesis that this pervasive sadness is someone else's fault and there's someone else to blame. You are our leaders! However, when those of us on the 'outside' look to you and your counterparts for leadership, compassion and a sense of belonging what do you do? You point fingers at others simply because they belong to a different political party, blaming them and our institutions for the sadness, loneliness and fatigue that pervades America."

'V' was spellbinding as heads bobbed in affirmation and he continued. "The brilliance of my father is not his knowledge! The brilliance of my father is not his wealth! The brilliance of my father is his profound compassion and innate ability to take those who were once disaffected and make them believe in common goals. Goals, that are nothing more than the betterment of all living species. His majesty lies in his ability to sincerely show these people the respect they deserve by simply creating a sense of family. If this is wrong, then America and the world are wrong! If we have violated the covenants of life or religion, then they, too, are wrong!"

'V' stopped for a moment and lowered his voice to almost a whisper as he added, "Yesterday, Dr. Borgwardt degraded and demeaned ten acres of land that has been the inspiration for those who have shared in the experience. This priceless parcel has transformed those who were sad, those who were lonely and those who only needed to believe in someone or something and made them whole, where all their anger, all their frustration and all their pain that they, and we all suffer, is lifted, such that we are exposed to the beauty of innocence."

"What is profoundly sad! What is the biggest tragedy! What grieves my heart the most, is that Dr. Borgwardt has never been to The Forest, has never experienced the feelings that many of us have, nor has the Doctor ever tasted the nectar of purity that trickles from within Mother Earth. Yet, he stood before my father and literally accused him a heresy, chastising him, belittling him and denigrating him for simply trying to follow the teachings of the book that he professes to holds dear – the Holy Bible."

"I ask you, is it wrong to simply try to follow it's teachings? Is it wrong to look for goodness and honesty? Is it wrong to practice humility, generosity, compassion and forgiveness? If it is, then we stand guilty as accused."

"Senator Fitzgerald, you chastised my father and accused him of being the leader of a cult and yet each person comes of free will, each person has had the opportunity to make their lives better! Each person shares in the beauty that comes when you sincerely feel wanted, needed, love and finally accepted for **who** they are instead of being judged by **what** they are. For this, each of these men has an equal share in the direction the Foundation takes where the only difference is that my father does not reap the financial reward they have earned for their time, talent and commitment, simply because he has enough."

"Finally and more importantly, Senator, none of these men, including my father, and I must emphasize the word **none**, has the ability to channel any sort of avarice or destructive propaganda towards the United States of America, its people or those of any other nation. Because of this, we have the global commitment and support of 214 of the 215 nations of the world, where the only exception appears to be our own country - the United States of America – land of the free and home of the brave!"

'V' turned his back on the panel and then slowly turned around and faced them once again, "Perhaps, just perhaps, if America would look at the betterment of mankind instead of just the betterment of those who hold its wealth and power, the aspects of war and global annihilation would be less. And yet, because we have made the choice to help **all mankind** and not just Americans, we feel threatened."

"Why do we feel threatened? Because we sense that our freedoms as American's are being slowly eroded in the name of protection and the insipient greed that undermines virtually everything we do today."

'V' paused for a moment and then looked at Fitzgerald and continued, "If you don't mind, let's look at the concept of freedom. There are two critical elements within that concept that must always be in place that are inextricably linked together. The first is that each and every individual is treated with dignity, that is spelled out time and time again - life, liberty and the pursuit of happiness."

"Life, means affordable health care so that events such as the death of my grandfather can be avoided because he could not afford a physical exam."

"Liberty! Where our government should not be in the business of setting down ultimate truths, nor defining who is worthy or not worthy of life, where it cannot, should not and will not be allowed to decide who is saved and who is damned, simply because of the power of a few who look at return-on-investment over quality of life!"

"Senator Fitzgerald, our government should be a tool to **preserve order** and the opportunity for free minds to wrestle with questions and answers regarding ways to make life better for everyone and **not** fear the threat of being impugned when those goals do not parallel those in power. Our government should **never** be the center of life. It should be the framework that enables **all of us** to enjoy the prosperity of freedom and the way we live."

'V' stopped for a moment to allow what he had said sink in. The Senators sat and pondered his words before he began again. "The capitol of Wisconsin is named Madison, after the fourth president of the United States. President Madison was a thinker beyond his times and if you have had the honor of reading some of his thoughts, you can see that Madison, like his contemporaries, had profound views on who we are, that has led our nation to the greatness it enjoys."

"In Madison's writings, he communicates that our system of government rests on a core conviction that human beings are fundamentally fallen, selfish and inclined to let our passions run roughshod over reason." This got a concerned look from his intended audience as he continued. "Madison once wrote that a zeal for different opinions concerning religion, government and many other points has always divided mankind into parties, inflamed them with mutual animosity and rendered them much more disposed to vexation and oppression of each other, than to cooperate for their common good. This is normal! This is natural! This is why we are here today!"

'V' spread his arms as if to indicate inclusion of all present and continued. "Madison, grasping at our inadequacies stated, '*As long as the reason of man continues fallible, and he is at liberty to exercise it, different opinions will be formed. As long as connection subsists between his reason and his self-love, his opinions and his passions will have reciprocal influence on each other; and the former will be objects to which the latter will attach themselves.*'"

'V' paused for a moment and continued. "What was Madison saying? He was stating that, it is through the difference of opinion that progress can prevail. It is through dialogue that we can learn and adjust. It is through tolerance and understanding that tomorrow can be better than today. It was Madison who proposed the concept of the Amendments to the Constitution as he knew that times would change, people would change, ideas would change, but the core concept of America could prevail."

"You, Senators, represent the people and serve as liaison to the government. It is my belief that your mission must be to preserve the **right kind** of government that will constrain people who try to deprive citizens of their rights, while being a government that, in itself, is constrained so that it does not deprive citizens of their rights as well. Your challenge must be to enable the government to control the governed, while it controls itself. We cannot allow government to dictate! We cannot allow government to take away individual rights for the benefits of a few! Finally, we cannot accept pressure for pressure's sake where the behemoth is so great as to impede the rights and freedoms of those it is intended to protect."

"I ask you, what has our Foundation done to admonish the rights of the people? What has it done that impedes the authority of government? What has it done to debilitate the process of freedom? We stand before you as honest men who have as their goal the betterment of mankind! Not once have we ever attempted to inculcate those who have committed their knowledge to the betterment of all. In the end, who has challenged us? - You! Our own government!"

'V' stood, looking at the floor and shaking his head. "Unless we are mistaken, government is not in the business of setting down ultimate truths and should never evolve to the point that it decides who is saved and who is damned. Your role as leaders is to use government as a tool to preserve order and create space for free minds to wrestle with the big questions, none of which is greater than the quality of life - not for a few people, but for everyone. Not just the rich! Not just the powerful, Not just the connected! Everyone!"

'V' looked at the ground for moment and then at me and then at the Senators as he added, "Government is **not** the center of life, but government should be the framework that enables lives to be lived in the true center of our cherished existence which is freedom - freedom to live, freedom to seek out treatments that might, and I emphasize the word **might**, improve the quality of the life we all live. The basic premise of our foundation, was, is and will always be, to enhance the quality of life and not its extension."

"Those who have challenged us, have attempted to point us out as some sort of religious zealots. We are not God, nor do we pretend to be! We are only trying to do God's work which is to bring peace, love and dignity to life and help everyone we can. If we are wrong, then America is wrong! If we have failed, then mankind will fail. If you sincerely believe that developing a product that might help people lead better, healthier lives is wrong, then perhaps, there needs to be a change in thought, process and perhaps leadership."

Applause rang through the meeting room as Fitzgerald banged his gavel for silence as 'V' continued. "I am but a young man. Yet, I understand that deep, enduring change does not come through legislation or elections. Meaningful changes come when minds are persuaded and above all else, hearts are changed as well. We need change in America. We need to right the ship and take special interest groups out of governance. We are on the cusp of enormous challenges, not just to the powers of control, but what it means to be a human being. We cannot close the opened door of tomorrow's technology that is currently impeded by rules and regulations of the past, as the pace will always be behind us. Progress is like a never-ending stream that is indefatigable – never wavering, tiring or faltering."

"People, citizens, voters who have exhausted all current medical procedures designed to save their lives, must be given the opportunity, at their own volition, to examine alternatives and determine for **themselves** what is the best course of action that may or may not improve their existence or extend their lives. Our foundation has done nothing wrong! Our foundation had abided by the rules and regulations and yet, we have been impeded inextricably by the limitations it has put upon itself and, in so doing, we have seen people who we might have been able to help pass away."

"I want you to close your eyes and envision yourself lying in a hospital bed and being told that you are about to die. I want you to feel what it's like to realize there might be a cure that, had it been implemented, would have allowed the time needed to extend life's joy with your spouse, children or grandchildren. Now I want you to feel the frustration of knowing that your government has said 'no' you can't have that procedure, you can't participate in that process, and you cannot continue to live, simply because someone, somewhere hasn't made enough money off their product, their procedure or their prescription to generate their desired return on investment. This is not a unique situation, but interminably endless!"

"To stand in the room of a dying person and listen to their last rasps of breath knowing that, perhaps, just perhaps, we could have helped is one of the greatest tragedies a person can ever experience, only superseded by the need to stand in front of you and justify a goal of simply wanting to help people live better lives."

'V' looked at me as I wiped the tears from my eyes and nodded in approval as he spoke.

He looked at the audience and then turned back to the Senators. "We stand before you, not as enemies, but as advocates; not to challenge, but to cooperate; not thwart our great country, but to work with you to help the American dream come true as we pledge allegiance to the United States of America and to its people, but also to those of other nations, other religions, other races and other orientations, where our only goal is to help all living things lead a better life."

"If our goal is wrong, then we are wrong. If our achievements are wrong, then we have no idea what right means anymore. My father began with a dream – a dream to help all people lead a better life. If this is not a positive dream, then it is a nightmare. If helping someone. - make that everyone - is not noble, then I have no idea what nobility is. You have challenged him and those who have chosen to follow. You have denigrated him and attempted to create someone who is totally contrary to what he really is. You have taken what is hallowed ground and besmirched it as if it means nothing to those who have been moved by its purity and innocence."

"I ask you Senators, what have we done wrong? How have we been impossible? Who have we hurt? Why is it that when someone comes along who doesn't care about money and is filled with the generosity and compassion summarized in a book that you all placed your hands upon when you swore to uphold the Constitution of the United States and you chastise him, belittle him and challenge his innocence and decency. Is that not worse than what he has done?"

'V' stopped for a moment and then stepped in front of the desk and microphone. This was not an ordinary move, but an extraordinary way of showing the importance of what he was about to say as he continued, "The other day, I went to visit the National Archives. In that hallowed hall, I bowed my head as if in prayer. As I made my way past the Constitution and examined the signatures of the brave men who signed it, I stopped at the Declaration of Independence and examined its majesty and reflected upon those precious words."

'V' paused for a moment for effect and then, without any notes, recited the entire second paragraph from memory. *"We hold these truths to be self-evident, that **all men** are created equal, that they are endowed by their Creator with certain unalienable Rights, that among these are Life, Liberty and the pursuit of Happiness.-That to secure these rights, Governments are instituted among Men, deriving their just powers from the* consent of the governed, -That whenever any Form of Government becomes destructive of these ends, it is the Right of the People to alter or to abolish it, and to institute new Government, laying its foundation on such principles and organizing its powers in such form, as to them shall seem most likely to effect their Safety and Happiness. Prudence, indeed, will dictate that Governments long established should not be changed for light and transient causes; and accordingly all experience hath shewn, that mankind are more disposed to suffer, while evils are sufferable, than to right themselves by abolishing the forms to which they are accustomed. But when a long train of abuses and usurpations, pursuing invariably the same Object evinces a design to reduce them under absolute Despotism, it is their right, it is their duty, to throw off such Government, and to provide new Guards for their future security."*

'V' paused for a moment and looked at the assemblage facing him adding, "We did not act with avarice! We did not act with greed! We acted and continue to act with those words emblazoned in our hearts – *life, liberty and the pursuit of happiness.* If you sincerely believe we have done wrong, we shall abide. If however, you look at the one billion people whose lives we touch – in a positive way - where we provide health and medical security, then you must agree that there has been no attempt to usurp the laws of the land and you must determine that our goals, intent and destiny is for the good of **all people** and not just a few. I thank you for your time and God Bless America."

My mind came back into focus. I was no longer traveling through the past. A soft smile crossed my face and I thanked God for all those who were with me in body or in spirit as the room erupted in round after round of applause.

'V' turned and our eyes met, if only for an instant. I then looked at those who had experienced his exhortation. As I turned back, I realized 'V' was already gone, escaping through a side chamber door, away from the congratulatory onslaught that would have prevailed. I realized that 'V' didn't want notoriety, nor allow the intensity of what he shared to be dissipated by the simple acts of gratitude so many people wanted to share. His absence was intentional! 'V' simply wanted the intensity of thought to remain in the room as a cloak over those who stood in total silence, comprehending all that he had said.

I took a deep breath and realized that Fitzgerald had been put in his place. Fitzgerald, who had used the system to make himself rich, was about to see what the wrath of people who trusted him and feel what it felt was like to squander all the goodness and consume all the honor that had been bestowed upon him. Word spread like wildfire. All the truths about where he lived and his lifestyle came out. The days until he was done were marked with words such as impeachment, imprisonment and dishonor.

Truth and Consequence:

It was agreed that the Derrick Williams Foundation would work with the government to ensure that the data harvested remained secure and to share our technology such that SIMON was equal to the systems needed to protect and defend our freedom. We did not agree to share the medical and personal data we had on those who trusted us and even the government realized that our mission was goodness. For these concessions, the Derrick Williams Foundation was commended by the President for its dedication to the betterment of all living beings.

There was relief. There was joy. There was closure to what had been a profoundly grueling experience and it was then that I knew my days were numbered. We had won the battle and even the war, but the scars on my soul were so deep, I didn't know if I would ever have the passion to keep going, keep fighting, keep dreaming that tomorrow could be a better than today. I remember what George the First had stated, that the weight of oppression can do that. It can usurp your life and make everything feel as if it is nothing, to the point that you feel smothered by those who don't feel the warmth of goodness and generosity.

Life is all about transitions from one generation to the next, from one person to another, from one idea, one concept, one belief to those cherished by the next generation. Two Feathers had already begun his journey that would take him beyond here and now, to a point where the goodness of heart was simply replaced by his greatness of compassion.

Perhaps, just perhaps, my dreams would come true. Perhaps just perhaps, all that the medicine man had predicted would actually happen. Perhaps just perhaps, goodness could prevail and the prevalence of self-interest that had withered so many dreams and taken our government from a body intended to defend and protect to nothing more than a great big, ugly machine who took from all for the benefit of a few, could begin the slow turn back towards the innocence from whence it came. My eyes closed and when they opened my Amy was standing there with tears in her eyes. All that I had hoped for. All that I had prayed for. All that I had ever dreamed about was coming true. We were making a difference for **everyone.**

Surprise:

We returned to Milwaukee and life began again. The drama of Washington slowly evaporated and we went back to our projects. Mediglove was continuing to grow and was accepted by more people throughout the world. Rover the Kaleidoscope, was patented and submitted to the FDA for approval. The Nanospheres and lithium cloth were being touted as incredible innovations that we licensed to a myriad of companies. We knew some of the projects would take a long time before they could be used, but the exposure at the Senate hearing had driven demand through the roof.

It was agreed that the generated revenue would be divided amongst other projects and charities that would not only help underdeveloped nations and American neighborhoods lead better lives, but do so through clean water, better health care and a more effective system of education throughout the world.

Mineral Point and Waldwick began being added to every map as cartographers realized that it truly was the center of medical research and achievement in the world. Pilgrims began arriving and walking the path in The Forest to drink of the pure water, where the only requirement was respect for land and the people who gave their lives for the betterment of all.

A few months later, as I was sitting in my office in Pewaukee, a courier came to the door. Ceclia looked at him and wondered if it was yet another "serving" by some competitor or disgruntled individual who thought we were a panacea willing to give them millions, or yet, another company who wanted to purchase the rights to Nanochip.

Instead, Cecelia signed for a letter and gingerly slid her antique letter opener through the envelope seam. She unfolded the letter and began reading it. She looked up and tears filled her eyes. There was a soft smile as she simply shook her head. She tried to stand but couldn't. All of her energy was being consumed by the contents of the words she held.

Cecelia caught her breath and looked at me, saying "George, you'd better sit down!"

"I am sitting!" I replied.

"You better sit on that old chest," was her reply.

I must have had a concerned look on my face as I watched her nod in approval of my motion. As I sat upon the old chest, Cecelia handed me the letter. The paper was beige parchment, embossed with a gold logo and a thin blue stripe around the edges. My mouth dropped open in disbelief. This simply couldn't be.

Dear Mr. George Terrill IV,

This letter is to formally notify you that you have been awarded the Nobel Peace Prize.

Your nomination was submitted by members of a national assembly, government, and/or international court of law consisting of university chancellors, professors of social science, history, philosophy, law and theology; leaders of peace research institutes and institutes of foreign affairs, previous Nobel Peace Prize Laureates, board members of organizations that have received the Nobel Peace Prize, present and past members of the Norwegian Nobel Committee and former advisers of the Norwegian Nobel Institute.

The Norwegian Nobel Committee, responsible for the selection of eligible candidates and the choice of the Nobel Peace Prize Laureates, has reviewed your nomination and is pleased to announce that you have been chosen to represent the Derrick Williams Foundation for your dedication and commitment to the betterment of all living species and looks forward to meeting you in person in December.

Sincerely,

Nobel Peace Prize Committee

Norway:

We flew the entire team to Norway and it was strange to see the MadCity Boys and the entire group dressed in tuxedos. Big Brother and Ann were there, along with Ceclia and her husband John, our son Derrick and his wife Andrea, 'V' and his wife Amelia and, of course, our Dr. Melia.

The photos taken are some of my most cherished possessions I look at every day. My eyes continue to dart from face-to-face, all frozen in time, all resplendent in the joy that comes from achievement and that makes me proud. I peer at the smiling faces of Peter and Tommie, Luke, Matt, Mark, Tad, James and Philip and my heart fills with pride. I think of mom and dad, Dr. Williams and The Duke, Great Grandfather and the Medicine Man, George the First, Francis and Aristotle and my little buddy Jake and wonder if they are looking down and smiling, knowing that some smart-ass kid from Waldwick, Wisconsin turned out all right after all. My thoughts turn to The Forest and I reflect on all that it has meant to me. How one small enclave could affect so many, where its purity has come to represent goodness and joy of giving of oneself.

As I stood before the Nobel Committee, my thoughts reflected on those who meant so much. While I was speaking to everyone, I hope and pray it was realized that the words were meant for all those who had made the journey with me.

"Ladies and Gentlemen of the Nobel Committee. I stand before you humbled by the honor bestowed upon the Derrick Williams Foundation. I am but a common man, who only had dreams common to all - simply a better life for the living. I have not made this journey alone, for the burden would have been far too great for any man. The gift I was given, was bestowed upon me long ago and it was the gift of giving, not of myself, but those who have given so much, that allowed all of us to achieve our first steps towards a better tomorrow.

To be recognized by you is something I will never forget. However, beyond this glorious award is the majesty that comes from sincerely feeling wanted, needed and loved by other human beings and that is what I am most grateful for. My life has been filled with so much joy, built not on accomplishment, but on people. People who taught me the beauty of giving of oneself. People who showed me the majesty of humility, generosity, compassion and forgiveness. Finally, people who have walked with me and given me the strength and wisdom needed to carry on when it seemed the road had come to an end.

As my head turns and I see my own footprints in the sands of time, I realize that what we have accomplished is only the beginning of what can be done when people believe - in themselves, in those around them and in the inherent goodness of man. To my family! To my friends! To those who have shared the passion. And to you, I simply say thank you for giving of yourselves, which is a gift much greater than us all."

The Baton:

We returned home and the glory and excitement of the Nobel Peace Prize slowly faded and with it my decision to retire became that much stronger.

One morning, as we lay in bed, I looked at my Amy sleeping next to me and thanked God for the life we shared. Without Amy, I would have never realized the beauty of acceptance, the nobility of tolerance, nor felt the majesty of love. They say that any good long-term relationship is based on seven criteria – attraction, association, communication, understanding, trust, compromise and forgiveness from which the net sum is respect.

Yes, there were times when things weren't right! Yes, there were times when I wondered if it was all worth it! Yes, there were times when I was filled with sadness. Yet, I wouldn't trade any of it for what I got in return, which was and remains love. I thought back to our vows and whispered.

"Do not press me to leave you or to turn back from following you!

Where you go, I will go; where you lodge I will lodge;
Your people shall be my people, and your God my God.
Where you die, I will die — there will I be buried.

As Amy's eyes opened, I announced "The day has come". She quietly nodded, as she knew what it meant.

Loose Ends:

I went to the office, pulled up the old chest and thought back to that first time at Hochunk and Big Brother. I thought about how we fought for a spit of land and the dignity it represented. I thought about Great Grandfather, knowing he was looking down on me with a gentle smile upon his face. I thought about those who had given so much of themselves for the betterment of others. I thought of Amy, Derrick, Melia and 'V' and how proud I was of all they were giving back. I thought about Dr. Williams, The Duke, mom and dad and prayed that I deserved the honor bestowed upon me. I thought about Ceclia in the office who had been so kind, so gracious and so loyal for so many years.

I called Cecelia in and thanked her for all that she had done and for putting up with me. I handed her an envelope and thought she was going to faint. Amy and I had written a check in her and John's name as a token of our gratitude ensuring that she and John were financially safe and secure for the rest of their lives. There were tears and hugs all around and I think she knew things were about to change.

A little later, I called Peter and told him, the time had come. He knew what I was referring to and, in the matter of minutes, things changed. After that call, I contacted 'V' and requested that he come to the office, where I handed him the box. As he opened it, tears came to both sets of eyes as he looked at the two white eagle feathers. "They're yours' son! It's an honor to be in the presence of Two Feathers. May you lead wisely."

'V' knew the baton was being passed. He had earned the honor and dignity that was bestowed upon him and knew I was turning down the intensity of the limelight and heading into the shadows of life and doing so willingly.

All I ever wanted to be was a writer. All I ever hoped to be was happy! All I ever dreamed about had come true and, as I sat upon the old wooden trunk, I knew the time had come and I stood and looked at my son and smiled. I spun the dial on the little lock until I heard 'click'. Slowly I opened the cover and beckoned him over. For a moment there was complete silence and then he gave me a hug. All the pain! All the suffering! All the misery that had been trapped in that white bear skin had evaporated and there was peace.

Later that afternoon, I got in my truck and drove Mineral Point. Along the way, I punched in the buttons for a radio station, any radio station and the Beatles "Blackbird" came on. I always thought the black bird Paul McCartney was referring to was death. (*all your life, you were only waiting for this moment to arise*), where we are all killing time until time kills us. The narrative *"broken wings/ sunken eyes"* crept into my psyche as I felt that existence behind death was the negative part. I thought of The Duke and then myself and surmised that *"people usually think of death as a bad thing"* and then realized that McCartney was saying that death is peaceful freedom - total bliss and tranquility – where one escapes from Earth's burden and that life is the hardest part of total existence and death, the easiest.

I arrived in Mineral Point and bypassed High Street going directly to the cemetery to pay my respects to grandma, mom, dad and all my ancestors buried there who had the peace we all aspire. After a few moments of reflection, I drove to Waldwick, parked near the farm house and slowly made my way to the family plot still surrounded by the limestone fence that had once been the family home. Slowly, I looked at the weathered headstones of those who came before me and those of Aristotle and Francis and my little buddy Jake and nodded my respect and appreciation for they had shown me the beauty of acceptance.

It was almost dark on a very cold wintery night, but I didn't care. Wisconsin's winter weather can be bitter and tonight was one of those nights. For some, the cold is an intrusion. For me, it's a time of solitude, that represents the majesty of silence as the crystal-clear air envelopes one in a sense of singularity that cannot be measured or appreciated, unless you've been there.

For some reason, the coldest nights always seem to happen when there is a full moon and tonight that was also case. As I walked the path to the Forest, the soft crunch of the light snow that had fallen in the afternoon when the cold front went through, kept cadence with my emotions. The clouds were gone and the sky was pitch black as the moon had just begun to rise. Each finger of the tree's barren branches ahead of me poked their solitary exclamation towards God, welcoming me back to my sanctuary.

As I reached the edge of the Forest, I looked above the trees at the silent majesty of space, sprinkled with small specs beyond which stood heaven, where I imagined arms were open wide, awaiting those making the journey that would reunite them with loved ones who had gone before.

I walked further into The Forest and bowed my head in reverence at the remnants of the old stone foundation of Skunk Hollow School. I paused for a moment and reflected on the goodness that began there, remembering just how much had transpired, where laughter and tears were gently blended with hopes and dreams and aspirations only of tomorrow. I felt as if I could hear the children laughing and it put joy in my heart.

After an instant, I walked to Great Grandfather's memorial and sat on the bench and thanked him for his wisdom. I closed my eyes and his goodness shrouded in the bright light of honor and dignity and I thanked him for all that he had done. My eyes were closed only for a moment and when I looked up, the big buck was there, quietly staring at me, nodding in the affirmative, before simply walking away.

The full moon was just climbing over the trees and its brightness illuminated all that was around me with beams so intense that they cast black shadows of the limbs on the pure, white, winter snow.

I arose and turned to make my way down the cinder path. Looking down I was surprised to see a fresh set of footprints and wondered who was there and why would they come on such a cold winter's night.

I made my way to the spring thinking of Amy and our first time here and how the joy of that day had lasted forever. I thought of Derrick and Melia and 'V' and how they had given us so much. I thought of all those who had given my life meaning and realized how really lucky I really was.

Slowly I traversed, never taking my eyes off the footprints in front of me – curious-yet-cautious, anxious-yet-concerned, wondering who and why they were there. As I arrived at the spring, I realized the footprints stopped with their imprints stamped only in my soul. Proceeding neither further, nor retreating from whence they came, I slowly shook my head. How could this be?

I bent down and filled the old tin cup with the purity that sprang forth from Mother earth and took the vessel and pressed it to my lips. Slowly sipping the cool freshness, I paused for a moment to thank God for all that he or she had given me and looked up at the darkened, winter sky, only to notice a shooting star silently traversing the horizon. It was then I knew Great Grandfather had found peace and was finally on his way home.

The Waldwick Series: The ten-book series spans nearly 200 years and are independent yet intertwined in several ways including, characters, location and thematic objectives that examine current social issues from different perspectives. Regardless of the time period or the characters in question, the core component - judging people by who they are instead, of what they are, remains paramount.

Waldwick addresses the subject of physical, social, economic and political oppression in the 1800's. Set in Cornwall, England, Virginia and Southwestern Wisconsin, *Waldwick* frankly discusses what one family was willing to do to overcome oppression, as told through the eyes of the narrator, George Terrill. *Waldwick* then summarizes what happens when the oppression is removed and opportunity arises. Integrated into the story line are actual events and people and how the main characters are affected by their existence and their interaction with these people and events. Above all else, *Waldwick* is a love story … love of the land, love of one another and the love of freedom, woven in a tapestry of acceptance, tolerance and justice. *Award Winner*

War of My Brothers examines America of the early 20th century and how and why it changed as seen through the eyes of Hank Terrill, great grandson of George Terrill from the original Waldwick. Ride along as Hank witnesses World War I, the Spanish Flu, the 19th Amendment, that gave women the right to vote, the Great Depression, World War II, Korean War and Viet Nam and how life changed, people changed and those who govern changed, as well. Experience the traumas of life and the joys of the living as you thank God that it didn't happen to you.

The King of Hearts has been reviewed as *"ambitious, extensively researched and deeply engrossing"*…a story that traces the actual Terrill family through 60 generations as it learns the consequence of wealth, power and prestige over 700 years only to have it all collapse around them. Using a blend of magic realism, lyrical prose and imagery *The King of Hearts* weaves a complex tapestry of a family's history from 65 BCE through sixty generations. Beneath it all, the book is about friendship and the deep, mutual bond between people based on trust, support, and genuine connection that goes beyond just companionship—it's about understanding, loyalty, and being there for each other through life's ups and downs.

Little Spirit Based in contemporary Wisconsin, *Little Spirit* examines the concept of eminent domain and the taking of land and dignity, first from the Indian's perspective and then today, as seen through the eyes of George Terrill IV a descendant of the original George Terrill. Using flashbacks through a 94-year-old, blind, Ho-Chunk Indian elder, named Great Grandfather, George learns about the feelings and challenges of the Ho-Chunk nation and the taking of their land and also how contemporary America hasn't changed that much in terms of citizen rights.

Driftless revisits George and his wife fifteen years into their marriage. Reflecting on the challenges they face when their marriage becomes mundane while examining the profound question of which is worse… having nothing or everything. As the mystery of the Forest is revealed *Driftless* examines the consequence of technology and the power of special interest groups to control the status-quo for their financial gain, while addressing the issue of individual rights in time of personal need, where the one thing all people have in common is … time!

The Hayflick Limit addresses the challenges of parenthood, while discussing a person's rights to live and die. When affected by an incurable malady the question becomes *"Would you choose five-to-seven years of normal mental acuity, at which time you would abruptly expire, or risk everything and allow for the slow, gradual decline with hope that a different, longer-lasting cure might come along?"* The Hayflick Limit addresses the role of government in establishing the validity of the Hippocratic Oath?

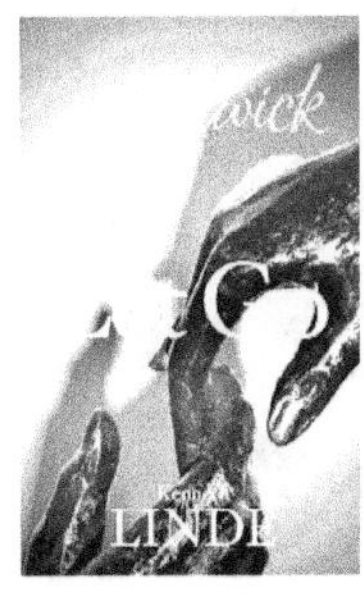

Let Go examines the consequence of bullying as Melia Terrill is affected by the verbal onslaught and her commitment to the only friend who has shown her the beauty of acceptance for who she is. The books examines the perks and perils of extreme wealth, the solitude of loneliness and frustration of achieving one's goals only to realize that all dreams can become nightmares when one risks everything for perhaps nothing as it delves into thoughts, emotions, joys, sorrow and consequences of being a captive of one's own past and fleeting fame.

Survivor...How Death Saved My Life looks at the consequence of an altered set of priorities and how it can take a near-death experience to "right the ship". Totally immobilized for six days, George Terrill examines his life and it's mistakes and vows, if he survives, to make things right. *Survivor* addresses the psychology of fear, the challenges of being told you have less than a 5% chance of living three hours and what you think about when you sincerely believe you're going to die.

Greed is a thought-provoking literary tale of ambition gone awry, exposing how the pursuit of wealth can fracture family relationships. This intense novel, explores the intricacies of human nature and the pursuit of meaning. It serves as a critique of modern society's obsession with wealth and status that challenges readers to reconsider what success truly means, making this book not just an exhilarating journey but a profound reflection on the human condition.

And/Or Using Newton's Third Law as a lens to explore relationships where every action sets off a chain reaction, *And/Or* journeys in ways no one can predict or control while asking difficult questions about resilience, identity, and redemption. As such, it ponders deep philosophical reflections and existential questions by drawing sharp connections between science and human nature, asking such profound questions as...Is it possible for a person to truly recover from betrayal? Can love survive after it's been broken? And when one loses everything, what's left? *And/Or* is a gripping, thought-provoking read that will linger long after the final page.

Disclaimer: This book is a work of fiction. Some of the events and experiences detailed herein may be true and have been faithfully rendered as researched by the author to the best of his abilities. The information contained in this book is intended to provide helpful and informative material on the subjects and events addressed and written as an interpretation of his learning.

The author is a descendant of miners from Cornwall. There is a town called Mineral Point, Wisconsin, where his childhood was filled with magical moments and marvelous memories. There is a village called Waldwick that remains nearby and is the birthplace of his grandmother and mother. There are many Terrills living in the area who are his relatives and the author hopes and prays that he has done the family name justice by what he has written, for they are the kindred spirit upon which our country was created. There is no reality to the names used, as they are all of consequence.

If the tale he weaves meets your fancy and your interest is piqued, the author highly recommends visiting the wonderful area just southwest of Madison, Wisconsin. The scenery is spectacular and is only exceeded by the honor, dignity, and warmth of the people who reside there.

The author has written this book as a tribute to those who have suffered from the profound sadness of losing a loved one to Alzheimer's disease. For some, the experience reinforces the value of integrity and honesty and the joy of acceptance that only comes from an open heart and a profound sense of decency that is now emanated with each breath.

No part of this text may be reproduced, transmitted, downloaded, decompiled, reverse-engineered, or stored in or introduced into any information storage and retrieval system, in any form or by any means, whether electronic or mechanical, now known or hereafter invented, without the express written permission of the author.

All rights are reserved under International and Pan-American Copyright Conventions. By payment of the required fees, you have been granted the nonexclusive, nontransferable right to access and read the text of this e-book on-screen. For additional information www.WaldwickBooks.com.

www.ingramcontent.com/pod-product-compliance
Lightning Source LLC
Chambersburg PA
CBHW070307310726
48976CB00005B/1607